EMMA WHO SAVED MY LIFE

EMMA WHO SAVED MY LIFE

WILTON BARNHARDT

ST. MARTIN'S PRESS ♦ NEW YORK

Design by Glen M. Edelstein

Endpaper photograph by Jerry Speier, hand-colored by Doris Borowsky

Library of Congress Cataloging-in-Publication Data

Barnhardt, Wilton.
Emma who saved my life / Wilton Barnhardt.
p. cm.
ISBN 0–312–02911–X
I. Title.
PS3552.A6994E4 1989
813′.54—dc19 89–30158

First Edition
10 9 8 7 6 5 4 3 2 1

TO
Greenpoint, Brooklyn
(1982–1985)
For those who were there.
And for those who missed it.

EMMA WHO SAVED MY LIFE

BEGINNING

IF I had it to do all over again, I think I'd try to find some way to skip being nine years old. Because that's when it bit me—the Theater Bug, I mean. I ended up devoting twenty-one of my thirty-five years to pursuing stardom on the stage and, looking back, I wonder if the height of my career might not have been when I was nine. It may have been the last time I was totally, utterly secure in the theater.

For those of you that missed my performance, I played Little Jimmy in *The Parson Comes to Dinner*, a 100% amateur theatrical put on at the Oak Park Community Playhouse, in the suburbs of Chicago. I don't think I knew the sheer depth and scope of my role until the first night's curtain call. They clapped at me. I know people generally do that at the end of plays but at nine I hadn't worked out the finer points and, frankly, I took it very personally.

SO, the next night I figured out that the more I did onstage, the more they might clap for me. The French maid did her scene while I titillated the audience with untying her sash. The woman who played my mother walked on and delivered her monologue while I intrigued the audience with whether, behind her, I was going to knock over a vase. I had one little line: *Ooooh Mom, it's not my bedtime yet*, which was to be delivered in a kiddie whine. You'd be surprised how long you can make that line last when you put your mind to it. *Oooooooooooh Mahhhhm* . . . About here I shifted my little weight back and forth and looked adorably at the audience in a way that I perfected in our bathroom mirror, and I'd continue *it's not . . . I mean it caaaan't be* (what a pro! already improvising) *my beeddddtiiiiime, right nowww.* "Right now" works out to a few milliseconds longer than "yet."

You might have thought this scenery-chewing would have earned the enmity of my fellow thespians but this was, after all, *The Parson Comes to Dinner* and I think they sort of liked it (since the audience liked it) and when it came time for my little step forward at the curtain call, the audience clapped even louder than they did the first night, and when everyone had had their portion of allotted applause, the man who played the Parson in *The Parson Comes to Dinner* scooted me out for MY VERY OWN INDIVIDUAL BURST OF APPLAUSE . . . and well, that was that. We were off and running. Toward the bright lights of the theater, in summerstock local theatricals, in church camp musicals, in high school productions (I was Joe Football in the *Oak Park Follies of 1972*, which was revenge since the football-types called me a faggot all the time), then to college at Southwestern Illinois where I was a theater major. I even dropped out of college as a sophomore to go make my fortune in New York, for ten long years, hoping, dreaming, struggling, scheming . . . and I think, if I'm honest, waiting for it again: that embracing, completely saturating very own individual burst of applause. These days, however—

"Is that typing I hear?"

(That's my wife, home from work, just walking in the door.) Yes, dear. The autobiography is under way.

"About time! I was tired of hearing you talk about it. How far along are you?"

I'm nine, it's page two, and would you mind fixing dinner tonight? I'm on a roll here.

"I suppose your starting this project at 4:45 p.m. was not part of a larger strategy to put me in the kitchen, was it?"

Of course not. (This woman knows me pretty well.)

"It'll mean just sandwiches if I fix it. Poor worn-out fragile pregnant woman that I am . . ."

She's not even two months into this and already meeting her demands has become a challenge. Last night I got rooked into driving up to Skokie for Chinese take-out. I can only imagine what the seventh and eighth months will be like around here.

Actually, I can't imagine it.

I can't imagine being a father. Between you and me, I thought kids were something other people had. But we agreed this was the right age and the time was right and . . . I guess the problem is I still have New York on the brain, residual theateritis. No, I'm not going back—I'm happily married, I've been working out here for four and a half years now, and I'm looking forward in an abstract way to being the world's greatest father to the world's greatest son or daughter. But I was a different person in New York.

"What kind do you want?" she's yelling from the kitchen. "The management's pushing baloney tonight. It's forming a wall in the back of the fridge."

Peanut butter and mayonnaise on white Wonder-type bread.

Silence. I wait for the comment.

"As if the morning sickness wasn't bad enough. That I have to craft such atrocities with mine own hands . . ."

You know when I said I was only secure in the theater once, when I was nine years old? I can think of another time. When I decided it was time to leave New York and take a long break. Maybe for the first time in ten years I really felt like my own person, in control of events for once, and part of my happiness was having the theater in proper perspective. Also, I was probably looking for an excuse to go home. Which is ironic. Because sometimes here in Evanston with the next few decades of my life chiseled in stone before me—well, the rest of my life, really—I wonder if lately I haven't been looking for an excuse to *go back*.

1974

IT was still a time when people moved around the country by Greyhound bus. That's how I moved east, and it meant my introduction to New York City was through the Port Authority Bus Terminal. Lisa, my only friend in New York, was going to meet me at 2:30. She showed up at 3:15, but forty-five minutes late is pretty good for Lisa.

Now I very much wanted to look like Coolness Itself so I went to Male Prostitute/Pot-Heroin-Cocaine Central, the men's room, to Freshen Up, and there I am before a dingy mirror trying to look tough, New York tough, Gil in the big city . . . nope, it's not gonna work. I'm still five-ten, I'm still a wimp, I can barely lift my suitcase. I am however a man in my own time: brown, aggressively tangled hair to the shoulders, a tie-dyed T-shirt (yellow with bursts of white—I loved that old thing), a denim jacket, a very patched-up thin pair of ratty jeans, my peace-sign belt-buckle and, for christ's sake, my HEADBAND—just for New York, to let the nine million know how *with it* I was. God. You know that bank robbery in Tulsa?

That series of liquor-store holdups in Nebraska? The old couple in the trailer park I killed for 50¢? That I can live with. What I've never been able to forgive myself was being so obviously a just-off-the-bus, immature twenty-year-old.

Because Lisa was late I decided, unchaperoned, unassisted, I would take a first step outside into the metropolis. The bus station is right on 42nd Street so there I was five seconds later walking against the tide of teenage hooker runaways, fourteen-year-old junkies, police busting some black guy for something, old men stumbling out of the porn-sex shops. I beat a retreat when this over-made-up transvestite tried to put his arm around me ("Nice headband, sugar"). Gosh, New York City. Mom will be so thrilled when I write her all about it. We're going to have to take this city, your new home, Gil, slowly, in small doses. Back to the bus station coffee shop to wait for Lisa.

Lisa.

Oh I cringe when I tell you what was most on my little mind as I entered New York, riding in through the Lincoln Tunnel, my face pressed to the green bus glass trying to take it all in from the Jersey side of the Hudson. My name in lights? How was I going to be a star in record time? Nooo, my big concern was if I could kiss Lisa on the lips. I never had. This was a good excuse, I figured, since I hadn't seen her in four months. We would be sharing her sublet for a year, after all. I had decided not to return to my junior year of college and instead come to make my fortune in the big city and, while I was being romantic, why not kiss Lisa with a Big Romantic I'm-a-Man-Now Kiss. Adults did that kind of thing and I was an adult. Somewhere on the bus ride between Southwestern Illinois University and Port Authority, I can assure you Lisa, I ceased being the theater-department sophomore jerk and became a full-fledged budding-actor-in-New-York jerk.

At 3:15, there she was.

"Gil!" She ran to give me a hug.

Lisa! (All right, get those lips into position . . .)

"Let me look at you," she said, holding me at arm's length, hands on my shoulders. Damn. Kiss was out. "You're early . . ."

No, I'm not—I said 2:30.

"I thought you said 3:30, honey. Sorry. Where's your junk?"

It was one overpacked suitcase, in a locker.

"Look, let's drag it to Seventh Avenue and hail a cab there," she said, tossing her hair, her beautiful long frizzy blond natural '70s full head of hair. "Never," she said, "try to go crosstown in a cab or it'll cost a fortune. Stick to going up or down the avenues—you're there in no time."

Three months in New York, and she was an expert, she was a zany-madcap-young-girl-in-New-York, and boy did I want to fall in love with that.

We got our cab. I'm in the back with my suitcase, head out a window, looking at skyscrapers, the mark of the newcomer.

"Headband's new, isn't it?" Lisa asked.

No, had it forever. (Okay, that was IT for the goddam headband.)

I was fascinated by everything that passed by, Lisa was jaded and blasé. I asked questions, she answered them . . .

"Oh this? This is the garment district, actually. Oooh look at that rack of fur coats. Still waiting for a rich man to give me one."

And then the Village, western half, not yet yuppified in 1974. Following a brief tour of Lisa's sublet, owned by a single mother with two kids who were in Europe for a year, we went to Lisa's favorite Village café and sat at an outside table.

"Think he'll do it tonight?"

Who do what?

"Nixon resign. Where've you been?" Lisa pulled out the last of her cigarettes. "I'm quitting you know. This . . . this is the last cigarette I'll smoke during the Nixon administration. Emma's got a friend at *Newsweek* who says it's a sure thing, he'll step down tonight. Which oughta be a relief for Susan."

Susan wasn't a Nixon fan?

"No, I mean her party—she's the person whose party we're going to tonight. I wrote you about her parties. They're famous. Susan's Soho Parties. I wrote you all about them, how incredible and bad they were, remember?"

No she didn't. I only got one letter from Lisa the whole summer and that was the one that invited me out to move in with her.

"I did *too* write about Susan's parties. Anyway, we're going to one, so, uh, psychologically prepare yourself. You're gonna meet every loser in New York tonight—these parties are great for the old ego, I'll tell ya that." The waitress made a near pass and Lisa leaned out to flag her down to no avail. "You saw that, didn't you? She saw me, she saw me . . ."

I could get used to Café Life, I thought. This was the Café Prato and if the waitress noticed us we were going to have cappuccinos. Lisa went on talking about work and herself and her new easel and other stuff, while I thought about my luck. Lisa (two years older than I was, a graduate of SWIU), had left for the big city upon graduation, got a sublet for a year in the Village. June 1974 to June 1975. She'd had two roommates lined up but they had a big falling out and weren't speaking, so there was Lisa left holding the lease. I wrote her and said—I'm cringing again—how Southwestern Illinois was holding me back, how I should move to New York and take my chances, how I was better than any of my classmates, knew more than the directors, etc. And then surprise: Lisa writes back and says, DO IT, drop out, come move in with me and this girl I met named Emma. Would I mind living with two women? Me, a sexually frustrated college sophomore with a strong crush on Lisa, object to moving in with two women in New York City in a snazzy sublet in the Village? WOULD I MIND?

"Anyway, it's a Nixon Resignation party tonight at Susan's," Lisa said, inhaling and exhaling her last cigarette seriously. "She was going to make us dress up like Watergate criminals or Pat Nixon or something, but I talked her out of that."

I wanted to know more about Susan.

"No you don't," Lisa said, smashing her cigarette out in the ashtray. "You don't know what a state of grace you are in right now. She's four hundred pounds and she wears these . . ." She shook her head. "No describing her. You have to meet her."

The waitress passed by again, ignoring Lisa's exaggerated semaphore to get her attention. "Did you see that? They hate me here. I spend all my money here and they hate me."

I ventured: Susan is sort of a friend?

"Oh god no. No one really likes her, we just like going to her loft parties. She's rich. I can't feel guilt about despising her and drinking her booze because she can afford it. Can't feel sorry for anybody rich for some reason." Lisa looked sadly at the smoldering butt. Then she went inside the café.

I sat there alone a minute, reviewing the essential fact of the day: I was in New York. Ta-da.

"They're snotty *inside* this place as well," said Lisa, returning with a pack of cigarettes. Before I could ask if Nixon had resigned: "There is obviously some confusion about what I said earlier." She flung the cellophane wrapper off in a single gesture. "I was referring to *this* pack of cigarettes. I don't buy another pack until what's-his-name is sworn in. Actually," she went on, as she lit up, "I'm really chain-smoking to celebrate your being here and rescuing your college chum from bankruptcy and eviction." Then she sunk her sharp fingernails into my arm. "You ARE moving in, aren't you?"

Yes yes yes. No turning back now.

For Our Audience at Home: Yeah, Lisa knew I had a crush on her. She enjoyed it. No intention of letting me do anything about it, of course, but it certainly didn't bother her that I was going to be adoring and worshiping around the house each day. Give it time, I thought. I grow on people; I'm like an industrial solvent, I'll wear you down . . .

Lisa licked her lips and tossed her hair back characteristically. "What did your parents say when you told them you were moving in with me, a Modern Woman of the World?"

It wouldn't matter what they thought, I told her. They weren't happy about my dropping out and they were set against my moving here and I'm sure Mom didn't care much for my living with a Woman of the World, but HEY, what am I, a kid? I told Lisa I was on my own and I didn't care what my parents thought one way or the other.

Which wasn't entirely true. I moved out with $400 I had saved and Mom gave me another $400 and I never told anyone that she gave it to me, lest I seem less independent. They *really* hated the whole idea—for them New York was where you went to be killed while your neighbors looked on, land of drugs and garbage strikes and—you had to hear my mother pronounce this for what was probably the first time in her life—hoe-moe-sex-yoo-uhls, which would be chasing her son down Broadway and back, day and night. Hey man, like, they wanted me to finish my degree, and that wasn't my scene man; you know, get a haircut, get a job, a concept right up there with Peace With Honor—the Establishment, man. I shouldn't parody how I felt at the time. Sorry.

"I guess your parents think we're sleeping together or something," said Lisa. (What was this—Parent's Day?) "They probably think I'm leading their little boy astray."

Wasn't it obvious I was so astray already? We laughed together, ha ha ha. Sex with Gil. What an idea.

Lisa and Gilbert, Their Early Years:

I met Lisa my first year at Southwestern Illinois. She was the resident advisor on the girl's hall in the same dorm, for our Sister Floor, and there was this Hayride Hoe-down Night and each guy was assigned a Pixie and we had to buy little gifts for . . .

NO, THIS IS TOO STUPID. Let's just say she was a junior, I was a freshman, and we liked each other a lot and I went and sat in her room a lot and ate her homemade cookies a lot and I was flattered that she didn't throw me out and thought I was mature enough to be seen with her, and I don't know what she got out of it, but you might just have to accept the fact I'm a Fun Guy and people sometimes like me. Anyway there was this fellow, Ted, and they were going out for—no, correct that: they were *breaking up* for years, longer than most marriages last. Nations rise and fall in the time it took for them to work out the fine details of breaking up. *Now* I see they were very immature, but back then that struck me as Real Life Drama because sex was involved which meant it was mature and important, which shows you how little *I* was involved with sex at the time.

Didn't take long, huh? Onto SEX, this author's almost-favorite topic. I'm warning you now—I like making lists, categorizing, analyzing, and I also warn you everytime I'm sure I've gotten it sorted out, I'm wrong. Nevertheless (and I'm not alone here) women in my early twenties fell into three distinct categories. We got room here, don't we?

1. The Only-Good-For-One-Thing Girl who is only good for one thing, and it was the '70s and everyone was rushing around telling me this was unliberated and sleazy and dishonest, and there's more to life than losing your virginity which is what I spent my late teenage years trying to do. I lost it over and over again with girls like this. But what the sensitive young man of my era *should* desire, I knew, was

2. The You're-Like-A-Sister-To-Me Woman who is like a sister to you. Now you should just never NEVER go to bed with a woman who is your friend but you feel *zilchola* for sexually because at that early stage in your sexual life it's going to mess with you in a big way. I don't think young guys these days feel compelled anymore to sleep with their wonderful female friends who don't happen to be lucky enough to look like *Vogue* models. But I did. I was the Sensitive Young Man of the New Age, struggling toward enlightenment, dealing with outmoded but latent sexism, trying to meet the New Woman on her own turf, pursuing a caring, nurturing relationship with someone I admired for her mind, someone as exciting to me as Mamie Eisenhower.

And this was where I got depressed. What I wanted to come along was a woman with whom the sex would be as stupendous as the intellectual companionship, and she had a name, the concept of her is legend, she's out there . . . the Quality Item . . .

Someone should have lowered a sign saying: you think Early-Twenties Heterosexual Average Middle-Class American Male Problems are bad, just wait until the *Late*-Twenties Heterosexual Average Middle-Class American Male Problems strike, chiefly, getting ANYONE to sleep with you. It is never as easy as college EVER AGAIN. As a younger guy I was obsessed with why things weren't 100% perfect, why sex wasn't all they said it would be, whether I should trade in someone good for someone potentially perfect, what the other guys were thinking. God, you hit the early thirties and you . . . you just want someone to have a hamburger with, you know? You develop an affection for human frailty and women who look like human beings live in their bodies, and you find yourself wanting to hug the middle-aged woman on the bus or get to the plain-looking sixteen-year-old before her tenuous adolescent confidence is defeated, you stop thinking of *Playboy* Centerfolds, Ideal Women and pedestals and rectifying all that's imperfect and disillusioning in the world on the battleground of a relationship with some poor unsuspecting GIRL. But back to

Lisa: Lisa was such a ticket, and I knew it from the moment I saw her. She was

3. The Quality Item who is, to repeat, the first woman you meet in whom erotic beauty meets the class act, the girl with the brains, admirable, adorable in every way *plus* she is of an order of beauty, intelligence, worth, sense, taste, etc., that is usually—and here is the key, so listen up—OUT OF YOUR LEAGUE. The male ego's gotta make a beeline for this one and has to be loved back in return, or that's it for you, you've had it, you're nothing, you're condemned to a life of barfly ex-cheerleaders, one-night stands, misery. I know guys who spent a decade pursuing their Quality Item Fixation—no one (thank god) is as important as that first, hotly pursued Quality Item. After you get her and see whoopdiedoo, no big deal (or marry her and live happily ever after—it happens I guess), you don't run after women on pedestals anymore. Women, yes; pedestals, no.

And so there I was that day in the Village, just two hours off the bus, my suitcase a block away in her Carmine Street sublet, I was sitting at an open-air café as the light grew longer and more orange, the evening turned a touch cooler, and there was Lisa (who was just soooo New York to me, even though she'd been there three months), adventurous and rebellious (she had moved to New York City, like me, over the objections of her parents) and talented and trying to make it as a painter, doing commercial art jobs and temporary work by day, and she was in the Village (which was a distillation of all that was wild and exciting in New York) and I wanted to make my life the equal of hers, I wanted to be an actor working in New York, an actor of some success and note, and I would do it so perhaps there would come a time, somewhere in the future, that the Quality Item would look up at me from across our shared breakfast table and say: yes, it is you, isn't it? YOU'RE THE ONE AFTER ALL, GIL. You are MY Quality Item.

"A man showed me his penis on the bus yesterday," Lisa said, staring out blankly into the square.

Yeah?

"This town's a toilet bowl, Gil," she said lazily, almost stifling a yawn. "Mayor Beame says it's the Big Apple but it's just as often the Big Toilet Bowl. I was reading today some expert saying the city was going to have to declare bankruptcy soon. If that happens it'll sink even deeper in its craziness. But Emma says you have to learn to love the squalor," she added, taking a deep drag on the second cigarette in the Nixon pack. She laughed a private laugh, thinking again about Emma, soon to be the third person in our sublet. "You're gonna love Emma," she said. "You won't know what hit you."

There was a flurry of pigeons in the square across the street from us as this old baglady tossed up a dirty hotdog bun, watching it fall, waiting for all the pigeons to swoop around it; then shooing them away, retrieving what was left of the bun, throwing it into the air again, repeating the process with a cackle.

"That's the Pigeon Lady," said Lisa, familiar already with the locals. "She goes around in the gutters and in the trash cans hunting for bread crumbs for her babies, her pigeons in Father Demo Square." The woman cackled again, scuffling amid the fluttering pigeons. "And look," Lisa said, nudging me, "there's a weird one."

This old, grizzled man, like so many of the old downtown bums, a scarecrow-man, tattered clothes, gray with unwashed years of soot and street-sleeping, would go up behind someone and lecture them, yell at them, use impassioned gestures, like a Southern senator, except no sound ever came out—it was just a mute pantomime. If anyone turned around, he mouthed "Sorry" meekly and backed away, only to begin haranguing again. We watched him do this until the man reading a paperback got up and left, irritated.

"Yet I don't feel that sorry for him," said Lisa, musing. "It's hard to feel sorry for someone whose delusions are . . . I dunno, authoritarian. What gets you is someone like Dolly."

Eventually I saw Dolly. Dolly was the Queen of the Pathetic, one of the regulars on Carmine Street. She was this obese black woman who searched the trash cans of New York City for tattered dresses—*thin* women's dresses, little girl clothes, baby clothes even—and she would parade around, holding her find up, press it to her chest, smooth it out, and stop you as you walked by: "You like my dress, my pretty dress? I'm gonna wear this dress. It's good on me, my new dress, it looks so good on me. You like my dress?" And so forth. After a month you got used to the sounds under your window, six in the morning, "My name is Dolly and this is my pretty new dress. You like my new dress?"

Lisa sent up a hand for the waitress again, who turned as Lisa mouthed "Check." "No tip for you, baby," said Lisa under her breath. "I learned a lesson the other day," she went on. "I was on the subway and there was this kid, twenty-one or so I guess, but he looked like a sad twelve-year-old. And as the subway got going under the river to Queens where I was looking for a studio to paint in, he got up and, looking weak and sickly, gave this speech: 'I'm Tim and, like, I'm a heroin addict and, like, it happened in Vietnam and I'm sorry about it but I gotta ask you people for money 'cause, well, like, I gotta eat and, you know, get some stuff. I don't wanna commit no crimes or nuthin' . . .' Gil, I tell you, my guilty white bourgeois heart went out to this kid and I dug deep and gave him a dollar and I looked around me, and all these cold bastard New Yorkers weren't even looking or listening, pretending he wasn't there. When they looked they looked at *me* as if I was the weird one for giving him money."

Well it's a jungle out there.

"Yeah right," she said, rolling her eyes, "and that kid was a con, because last week I saw him again doing a routine about being thrown out of retarded school and his mother being sick and in intensive care and how he can't take care of his mama. I mean, if you didn't know, this stuff would break your heart. This one woman across from me just coughed up a handful of coins. I was thinking, hm, first week in town, huh?"

Strange city.

"This town," she said lighting cigarette number three, "particularly the crime, the streetcrud harassing you, the panhandlers and the goddam hippie leftovers—it gets to you, as you trudge back from your $2.50 an hour job, you know? If you stay here long enough, you wanna form a vigilante squad, you want Dirty

Harry to come clean the streets. You're ready for a Goldwater comeback."

Now now.

"Three months ago I was a McGovern Liberal. I would have given my body to Eugene McCarthy. Now I sound like my mother back in Milwaukee, for christ's sakes."

Speaking of family, how was her brother?

"Don't ask," she said. "He's still doing his Love Generation routine in San Francisco. It's just like Washington Square, over a block or two. We'll walk through it on the way to see Emma. I mean, hey, that stuff's nice, beads and sitar music and people selling earrings made out of tinfoil and all, but come on, you can't keep living that way. Aren't you glad we had our older brothers and sisters to do all that dumb shit so we didn't have to?"

The waitress slung the check on the table: "Have a nice day."

"Well I wasn't planning on it," said Lisa, "but if you insist."

It was great then, that afternoon—I hadn't one *ounce* of an idea of the sheer grind of living in New York, day to day. Walking around Washington Square, with Lisa narrating, seeing the colony of activists, artists, jewelry-makers, guitarists, people selling beads and African batiked cloths, pottery, their knitting, the pamphleteers, people waving petitions, Jews for Jesus, brochures about federally funded abortions and harassment of homosexuals by police; someone pinned a flower on me asking for a donation to the Temple of Universal Love, whatever that was; there were the better-dressed hippies sidling up and offering one-word drug pitches ("Snow? Hash? Weed? Pills? Horse? . . . "), the teenage juggler with a hat full of coins in front of him because he was very good, the buskers harmonizing only half as good as Peter, Paul and Mary on the song they were attempting, the ill-nourished runaway who was beyond persuasion, circles under his eyes, pallid, on something, "Can you give me some money, man, huh, can you?" Lisa put a quarter into his hands, thinking perhaps of her brother in San Francisco (who got messed up really bad on drugs), and he pocketed the money without acknowledgment and stumbled through the crowd, intent on the next handout. Washington Square in 1974, the last hurrah of the dying '60s. Even more mysterious than how the Love Generation came about in the U S of A, God's Country, was how completely it was to disappear without a trace by the mid-'70s. Yeah, I know, a lot of the "idealism" was self-serving and self-indulgent, but you look around now at every smart, talented person rushing to get in the door of the nearest investment bank and you can't help but think back on August evenings as late as 1974 when there was something beyond the color and the music, a spirit (I know, yucky word, but what else do you call it?) that the United States might have done well to hang on to a little longer. This seems a long time ago.

"Playtime's over," said Lisa, pulling at my sleeve, "we'll come back and mess around later. Let's get something to eat."

I followed Lisa as we approached the eastern edge of the Village, where things began to look even seedier, the shops untrendy; the posters and signs turned more ethnic (Ukrainian and Italian, with misspelled English translations underneath), the people a little more worn-looking either from having to work grueling daily jobs, or from being unemployed.

"We're headed toward Baldo's Pizza, if I can remember where it is. That's where Emma works."

In a pizza place?

"Yeah," said Lisa, "because poetry-writing doesn't bring in too much. Gotta support your habit."

Was Emma any good?

Lisa slowed the pace a bit. "Yeah I think so. Then I don't know anything about poetry. Or theater for that matter—so you're safe too from critical opinion."

Did Emma know about art?

"Good god, Emma knows about everything. More than me about art, more than you about theater. She's scary. Sometimes I have second thoughts about asking her to move in as our third—I'm going to feel so stupid."

Tell me again, I said, how you met Emma.

"I put all that in a letter to you —what were you doing with my letters?"

Lisa NEVER wrote ANYTHING TO ANYBODY—pay no attention to her.

"How I met Emma?" Lisa paused and decided which rundown, dangerous-looking street to take. "I met her at a Susan-party. She's staying with Susan—poor girl—until she moves in with us. Emma wanted to meet you first before she moved in, though, so make a good impression . . . we've passed this porno bookshop thing before haven't we?"

We found it after fifty wrong turns: BALDO'S PIZZA, in flashing pink neon. Inside there was a waiting area with green and white and red patterned floortiles, Italian flags, several posters of a national soccer team on the walls, postcards from awful places, and one-dollar bills glued to the cash register under a sheet of faded yellow tape. There was a sample pizza out on display that looked like some modern art conceptual-thing, all dried out, the tomato and cheese a surreal red and yellow, all sort of glazed over in grease.

"You think it looks bad," said a woman behind the counter, "you oughta taste it."

And that was Emma Gennaro.

She was covered in flour (one got the impression more flour lingered in the air than ever went into the pizza at Baldo's), but I could still make out that she was about an inch taller than me—a tall girl, lean, angular, with long straight brown hair that got tossed back angrily a lot, or in disgust—a trademark gesture. I'm not good at describing people. Just think of a pretty Italian American girl who is not an immediate knockout—not Sophia Loren—but in five minutes or so, after getting used to her, she's quite striking, made very striking by her hand gestures and expressions that seem to take up all the space in the room. Give her ten minutes and you'd be convinced she was a beauty, but now that I think back I'm not so sure anymore—the photos could go either way. I'm not much help, am I?

Gee, I haven't described Lisa either. Let's see . . . Lisa was the pretty girl in high school who was popular and Class Secretary, looked like she belonged in an Ivy League college recruitment catalogue, the girl in the stylish outfit—yes, she wore outfits—sitting by the river that reflected willows and rowers and swans; and she looked like the kind of girl who might be the only cool member in her sorority but dropped out of it once it got too cliquish and stupid but she might not mind your knowing that she got into it in the first place. You could see her as a woman in business, but you could take her camping too—she wasn't conservative-looking, really, just clean and bright and dressed tastefully, just not her own tastes. Even when she had a punk phase (that's later on) she looked stylish, nothing too outrageous or jarring. It doesn't seem like someone who would want to be an artist, does it? She should own a bookstore or something.

"What is this, the UN?" yelled a big man with hairy shoulders who stormed out of the back room in a U-necked T-shirt, he too covered in flour. "I pay you Emma to talk or to dish out pizza?"

"Yeah, you pay me next to nothing to dish out the worst pizza in town," she said, waving a finger at him provocatively.

"Whadya mean woise pizza?"

"I mean when I wanna pizza I go down the street for some; that's what I mean by the woise pizza."

When she wanted to, Emma could really lay on the Italian-American routine, the singing insults, the exaggerations and drama, the gestures. She was a quarter Italian and she told me the family history a few times, full of hard work and immigration and American Dream and bootstraps and fingers being worked to the bone. Gennaro is Neapolitan, but in the late 1800s her family moved north so they could make something of themselves, married Milanese, then took on America, Ellis Island and all that, settled in New Jersey, then Indianapolis as of the last generation, her hometown. Catholic guilt? "Nah," she'd say, "I wish I had been brought up stricter—I'd have an excuse for being so screwed up. I went to a suburban Catholic church, never confessed anything, went to mass at Easter and Christmas." Any longings for the Old Country? "What old country?" she'd ask. "New Jersey? I wish I had had a richer ethnic upbringing—it'd give me an excuse for being so screwed up. My folks tried hard *not* to be Italian—I can't speak Italian worth beans. Some people here in New York get fish on Fridays and Grandma telling folk tales and Grandpa drinking grappa after mass, and all that, but nyehh, I had Indianapolis and shopping malls, Girl Scouts, all kinds of Americana and crap." Difficult childhood in conservative Indianapolis? "Not really. It's a nice place, a nice boring place. I was too boring back there to mind it. But I'm interesting now. Sorta wished I had grown up in Little Italy, the mean streets with all the passion and drama." We looked at each other and simultaneously said: "It'd give me an excuse for being so screwed up."

"Do me a favor," Emma was saying, "and fire me—do me a big fat goddam favor and fire me, get me outa this place, willya do that for me? You think I like seeing people come in here all the time, DYING for a pizza, hungry, starved for pizza, and take a pathetic look at this garbage and whisper, gee, let's go someplace else, it doesn't look very good here? Hey, and don't walk away while I'ma talkin' to you!"

Baldo came back from the kitchen: "You're talkin' to me?"

"Yeah I'ma talkin' to you."

Baldo locked Emma in a big embrace, a cloud of flour flying up from the apron: "You gonna apologize 'bout my pizza, ey?"

"Hands off, hands off—you mess me up like you mess up your pizza . . ." Both were laughing at this point; Baldo was tickling Emma. "You gotta meet my roommates," she said, fighting him off. "This is Lisa, this is Gilbert."

Baldo tipped his silly Italian pizza-chef's hat to Lisa. "Her I seen before here. Pretty face, I remember that. You—" He meant me. "—You I don't know. You livin' with these two? You are? A baby like you? Gonna be nothin' left of you, sonny boy. This one'll kill you—" He recommenced his tickling attack on Emma who was now armed with a garlic shaker.

"How 'bout a faceful, huh? Get your hands away from me. I think it'd be nice if you gave my friends a pizza slice. It's Gil's first slice of pizza in New York. Not that this shit is pizza." She dodged another lunge of Baldo.

"Free slice?" he cried, slapping his forehead, looking to the ceiling, beseeching the gods. "What am I? The return of Mayor Goddam Lindsay? I look like Welfare to you little gurl? Scuze me but the soup kitchen is that way to the Bowery, ey?"

We got three free slices and they were terrible, but even bad New York pizza is better than a lot of good things and I was happy to be eating a slice of it, walking along the East Village, down St. Mark's Place, where the trendy, filthy, fashionable and wretched all meet and intermingle to this day ("very NYC," as Lisa would say), with Lisa on one side of me, Emma on the other. Wow, Gil in New York with TWO WHOLE WOMEN!

"Let's get drunk," said Emma, holding her hands to her face. "God, my hands have permanent pizza smell. I go to sleep smelling this stuff—I dream about oregano. Every night, pizza dreams, like Disney—little pepperonis jumping on my pillow, the Dance of the Garlics—"

"You're right, let's get drunk," interrupted Lisa.

I was on a budget so I asked why we should buy drinks if there was free booze at Susan's party.

"Yeah, but you need to be drunk," said Lisa, "even to go drink her booze. You need serious alcoholic conditioning beforehand. And sometimes the drinks there are atrocious."

Emma nodded. "On St. Patrick's Day she had a green Irish whiskey crushed ice punch, which . . . ulllch, it looked the same coming up as going down."

Lisa added, "And the refreshments—good lord. Third world African nut paste, and Indian grain mix and, oh god, if it's vile and sick-making it's out on the table."

"Joan's in charge of food tonight," said Emma, which set off a string of curses from Lisa.

We settled on an Irish bar called The Irish Bar and it was done up in green foil and shamrocks and little plastic leprechauns hung from the liquor racks and the gruff man behind the counter and the quietly sodden lot inside didn't seem connected to or responsible for the frivolous decorations. We found a booth with lumpy, badly stuffed vinyl upholstery, but it was toward the back. Emma went to get three 50¢ beers.

"This is a drinkin' bar," said Lisa, scooting into the booth beside me. "It's a drinkin' man's jukebox too. About ten versions of 'Danny Boy.' "

Emma put down the beers; Lisa lit up a smoke. As we had no mutual acquaintances, Lisa and Emma began telling Susan stories and Susan Party stories, giving me a rundown of the legend of Susan before our eventual meeting.

Three Most Popular Susan Stories:

* * *

1. He Was Masterful, a.k.a. I Came Seven Times

Time: A Susan Party, sometime in the spring

Place: Soho loft

There was Hervé who was a male model and very gay and very stuck on himself and he began to brag that he could screw anything that moved and perform admirably and that he should be a gigolo, etc., so after a while his friends prodded him in the direction of Susan and said "What about her?" and he said he *could* do it but he wasn't going to, but then his friends accused him of lack of resolve, that perhaps he had met his match, so he got real drunk and stumbled over to make a pass at Susan, who had never had a chance with such a hunk before. Susan ran around soliciting advice, making sure everybody knew about it—of course, she was really a lesbian separatist as she had made clear many times before and she hated men but for the experiment of it, the wildness of it—and she was wild ("You know me, I'm just crazy—I'm mad, I'm perfectly mad! I do all kinds of crazy things; I'm that way, you know?)—so she should just go ahead and do it, and it was politically correct sleeping with a gay man anyway, she figured. Well the core group of her acquaintances (couldn't quite say "friends") all agreed that no matter how bad Susan wanted to tell them allllll about it, they would act like it was no big deal, which made sense because Susan had claimed "hundreds" of lovers and there was no reason for her to run around as if this were her Big Score. It just about drove her crazy—she tried to work her Night of Passion into every conversation, she'd start discussions with strangers about it but she couldn't get much of a reaction out of anyone. So her story, which she told repeatedly, got more honed, more sensational. "Wellllll," (Emma did the imitation, low raspy smoker's alto) ". . . he was masterful, an artist . . ." (Emma did a long draw on the pretend cigarette, a disinterested look into the distance) ". . . a craftsman. I was like a block of marble, a *big* block of marble and he was, like, a sculptor . . ."

I interrupted: No one talks that way.

Lisa was laughing uncontrollably at Emma's apparently accurate imitation. "No, you're wrong," Emma said. "One person *does* talk like that."

Anyway, in her quest for a reaction, Susan would put a hand on your arm and say, that worldly look in her eyes, one omniscience confiding to another, "You know, he was so *good* . . . I came three times. He knew what a woman wanted—these gay men, believe you me. Sensitive. Not ANIMALS like so many . . ." (in utter disgust) "mennnnn . . ." Anyway, by the time the story reached Lisa she had come six times, and Emma (who had heard it earlier when it was up to four) heard her say "I came seven times."

Lisa stopped laughing to add, "Mandy, a friend of ours, has an open bet that it'll be up to nine before's year's end."

Emma shook her head, adding, "Yeah and the punchline, of course, is that Hervé, sober and utterly embarrassed the next morning, said he was too drunk to do anything, he just sort of fell asleep on top of her. God knows how her mind works."

Lisa said, "She's obviously never HAD an orgasm to tick 'em off like that. Or else, maybe it's the opposite—maybe she's such an easy mark, you just put your hand anywhere on her and BANG."

We all laughed, ha ha. I couldn't have sworn what a woman having an orgasm was like either, so I laughed loudest of all.

2. Truth or Dare, a.k.a. I Want to Show You My Breasts.

Time: a month previous

Place: an uptown theater party, 2:30 a.m.-ish

Susan's favorite game was Truth or Dare in which she only had one line of questioning: everybody else's sexual experiences, which when listened to allowed her a chance to tell about hers (whether she had them or thought she had them or made them up and forgot she made them up, wasn't known). If you didn't tell the truth in Truth or Dare you had to do the dare, which was usually something harmless like downing your beer in one. But Susan kept saying things like "Oh god, I mean, just don't dare me to take off my top, I'd be so embarrassed!" and "I'm going to dare you, Cindy, to take off your top—just don't dare me!" Soon it became obvious that the game would not proceed until Susan was allowed under some pretext to take off her top. So someone challenged her and she took off her top, exposing this big fat pair of meaty breasts. "I'm really comfortable with my body weight. I like being this size," etc. Finally, being persuaded to put her top back on, she started asking questions like "How would you react if I took off *all* my clothes?" The Truth or Dare players insisted there had been enough exhibitionism for the night, but one guy (the guy who dared her to take off her top) was intrigued and dared her to take off all her clothes, and of course she just couldn't bring herself to answer the question. "Oh my god, you mean I have to take off . . . take off ALL MY CLOTHES?" Machine-gun laugh. So she retreats to the bathroom and a sizable percentage of the party clears out, heads for the door, has had enough, etc., and the rest stay to see Susan emerge from the bathroom which she does. The game never got back to normal after that with Susan asking impossible to answer questions ("Would you kiss my breasts?") with follow-up dares ("You have to take off all your clothes too and run down the hall and back with me . . .").

"She was drunk, but still," sighed Lisa, barely able to sip her second beer from giggling.

Sounds a bit pathetic, I said.

"You're making the mistake of taking Susan seriously as a human being," said Emma, "which once you meet her, you won't do anymore. She's impervious. You could walk right up to her and go: Susan, you're a fat pig and the most ridiculous person in the world. It wouldn't register—her mind omits any negative input."

Lisa kept giggling, almost spewing her beer. "Tell . . . tell Gil about her, uh, subscription . . ."

Emma put her head down on the table laughing.

What? What is it? I asked.

Emma reared up, tears in her eyes. "I don't know you well enough to tell you this one."

Come on, come on.

Lisa and Emma enjoyed some more convulsive laughter.

It's probably not that funny, I suggested.

"You're right, it's not," Emma said, before she and Lisa made eye-contact and slid off into hysterics again.

I went to the bathroom and came back and they had calmed down and had ordered more beers and a bowl of peanuts.

"There," said Lisa. "We're all right now."

And then they broke up again, virtually having to fall to the floor to hold onto themselves.

What? What? What? What?

"Okay, okay, okay," said Emma, fanning herself, trying to catch her breath.

3. Susan's Magazine Collection

Time: this week

Place: Susan's loft, the bedroom

Emma had come into the bedroom to ask Susan how to turn on the gas stove and as Susan couldn't explain it, Susan left to do it herself and Emma wandered absently around the room noticing that Susan had been reading this porn mag, lying there on the floor, by her bed.

Emma hid her face in her hands. "I don't know you well enough to tell you the title. Lisa, you do it."

Lisa tried to sober up and began to say with exaggerated dignity, It was called *Big* . . ." Then she couldn't.

Emma finished: "*Big Black Rods.*"

Lisa looked down into her beer. "It wasn't about motorcycles, Gil, if you know what I mean."

"And then Susan comes in and there I am looking at this thing," said Emma, "and of course she says she's a lesbian separatist and all that, but men have oppressed women through pornography for hundreds of years and she doesn't see why, now that men are in porno, that she can't buy an occasional mag to get even, blah blah blah. And then she went on to tell me about her . . . oh god."

You've already started this story, I reminded.

"Then she told me," Emma went on, rolling her eyes, "about her masturbation rituals. I mean, she just told me all kinds of things, things I could have lived very happily without knowing."

"I would love for twenty-four hours," said Lisa, "to go through my life with *one half* the confidence, the unashamed self-love that woman has. She has absolutely no shame. Emma, tell Gil about the cucumbers."

Emma buried her head in her hands again. "I can't tell him about the cucumbers."

I said I thought I understood already about the cucumbers.

"She's into cucumbers," Lisa began.

"And vice-versa," Emma added.

And she told all this to Emma?

"Yes, she goes shopping for them and she thinks it's more socially responsible than buying, you know, an aid, because that supports the female-oppressive sex industry. Besides, she said, a cucumber is natural, organic."

Lisa finished off her beer and said, "I feel like washing my hands after this conversation."

Emma turned up her glass as well. "I think it's time we go get ready for the party; it'll be an all-nighter, I bet. Old Tricky Dick must be down to his last moments in office, huh?"

We all trudged back to the Carmine Street sublet to clean up and Lisa hogged the bathroom for a half hour and came out looking just the same as when she went in (pretty as always), Emma plopped down in front of Lisa's tiny black-and-white TV checking for Nixon updates, and I went into what was going to be my room (the rich woman's little boy's room with a miniature desk and low-to-the-ground bed) and changed clothes. I didn't pull the door all the way shut and I heard Emma call out: "Let's see what Gil looks like in his underwear!" and I ran to slam the door and lock it to the sounds of giggling in the living room. "You'll get over your shyness one of these days," said Lisa. "You're living with two women now, remember?"

No, that fact had not slipped my mind.

It was twilight as we walked along a street that looked like a movie set of warehouses, fire escapes, run-down if not abandoned small factories. This was Soho?

"Yes," said Lisa, "designer ugliness for a new generation. A place for those who think the seediness and slum dwellings of the Village aren't quite bohemian enough."

We went up in a creaking, dangerous-looking elevator, enclosed only by a scant railing and metal screens, the shaft exposed completely (which wasn't comforting).

"What will Susan be wearing tonight?" Emma, making nervous conversation, asked Lisa.

"The muumuu with the Chinese dragon."

"You mean the mooooo-moooo?" said Emma, making cow noises.

Lisa laughed, ssssshhhing Emma because anyone could hear what we were saying and no telling where Susan was.

We clanged to a stop and got out on the sixth floor which was dark except for a shaft of light coming from underneath a door at the end of a long hall. We heard muffled party noises as we slowly, feeling the walls, approached the door. Then suddenly the door opened and we saw a great block of light which was soon eclipsed by a silhouetted, massive figure . . .

"*Emma* baby, come give Mother a kiss! Ahahahahaha . . ." This, I figured, was Susan. "Lisa you too!" Susan planted lingering kisses on my friends as they winced politely. "Lisa, always good to see you—and whoa hoa hoa, this must be the NEW BOY! A little fresh meat, huh?" The machine-gun laugh, followed by her hand on my behind. "Ooooh, *medium-rare*—how old is he? Looks sixteen, but the younger the better is what I say. Older women are more sexually compatible with a young man." She fired off another machine-gun laugh, shaking her head, she was just too much for herself: "I'm crazy, I'm *wild*, I really am. Oh kid, you'll get used to me in time—I'm completely mad, that's what everyone says." Her hand found my behind again and I was guided into the party. "Now don't you be offended at my wandering hands, you little sex object you. Men have treated women this way for centuries, so turnabout is fair play, and it's about time we women got some of our own back, you know? This is 1974, Bill, loosen up, loosen up. Are you a virgin?"

Emma and Lisa drifted away intentionally, as I was dragged into the vortex of the party . . . I turned briefly, seeing Emma waving a little bye-bye to me, Lisa blowing me a kiss.

"My parties are famous, Bill—famous. And wild things happen—I don't know how, god help me, but they just do . . ."

I was parked with a guy named Bruce while Susan promised she would get me a drink.

"We've met before, haven't we Bill? I'm Bruce. We talked about jazz last month at a party here, I'm sure."

No, I don't think so, I—

Hands on my behind again: "GUESS WHO??? Ahahahahaha . . ."

Susan put a gin and tonic into my hands and corralled me over to a group of skinny men with mustaches. "Boyyyys, oh boyyys," she cooed, "some new ass for you—boys, meet Bill, he's from the Midwest somewhere on a farm—"

Gil, I corrected.

"He's an actor," said Susan, raising one of her eyebrows with a pudgy finger, then winking, "and you know what that means, Tony don't you? Latent homosexuality."

I met everybody. I ventured a comment after Susan fluttered away. Something like: She's really something else, isn't she?

"I love that woman," said Tony. "She's stupendous, just tremendous . . ." Well he was right about that. "I'll tell you something: When I was coming out and trying to deal with certain aspects of my Gay Self, she was the best friend in the world to me. I mean, I can tell you stories, times when we held each other and cried ourselves to sleep, shared that kind of experience and pain. She even saved my life one time."

Another strike against Susan.

Emma, meanwhile, was setting off brushfires around the room, pulling everybody's chain, whipping the conscientious activists into a frenzy, which was good fun, as it seemed for some reason that everyone in 1974 under the age of thirty had the *same* opinions.

"You're crazy," I heard Emma say, as I sidled up to hear her conversation. "You're gonna miss Nixon when he's gone, and history is going to show he wasn't a half-bad president aside from his total moral corruption, which is probably a requisite of that office."

A woman with a very earnest, high, hollow voice, long stringy hair which she tossed back when she was about to make an intellectual point: "You can't mean that. You didn't vote for him, did you?"

"I always vote for entertainment value, because I don't take the system seriously and I certainly don't think my vote matters enough to take seriously either. Nixon has been amusement from day one. Nice as it would have been to see McGovern go to North Vietnam on his knees and beg for the end of the war—"

Someone else: "He never said that."

"—or distribute the wealth of the country and put a thousand dollars into my pocket, Nixon was the first bet for the entertainment-minded person. I mean, just look at all the entertainment he has provided: the greatest whodunit public television spectacle in history, better than the McCarthy hearings (which, significantly, he had a part in), better than your run-of-the-mill sex scandal. In fact, I'm going to be damn sorry to see him go."

Offended Superliberal: "What?!"

"You don't think Gerald Ford is going to be the laugh riot Dick Nixon was, do you? Oh the Golden Days of Presidential Entertainment are slipping away."

The first Someone: "And I suppose you think the Cambodians were entertained by his secret bombings?"

"I knew about 'em. You knew about 'em. The Cambodians knew about 'em."

Flustered: "It was a neutral country."

"With 40,000 Vietcong troops operating out of it, supplying their front lines."

Outraged: "What did that have to do with the innocent women and children whose villages we bombed?"

"Not much, but it had a lot to do with the innocent nineteen-year-old soldiers from Podunk, USA, who were being shot up by those weapons in South Vietnam. Given that we were fighting the war, what was wrong with defending our soldiers? We should have waited for Cambodia to stand up and go: hey guys we're not really neutral so you can bomb us now? Come on."

Emma Gennaro, radical anarchist, taking a hawk line at Susan's party. What she wouldn't do for intellectual exercise.

I drifted back and forth to the refreshment table—as predicted, full of mucks and pastes and goos and natural overripe brown cubes of vegetables on toothpicks to stick in the mucks and pastes and goos, and lots of slivers of bread with no yeast, salt or flavor, next to bowls of seeds and kernels and bran dust. Emma's voice rang out against the general din, as I noticed from time to time . . .

"You know, Susan, the antiabortion movement began on the left, for your information. Fetus rights were on many liberal agenda with antiwar, gay rights and socialism—in fact, I have a handicapped friend who feels like abortion will eventually rid the world of all human imperfection, as people will abort a fetus with any deformity or undesired characteristic, and he takes the line that abortion morality will do away with handicapped people altogether, denying humanity its variety, undermining the premise that a handicapped person can have a worthwhile existence. He saw a future where people breed for perfection like the Nazis, the whole eugenics lie . . ."

That got a few people going. She struck next in this pocket of people hanging on the words of a bearded Columbia-professor-type:

"I'm actually looking forward to nuclear war, in a strange way," Emma said. "I mean, for one thing, the suspense is killing me—a car backfires in the street at three a.m. and in my semiawake state I think: god, they've gone and done it. Secondly, if it were a limited exchange, or say, if India and Pakistan have a holy war and do each other in, it might do some good—"

Squeaky man: "What do you mean by some good?"

"Well, the population problem would certainly seem less threatening. And the effect would be so devastating that there might very well be in the aftermath a world disarmament; in order to recover from the collective effects of the war, the world would have to unite, work together, under one provisional government perhaps. Why I can envision a new postnuclear ethic and morality and order, a restructuring of society. A second Eden, a millennium of peace after Armageddon—"

"You must be kidding" said Susan, drifting over.

"Not at all. I also intend on surviving this limited Soviet-American exchange."

Someone broke in: "It wouldn't be worth living after a nuclear war. The radiation, the culture ruined, civilization gone, all your family burned to a crisp."

"Except for the radiation, all that sounds fine to me," said Emma. "And the radiation is going to go away, and you can stockpile food, canned goods, Cheese Whiz, Captain Crunch, all the staples. I envision coming out of the shelter in Maine or Oregon and getting on a motorcycle and driving around seeing what's left of everything. I see a whole neo-Romanticism growing out of the desolation, the ruins, the scavengers, the omnipresence of death. I envision doing the country with a band of my friends, weapons in hand for protection against the radiation-mad mutated humans who pursue us for our food, or perhaps to eat us—it'll be like a science-fiction movie . . .

And she never let up, until everyone was yelling and screaming at her. I wandered back to the drinks table. In the background I heard Emma say: "And what's so bad about genetic mutation? We'd all be chimpanzees without it . . ."

Lisa bumped into me, steadying herself on my arm. "I'm officially drunk Gil baby," she said. "This is my life now: coffee all morning, cappuccino and iced tea all afternoon, a caffeine high with a vengeance. Then"—Lisa used her hands in grand gestures that seemed to have little to do with what she was saying—"then at night, booze. The body is ready for drink, ready to come down. You giveth the body adrenaline and then you taketh it away . . ." Lisa had trouble with the *th*s on giveth and taketh.

I said Emma was in danger of being lynched by the party.

"What's great," said Lisa, "is that Emma really does *mean* these things. Everyone wakes up the next day and laughs, thinking she's kidding. She's not. Oh look. Look."

What?

"She's talking to Joan now. They got in this horrific fight two weeks ago over native Americans."

Native Americans?

"You know, Indians. Woo woo woo woo . . ."

Joan was in sandals, jeans, and a homemade knit blouse that she had made herself (as she was happy to tell everyone), and she sold her homemade handicrafts in order to buy the materials for a loom that she was going to make herself to produce crafts upon as it was the only moral alternative to buying textiles from un-unionized factories down in North Carolina where there were goons and Fascist tactics and union-busting and the loom was very important to her, as was her homemade knitwear business; i.e., her smock, which was the color of dirty, tawny, offwhite wool and had no sleeves but rather two big gaping holes at the shoulder and every time she gestured or got a drink or got a piece of flavorless brown bread, you couldn't help seeing her pointy small breasts when she bent forward. But then she seemed like she might not mind your seeing her pointy small breasts. I told Lisa that I couldn't help noticing her pointy small breasts.

"Yes," said Lisa seriously, "they're always pointy and sticking through her crocheted tops. Joan once gave me a speech on how dishonest I was because I shaved my underarms. Joan is that woman's roommate . . ." Lisa pointed her drink toward a brunette version of Joan, who had long dark hair as if she might think she looked like an Indian—wait: native American—with a leather headband (HOW unfashionable . . .) pulling her hair back, but from the neck down she was dressed like an almost-stylish secretary in a "midi" with white hose that looked strange between the midi and the leather boots.

"Sally's a classic," said Lisa, pulling me further back from the party so we could gossip. "Last month she had two analysts. Two. She had so many problems, you see, she went to one on Tuesdays and Thursdays, the other on Monday and Wednesdays. On weekends she went out and did self-destructive, stupid things to talk about Monday through Thursday."

Lisa was rehearsing her stand-up comedy routine, right?

"No, I couldn't make this story up," she went on, steadying herself on my arm. I led us both to a sofa that someone had spilled a drink on and therefore was deserted. "All her problems in life are because of Daddy," said Lisa. "Daddy who pays the rent on her $400 a month loft apartment I'd kill for, Daddy who pays her analysts' bills, Daddy who is a wealthy real-estate tycoon who sends her to Europe once a summer—"

Sounds like child abuse to me too, I said.

"Well Daddy," Lisa continued, "is the source of all her neuroses and when the Unification Church didn't help and the People's Love Temple didn't help and a retreat with the Mormons didn't help, she went to this high-priced analyst and told him about her daddy who raped her, abused her, and fondled her as a child and why this has caused her to be frigid with men today. Well the doctor came up with a therapy: sue Daddy. Take him to court, exorcise those demons, expose him for what he is, a public catharsis."

And she did?

Lisa smiled, "There was a problem," she continued, raising a finger. "Mainly that she made it all up. So she started going to Analyst No. 2 and told him about telling Analyst No. 1 the rape story. He asked her why she made it up, and she said that it was because Analyst No. 1 had made a pass at her and had molested her during a Valium treatment and she was so scared of him that in order to assert how vulnerable and fragile she was she created the whole father-rape story. It gets good here. Analyst No. 2 is outraged that Analyst No. 1 did these things and tells Sally that she should sue him, get his license revoked, expose him for the quack he is—it's analysts like that who give analysts a bad name, right? And so he was going to take this up with the New York Psychiatric Board."

She made up the second story as well?

"Yes, so she's in a bit of a spot. Now I can't remember what comes first here, the affair with Analyst No. 3, who I think I saw here at this party, or her botched suicide attempt—"

Suicide attempt?

"Yeah, she took too many pills, unfortunately. I mean, unfortunately because so many people want her loft. Anyway, Joan moved in with her and the details are foggy. It's been a long time since she told me all this stuff."

She TOLD Lisa all this?

"Honey, she'll tell *you* all this; any acquaintance, the mailman, for christ's sake. I was young and innocent, a scant *two* months ago. They warned me don't go out with Sally for lunch, you'll be sorry. But her daddy has an account with Four Seasons, and I was never going to get in the *door* there—so I went. A fair trade: lunch for her life story. It's not as if it's a dull life story."

Susan had dropped a sandwich of cress and refried beans and curried mayonnaise down her front, making a big stain on the Chinese dragon. So she made a big show of undressing and warning no one to come in because she would be NUDE and then she took minutes choosing something to wear, once peeking around the door and titillating us with a bare arm ("I can't decide what to wear! Joan come here . . . help me decide. No, come on . . . Tony, you, yes come here. What should I put on?"), and then after Tony went in to look through her wardrobe, she pulled the door closed yelling "Ahahahaha, I'm going to *convert* you!" I only relate this because now Susan was back in a bathrobe/evening jacket/smock-thing, sweeping through the room commanding silence, silence.

"It's time! It's time!" she cried.

Tony followed her, wheeling out a small black-and-white TV on a cart behind her. Much confusion as they hunted for a plug, and tried to tune it.

"Thank god," said Lisa, still next to me on the sofa. "I am down to three cigarettes. Now watch the bastard *not* resign. I'll impeach him myself."

"I mean I NEVER watch TV," said Susan defensively, "except for PBS and cultural things, of course. News and documentaries—"

"And *General Hospital* every afternoon," called out Emma, hidden behind a crowd.

Much laughter and finger-pointing; Susan laughed along, breathing drily, "Emma . . . ha ha ha, what a card."

The picture stunk. There were lines and snow and static and the sound wasn't good. People talked and didn't pay attention, and when Susan flipped the channel around hoping that would improve reception there was a major outcry to watch the Bogart movie on Channel 9. Finally, the commercials ended, the network news announcer came on, the White House appeared, and there he was: Nixon, looking a good deal older than two years before at his landslide re-election.

Good evening . . .

Someone: "Jesus Christ, he's gonna do it, isn't he? Can't believe it."

Someone else: "The man could not wear ties. Look at that awful tie."

Others; Ssssssshhhh!

This is the thirty-seventh time that I have spoken to you from this office . . .

Someone: "Thirty-seventh and last."

I no longer have a strong enough power base in Congress . . .

Joan: "The bastard, just look at the bastard."

Sally: "Next time we hear from you, I hope it's from behind bars."

Whoops were going up around the room. People embracing.

I would have preferred to carry through to the finish, whatever the personal agony it would have involved . . .

Susan exhaled her cigarette smoke, nodding: "Serves him right for the Fascists he put on the Court. Suffer, Dickie, eat your little heart out."

. . . and my family unanimously urged me to do so . . .

Someone: "Pat's probably putting the silverware in the suitcase now."

Someone: "With her cloth coat."

Sssssssssh!

Therefore, I shall resign the presidency

YEAH!! Screams, cheers, hoots, applause.

effective at noon tomorrow.

Someone gave Nixon the Bronx cheer.

"President Ford," said Lisa, trying it out.

Someone: "He's got it together. Do you think he's going to cry?"

Joan: "Next stop for you is Leavenworth, Mr. Nixon."

To have served in this office is to have felt a very personal kinship with each and every American . . .

"I can't believe it," Lisa said blankly.

Emma asked, "What are we going to do now that we've gotten Dickie out of office? An era is ending, for sure."

Most people had drifted back to the drink table, talking amongst themselves. ". . . it's nothing short of vindication for everything we've worked for," said some bearded man with thick glasses.

Susan said intently without removing the cigarette from her mouth: "C'mon Dick, for *me*. Say you're sorry."

In leaving, I do so with this prayer: May God's grace be with you all in the days ahead.

"That's it?" someone whined.

"Damn," said Emma, "I was waiting for a big scene, Checkers-style, not a dry eye in the house."

Nixon faded out, the commentators took over, and the party cheered distractedly. "Bring out the pot!" someone yelled, and there was a general drift to Susan's bedroom, repository of the marijuana.

Susan crushed her cigarette into an ashtray, shaking her head in dissatisfacton. "He didn't say he was sorry. I wanted him to say he was sorry."

The party at large: "Susan, get over here and get your pot!"

Lisa and I were still on the sofa. Emma went to get another drink, leaving us with a thought: "Watch for a Nixon comeback in the '80s, mark my words."

Lisa slapped her knee. "Well," she sighed, still thinking about the speech, "that was short and sweet. No grandstand play."

There was brief drama as two guys attempted to hijack the TV to watch the Bogart movie on Channel 9, while Sally and Joan demanded to watch the followup and news analyses of The Resignation on PBS. Then Susan swept in—"Here it is, gang! I bet Dick is doing some serious drugs tonight, too!"—and a group of potheads devoted themselves to rolling joints for the party. Susan turned her attention to the TV squabble: "*No* TV at my party! Put that away and come with Mother Susan . . . "

I expected something longer, I said to Lisa, concerning The Resignation.

"It's like *Richard the Second* by Shakespeare," said Emma,

descending on us from out of the blue, sitting right on top of the drinkstain on the sofa, oblivious. "A man presiding over his own disintegration, his kingdom going to hell while he makes speeches, postures, eloquently defends himself—does everything but save his ass like a normal human being. Oscar Wilde too."

"You are probably the first person in history to compare Nixon to Oscar Wilde," said Lisa.

"You know what I mean, the idea of setting up your own downfall and then playing out this grand tragedy as you martyr yourself. Remember Oscar brought it upon himself—he was the one who sued his boyfriend's daddy for libel. At the trial, of course, Wilde loses, loses everything, his respect, his career, his wife and kid, throws it away so he can sit up on the witness stand being witty and brilliant. It's like Nixon and the tapes. Both men insisted they were innocent, eloquently, authoritatively, and yet they *knew* they weren't, they knew their very 'proofs' of innocence were going to condemn them. You need to be more of a psychologist than I am to figure out that one." Emma hit me gently on the knee. "But you know all this, huh? Being in the theater: Oscar and *Richard the Second*."

Yeah sure.

Emma was about the smartest person I'd ever met up to that point. Maybe even after that point—intelligent, I mean. I should mention that I was officially drunk at this point too. In fact, I told Emma artlessly that she was the most intelligent person I'd ever met.

"Well you must not get out much," she said, patting my knee again.

Lisa and someone I really had to meet when they got back from buying cigarettes named Mandy were gone. So I tagged along beside Emma, who left me standing outside the bathroom. I thought about making a pass at her. NO, that would mean abject mortification. Just the first day in town. Unless I came up with a really good line. How about: you know, I think I'm sexually attracted to intelligence. Flattering, different, sincere. No, on second thought, that was CRAP. I could pretend to be interested in Lisa and ask her advice. Waitaminute. I *was* interested in Lisa. That was three hours ago. Now I was interested in Emma. No. I'm just going to tell her outright, when she comes out of the bathroom.

"You waitin' for me?" she asked, emerging from the bathroom. "No towels of course—turn around." She wiped her just-washed hands on my T-shirt. I recall at the time I found this arousing.

"I like you, Gil," she said.

Good I like you too.

"If I was a normal person and not so screwed up—oh good god, look at that." Emma nudged me to look across the room where Susan was putting makeup and lipstick on her male friends, everybody drunk.

(C'mon, Emma—finish your sentence!)

"You're next Bill!" Susan called, spotting me. "You'd look lovely with a little eyeliner."

But Emma, when I turned back, was gone, off to talk to a woman named Janet. Janet and Mandy-I-had-to-meet worked for this feminist gazette called the *Womynpaper*—smart, urban women, new women of the '70s, women who wouldn't put up with any male nonsense from me, no ma'am. Emma promised to come retrieve me in a few minutes.

All right, leave me then.

I'm independent, I can hold my own here at a New York loft party. I'll mingle. I'll meet exciting people. Maybe a woman, the woman I've waited all my life to meet, someone I could fall in love with—

"Oh shit . . ." moaned the woman Cindy as she threw up beside the sofa. Everyone groaned, turned away, Susan ran to the rescue.

Suddenly, I was not in the mood for love.

Anyway, Operation Mingle.

I found myself talking to someone who was writing a book.

"It's this book, and I've been working on it, oh hell, say, three or four years," he said. "*In my head,* I mean. In my head only—I haven't put any of it down on paper yet; it will come rushing out at the right time when I've let it gestate." Yeah.

"It's about this film director and how the films he makes become indistinguishable from his own life; it's called *Lights Camera Action*."

Wasn't there something called that already?

"No, no," he said excitedly, almost spilling his drink, gesturing, "that's the amazing thing! Not for fiction, I looked it up in the Library of Congress catalogue—can you believe it? No one's thought of it. And I think film is such a good metaphor for life. It has a beginning and an end and you gotta fill up the space in between; it's also visual just like life . . . "

I drifted away after a while and ran into one of the skinny gay guys I had met at the beginning of the party talking opera with a bored-drunk woman.

"Oh christ, honey no, she's awwwwwful—you like her? She can't sing a note. How can you mention her in the same *breath* as Sutherland? Her *Tosca*—good god, take her out and SHOOT her. Name me one thing she can sing . . ."

The bored-drunk woman said a role and he nearly went through the ceiling: "Chriiiist, you bought her in THAT? Oh if you'd ever seen Caballé in that, my dear, you wouldn't even breeeeeathe her NAME . . ."

Susan was screaming with hysterical laughter, asking someone "Do you think I should? Do you? Should I?" Instinctively, drunkenly I drifted in an opposite direction, toward two older women, two nice-looking, serious-looking women who . . . no this was a mistake.

"What does she mean *too old*? I'm not old—what? She thinks I'm old? You know I'm not old, don'tcha baby, huh?" The older woman began to french-kiss the other woman. These are lesbians, I said to myself. "She said what? What, I'm dried out, am I? I can bleed, I can goddam bleed—I'll spread my legs and bleed with the best of 'em . . ."

Bad drunk. Embarrassing drunk. Take this woman away.

Somewhere in here I was seized by Susan who was making a full-party sweep, devastating all in her wake. "Anyone a virgin in here? Come on, any virgins? 'Fess up! I'll cure that right away—oh you think I'm kidding Julian, I'm not, I'm not. You dare me to do what? Look, I don't care—man or woman, I'll take you on right now . . . Wait, where was that Bill farmboy? Farmboy, where are yooooo? Ahahahahaha. Sooey sooey sooey—I can smell a virgin a mile off! Bill, there you are!"

Oh god oh god oh god—

"Billy's a virgin isn't he? Look at him blush! Oh he is, he *is*! I'll fix that honeylamb!" She made a lunge for me as I dodged, slipping behind someone I'd seen before as she rampaged in another direction, after another victim. I made conversation with the someone—god, please be normal . . .

"Hi. I'm Bruce. Hey, haven't we met? Wait we met a month ago at this party."

No I just—

"Don'tcha remember? We talked about jazz."

I don't know shit about jazz but we talked about it and then I excused myself to the bathroom where I threw cold water on my face and heard through the bathroom wall: "C'mon Dave! Show us—don't be shy!" Followed by: "Oh Susan you're wild—you're a madwoman!" And then (I was waiting for it): "Ahahahahahahahaha . . ."

I'd gotten high in here somewhere and now I was starving. I went to the refreshment table. I gnawed on a crust of flavorless, yeastless, dusty-tasting natural brown bread.

"Good isn't it?" said Joan, extending her hand. "I'm Joan and I don't think we've met."

I said I was with Lisa and Emma.

"Oh," she said grimacing. She bent down to make a sandwich out of sprouts and bran dust, natural mustard and the flavorless bread, and I happened to look down her front as her loose homemade knit top sagged forward.

Interesting breast—uh, *bread*, I noted.

"I made this bread," said Joan, eating her creation. "And I made this top myself. I'm trying to earn money for a loom. If you need a scarf or anything, give me a call."

Susan from the bedroom, after a whooping laugh: "Oh come on, we allll masturbate . . ."

Then suddenly: *AAAAAIIIIIIII!*

Sally was in the middle of the room, standing like a zombie, screaming at the top of her lungs. Everything fell silent at the party. Joan ran up to her, and others followed . . . Sally, what's wrong? Honey tell us . . . Please, speak to us . . .

"What?" Sally said, as if awakened from a dream.

"Why did you scream, baby?" said Joan, holding her.

"Scream?"

Others in the support group, taking her hand, stroking her hair, asked her why she had screamed.

"Did I scream? Yes, I think I did . . . I . . . I don't know why I did that. I just . . ." Tears formed in her eyes.

"Talk to me," said one heavy-set woman, beseeching.

"I don't know . . . I just don't know . . ."

WHERE WAS EMMA? WHERE WAS LISA? WHERE WERE THE WOMEN I LOVED? I wandered about desperately, dodging the bores, avoiding the intimates of Susan. There was a partition in the far darkest reaches of the loft and a gray, flickering light emanated from behind it. I peeked around it and Emma was watching TV; Lisa was beside her in a beanbag chair, mouth open, lightly snoring, dead to the world, a spilled drink to her side.

"Oh it's you," said Emma, looking up and starting a little. "I thought you were Susan. I am acting in violation of the Hostesse." She patted the floor beside her. "Sit down. Come be my co-conspirator."

I told her Susan was looking for her; she shrugged.

"This is Channel 6," she said, nodding to the TV. "All night long they rerun all the great old shows, when everybody else is off the air. Situation comedies, black-and-whites, and *The Family Compton* which I never miss. I love that old show—just got turned on to it a few months ago—don't make 'em like that anymore. Lots of sex and sadness and death, they kill off someone all the time, someone is always critically ill, such good melodrama and I always cry. Tears running down my face. The show is so old that most of the illnesses can be cured now, so it doesn't affect my Perpetual Death Obsession which flares up from time to time."

Susan made a brief pass near the partition. Emma turned down the volume and the brightness so all was dark and quiet. Susan left our vicinity shrieking, "Wait for me, wait for me!"

Emma turned the volume, brightness back up. "I hope the Harpies aren't having an orgy. No, you laugh, you think I'm kidding—last month they did. Three fat women all kissing each other and caressing each other's flab. You had to see it." Emma's show was over, the credits and music whined from the small black-and-white TV. "Okay, here is the big moment."

What was, I asked.

"To see if *Lollipop* comes on."

Lollipop was this old, bad sitcom with a little adorable tyke named Laliana Papadopolous (Greek ethnic-stereotype family) and she was called Lollipop for short and she went around the tenement making people's days and patching up quarrels and all things would be resolved because of her, and each episode would end with people hugging Lollipop and saying she was an angel and Lollipop would cock a smarmy little childstar smile at the camera which would zoom in on her, and the theme music would come in for the final credits, amidst the sound of canned clapping . . . *Lollipop, Lollipop, Lala La Lollipop / Lollipop, Lollipop, Lala La Lollipop* . . . all sung by this '50s nebulous chorus of children. It was the worst TV show in the History of the World.

"I'd like to find that Felicity Glenn, or whatever her name was," said Emma, glaring at the child actress, "and personally annihilate her. You see Gil, I wrote Channel 6 and told them that what they should do is run two *The Family Compton*s and can the godawful *Lollipop*s, and they wrote back and said they appreciated my letter, blah blah blah, but no. So I was looking through this *Channel Six Fan Club Magazine* which they put out for old movie and TV show buffs and they always feature a staff member and there was this middle-aged man named Harry Langston who was their nighttime engineer and button pusher and I wrote him and I told him I would give myself to him, sleep with him unconditionally, if he'd run back-to-back *Family Compton*s and scratch the *Lollipop* show—and he DID, because next week there were two in a row. Well I wrote again and told him thank you, I knew he couldn't do it every night, but if he could JUST see his way to doing it one more night that next week . . ."

Did he do it?

"That's what we're going to find out tonight."

The commercials were over. The TV went black for a second and then: *Lollipop, Lollipop, Lala La Lollipop* . . .

"Shit," said Emma, "not tonight."

Well you can't have your way every night, I said.

"Some people want to run the world. Some people want power, wealth, fame, influence. This is what I want. To every once in a while alter the New York Channel 6 TV schedule, little triumphs like that, played out before millions of people who don't know what's going on."

"*Ahaaaa!*" said Susan, seizing upon us. "I've found you! No hiding from the Hostesse!" Lisa stirred in the beanbag chair, not able to wake up. "Lisa, Lisa, Lisa," Susan said, shaking her, placing her hands on her shoulders, then her back, putting a firm hand on her thigh. "Time to get up, the party rolls on!"

Emma flicked off the TV.

"Oh was that *Lollipop*? I wish they'd put it on earlier," said Susan. "I loved that show as a kid . . ."

Emma looked at me, raising one eyebrow.

"Billllll, baby," Susan began.

Gil.

"Gilllllll, baby," Susan went on, "the evening's young. Lonely for the Midwest already? You Midwestern farmboys!"

Emma suggested we go to the roof and look at the city and Susan said she'd join us later, but fortunately she didn't. We left Lisa asleep on the beanbag chair, passed out. We took the creaking Death Elevator to the top floor, stepped out, wandered around in darkness, using Emma's cigarette lighter for guidance, found the fire door to the roof and then propped it open with a brick. You couldn't see much of the city because to the north was a taller building, the Empire State Building stuck up above it; to the south were the Twin Towers, lit up all night long.

"It costs more to turn the lights off and start the power flowing again the next morning," said Emma, "so they just keep the lights on all night. I worked there once."

Doing what?

"Well, before Baldo's, I worked temporary work, filing and typing and making coffee, playing secretary for $2.50

an hour. I get $2.75 at Baldo's which isn't much more but I can work all day and all night if I want. How are you going to get money?"

By working in the theater, I said, I hoped.

"Got a job lined up already?"

Not exactly.

Emma gave me a sympathetic look. "I'll have my Aunt Leonie back in Indianapolis say a novena for you."

But I had a connection, I said, an ex-roommate of a drama instructor at Southwestern Illinois who was a casting director at an off-Broadway theater. I'll be working within the week!

"None of my theater friends like the theater very much," Emma said. "In fact, I don't like my theater friends very much. You're not like most actors."

Thanks. I think.

We went over to the edge of the roof to look down and then we decided we'd really enjoy throwing something off the roof, so we looked around for something to throw off the roof but there was nothing small and convenient to throw. We thought about climbing down the fire escape—High Adventure—and climbing into Susan's bedroom window . . . and then we thought of fifty reasons why that was a bad idea.

"I'm never having sex again. Did Lisa tell you that?" At this juncture, I figured Emma was officially drunk too.

No, I said, Lisa hadn't told me.

"I'm not. I've joined this Celibacy Support Group which meets down here in Soho." Then she said the next thing in a rehearsed tone, so I figured she'd given the speech before: "One is persecuted these days for *not* having sex—if you're not engaging in orgies every night, you're obviously out of it."

Yeah, I know what you mean. (Whose side am I on here?)

"I've certainly had enough bad Midwestern sex to last me a lifetime, in high school, at Purdue."

(I was sort of hoping she was inexperienced and shy, which shows I was inexperienced and shy, I guess.)

"Nope," she said, finishing off her cocktail. "That was my Sex Phase and it's over—I'm disgusted with the whole thing. Exchanging bodily fluids. Body parts. Viscosities."

Viscosities?

"Lots of viscosities. Can't stand viscosities."

A church in Little Italy rang the time.

"It'll be dawn soon," Emma said, sighing, looking down into her empty plastic cocktail glass. "One drink in Emma and it's just True Confessions. One good reason for going back to sex would be to have something to confess when I get confessional. Hey, the glass." I didn't understand. "Let's throw it over the side," she said, and we ran to the edge of the roof and did it and it was excitement galore.

"Better take me downstairs before I pass out," she said, steadying herself against me at the roof's edge.

Sure, I said, and I put my arm around her waist. Emma was always weird about being touched. You'd hold her arm and it would go limp; you'd hug her goodbye and she'd go strangely stiff—it was automatic, I don't think she was trying to do it. As we made it back to the elevator, staggering together, I stopped us both and looked at Emma in the moonlight—no, no it wasn't moonlight, it was streetlamp light, the collected nighttime neon haze that hangs over Manhattan, but Emma was still pretty in it. I got some class, I didn't maul her—I kissed her on the cheek.

She giggled, stepped back from me, folded her arms around herself. "I'm taller than you," she said, laughing again.

Just by an inch or two.

"I mean I can't go with someone who . . . I mean I don't . . . "

Too short for you, huh?

She said softly, "I just better get back to the party, that's all."

And we went back to the party, which was in its death throes. We went back to the TV room and as Emma flopped down on some cushions I was very authoritative about how to avoid a hangover, take two aspirin, drink lots of water . . . I passed out first though, I'm fairly sure.

The next morning was the definition of hangover.

I awaken. Where am I? I tick through the list: Oak Park, Southwestern Illinois's Stephen Douglas Hall, Grandma's house . . . Nope, nope, nope. Oh yeah: New York. I call Lisa's name.

"She's not here . . ." That was Emma's voice, subdued. I lifted my head slightly. Emma was watching the TV again.

This is the morning, right?

"Yes, it's the morning," she said, turning to look at me. "I don't know who looks rougher, you or Nixon."

Nixon was on the TV again, making a last statement, saying goodbye to the staff.

You know what my father was? He was a streetcar motorman first, and then he was a farmer, and then he had a lemon ranch. It was the poorest lemon ranch in California, I can assure you. He sold it before they found oil on it . . .

Pat was crying, Nixon was about to cry. Emma sat there snivelling too, reaching for the Kleenex. What was going on? I asked.

Emma turned around briefly. "It's his last press conference, and it's a killer. God, the man could work TV. Why didn't he use this material before he had to resign?"

Nobody will ever write a book, probably, about my mother . . . My mother was a saint. And I think of her, two boys dying of tuberculosis, nursing four others in order that she could take care of my older brother for three years in Arizona, and seeing each of them die, and when they died, it was like one of her own. Yes, she will have no books written about her . . .

It was sad.

"I've got a new theory about why we hate and love this man," Emma said. "He's everybody's Uncle Richard. Uncle Richard with the carpet outlet or used-car dealership, the guy who got things working and yet always blew it, always screwed things up, went bust time and time again only to get back up and take it again. Oh look, that's it. I'm relieved, I thought he was going to break down and that would have been embarrassing."

Commentator: . . . *The helicopter will take the former president to Andrews Air Force Base where he will fly to San Clemente, while the vice president, Gerald R. Ford, will be sworn into office by Chief Justice Burger . . .*

I asked where everybody was.

"Most everyone's gone," Emma said, passing me a bowl of

greasy chips she had been munching. "Have some breakfast. The dip is great—only good thing at the party." She slid a bowl of white dip over to me. I ate automatically. "Hungover?" Emma asked.

Yep.

"You know that famous chart we got in biology class of man evolving? Starts off on all fours and then through early man and ends up at Homo sapiens?" Yes. "Well I'm at Australopithecus about now. I expect modern man by this afternoon sometime."

I said I wasn't going to be erect anytime soon.

"Ha ha, that's good. It's gonna be the Emma and Gil Show around the apartment I see."

Gil and Emma Show, I corrected.

"Look, there he goes," Emma said, looking back at Nixon going up the steps of the waiting helicopter. "Come on, Dickie baby, give it to me . . ." And then Nixon, his last gesture in office, gave America the victory sign, two outstretched arms, two Vs, Nixon of the Nixon Imitations. Emma shrieked with joy. "Oh he's a classic! Look at him, walking away from the mess he made! Oh I'm gonna miss him—we won't see his like again . . ."

And Nixon flew away.

We heard a stumbling, a plodding. It was Susan who in a moment peered around the corner of the partition. "God, I can hear you two in the bedroom. Ask me if I'm hungover. I'm hungover—don't ask. I don't know what I did last night. Did I disgrace myself, Em?"

"One hundred forty-two times, Sue."

"Par for the course . . ." She turned to plod to the kitchen. "There are a lot of passed-out people in my bedroom and one might be dead. You'll help identify them, won't you Emma?"

Emma said sure.

"That dip's good isn't it?" she said, pointing to the bowl we'd nearly finished off. "All night long people were asking for my recipe. It's famous—I do it every time! Susan's famous *Cucumber Delight*!"

1975

IT'S 1975 and I didn't know *anything* before I moved to New York. Am I in Actors Equity? No. Does my résumé impress anybody, including my mother ("Come home son, come home . . .")? No. I go door to door, theater to theater, look I'll do anything, I say. Well, so will 300,000 other struggling actors. Who do you know? I don't know anybody. My connection, the casting director guy, didn't work in theater anymore, as it turned out. You don't know the New York Struggling Experience unless you've been faced with: the Possibility of Having to Crawl Home. You opened your BIG MOUTH and now you have to crawl home, with your high-school class going: "Ha ha ha Gil, you loser—guess you couldn't DO IT," followed by girlish, derisive laughter. No way. I was not going home. I might die on the streets of Manhattan sharing Ripple with the winos, but that's all right. I'm not going home. Discouraging as it was, heartbreaking and grinding and dispiriting as it was, I would continue to march to audition after audition.

The Time I went to the Audition from Another Planet:

"Hello people, my name is Ira Forrest and this production we're casting is *Experience 27*." Ira Forrest was a middle-aged hippie, his thinning hair combed over his bald head. He had the beginnings of a potbelly which didn't prevent him from wearing a tight muscle T-shirt with *Experience 26* lettered across it. As he paced with his clipboard giving us his résumé, we noticed his assistant, this zitty, pale twenty-year-old (maybe) who was unhealthily emaciated, wearing shorts which exposed these hairy toothpick legs. ". . . And some of you have been, no doubt, following the *Experience* series which I've authored, and perhaps you've heard of my work with the Northwest Co-op Theater Consortium in Portland, Oregon . . ."

Nope.

"This is Ryke, my assistant, and his input will be invaluable in our selection today." Ryke stiffened his neck as we observed him.

"You're wondering, I suppose," Ira said laughing slightly, "why all of you are together out here on the stage. We're not going to audition one by one—that's old, that's regressive theater. We're going to go through a series of exercises and through my observations—"

Ryke cleared his throat.

"Through *our* observations, we will make our selection. But first two cardinal rules of this process. One, this is *not* competitive. Yes, some people will get a part, others will not"—and here he raised his voice until it filled the hall—"but that is not, NOT to say that you don't have *worth*, have value, have talent. I want that understood. All of you repeat after me: I have worth."

We have worth.

"I have value."

We have value.

"I have talent."

Yeah yeah, we got talent. We also were told to shake the hand of the person beside us and introduce ourselves. I'm Gil. The woman beside me—good-looking, about my age—was Francine Jarvis.

"And the other cardinal rule of this process"—and here he seemed to melt, to look imploringly, vulnerably up at us—"is that I'm your friend. Yep. It's that simple. What we have here, yes, is an audition, but it's also the beginning of a long and sincere . . . friendship."

"Geeeeez," muttered Francine.

"Any questions?" yelled Ira.

Someone from the back row spoke up. "Uh, Mr. Director—"

"*Ira*, please. And if you see me on the street, I would hope you'd stop me and say hello Ira, because look people . . ." He seemed to get serious and almost choked up. "I'm here for *you*. My ideas are a conduit, a platform for *your* talents. I'm *nothing* without you."

("He's nothing anyway," whispered Francine beside me.)

"You got that? Good," he said, sitting down with his clipboard, having not answered whatever question the boy on the back row wanted to ask. "Now. We'll start with a teamwork exercise. You are . . ." And then the artistry of his idea carried him to his feet again. ". . . You are a pond. Close your eyes. Yes, right now, close your eyes. It's autumn. It's autumn in the woods, in the woods near a pond. Can you see it? Now all of you are the pond. Now I'm going to take these Styrofoam balls . . . Ryke, where are my Styrofoam balls? Have you seen my Styrofoam balls?"

Ryke: "How would I know what you did with them? I guess wherever you left them."

Ira, under his breath: "I was hoping for a spirit of cooperation, Ryke deeeeearest, but if you're going to be sniffy about every little request—"

"Who's being sniffy? You don't value my input anyway. You've been blocking me, Ira. You've been blocking me all day—"

"I have *not* been blocking you. What makes you think I'm blocking you?"

"I'm not going to discuss it now."

Then more tense whisperings passed between them, as we shuffled on stage. Ira was back soon enough:

"All right, you're a pond—all of you the surface of the still autumnal pond. Now everyone stand in circles, touching—I want touching, I want connections . . ."

We connected.

Ira found his box of Styrofoam balls and pitched one after the other into various parts of our pond. We shimmied and jiggled and hula-ed pretending to be a rippling pond, depending on where the balls landed (that is, when Ira's throws reached the stage).

"Next exercise . . ." Ira came from the wings of the stage with a ratty-looking blanket. "Everyone under the blanket! Ryke, will you help me spread this out?" Ryke reluctantly made his way to the stage, complaining at the lack of support, the blocking, there were denials of blocking, accusations of suppression, denials of suppression, and after a tense private three-minute meeting offstage, Ira returned all strained smiles, with instructions.

"We are now going to enact Evolution! You will be creatures progressing from the slime, on your bellies, crawling from under the blanket, and evolving, growing, changing . . ." As he said these words *he* evolved and allowed his gesturing hands to grow and change and flutter. "Some of you will be birds, some of you will evolve into mammals feeding your young, I want to see suckling, nurturing, we'll see primates, some horses, some . . ." Ira seemed stuck for an animal.

"Gerbils," suggested Ryke.

"*Yes*, gerbils," cried Ira, enthusiastically. "I'm glad you contributed that, Ryke. Thank you, I want to thank you for your input."

Ryke looked slightly mollified.

"What are you going to evolve to?" Francine asked me in a whisper. "I think I'll be a kitty cat."

Just as joylessly, I said I'd stay primordial slime—I mean, someone has to stay behind and be protozoa. I noticed a few auditionees slipping away toward the door.

"Everyone under the blanket!" yelled Ira. He then began to narrate the big bang, the history of the universe, the earth cooling down, volcanos erupting (he would erupt, making noises like:

KUSSSHHHHH, BRRRRRRRGGGG, BOOOOMMMM), then the age of the dinosaurs, squawking beasts . . .

"Now everyone," he said, coaching, "put the noises of your animal with your gestures . . ." The stage exploded in a melee of meows and moos and barks and grunts. "Yes! Yes! That's wonderful! I see . . . yes, I see you, young man, that is a fine lion—beautiful roar—yes, you've thrown yourself into it . . . I see you're going to attack that—what are you dear? An ibex? Yes, they attack, they kill—it's the jungle!" The auditionees started rolling around pawing and scratching each other. All except Francine who was doubled over in laughter.

THEN we got to be circus performers and we all were free to pick what we were (I, fittingly, was a clown). THEN we were a machine and we had to touch each other and interconnect (I was a piston going up and down). THEN we were all sea creatures under the ocean (I decided to be a motionless bed of kelp). THEN we had to be forms and shapes—each of us had to *be* a gesture that expressed our innermost soul: "No blocking allowed!"

Ira clapped his hands after this to bring us to attention. Then he raised his hands high above his head so we could see the giant sweat stains on his T-shirt. "Bravo! Bravo! You're *working* for me! Bravo, I say. There was some superb inter-relating—didn't you think so, Ryke?"

Ryke, sulking again, barely audible: "Uh-huh."

"And now," said Ira, lifting himself, huffing and puffing, onstage. "Now, the centerpiece of *Experience 27*, like in *18* and *24* of the series, will be the Assumption of the Earth Chief, in which the Earth Chief, the prime Speaker, the bearer of the *logos,* is conveyed by the supporting tribe . . ." Far from the confusion I felt, some of my fellow auditionees were nodding seriously, *understanding* this drivel. "So what we're after now is the bearing, the assumption of the master. Now I . . ." Ira cleared his throat, and shuffled a bit, "*I* will be the Master of *Experience 27,* re-creating my role of chieftain from *18* and *24* which had a similar processional—"

"It was *Experience 17,*" Ryke said from the orchestra seats.

"It was *18*, Ryke," snapped Ira. "I wrote it, I ought to know which experience it was—"

"Oh you're always right, aren't you? It was *17* where the troupe carried you around the stage and up and down the aisles—I'm sure of this Ira, because I helped co-write some of that."

Ira, now irritated, repeatedly cleared his throat in short bursts: "No Ryke, if I'm not mistaken it was *Experience 16* I allowed you to help me construct—"

"ALLOWED me?"

After Ryke eventually stormed off to the printer's office ("I might be back tonight and then again I might not . . ."), Ira had himself picked up by the assembled auditionees and passed around between groups of people, who held him high as they could overhead. The auditionees were told to make a chanting wooooooing noise as they held him aloft, and Ira recited something like poetry: "We touch . . . we hold . . . we touch . . . we are a oneness . . . we celebrate the beingness of being . . ." This part of the audition came to a close when a fragile contingent of short men and slender women couldn't support Ira's weight and dropped him, all of them crumbling into a heap on the stage. Ira just laughed:

"Mercy me! These things happen . . ." Then he clutched the arm of one of the boys, ruffled his hair. "I love the *physicality* of the theater, the touching, the inter-relating . . ." He slapped the boy's thigh, then put an arm around his shoulder.

Francine whispered: "Byyye-bye, Ira. Time to split."

Yeah, let's get out while we can, I said.

Francine and I walked to the subway stop together and we laughed about what had happened and shared all our other crackpot stories from auditions. I ventured we ought to get together sometime. She said yeah, wasn't it a shame she had to rush off. I said, can I call you? She said yeah, sure, and had a pen in her purse but no paper. I hoped she'd write her phone number on the balled-up Kleenex and she did and gave it to me.

My first phone number in New York! You'd have thought I would have gone home and had it plated in gold, had it raised upon a DAIS, built a SHRINE for it, but instead I managed to lose it. Probably used it to blow my nose. I'm sure, by the way, Francine Jarvis was the Great Love of My Life—if I'd not lost that Kleenex, history would have changed, like Abraham we'd have founded a nation, a people . . .

There was the Time I was standing in line to go out onstage, and I made idle conversation with the guy before me and discovered we had the same audition piece. There was the Time the audition was a private audience with the director who explained how he could not direct someone he hadn't known sexually at least once. There was the Time it was so hot and miserable backstage waiting to be called, that I fell asleep and missed my audition slot. There were countless times that I traveled down to the theater to learn the play was cast, the audition was canceled, my résumé (all lies) didn't get by the audition manager.

There was the Time I Walked Out of An Audition:

There was this petite little blond woman who went onstage before me. We were auditioning for this experimental work and the call was for lots of young people. Here we were.

"All right, love," said the director, this paunchy man in a flowered shirt, a gold chain around his neck, rose-colored sunglasses, very earnest, very pleading. "Tell me about yourself, Diane . . ."

"Uh, don't you want me to do my piece?"

"No, I don't, dear. Tell me about yourself."

This revealed that the girl had been brought up in Jersey, went to high school, got started in acting, she and her mother still lived in Weehawken—"

"Your mother's divorced?" asked the director.

"No," she said, "my father passed away—"

"How?"

She looked around as if for support. "Well he, uh, had cancer. Lung cancer. He was a heavy smoker, he—"

"Did you love him?"

"Well yes, I—"

"Did you tell him? Before he died?"

She was a bit irritated now. "Well yes, I did but I don't see what this all has to do with—"

"Tell me about the night he died. I want to hear about it." The girl was quiet a minute. "If you can't share pain, if you can't bring us inside your life, the door's over there, you have no place in this production." The girl cleared her throat. "Go ahead, leave if you want to—"

"No, it's all right," she began unsurely. "My father—"

"You didn't call him Dad?"

"No, not really. We said Father in our family—"

"You weren't close to him were you? You were distant, you were a stranger when he died."

"No," she said defensively, "it wasn't a perfect relationship but I'm sure he knew I loved him—"

"*Not* if you didn't tell him, baby!"

"What the hell business is it of yours?"

The director, now energized, laughed. "That's right—fight me, fight me. Come on—tell me you loved him and he knew it all his life. You wanna fight, we'll fight . . ."

This director closed in and intimidated and needled her into telling him about the night of her father's death and as tears rolled down her cheeks she mentioned that since she had been caught as a teenager in bed with a boyfriend by her father that he had never been warm to her and he had always preferred her little sister for some reason . . .

"Say it, say it!" said the director, who must have thought these catharses were important, that he was doing good necessary work.

"I never said I loved him," she sobbed, breaking down and bending over, holding herself.

I left before my turn.

The Time I Almost Got a Role but Walked Away:

"That's great!" yelled the director in this particular audition, a young wiry man with a pointed beard. "I don't have to see any more." He pointed at me. "I don't care if you can act. I want someone who looks like *you*—I want your body type, your looks. I don't care if you're a grocery clerk."

Gee, thanks a lot.

"Now let's get Pamela out here—Pamela!" Pamela, I gathered

was my possible co-star. "Pamela, this is . . ." The director checked his clipboard. "This is Gilbert Freeman. Kiss him."

Pamela kissed me, without hesitation. "Okay, Mr. Limpermann."

She had flat, bitter breath, this big groping teethy mouth—

"And again and again and again . . ."

More kissing. Pamela groaned with pretend passion. It seemed like bad porn-film acting to me.

"Are you hot for her, Gilbert? You want her, you have to have her, here, right here on the stage!"

I thought he just meant figuratively.

Pamela started unbuttoning her blouse.

WAAAAIIIIT a minute, I say. I didn't think this was a production with nude scenes.

"It may be, it may not be, I have to see," said the wiry director, all seriousness. "I have to see if you work together. Can you make *heat* for me, people?"

I said my clothes were not coming off and I was not copulating with Pamela onstage, I was sorry. And everyone looked at me as if I was some fugitive axe-murderer. *Look* New York, I didn't want to be psychoanalyzed, I didn't want to cry, I didn't want to screw onstage, I didn't want to show my naked body, I didn't want to sleep with all the directors in town. Acting? You remember acting, don't you? The thing they do onstage? The thing auditions—I assumed—were all about? ISN'T ANYONE IN 1975 INTERESTED IN MY ACTING TALENT?

The Time I Got Asked to Leave the Stage:

I had seen a part advertised for someone in their mid-thirties for a family drama and I got it into my head that, weary and defeated as I was, I could convince people I was early thirties. Quite horribly, I had this idea it was perfectly zany and wild and one-of-those-experiences to audition for something I wasn't quite right for. If it paid off then it was one of those gutsy moves you hear about, one of those audacious famous auditions, like Brando's. I acted my little heart out, I gave them anger, rage, hurt, pride—

"*Excuse* me," said the director, clapping his hand on the back of his clipboard, now standing, looking angry. I suspect I've done something wrong here and so I quit acting.

"You're answering the ad in *Backstage*?"

Uh, yes sir, I—

"You don't look thirty-five with ten years of marriage under your belt."

Well I think I could play—

"Little boy, you can't convince me you're SIXTEEN—you've got a baby face, anyone ever tell you that? If there was a role up for a fourteen-year-old I'd be happy to see you . . . How old are you?"

Uh twenty-five, I lie, adding four years.

"Oh great, twenty-five!" said the director, laughing a he-is-not-really-amused laugh. "What's your name?"

Gil Freeman, sir and I—

"You are wasting our time, Gil Freeman, and we don't have a lot of time. We said thirty-five, we meant thirty-five. Do you know how to read? Learning how to read will help you in this business . . ." And he went on, sarcastic, grouchy, tired at the end of his long day, not abusive enough to make me dismiss him as a jerk, but just abusive enough to make me dismiss *me* as a jerk for being there. I just wanted to die and be quietly buried back in Oak Park.

On the way home on the subway I dealt with the major issue of the moment: was I going to cry about this? Before I got home, was I going to get all my frustration out of my system and cry like a five-year-old? Yes, I decided I would and slunk off to a corner of the Christopher Street station and did so.

The only place I was happy was back in the apartment. But that didn't stop me from taking all my misery out on Lisa and Emma:

"C'mon, c'mon," said Lisa, bouncing about in front of me as I tried my hardest to be Byronic and morose, "I'm not leaving until I make you laugh." She made a silly face like she might for an infant. "Oh geez, Gil, c'mon, you've only been at this for . . . for not even a year yet. You'll get a break. Cheer up!"

I'm out of cash.

"Look," said Lisa, "just get any kind of job. Lesson One in New York is *have no pride*. Do anything for rent money."

Do you know what anything is in New York? It's going to a temporary help agency and volunteering to file note cards, account slips, that kind of thing. You go in and the people running the agency look at you with disdain: Can you type? No. Can you work any kind of computer? No, since I can't type. Can you do stenography? No, since this is 1975 and I'm a guy. Do you do light accounting? If you saw my checkbook you wouldn't ask stupid questions. What *could* I do? I could file things in alphabetical order.

"Can you alphabetize?" asked the fat, immobile woman with the slicked-down hair at the temporary agency, and I said yes (mind you, I got dressed up in my suit for this), and then I was ushered into an inner sanctum to take a test. The assignment is to alphabetize the following ten things: wheelbarrow, lemon, toy, Albert Jones, baseball, Kansas . . .

"Well done, Mr. Freeman! You got them all right!"

Two fifteen an hour. And I took it. That spring morale was not high. I came home one day to pass a fleeing, crying Oriental woman in our hall. When I got inside our apartment Emma explained:

"That's Kim Li. A friend of Mandy's. She's from Vietnam. I met her last night at Mandy's and I thought I'd be noble and ask her around for coffee today." Emma stood up and walked over to the TV. "Saigon is falling and the TV was on and she got upset."

I watched the TV showing the evacuation of troops and civilians and anyone who could pay anything to get out before the Vietcong made it to the city and meted out justice. People hanging from helicopters as they took off, their suitcases tumbling to the ground . . .

"Kim Li has wealthy parents and they all got out in time," Emma went on, now going to the kitchen. "I invited her over for penance, Gil. I'm American, I wanted to say, yell at me, hate me, throw things at me, trash our apartment—I'm so sorry what we did to your country."

Did you get your way?

"Nah, she was all for the war, ruling class and all. And you'd think someone from Vietnam could at least be *interesting,* but she's not. She wanted to know where to *shop* in New York. I mean, me, Emma Gennaro, fashion consultant. Gil, where are the Fritos?"

I didn't buy them because I didn't have any money. I stood transfixed before the TV and the rioting crowds, the desperate push to get to the roof of the US Embassy and possibly away by helicopter. If I'd been born a few years earlier, I'd be over there helping them pack, I mentioned.

Emma stood in the kitchen doorway, arms crossed. "Your death would have been a tragedy but not nearly on the scale of my NOT GETTING TO EAT MY FRITOS after a hard day at temping."

I stared mindlessly at the TV and shook my head. What a mess. Another sterling, incomparable first-class job done by that long-running comedy act, the American Military Community After World War II. No good, I said, was going to come out of this fiasco.

"Take-out Vietnamese restaurants," Emma suggested.

I flopped on the sofa and went into brooding-actor mode: I have no money. I have a stupid job which pays next to no money. I am a failure in the theater. I have no career. I will take out an insurance policy, kill myself, and leave the money to Emma so she can eat Fritos for a month.

"Gil, you *know* how I am about nutrition." Emma went over to the TV and gave Saigon a last glance before turning off the set: "I guess this means goodbye."

You can eat all my cereal, I suggest—finish out the box of Fruit Loops. I'll just quietly waste away here on the sofa.

Emma sat on the arm of the sofa. "Gil, Fritos are important to me. It is important in the daily diet to have one representative from each of the Four Food Groups. A caffeine, a sugar, a booze and a grease. Now I had coffee and a doughnut this morning, and I'm going to drink cheap beer tonight. That leaves a grease. I haven't had my grease today—I was counting on it. You said you'd buy some Fritos since it was your turn."

I groaned unmoved into the sofa pillow.

"Gil," she said after a moment. "New York doesn't get much better than this, I hate to tell you. You know where I temped this morning? Excellence Products, Inc. Do you know what they make?"

I silently shook my head.

"Those little plastic guns you can fire candy BBs into your mouth with? They make those. Lisa's part-time job is Xeroxing other people's drawings for the new 1975 image for the milkmaid on Little Milkmaid condensed milk. This is how we get by."

Yeah, but you can write poetry, Emma, when you get home, and Lisa can paint. I can't act without being up on a stage.

Emma thought about this. "All right, I wasn't going to do this unless things got desperate . . ." They're desperate, they're desperate. ". . . But I know this, this COW, Rachel Dennis. She was at my last temp agency. Her husband is a casting director at some off-Broadway theater."

I sat up. Call him, pay him off, sleep with him! I suggested.

"Gil, this is going to cost me . . ." She winced. "Before I left the agency I reported her to the president for being utterly worthless and incompetent. I called her a cow to her face. I'd have to grovel, to abase myself."

I looked at her wide-eyed, all puppy-dog sadness.

"God, she was pretentious," mused Emma, thinking back. "She always name-dropped about the people she met at her husband's theater. And they were all nobodies too. If you're gonna name-drop name-drop Rosemary Harris and Al Pacino. She would go on and on about Bobby Carew—last night at the opening, I saw Bobby Carew, you know, Bobby, Bobby Carew. I mean, geez, the guy plays the salty sailor on the Chunk-a-Chunk Tuna ads."

He's higher up the show business ladder than I am, I reminded.

Emma stared hard at me.

I'll probably have to move back to Oak Park, I threatened, adding incentive.

She reached for the phone. "Oh no you don't . . . no one's breaking up the Apartment of the Gods." She dialed, muttering, "And NO ONE moves back to the Midwest while I'm around—is that understood?"

Yes ma'am.

And that phone call began a chain of events that led to my first job in the theater, the Venice Theater, scourge of off-Broadway. Wait. That sounds ungrateful. Ungrateful to Emma, to Dewey and Rachel Dennis, to all the good people (two or three of them) at the Venice. I thank you all. Thanks to you, Venice Theater, I survived my first few years.

Now. THAT BEING SAID:

The Venice Theater, where I worked, where I slaved, where I hauled stones on my back and built pyramids and dug canals and comprised a sizable percentage of the American workforce—the Venice Theater was the WORST, the dregs, the nadir, the lowest ebb of New York theater imaginable. It was antitheater. If you worked there long enough, you would get less talented. It was a void to which the outcasts, the losers, the hopeless of the New York theater world made their way to die, to fade away, gracelessly, a place of ignominy . . . It began that spring, after nearly nine months of filing files for $2.15 an hour. I was interviewed by Rachel Dennis's husband, Dewey, Assistant Director of the Venice Theater, a big bearish guy, a beard and potbelly, a loud laugher, radiating opinionatedness. Dislikable on sight. He talked at me and talked at me and asked about my feelings concerning the ART of the Theatuh, what purer higher sentiments drew me toward this magical wonderland of stagecraft and, for my part, I agreed with everything he said, I licked his boots, humiliated my flesh, I sucked up to his pencil sharpener, I would have performed sexual acts on his *stapler*—

"Well," says Dewey, "I see you'd fit in real good around here. We'll be in touch."

That was the big kiss-off. You may have recognized it.

Time goes on. I get a call in May that Mr. Dennis has put my name in a file for possible replacements since two people were leaving before the summer. I called back and talked to a raspy-voiced secretary who sympathetically explained the positions had been filled so I figured that was that. Then I got another call a few weeks later, and the same raspy secretary said one of the guys had left for Yale School of Drama and had jumped ship (no doubt recognizing the *Titanic* when he saw it) and would I consider joining the Venice?

Job description: Sweeping up, helping out, finding props, working costumes, subbing for dressers, working in the shop to build scenery, printing and proofreading programs, phone sales in the advertising department, doing admissions, working in the ticket booth, matinee ushering, and as New Boy in the theater, bringing in the standing order of doughnuts for Saturday mornings. The pay? $60 a week, and it could have been worse . . . but, son, this is The Thee-ah-tuh, fill in the speech about A Great Future Lies Ahead.

And I was ONE HAPPY BOY, I tell you. I ran all the way back to Carmine Street, proudly down the streets of Manhattan which had become the place *I* worked, the place *I* lived in officially now for real, and I wanted to take Emma in my arms and mess up that shoulder-length dark hair and kiss her one hundred times on the lips. (I always wanted to do that anyway, but now I had an excuse.) Emma was not home, however, and Lisa was, so I did it to her.

"God, this is news—this is your big break!" said Lisa. "Do we have enough change to get a bottle of wine and get drunk?"

We had just enough, $1.99. Enough for the jug of Chianti-flavored wine you could get at Gino's Delicatessen down the block. We ran there together and counted out our pennies for Gino.

"When are you going to get to act?" Lisa said, taking my arm for the walk back.

Not right away, I figured. (Boy, was THAT right.)

"Aren't you excited?" she kept asking over and over.

Yeah, I was excited. An illustration: Me, sitting outside the Venice Theater, the day before I start work, in the pouring rain, 45 degrees, watching the personnel file in and out of My New Home, the new place I belonged, imagining myself in that actress's arms, imagining myself impressing that important-looking director (it was the janitor), wondering who that jerk was and what they said about him (it was the executive director), making friends that (enter string music, swelling violins) would last my whole life long, characters in my memoirs, already being written. In the euphoria of my new employment, I extrapolated (1) understudying, (2) the long-awaited Big Break, (3) being the director's pet ("Who'd have thought that stockboy was going to be such a talent? I want him for everything we do here—he's a draw"), (4) great notices, (5) dumping the Venice Theater, getting an agent, moving up to Playwrights Horizons or Circle in the Square, (6) my Tony acceptance speech ("When I began work in 1975 at the Venice Theater, who would have thought I was going to be here, accepting this, tonight? Dewey Dennis, I love you man, I owe it all to you. But mostly, let me say that I share this award with my best friends—Lisa, Emma . . . this is for you too . . ." *Orgasmic* applause), (7) movies, going Hollywood, which is so laid-back after the New York scene—

Slam of door. "I'm home, fan club!" Emma was back.

"Gil has news," Lisa blurted out. I told her about my job before Lisa got a chance to and then I got to give Emma a big kiss. Emma, you saved my life.

She shrugged, smiling. "Nyehhh . . ."

No really, you're a lifesaver.

"Well, just let me watch what I want on TV all the time."

Lisa ran into the kitchen and then out again brandishing the Chianti bottle: "Ta-dah! Party time! Where's the corkscrew?"

And then, on my night of triumph, a crisis. We couldn't find the corkscrew.

"It's not in the bathroom," yelled Emma.

". . . Or under the sofa," said Lisa, on her hands and knees. "Oh hell, I think we left it at Janet's. We could call Janet."

"No, she's as poor as we are and she'd want to come over *with* our corkscrew and there'd be less wine for us."

Do your trick, Emma, I suggested.

"What trick?"

The swordsmen-in-the-Italian-cavalry trick you were telling us about. It was in some book. If you take your sword and slide it down the neck of the bottle, hitting the rim consistently from all sides, the cork will break off with the rim of the bottle evenly. Or so Emma said.

"Gee, my sword's at the cleaners," said Lisa.

Will a kitchen knife do?

"No," said Emma, looking about the apartment, "we need something heavy and metal and . . . hey, how about the shower attachment in the bathtub?"

So there we were, standing above the bathtub, huddled in the bathroom, watching Emma clink away at the Chianti bottle with the attachment-hose thing you use to wash your hair with—

SMASH. Glass everywhere.

"Goddam it . . ." Emma muttered, inspecting her hands for splinters of glass.

"Don't spill any of the wine, whatever you do," said Lisa.

"I could be bleeding to death and you're worried about the wine . . . Shit. There are probably glass fragments in the wine now."

A gloomy pause.

"Wait a minute," said Lisa.

She came back with some Wipe-Away Paper Towels and a bowl. Lisa was at New Marketing Ideas Ltd. making cardboard display racks for Wipe-Away Paper Towels, so consequently we had a gross of paper towels which we used for everything, including stationery.

"We're gonna strain the wine," said Lisa. "We are not pouring that wine out—we can't afford another bottle."

Lisa held the paper towel taut and Emma poured the wine through it and it drained into the bowl below. But Emma got worried that some small glass fragments had gotten through, and after all, popes and Chinese emperors and Caesars were always putting ground glass in people's food to kill them, so we strained it again with a new towel and Emma poured Bowl No. 1 onto the paper towel to drain into Bowl No. 2.

"Strange taste," said Lisa, after toasting My Glorious Future.

"Tastes like Wipe-Away," said Emma. "Absorbent but not precocious, a distinct aftertaste . . . a two-ply wine."

Well, when you don't eat, a third of a bottle of Chianti can hit you pretty hard and make you giddy, and our drunken evenings, like this one, usually ended up on the roof, up the fire escape. The Carmine Street roof wasn't as good as Susan's, it was blocked in on all sides, but you could look over to the street. It was ten p.m., the street was still hopping, a vendor on the corner selling beads and belt buckles, down below a busker we called the Tambourine Man because he could only play two songs over and over, "Mr. Tambourine Man" and "Blowin' in the Wind."

"Here's our chance to kill that guy," Emma said, "we bean him with a flowerpot. He's *got* to get a bigger repertoire if he's going to play outside our window."

"It's cold up here," said Lisa. "I'm going down, bye-bye."

Emma and I lingered.

" 'Hey Mr. Tambourine Man,' " recited Emma, " 'play a song for me.' Now what kind of song *can* a tambourine man play? Dylan is God, but have you ever thought of that?"

I put my hand on Emma's shoulder. She seemed to freeze. I told her thank you again for helping me get employed. After I'd kissed her on the roof at Susan's party she had followed up that encounter with so much celibacy talk, so much I'm-through-with-sex I got the message: you don't do it for me, Gil. So I laid off. But she'd kissed me congratulations that night. Pretty pathetic, huh? We get two kisses in almost a *year* of time, both platonic, and I'm rushing back for more rejection. I kiss her again; I aim at the lips but she turns her head just a bit, so I get the right half of the mouth, and she tries, so it won't embarrass me, to kiss back a little.

"Gil, you know . . ." she began in that you're-just-my-friend tone of voice all women have perfected by the age of sixteen.

That wasn't a romantic kiss, I said, that was a thank-you friendship kiss. (Which was a lie; I shouldn't have ducked out there.)

She breathed heavily. "Look I just gotta get some things straightened out in my life first, you know? I'm happy for you and all that, but I'm still where you were a month ago: nowhere.

My journals suck, my poetry should line the bottom of a birdcage. I'm getting uglier each year—"

That's crap, Emma.

"I am not pretty enough or talented enough to have sex at the moment. Or at least enjoy it if I had it." She smiled and turned to the back fire escape to go back down. "I publish a book of poems next year, I'll sleep with the New York Giants."

I'll try out tomorrow. Does this offer extend to the waterboy?

She shook her head, laughing. "Don't mess things up, Freeman! It's great, the three of us, just as it is."

Not an auspicious celebration, but we're talking about the Venice Theater so maybe it was appropriate. And I can't even drink Chianti anymore. Living on the fringes of Italian neighborhoods and buying countless bottles of $1.99 Chianti ("Uh-oh, this Chianti is made in Ohio," said Emma once, dourly looking at the fine print) finished off my appetite for that wine. An exception, however, could be made for the San Gennaro Festival in Little Italy, during which great quantities of Chianti were necessary for getting Emma drunk. Emma Gennaro, predictably, considered this saint's celebration her personal holiday.

Emma explained it to us as we walked along the crowded streets of Little Italy, the sidewalks taken over by booths and amusements and foodstands. "Everyone knows the San Gennaro Festival is in honor of me, but some will tell you it honors an obscure Neapolitan saint who stopped the lava from Vesuvius at the gates of the city or predicted an earthquake or whose body refused to rot—I forget which."

"I want *that*," Lisa said, interrupting, pointing to a van selling deep-fried pastries. "That pastry thing in that . . . passticker . . . passticher . . ."

"*Pasticceria*," said Emma, using an elaborate Italian hand gesture.

We goaded Emma into ordering the triangular cake-thing in Italian, but she got shy. "Nah, I can do my tourist Italian around the apartment but not here—"

"Ey? Whatsa mattuh?" said Lisa doing a Godfather imitation. "You no part of the Family anymore?"

"Ssssssh," said Emma, restraining Lisa. "This ain't the neighborhood for Godfather jokes." Emma pointed to the pastry. "*Una sfogliatella, per favore, signora.*"

"Whut?" said the large woman in the van.

"That thing, there," Emma said surrendering.

Emma explained that Little Italy Italian wasn't schoolbook Italian. "Besides," she added, taking a swig from our mutual jug of Chianti, "you try saying *sfogliatella.*" And on we walked to take our positions on Mott Street for the big parade. "Anyway, are you guys gonna let me finish this or what?" Emma went on. "San Gennaro died and they drained off some of his blood, and every September nineteenth, in Naples, the priest comes out with this vial of dried blood and shakes it and dances with it and prays over it and puts it up various orifices and eventually they either give up *or* the blood liquefies. And that means it's going to be a good year for Naples . . . which means plague deaths, Camorra shootings, murders and rapes will only be in the tens of thousands."

The parade was amazing: they had this five-story model of the Madonna and another one of San Gennaro, and the Madonna one was draped in expensive relics and jewelry from the local church.

"Looks like a bunch of tinfoil to me," said Lisa.

And more amazingly, the Madonna was cloaked in a long robe of dollar bills, each strand of cash joined end to end, representing the parish's contributions. The Virgin strode by us (supported unsteadily by a group of young men in T-shirts, all desired physically by Lisa); we watched the train of dollar bills flag by.

"That is just beautiful," said Emma, after a long swig of Chianti. "I like it when the Catholic church is upfront about its materialism. I expect to be cloaked in dollar bills when we get home."

Here I can tell you about what became Emma's One Annual Joke, which she made as if she had forgotten that she'd done it all the years before. Come Sunday morning, parallel with the festival in Naples, she would rise and present herself to her friends and if she had a hangover (and her blood hadn't liquefied) then it was a bad year for her and her friends, the surrounding metropolitan area and the world at large; if her blood had liquefied and she bounced out of bed without a trace of Chianti hangover, then there was to be prosperity and happiness. She was generally accurate—at any rate, after her Saturday night bottle of Chianti, two greasy hot sausages on an Italian crust of bread smothered in peppers, a take-out spaghetti carbonara, lots of deep-fried pastry things in powdered sugar, and three cans of beer we had waiting for us back in Brooklyn, Emma emerged from her bedroom unhungover, dispensing blessings for her idolators.

Brooklyn.

For the historians taking notes, let it be recorded that it was Emma and I who found the new apartment. Lisa had the only daytime job of any of us, and the only one that didn't pay shit, although she swore she was leaving New Ideas Marketing Ltd. any day now but the thing about makeshift, just-for-a-few-months jobs is that they always pay enough money to seduce you into staying, into putting off artistic struggle/starvation another month, just until you get enough money to go home at Christmas, that vacation to New Jersey, a color TV, etc. Lisa spent the day in the Tri-State Area supermarkets sticking happy-face decals on Smile-So-Bright toothpaste buy-now-get-a-second-tube-free display racks. Once we all three were shopping in the Associated for our staples (cookies, cheesey puff things, generic pasta, liters of diet cola, generic beer, tons of Associated homebrand peanut butter, and one special piece of junkfood apiece, which we allowed ourselves) and Lisa saw one of her display racks, her "artwork," her Claim to Immortality; she sneaked up with a pen and autographed it. Which is to say that house hunting was left up to Emma and myself (I worked nights doing horrible, menial things at the Venice Theater; Emma was at Baldo's from 10 p.m. until 3 a.m.). To be honest, throughout the spring we got lazy, always figuring we had *months* to go before June came and we got thrown out of the Village sublet.

"You know, I'm not entirely unreligious," Emma said once. "I do pray on occasion, suburban Catholic upbringing notwithstanding. I've been praying for the woman and her two little brats to die in a plane crash coming back from Provence and leave us this apartment. We could be squatters."

There were no plane crashes and slowly, grudgingly we started hauling ourselves all over the rat-infested, lousy, overpriced, dilapidated, dangerous world of cheap New York apartment hunting. We would sit in the Prato, Emma and I, and circle ads with a red crayon and then look at the paper, go nahhhhh, and talk ourselves out of getting up and going to look at the place.

"Don't hand me this garbage," said Lisa, being a bitch one day. "You're not looking hard enough. Stop messing around." So she joined us next weekend, and then we were all irritable and frustrated.

We packed up completely, everything in boxes, and we were reduced to living out of crates, suitcases, and overnight bags. Emma arranged to stay with Mandy, who was going through some changes and wanted company, even if it was Emma on the couch. Lisa bit the bullet and asked to stay with Susan. Lisa chipped in and I stayed at the YMCA. Three people not having any fun.

So we met at Mario's Coffee Shop in the East Village to compare notes after living separately and apartment-searching for four fruitless days. Lisa hugged me for a whole thirty seconds, a defeated woman. And Emma shocked us both—she showed up last—by giving us a big hug and a kiss each.

"God, I missed you both," she said, turning red a moment later, checking my eyes to make sure I didn't make too much out of the platonic kiss. We're up to *three* kisses now. Yes, I was keeping score. "Our apartment," Emma continued, "must never die. As God is my witness we will be roommates for life. I love Mandy but I'm going crazy over there." She sank into the booth at Mario's beside me. "And every place I've looked at is a slum dwelling."

It had been a typical week of apartment hunting: Lisa had almost been raped by a landlord, Emma saw a great place except for the rats that came running out of the bathroom when she opened the door, I opened up a kitchen cabinet which contained no fewer than one million cockroaches which went up my arm and you can envision my unmanly screams, dancing about trying to get them all off me.

"But there is some good news," added Emma to our tales. "Mandy has discovered her Lesbian Self."

But we thought she was in Emma's Celibacy Support Group.

"Well she was," Emma explained, "but Mandy decided she wasn't really celibate, but rather that she had been repressing her lesbian tendencies. So she's going out now with Kim Li—"

Your Vietnamese friend?

"Well there are so many Kim Lis in my life. Yes, my Vietnamese friend."

Lisa smiled for one second. "Great. I'm happy for them. What does that have to do with us?"

"Kim Li, wealthy refugee that she is, has a *car*. And Mandy asked if we could use it, and we can. We can hunt for apartments with a car! That oughta spice up apartment hunting."

It sure did. And slowed it down more than ever. Our borrowed car was a NEW TOY to play with, wheels, automotivation, the road before us, the highway song, bridges, tunnels, intersections, places we'd never seen . . .

"I want to go to that place called Fresh Kills," said Emma, looking at the city map and the Dutch-named inlets on Staten Island. "I envision a gritty cop movie, some serial killer who deposits the bodies of his victims at Fresh Kills. I see Sinatra or William Holden as the crusty detective standing over the corpses, police cars, sirens, he looks up, shakes his head, 'Someone has a real sick sense of humor, sergeant . . .' I could sell this screenplay, Gil, don't laugh."

July 10, 1975. Ten days had elapsed.

"You *are* looking, aren't you?" Lisa asked, running out of patience with us. She said Susan billed her stay as "one big slumber party," and was overly affectionate, and spoke eloquently about women sleeping beside each other, an openness between them, something foreign to men . . . "Just find a place goddam soon," she added on the phone to Emma and me, huddled in a pay booth. Lisa was desperate for money as well, none of us having really enough for a down payment, so she took on extra weekend work, going out to supermarkets herself and standing behind a display booth for Connecticut cheese and the Connecticut Cheese Association which was pushing something called Connecticut Edam. She would go out to Queens and stand there in a red and yellow uniform with a big sweatshirt with CONNECTICUT CHEESES: EAT 'EM! on it passing out cubes of Edam cheese on the ends of toothpicks; she was asked to write down occasional comments which no one gave her so she had to make them up. She told us about bending down to put an I LOVE CONNECTICUT CHEESE hat on a little kindergarten-age boy when she had a moral qualm about children walking around with advertisements on them, oblivious instruments of capitalism. "And on top of all that," said Lisa as her phone money ran out, "I'm constipated like you wouldn't believe from eating all that goddam—" Click, dial tone.

Lisa wasn't the only one desperate. Emma was staying at Mandy's, and three was a crowd where the new young lovers were concerned and in the last two days they had begun fighting about what Americans knew at home about the war, then over whose turn it was to do the dishes.

"I'm not going back to the DMZ tonight," said Emma as we were driving around. "I know what. We're spending the night in Jersey. I have some real cool cousins there. Haven't seen 'em in a while but they are real cool—really, I promise." However, a little drunk and in the dark with both of us tired Emma got lost and couldn't remember anyway whether it was Mayfair, Montclair, Montrose, Madison, Middleborough, Morristown, whatever M they lived in, and all the expressway exits looked like the one. So at 11:30, utterly used up, we pulled into the Admiral Halsey Rest Area on the New Jersey Turnpike to spend the night.

I pointed out that everything we owned was in the trunk and, as I climbed in the backseat, that we might get raped by motorcycle gangs.

"Nobody pays toll to come rob people, Gil. We're safe here," Emma insisted, struggling to get comfortable in the front seat, dodging the handbrake.

We were quiet a minute.

"I was about to wreck the car I was so sleepy," said Emma. Pause. "But I'm not sleepy now."

If we were quiet we could get to sleep, I said.

Emma clinked change around in the front seat. "I got some more good news," she said. "We don't have enough change for the toll tomorrow."

Shouldn't have had that coffee and candy bar at the Quick Stop Restaurant. The Quick Stop was part of the Admiral Halsey Rest Area.

"I don't suppose these fluorescent lights ever go off, huh?" she asked. This began a series of comments at ten-minute intervals designed so she wouldn't be the only one awake . . .

"I'm not comfortable, Gil. I hate this. Is the backseat better?"

Later: "When I'm famous, I hope Indiana will name a rest area after me. Think they will? I'll insist on that. No cash awards, no plaques, no statues, no foundations or scholarships—I want a rest area. With a Quick Stop Restaurant. Restrooms where gay men can meet."

Later: "We're under the flightpath for Newark Airport. Do you remember the plane landing on the Van Wyck Expressway? What if this is the night a plane mistakes the rest area lights for the runway lights? Something to think about."

Later: "Did you fart?"

No I did not fart; it was New Jersey. The refineries and chemical firms and gasworks. We were dying from toxic fumes, I suggested. Good night, Emma.

"Yeah we gotta stop talking."

Good night, Emma.

"By the way," she added, repositioning herself once again in relation to the handbrake, "I think this qualifies as the Official Low Point in our New York Years, the *nadir*."

And when I was drifting off, almost asleep . . .

"I don't understand how people fuck in cars. I can't even straighten out my legs . . . it's like that room in the Bastille, that Room of Little Ease where you couldn't stand, sit, straighten up. All across Nebraska and the Great Heartland tonight people are *doing it* in cars, defying all odds, all physical laws."

I volunteered to show Emma how it was done.

"Ha, ha, make me laugh, in the Rest Stop. Halsey wouldn't approve."

In a spirit of futility: Good night, Emma.

"Night."

Sound of a plane passing over.

"Gil?"

Yes.

"I have to pee."

I must have shut my eyes and hours passed but I wouldn't term what I had as *sleep*. It got light and trucks started noisily pulling out, planes landed every two minutes at Newark, and so we got up thinking it was nine or something, but it was five a.m. We spent the rest of our insufficient toll money on more coffee at the Quick Stop where Emma tried to flirt with a zitty teenage busboy, asking him how we got off the turnpike without paying toll. We surrendered to the inevitable and Emma got issued a ticket at the tollbooth and the license number and registration were taken down for the files.

"Kim Li is not going to be happy about this," said Emma as we drove out of sight of the tollbooth. She tossed the ticket out the window, so I imagine by now Kim Li is really unhappy about it. "First the napalm, then parking tickets. A raw deal all around," she added.

It was 6:30 and we were up with the commuters, actually preceding them a little. We went to Brooklyn (via the free Brooklyn Bridge) and Emma with her new money-machine bankcard volunteered to pay for breakfast. We parked the car in Brooklyn Heights, the richest neighborhood in Brooklyn, where all the writers lived (Emma said), and we walked around waiting for something to open, heading south past the Arab section, then back around to the city hall and down an urban warehouse-filled street until we came to a wonderful diner with a chrome façade, a real workin' man's diner, Sal's, a place of breakfast specials and taxi drivers finished with the night shift, plump waitresses in tight polyester uniforms you could see the bra straps through, big cantilevered Brooklyn waitress bras, women who got all the orders right, knew how the boys wanted their eggs, attended with unconscious precision to the refilling of the coffee cup.

"To hell with Manhattan," said Emma, drinking in a deep draught of working-class pre–7 a.m. coffee. "Let's live in Brooklyn."

We turned to the Brooklyn real estate pages in the *Times*, out came the Official Red Crayon, and we circled away. Emma's eyes wandered to the Queens listings. "Far Rockaway. One block from beach, two bedroom, back yard. One fifty per month," she read. "Where is that? Far Rockaway."

The waitress coming by to refill our coffee answered, "Oh you don't wanna live out there dearie. Furtherest point on the New York subway system—George!" she yelled, looking over her shoulder, "your mother's in Rockaway Park—how long's it take by subway?"

George, a cab driver, said two and a half hours unless you got an express during rush hours. But still, two hours, easy to the City.

"But the name is nice," Emma said, musing.

"There's Rockaway Beach," said the waitress, topping off my coffee, "then Rockaway, then Far Rockaway because it's the furtherest away. Furtherest stop on the New York subway system. It's out on the island across from Jamaica Bay. You got milk in there, honey?" she asked, looking at the milk tin. There wasn't and she went to get more.

"You looking for a place?" said the cook behind the counter.

"Yes," said Emma, playing the situation artfully, "but here in Brooklyn. My mother was born here, and we had to move to California 'cause my Dad worked in the press office for the Brooklyn Dodgers . . ."

THAT WAS GENIUS. We had no fewer than five numbers when we left Sal's ("You tell my sister, I sent you, her brother Harold," said a bus driver from South Brooklyn) and we went to work.

South Brooklyn, south of the Heights but north of almost everything else in Brooklyn, is almost as nice as the Heights but not quite. We made our way to Harold the Bus Driver's sister's place along tree-lined streets. This place *was the one*.

It had four rooms and a cramped bathroom—a living room, a kitchen, two bedrooms, and Mrs. Dellafini said Lisa could use the basement for painting as nothing was down there but the heater and the fuse box and a utility closet (and rats and mice, Lisa would later report), and Mrs. Dellafini also said she'd rather have two than three but since we were nice (Emma gave the Brooklyn-roots routine again, plus told her I was her brother) that would be all right but the rent had to go up $40 a month to $240 (which sounded steep to us then) and Mrs. Dellafini said she was a widow and her husband died in the first-floor apartment where she still lives (and where we kids were to come if we had a problem) and she lived with him for thirty-five years and she had some good times and some bad times but she saw him through and she loved him very much but he was dead and Life Went On and she was taking a pottery class now.

My memory's pretty good, huh? No, I didn't keep a journal—I kept someone else's journals, Emma's. She'd kill me if she knew (well, she wants to kill me anyway, but we'll get around to that). I didn't steal them. Emma kept throwing them out, cursing her poetic/writing talents, so once in the trashcan, I figured they were public domain.

Periodically Emma declared herself utterly unreadable and worthless, a Major No-Talent, or—and this was a favorite term for others—"Multi-Untalented," and that her writing was garbage—there was no hope for her, she'd scream. These fits of self-disgust (where her own bad passages were read loudly until Lisa or I smirked or betrayed the slightest sign of not liking something) ended in Emma opening the window facing the street and announcing to the neighborhood at large: "Here Brooklyn! Here's some more trash for your street!" And she would hurl her latest work to the wastecans below, page by page.

"Emma, stop!" Lisa would yell, wrestling Emma to a sofa, debilitating her by tickling until they both were laughing. "You'll get arrested for littering. You'll publish one day!"

Emma through pained laughter: "If I published *that* I *would* be arrested for littering . . ." I'd run down to the street and collect the pages. We'd chalk this behavior up to Emma's creative process.

In the midst of all this, she produced a "Brooklyn Journal" which, before she'd written a word in it, was going to be the century's only rival to Thomas Wolfe, and after she'd filled half of it, was declared "toiletworthy," and was flushed page by page down the toilet until the water pressure and Emma's interest in her dramatic gesture gave out. And so I have it now, that and a number of other excommunicated papers, odds and ends. They were thrown away, I think now, because they were sincere and sometimes awkward and always sentimental—everything Emma fought so hard not to be in conversation, in life, in front of us. It all went in the journals and spiral notebooks, and then the trashcan. I've kept something called "Brooklyn Serenade." Here's a piece of it:

> . . . To live in Brooklyn, even as an interloper, a refugee from the outrageous rents of the City, is to be born there; it holds you like the unwelcome grip of a Great Aunt who doesn't speak English very well, it adopts you, it converts you to its pace, its poverty, its tremendous dreams hand in hand with meager expectations. You find yourself defending it at the Soho loft party, speaking of its virtues to someone without a place to live in the fall, you find yourself regularly at your window staring unthinkingly, accepting what plays before you. If you watch for it, observe carefully, you may see something flash, something catch the light momentarily, something beautiful have a brief life in the rude and filthy streets: innocence (the girl in the Catholic-school skirt twirling her hair, watching the boys play ball), faith (the mother storming from the house to retrieve her daughter out playing in her confirmation dress), hope (the adolescent boy standing on a crate, using a stick for a microphone, being Elvis, English his second language), and love, disguised and disfigured by explosive family fights heard up and down the block, borne in the faces of banished daughters, sons who said no to fathers, wives who went away but now are back, husbands trudging home from a second job.
>
> And when the sun begins to lower, behind that wall of haze over Jersey and Manhattan, and when it spills into the brick

> and brownstone canyons of Brooklyn, all tired and dirty with the industry of Jersey, the exhaust of Manhattan, and when—at the same time—you emerge from the hot, crowded subway and come up for air in what has become your neighborhood, and you stand there amidst the quiet bustle, its obliviousness to the sordid goings-on across the river, it is enough to stir in you an affection for this naked and therefore most ashamed part of America, and you too will share a sense of loss for a way of life fading as it thrives, fading in that second-hand light, around you a sepia photograph brought to life, warm and inclusive and as sentimental as an immigrant's memory of home.

About a week after she wrote it and liked it, Emma decided it was trash, written by someone, she said, who stayed up too late a little drunk, some twenty-two-year-old at three a.m.

Those *are* the circumstances, I reminded her.

"It's not supposed to read like that," she whined. "It's supposed to read like George Eliot already. I refuse to *grow* as a writer—it'll come out perfect right at the start or to hell with it. 'Brooklyn *Serenade*'—MY GOD!"

Okay, maybe calling it a "serenade" wasn't so hot. I'm laughing a bit, because to read all this stuff, some of the short-story fragments, some of the poems, you'd have thought we were living in the heart of Hasidic Williamsburgh, the lone English-speakers amid a world of immigrants fresh from Ellis Island, women dressed in black trudging to mass, Poles over here, Lithuanians over there. Carroll Gardens wasn't *that* exciting. Emma, just like me, you had a bit of the theater in you, you old fake.

I picture her writing. We had this tree-lined street and our own tree in front of our window, a big turn-of-the-century ten-foot window with a window seat, sort of a Victorian projected window box, and this tree displayed autumn for a precious single week that fall and we mourned its passing, until we saw snow on the branches that December, which was to be only upstaged by the yellow-green buds that came the next spring, our own little Reminder of Nature, virtually in our living room. Emma no doubt sensed the clothesline Ellis Island Brooklyn out there somewhere, sitting in her window seat, her and the tree, gray Sunday afternoons, chain-drinking tea, pad in hand. Like this unfinished poem—

I AM THE IMMIGRANT

They arrive on jetplanes now.
No babushkas, no more lives in a single
    suitcase.
No more Ellis Island bureaucrat changing
    Padnowczynski to Patterson,
No more lore and legend.
Just green cards and a grocery to work in.
And they don't matter anymore.
Now the story has been passed within,
And the young of the country file into
    the City,
From the small towns and flatlands.
They've heard the streets are paved with
    gold,
That silly statue speaks to them,
They talk of dreams, American and otherwise,
And they are willing to work and collapse
    for the bother, for the glory
    that comes from putting one's hands
    on one's future.
The young actress, once Padnowczynski,
    now Patterson,
Can tell you stories.

I am the immigrant.
I have come for

And the poem runs out there, with a pencil scratching through most of it, abandoned to the trashcan, and maybe she was right to give that one up—what do I know about poetry?—but still. Still, that's what I was thinking too, sort of. That's why we all came there, and I recall thinking: thank god, in this generally cultureless, boring, narrow-minded grab-bag of a country we got it right once: New York City. What wouldn't we do to appease the place? What wouldn't we sacrifice? (The answers to these and other questions ahead . . .)

But Emma's writing angst was an acceptable part of the routine; it would have seemed emptier somehow without all her artistic suffering and self-mockery. Certainly Lisa (who'd never gotten a picture in a gallery) and myself (about as close to Broadway as Saturn) could sympathize. The routine changed, though, because in mid-summer I was given a chance to go daytime at the Venice Theater. That meant getting to politick and ingratiate myself with the directors and casting people. That meant leading a normalish life with nighttimes to play around with again. That meant the end to Emma's and my truancy all day, dragging it out of bed at noon, drinking until four a.m. or until Lisa stormed out of the bedroom to tell us to go to bed as SOME PEOPLE had to get up in the morning.

"Your going daytime," said Emma, "is ruining our lives. There's no sense in my not working every morning now, just like you—it's back to temping, filing papers, making coffee. See what you've condemned me to? Think of all our projects we didn't get to finish, all our plans."

Which included:

1. Riding all the subways in New York. We'd already made our way, for the hell of it, to the amazing Broadway Junction in Brooklyn where the L and J trains, both elevated, met in a tangle of ramps and merging railways, with a railyard attached to make all the intersections even more confusing. We had stayed on the 6 line where, after everyone was asked to get out, the train turned around in an old unused station under City Hall, one of the first subway stations in New York (chandeliers, gaslight fixtures, baroque tiles like it was some kind of Turkish bath)—Emma and Lisa and I were glued to the window, our hands shielding out the light of the train so we could see the ghost station. There was a ghost station on the 4-5-6 lines at 18th Street too. Nothing could beat the 5 line across the wastes of the South Bronx, square mile upon square mile of slumland, burned-out buildings unrecovered from the '60s riots; plus this trip had the added adventure of surviving a trek through that neighborhood, the heart did beat a little faster.

2. Eating cheap budget lunch-special lunches at every nationality of restaurant in New York; getting out the yellow pages, Emma had made a list: Algerian, Argentine, Austrian, Australian ("Must be a beer garden," said Emma) . . . on through Zambesi.

3. Going to the live, free videotaping of our favorite local talk shows (the smarmier the better) and participating in all those sincere questions-from-the-audience, asking even stupider questions than the real people there . . . which was a challenge.

4. Decorating the apartment, painting, sanding, making messes.

"And lots lots more, Gil," Emma hounded. "But alas, your limitless ambition, your greed for power, for fame, takes you away to work all day long. You shall not be forgiven easily."

And so, there I was, in the thick of it, feeling at last that I was part of a theater and not a lackey consigned to the most menial chores (not that I stopped doing those either). I met all the actors and administrators and the one mainstay, my one support, rock, pillar, navigational aid, Joyce Jennings.

Everyone's best friend at the Venice Theater was Joyce Jennings, the secretary with the raspy voice. Joyce Jennings, in her day, had been a Broadway musical actress, a chorus girl, but that was when she was nineteen and it had been in shows with names like *Follies of 1939,* just as the Big Revue was going out of style and nobody seemed much in the mood for follies. Every theater has an ever-sympathetic, understanding mother figure, and also someone who has been around, and has SEEN IT ALL, and often an old-timer who *is* New York Theater and can evoke it in such a way that you never lose hope. The Venice Theater was lucky to have all these stock roles in one person: Joyce. The stereotype is the old stagehand who remembers Cohan, the crusty old night watchman or stage manager or custodian who is full of lore and history and warmth and good advice, but in my experience the old men who live their lives in the theater are cranks, embittered grouches who've lived hand-to-mouth for too long. It's the women who remain who retain the magic and the faded charm and nostalgic sense of the Theater. They also know what's going down.

"You see that one?" she'd say, arching an eyebrow in the direction of the auditions manager. "Watch out for him. Boys, girls, everybody, anybody." A slow drag on her cigarette. "Hands. In the hallway, in the dark. A mauler."

Joyce talked in what we called Joycespeak, a theater-gossip shorthand, abbreviated sentences we tried to imitate but never as successfully as Joyce doing Joyce. As administrative secretary, phone answerer, party organizer, all-purpose Competent Person, nothing much got around her, by her, near her without her knowing about it, and the directors of the theater themselves were careful to solicit her opinion. She had been in that one run-down theater for thirty-some years, and even though they could have fired her, there was some strange sense she projected of being able to survive everyone there, to be left still standing.

Thanks to endless mornings of cigarettes (the only time I took up smoking) and coffee at her desk, I now can present for Historians of the Theater, in all its glory, in all its resplendent stupidity . . .

THE HISTORY OF THE VENICE THEATER

by Gilbert Freeman

(compiled from reports of Joyce and hearsay)

The gilded, rococo-embellished kitsch that festoons the Beaux Arts façade of the Venice Theater (including a Venetian lion above the carved-in-stone TEATRO VENEZIA, two seraphim, the comedy and tragedy masks) gives the Venice the appearance of a faded 1920s movie palace. It *was*, in reality, a faded 1920s movie palace. (Hence the cramped changing rooms, the flats and props filling the narrow hallways, the unversatile stage . . .)

Back then, though, it was the Teatro Genovese, owned by an Italian not surprisingly from Genoa. In 1929, he made the bad decision (the first of many in the Venice) that movies were passé and theater was the future—this, right before the age of talkies. His new theater struggled with ethnic shows (Italian, Irish, Yiddish) before finally going bust in the mid-'30s, having to be sold to the owner's worst enemy, a loan shark of more southern Italian ancestry, who spent lots of money sandblasting the Genovese into the Teatro Amalfitano. It stayed that way for two years being the home of burlesque girlie shows and vaudeville acts. The owner's love of drink and gambling and womanizing with the showgirls bankrupted the place and soon it was sold to his worst enemy, who quickly changed the name to the Teatro Venezia (they kept using Italian names so they didn't have to pay to sandblast away the TEATRO), hoping to confuse people that this might be the once-famous Venice Theater of some note and repute that had folded in the late '30s). Such shows as *What Do I Look Like, Chopped Liver?* and *They Do It Every Time* and *Your Wife or Mine?* were not exactly hits but people drifted by to see them for want of anything else, I suppose. There was a major disaster, a musical called *Garfield,* about the unjustly forgotten president, etc., and people were laughing by the time President Garfield got shot, which wasn't promising for a long run. Mrs. Garfield was played by Lucille Lamont, who somehow connived the theater into producing a revue, a one-woman show where she was the one woman.

Lucille Lamont had one claim to fame, the only song she ever originated, "Come Back to My Arms," and there's a picture of Lucille, her ample, meaty arms outspread, her face glazed with a touched-up actress smile, in the Venice foyer. The revue was essentially Lucille singing everybody else's songs, songs written so long ago you might be tempted to think she had something to do with them. She opened the show with "Come Back to My Arms," and reprised it at the end of the show, and if there was an encore she would come out and do it again. The show was called *Come Back to My Arms: An Evening with Lucille Lamont, the Queen of Broadway.* The Queen of Broadway part was in fine print.

Interest waned after a week or so in the Queen of Broadway, and Lucille, to save face, asked her very rich husband to underwrite her revue, which he did. Figuring they'd never have another chance to unload the Venice Theater, the current owners approached Lucille's doting husband about buying the theater. He said yes—probably with Lucille's prodding; she envisioned vehicle after vehicle for herself—and soon the Venice changed its name: The Lucille Lamont Theater. No one called it that, but the name stayed until she died and the husband lost his passion for the theater and it passed on to their son, Dick Lamont, who was in real estate and unloaded it, writing the property off as a tax loss.

In 1961, the Venice/Lamont Theater was rented temporarily to a china/porcelain/dinnerware/tacky-yard-ornaments manufacturer who used the theater as his emporium.

In 1962 the theater was sold to a guy who had lent the porcelain business a great deal of money, who in turn sold it to a company called Smash Entertainment, Inc. (the name tells you all you need to know). They mounted a number of inexpensive musical flops before moving on to three big *expensive* musical flops: *Go-Go Beach,* an attempt to transfer the magic of bikini-beach movies to the musical stage; *World's Fair!* which tried to capitalize on the breathless anticipation New Yorkers shared for the upcoming 1964 World's Fair; and finally, *Cleo,* a bebop version of Anthony and Cleopatra.

Smash Entertainment, Inc., also had the notion of renaming the theater the John Fitzgerald Kennedy Memorial Theater, but a downtown theater had gotten there first and as it meant going to court, the Venice kept its name. Then it became a porn theater.

Thinking Broadway liberality had yet to reach its peak, they decided to stage a poor man's *Oh, Calcutta!* called *The Summer of '69* which ran from 1968 to 1970 with the same title. What started off as a risqué "adult entertainment" became your basic cheap, sleazo, Theater District LIVE SEX show with old men in raincoats, etc. "Oh what a time," Joyce recalled for those of us who couldn't conceive of Joyce in this environment. "Trash. Misery. The drinking, the drugs. Those girls were so messed up. I'd say, 'Sheila, Candy, get out of the business, give it up.' " A puff on her cigarette, a sigh. "Management told me they'd fire me if I tried to get any of the girls to leave." It apparently never occurred to Joyce that she might herself want to leave. "Ah," she'd say, wiping the issue aside, "you gotta be amoral in the theater if you want to survive in it. Immoral helps too, but definitely amoral."

Ownership of the theater then passed to the Schmeens and the porn stopped. After one tremendous bomb by a fairly well-known playwright, the Schmeens toyed with the idea that the Venice Theater was more valuable as a loss. And while they were investigating how to save on their taxes, their accountant ran across an option: public, grant-funded theater. So Schmeen, Sr., leased the place in 1971 to the New York Children's Theater Consortium, a group firmly convinced that children's theater was the future of New York Theater, and the gimmick—and you gotta hand it to 'em—actually worked for a while: a production of a nine-year-old, starring twelve and thirteen-year-olds, directed by a sixteen-year-old, billed naturally as the Future of New York Theater, a showcase of new young talent, and everyone associated with this project was deadly serious about their CRAFT. The *Times* did a big spread on this novel idea but a little children's theater goes a long way and soon the theater fell into endless seasonal repeats of *Hansel and Gretel, Amahl and the Night Visitors,* and *The Three Bears*. Then one of the Consortium got an idea, an idea of such genius and commercial magnitude that it is amazing that it could ever have occurred under the Venice's roof: Why not give *classes* for up-and-coming child actors/directors/playwrights? In other words, Stage Mothers of Manhattan, actual theater experience for your theater brat *right now* . . . think of the résumés. Think of the lines around the block, mothers and little darlings, think of the auditions, think of the checkbooks and the contributions and the money changing hands, all of it going to the New York Children's Theater Consortium and none of it to Schmeen.

Well it didn't stay that way for long.

The NYCTC was tossed out and Schmeen, shamelessly, set up his own Children's Theater Project, which he let his untalented son, Arnie Jr., direct. On the basis of the theater-brat profits, the Schmeens, father and son, decided to produce some new material, important new playwrights and radical theater, anything to improve the standing of the Venice among its fellow off-Broadway trendsetting neighbors. The 1974 season included *The Revolution Is Now*, which was being produced at the same time as another modern drama, *There Is No Now,* and curiously these titles ran together on a sign in front of the theater for a week before Joyce pointed it out. Weekends belonged to the kids and *Peter Cottontail,* featuring variable casts of kid actors and variable audiences of kid actors' mothers. It played for three years, on Saturday and Wednesday afternoons. Alternately the theater staged *Burn It Down* (an unsuccessful Black Rage play not as good as the others on off-Broadway that season) and *Fuck*, which was the height of MODERNITY and AVANT-GARDE and SOCIAL RELEVANCE of the mid-'70s. *Fuck* never made it to the stage—not because of bad publicity (no one cared, despite every attempt to court controversy)—but because there was an ad in the *Village Voice* that advertised *Peter Cottontail* on weekends and *Fuck* during the week and some of the mothers complained, so it was canned and the playwright threatened to sue before seething off somewhere, his vision, his art suppressed by filthy bourgeois interests . . .

Speaking of Black Theater, the Venice tried real hard but never could get it right. When I first joined, working nights at the Venice, there was a musical running called *Truckload of Dreams* which was all-black, a musical where a young wiry multitalented teenage girl who could sing, dance and act (1975 population of young, gifted and black teenage actresses was upward of 100,000, I think—where did they all go?) wanted to break off from her father's ministry and her mother's gospel choir to pursue her truckload of dreams in New York. The set was amazing: sort of a *Porgy and Bess* ghetto shack, somewhere in the South, and at the end of the play a truck came out onstage (let the props designer bore you stiff one day telling you how they assembled a fake truck on the second-floor shop of the Venice), and the truck was loaded up with all her belongings, and the boyfriend wouldn't forgive her for leaving Shacktown, and her father wasn't going to reconcile with her, only Mama knew she was pursuing her truckload of dreams, and they had this tearful denouement . . . "GO baby, go into that big world and pursue your . . . your *truckload of dreams* . . ." and then young, gifted daughter got in the truck and went away, and Mama had the show-stopper blues number where she wailed and rolled about and emoted. Our first Mama left after a month because she got a better offer from *The Wiz,* and the Schmeens turned up a popular nightclub artist from the Village who had a bit of a drinking problem. She would take a nip backstage, passing the bottle around to all of us, all of us gladly accepting, sick to death of this stupid musical. And one night before her big number, Roberta (the new Mama) got to laughing and couldn't stop. We asked her what it was, and she said no, she was going to go out onstage and laugh if she discussed it, so we didn't ask her, but she didn't stop laughing. "Truckload of dreams," she said, trying to catch her breath. "Have you ever heard anything more dumb in your life than *truckload of dreams*? Lord help me, I can't do it tonight." But she straightened up and went out there. "Mama," said the young, gifted and black musical actress of the moment, "I know you understand, I know you know I have to go to the City. Try to tell Papa that it has nothin' to do with him." And Roberta swept the actress up into her ample bosom, "I know baby, I know you gotta leave Shacktown . . ." And then she started smiling, fighting it, almost losing, no she was going to make it, nope, too late . . . "Go baby, go into that big world and pursue your . . . good God, I can't say it, your truck . . . your truckload of . . ." And she let up this tremendous whooping laugh, and in a minute the whole audience (a full house, all there to see her) knew that Roberta had lost it and this wasn't the real play, and soon watching this big woman laugh and laugh and try to say "Go baby, go after your truckload of dreams," they started laughing too, and soon everyone backstage was gone, and I swear, I never have seen such unity, such conspiracy in the theater, such mutual abject JOY at the idiocy of a production. She never lost it again like that, but that was the immortal performance, and I had the luck to run into someone at a boring theater-lobby opening party one time who mentioned Roberta's act downtown and I asked if he saw her in *Truckload of Dreams* and he said yes, suppressing a smile, and we both caught each other's eyes—YOU WERE THERE THAT NIGHT, we said simultaneously. At least I can't say there weren't some good moments at the Venice.

Oh wait. You gotta hear this one. As a promotion drive for the theater, Arnold Schmeen, Sr., decided to throw a big party, create a Friends of the Venice Society (for contributions, grants, sponsors who would get credit in the playbill) which was just one more scheme to sell season tickets and rake in money, and the cause of this party was to be the 100th Anniversary of the Venice. Now this was typical of Schmeen in that the 50th Anniversary (which was virtually true) would have been a worthy event and something no one would have questioned, but NO, he had to exaggerate and put together a program full of misinformation, wishful thinking, bald lies, that was supposed to impress the New York Theater World with the importance of the Venice. He spent hundreds with art people and advertising people and researchers preparing a souvenir program which had playbills and old ticket stubs and good reviews (it displayed six because that's all they could find), finding photos of Lucille Lamont, old snapshots from the vaudeville days, the Follies days—a complete whitewash. This came to a spectacular end when one of the unrelentingly savage theater critics, who knew damn well what had become of the Venice, rewrote Schmeen's souvenir program, lampooned him nationally, ridiculed the whole affair (including a fundraising $100-a-throw cocktail party) under the headline: TO FORGET VENICE. Another magazine did a retrospective as well, citing bomb after bomb with the headline DEATH IN VENICE. There was a time, I vaguely recall, during which I could hardly wait to put the Venice Theater on my résumé . . .

Now if someone had told me in those first days: "This is the Venice Theater and it is barely theater, and you will come to realize that no one here has any talent and that nothing that is done here is any good and that before it's all over, you will be jumping around in a bunny suit (*Peter Cottontail*, '77 season, summer, Sat. and Sun. matinees)," I don't think it would have mattered. Even knowing that now, it doesn't matter because it was important to learn and understand that the Theater is 5% (if that) Glory and Applause and Long-Running Hits, and 95%

Bunny Suit. And I remember when I had a part-time job as a dresser and there I was helping chorus boys slip in and out of tuxes and top hats in a show called *Deluxe* (a short-lived musical on the life of Busby Berkeley; the whole play was supposed to be a dream of Berkeley's but it wasn't clever or lavish enough to be anything but an insult to Berkeley) and there, in this flop, was Brenda Simpson, who had won a Tony for *Table for Five,* who was on the cast albums for half the Rodgers and Hammerstein ingenue roles, who was by anyone's standards an Established Presence on Broadway—mind you, not a household name across America, but a bona fide Theater Person—and here she was in this drivel, and I asked her why, very tactfully, during the show's intermission over coffee, and she smiled and said, "The object in the theater, if you love the theater, want to make your life in it, is not to become famous or only play roles that flatter you or be the Star of the World, or to become a Legend in Your Own Time. The goal is to *work,* simply and consistently work, and do good work when you work, do creditable work with bad parts, create a moment or two worth remembering, be the name in the program that the week-in week-out theatergoer sees and goes, 'Well thank god, she's in it; it won't be a total waste.' " And as Brenda Simpson told me that, I knew it was wise and good and true, and then she got up to run back out and sing "Busby, You Never Write Your Mother," and I sat there thinking that there must be shortcuts and there must be fame and glory and Tony acceptance speeches—I wanted the 5% Greatness and not the 95% Bunny Suit. Are there words enough to tell you how much in the theater, in New York, in love and in life, you get the Bunny Suit?

And so I began my Illustrious Career, doing all the things one does when one is Nobody Yet in the theater, the four mainstays of the bottom rung . . .

1. Office and Clerical Work.

Joyce made this tolerable. Basically all we did was drink coffee, listen to her reminisce, and chain-smoke. A pack a day, with ten little Styrofoam cups of instant coffee. "Smoking will do you good, kid," she said. "Lower your voice. You'll get the manly roles." Still waiting, Joyce babe.

2. Working Props.

I loved working props. Any fool could work props. I was always immensely relieved to see the weekly assignment sheet and see that I got to do the Easiest Job in the Theaterworld, and I was confident . . . until I forgot, one night, to put out an ashtray on a certain table for Garner Fuskins, our fifty-five-year-old prima donna, who played most of our stately gentleman roles. He was furious—he rampaged backstage, an elephant crashing through the underbrush, "Where is he, where is he, wait 'til I get my hands on him . . ." and although friends tried to lie and protect me, he found me, took me by the collar and snorted, "You little shit. I had my cigarette lit and I reached over to put it out and, what? Huh? There was NO ashtray." Here his voice got strained and intensely quiet. "Do you think a gentleman like Ashley DeCamp would put out his cigarette on the table, maybe stomp it on the carpet? Throw it out the window? Do you know what kind of *business* I had to invent to put out that lousy cigarette? Hm?"

I was terrified after that. I psyched myself out completely, showing up twenty minutes before I had to, double- and triple-checking the prop list. Later, I learned it was common to torture the actors that treated the underlings like garbage by removing their key props—it rarely got back to anyone important, and if your conspiracies did reach the ears of directors, they shrugged it off as tantrums of temperamental actors (that is, unless you *really* went and mangled the play). Let us review some of the favorites. Oldies, I admit, but goodies . . .

A. Absence of Actor's Favorite Piece of Business.

All ham actors create lots of business for themselves, dramatically smoking cigarettes, adjusting the cravat, reading a magazine with exaggerated interest—there is no end to what people will create to lengthen their time onstage, turn a small role into something the audience will remember. The trick here is to sabotage the piece of business. Fuskins elegantly pulls out his cigarette case, opens it with a flourish . . . and there's nothing inside, ha ha. One time Tim, one of my drinking buddies there, noticed that Fuskins was dragging out his time onstage by riffling through magazines on a table, so he put a *Penthouse* face down so that when Fuskins picked it up the audience could see what this turn-of-the-century gentleman was reading.

B. Shifting the Subject of a Key Line.

I.e., slightly moving something directly referred to every night by an actor. "Don't those flowers look nice, Reginald, under father's portrait . . . Ha ha ha, oh I mean, how nice the flowers *would* look under father's portrait. I'll move them right now . . . from this . . . table . . ."

C. The "They Can See It, the Audience Cannot" Gambit.

I.e., "Veronica, I swear to you, she looks just like little Albertine. Can't you see it in her eyes?" The actor pulls out a wallet to show a picture where the prop person has replaced it with a photo of Hitler, the actor's résumé photo, Arnold Schmeen, a cutting from *Blueboy* magazine . . . lots of possibilities, all of them good for getting the unbeloved victim to flub the next line. A corollary to this is the ever-popular quinine-and-Dr. Pepper in the Scotch bottle, or even better, real vodka in the decanter usually filled with water for the "I better fix myself a double" scene where the actor has to drink the shot straight.

You often hear from actors how worthless and menial and inessential the techies are, but of course, this is wrong. They hold all the power. Moral to this story, if you're an actor, is to remember that or else face unending conspiracies . . .

3. The Dresser.

This, I think, is the worst heart-attack work, therefore higher in the Backstage Hierarchy. Example: Thirty seconds. The actor runs offstage, throwing off his tear-away clothes—you are there with his next costume. He steps into it, you tie his tie, you fasten his pants . . . Fifteen seconds. The sole comes off the shoe, the zipper is stuck, the shirt won't button, the amulet (he has to look at meaningfully in Act Two) snaps at the chain-clasp—suddenly, he panics: "What's my line? I can't remember my fucking line—good god, help me Gil, what is it?" You give it to him . . . or was that his entrance line for Act Three? . . . Five, four, three, two, one, he's on. And in a musical with lots of numbers, it is not unusual to have this fun experience ten times a night—all of this misery compounded by the mind-numbing, embalming *boredom* of having to hang on the cues and lines of the same play every night. The dresser can recite the play by memory, unfailingly.

Actors and actresses with some pull get the same staff person each night, so they feel at ease, trust their dresser, don't have to worry about their clothes falling off while they're tap-dancing. I kept getting assigned the chorus line, usually chorus boys but sometimes chorus girls (there is no modesty backstage during a quick-change). Most chorus-people, sorry to say, are dime-a-dozen. Which is not to say they are untalented: they are enormously, frightfully adept and talented. There's just 100,000 of them in New York. You have to be soooo talented it's not funny to be the chorus-extra in the lousiest low-budget musical in New York (usually running at the Venice, I assure you). They are young (eighteen to twenty-threeish), naïve, they have been in dance classes since they were nine, vocal since fourteen, theater classes with Mr. Once-Famous in the Village since sixteen, they are from Riverdale and Mother has pushed them all the way, Mother is manager and agent and, yes, the sympathetic best friend.

How do these extras get in the door? Well, one of the regulars, Tony, has the flu and will be out for two weeks (what Tony is really doing is auditioning for another show in San Francisco, a big role with billing; no one has *ever* had the flu in the history of the theater, absence is due to something else always—you'd go on with the flu, for pete's sake). ANYWAY, so the theater calls some agency and gets sent Chorus Boy Clone No. 34,798, and Chorus Boy is very excited, happy to have another show on his résumé, and he has delusions of staying on, replacing old Tony. The Dresser is the main contact for the extra, and hence

I learned that the Chorus Boy substitute/Dresser relationship moves along this inevitable path:

First, the Dresser is the Chorus Boy's best friend. Remember, they think this two-week trial is their Big Break, someone famous may see them, so they're going to dance their little hearts out, sing the ooohs and ahhhs so beautifully that they will be asked to stay on . . . maybe a cast album credit. But they learned all the steps in a week, the words last night, the music from a badly recorded cassette, and they watched the play all last week to get the feel of the production. Then there they are. You know their cues and where they should be. They don't. At this stage it's "Thanks Gil," and "You're a real pal, Gil," and "I never woulda made it without you, Gil," and you get taken out for an occasional drink (not that these boys have one interesting thing to say—they're all chorus machines, automatons of talent).

Second phase, around the fourth day in the role. They have the feel of the thing, they're having fun, they're getting cocky now. Guess what, they tell you, I talked to the director and he really likes me. Uh-huh, you say, your mouth full of pins, doing an emergency hem-job on his formal trousers he ripped, kicking his heels in the finale. The Dresser is not as important as he once was; he is, it seems, subservient . . .

Third phase, the Chorus Boy manifests confidence, utter disregard, contempt, indifference, superiority: "Quickly, quickly," they snap, "I haven't got all day. Owww, that's too tight—can't you find me another necktie?"

End of story? Tony doesn't get the part of the second male lead in San Francisco, he is back. Tony is the director's nephew, by the way, which no one bothered to tell Chorus Boy. So, son, they tell him, we're sorry to see you go, you were good, real good, damn good (the Kiss of Death: "damn good") and, yes, of course, when something opens up, if someone leaves, he will be the very first person they immediately call.

Fourth phase, for the last two nights only. You, the Dresser, are once again his all-time best friend. You are inside the theater, lowly thing that you are, and he would pay anything just to be where you are, inside instead of outside, no more auditions, no more Mother in Riverdale ("I know it's 8 a.m. darling, but don't you think you ought to get up and practice your audition piece for Mother?"), no more sacrifice. And so you say goodbye and he is extra friendly and asks you to put in a good word for him if someone, ha ha, breaks a leg or something, and you say you will, and he gives you his phone number (or his mother's) for you to give to the director, and you take it, and there's a lot of real-nice-working-with-you and then they walk away, kit bag over the shoulder, perfectly assembled in I'm-a-professional-dancer-on-Broadway fashionable sweats. And you NEVER see them again, and they NEVER have any more personality than that, and they NEVER seem happy.

And finally:

4. The First Reader.

Everyone's a writer in New York, as Emma says, and when they're not working on their Great Novel, they're writing their Great Play and sending it to off-Broadway theaters. One in a million gets produced this way but theaters, particularly the Venice, don't want to miss out on a hit, and plus they like the "artistic interaction" with the community, and plus if they read free-lance submissions they get a little money from some playwright's guild and a state-funded grant, so this CHARADE of reading plays occurs, and this task is pawned off on the New Kids.

At first I thought I shouldn't be a First Reader because I didn't finish college and had a limited background in theater literature, but Joyce gave me this look that said: You don't think reading this crap takes any talent or smarts, do you? And I recall, god, with a blush now, that I told Joyce that I was looking forward to reading plays. Joyce smoked her cigarette impassively, with the merest shake of her head: "Gil, darling, they've been waiting for you to come along. For a long time."

Joyce would collect a week's worth and drop them in a pile in front of me and Monica, the second-to-last person to join the Venice, and Joyce would give a little spiel: "All right, here they are, one performance only before the Trashcan. Three piles. No Way in Hell. Not Half Bad. Might Work. Let me warn you I've seen only two "Might Work"s in twenty-five years here come over the transom. If the writer has an agent, we send it to Schmeen in case it's for real. If it's a real prize turkey, we keep it for our Classics file for the Christmas party."

At the Christmas party three things invariably happened, and having missed last year's, I got to hear all about them: 1) the Classics folder was read, some of the actors taking part in the dialogue (Him: You lied to me, Sylvia. I thought we had love! Her: Oh we did, we did, Jerome, but it went away, far far away . . ."); 2) Joyce was coerced into performing her tap-dance routine from *The Follies of 1939* and everyone loved it and everyone said her legs hadn't changed and they were still those of a nineteen-year-old and Joyce sat there and ate up her annual night of adulation; and 3) Arnie Schmeen, Sr., would get up to give a speech, drunk, and get sentimental ("But what *is* the Theater? I'll tell you what it is—it's Dreams, it's Hopes, it's Magic . . . and if anyone tells you, hey, it's just a business, well you tell 'em they're wrong, baby, wrong as can be . . .") and rousing and teary-eyed until the emotion overwhelmed him and he was led away, back to the table with the spiked punch and everyone was supposed to, at some point after it, go up and tell him how much what he said meant to them, and the actors cynically competed amongst themselves for who could lay the biggest pile of bullshit on Arnie ("Oh Mr. Schmeen, I . . . I don't think I ever understood why I was here, in the Theater, until you got up there and said what you just said . . ."), and woe unto the person who broke up laughing in midspeech. But anyway, in my days at the Venice, particularly in the summer as the Hot New Ideas for the Fall Season drifted in, and Monica and I sat there in the boiling hot practice room dragging ourselves through these things, I personally put quite a few Classics in the Classics folder.

Monica would read the one-paragraph description required on all submissions. At first we were conscientious and read some of each play, but finally we learned it wasn't necessary . . .

Monica would read: "Steve is married, but his ex-roommate John is gay; Mary is married to Steve but he doesn't know about her lesbian past! What happens when all three plus Mary's strident lover share a mountain cabin in New England for the weekend? A delightful romp, a comedy of manners—"

Not Half Bad pile, I'd say. At least there was a plot.

Next. Monica read on: "A musical based on the *Diary of Anne Frank*. It moves from light romantic comedy—"

You've gotta be kidding, I said. Classic folder.

"—to the tragedy that was Nazi Germany for the Jews. *Anna!* (yes, Gil, with an exclamation mark) will make you laugh, make you cry, fun for the whole family, heartwarming and educational . . ."

Is there a rundown of musical numbers, I asked.

Monica couldn't read she was giggling so hard, "Oh god yes, of course—he's even got a cassette tape for us. Oh Gil we've got to put it on and hear 'I Call My Closet Home.' "

I wanted to hear something called "Jawohl," and "Mama's Song." Monica and I put first dibs on performing "Maybe the Nazis Are People Too" at the Christmas party.

Slowly the pile would lessen. Monica and I were becoming friends through all this, and we gossiped about people, trusted each other sort of, discussed our eventual goals—a true TOP SECRET as, bizarrely, no one ever *admitted* to any ambition in the theater. It would be six o'clock and time to go home, or for a drink with Monica, and on some days we were clever enough to be so quiet, so unnoticed that we stayed up in the rehearsal room all afternoon unmissed, goofing off, avoiding other assignments.

Real life seldom intruded once I moved to daytime at the theater. There was a president named Ford who told New York City to drop dead, Nixon to go free, had a cool wife who said she knew her kids had sex and smoked dope, got shot at by someone in the Manson Family.

"Well well well," said Lisa, one night when I came in late, "look who's here. Our roommate. Our roommate, that is, when last we checked."

"I don't know this man," said Emma blankly. "Wait . . . a distant, ancestral memory returns . . . You are Gil . . . he walks among us."

Oh come on guys, I'm not gone that much.

"Why don't you bring your theater friends over?" asked Lisa.

Then Emma kicked in: "Why don't you invite us to hang out with your artsy fartsy THEATUH friends, huh? Ashamed of us?"

I haven't been keeping you from them or them from you, don't be ridiculous.

(But I had been, they were right. Unconsciously, I had kept my apartment life from my theater life, one as a retreat from the other. Besides, I didn't mind the idea that Emma might be thinking I was up to something behind her back. Nor did I mind having the theater think I was living with someone and being modern and with-it—I hid behind Emma and Lisa. If the loud unappealing actress or middle-aged gay director made a play for me I could say, gee, let me call my housemate and see if *she* has dinner ready. If all my acquaintances got together and compared notes nothing major would be exposed but I couldn't keep inventing my life with such confidence if that happened, so I made sure it didn't happen.)

And then one night, Emma walks into my bedroom and slams the door. She stands there with her arms crossed. I can't tell if she's really upset or not:

"WHO is Francine?"

Francine? Francine Jarvis, I repeat instinctively.

"You tell me."

Francine's an actress. Did you find a Kleenex with her phone number on it?

"Yes I did. I want to know if I've been paying a third of a phone bill rife with calls to Francine Jarvis. If so, I'm getting a separate line."

Well . . . I sit up in bed and I do what any man would do in the circumstances: I lie. I say: Francine and I met at an audition and we went out and I've seen her a few times, just friendly-like, for drinks, for coffee—

"*Coffee*?" Emma blanched. "You had coffee with a woman —an actress—and you didn't clear it with me?"

It was spontaneous.

"Don't let it happen again. No actresses—is that clear?"

Emma, what's the big deal?

"This apartment will not disintegrate into disgusting couples with Emma watching from the sidelines. I will not condone BIMBOS on your arm."

Francine's no bimbo, Emma, she . . . she uh has a degree from New York University and she's a good actress and—

Emma sternly wagged a finger at me: "Actress equals bimbo. There are no exceptions."

Can I have the Kleenex?

"I incinerated it in the ashtray. And another thing: Why don't you take me to any of the theater parties at the Venice?"

Because you say theater people are phoney and pretentious, all actors are jerks, all actresses are bimbos, all people associated with it are stupid, there hasn't been a good playwright since Aeschylus—

"I'll soften the rhetoric. Someone's got to keep an eye on you. It's my duty to work the Bimbo-Watch."

Remarks like that keep you at a distance from my social life—

"Pleeeeease take me to a theater party . . ." she begged. "I don't get to meet any *artistes* and bohemians in my boring life and my boring jobs. I never go out. Pleeeeeease."

All right, all right. You can come to the next one if you really want to. But you'll hate it.

The Time Emma Went to a Venice Theater Party:

Emma wore a slinky black dress, trying to be bohemian for the occasion. She spent all day frizzing out her long brown hair which made her look Bride of Frankensteinish but I didn't say anything. She was trying to look stylish for me. I think.

There she was, cornered by the cocktail bar, with Robbie the Mime. Robbie was immensely handsome with a perfect body flexing underneath his leotard, but nobody liked him because he wasn't funny and had no sense of humor and was vain about his work and the one thing you can't be as a mime is unlikable. I went to get a little cocktail sandwich when I heard Emma's voice ringing out:

"Is there anything worse than mime? I mean, that's NOT entertainment, if you ask me. Marceau has done it all anyway, and a little of it goes a long way, a long long way. There's this mime at Rockefeller Center where I'm temping that waits for people to walk by and then he follows them, imitates their walk behind them, so close that when they turn around, he darts around so they don't know he's back there. And the lunchtime crowds laugh and laugh at these poor victims. And one day . . ."

I was swimming through the crowd: Emma don't tell this story, God please, don't let her do it . . .

"And one day," she said laughing, "this guy who must have been on a break from a construction crew turns around and belts this mime who is making fun of his lumbering walk. The mime goes *down,* lemme tellya, and the guy says 'You little faggot. Why don't you get a job like normal people, huh?' I thought I was going to die laughing . . ."

I arrived too late. Robbie turned away without a comment; I told Emma he was a mime.

"Oh," she said, downing her drink in one, "sorry about that. I'm batting a thousand tonight. I told what's-his-name there that Tennessee Williams is unbearably swank sometimes—"

He's directing *Streetcar* in the fall, I mentioned.

"And I told what's-her-name that Americans massacre Ibsen, Shaw, and Chekhov by trying to play it for laughs."

Yes, well, that's what the reviewer said about her in *The Three Sisters,* and she must have thought you were rubbing it in, maybe.

"I told that guy there my theory on how homosexuals have made too much of the theater effete and precious, and how *A Chorus Line* is a bunch of gay neurotics performing for another bunch of gay neurotics . . .

You haven't even *seen* it yet, Emma.

"Don't worry, I never mention your name—your career is safe," she said. "And that's Monica, huh?" We both turned to look at Monica, who was dressed shabbily that night. "I don't suppose I have to worry about anybody falling in love with *her.*"

I've toyed with the idea, I said.

"Oh c'mon Gil," she said, folding her arms. "I at least have to approve. No actresses." She studied her a moment.

"Nice behind, that must be it. That's all it comes down to for men, right? The woman has a great behind, no wonder you love her."

I don't love her, she's just—

"Can we go?" Emma asked, distressed about something. "You're right, you're right, I don't fit in here; you said I wouldn't like it and you're right." She punched me playfully in the arm. "How about Sal's, huh? Don't you want some grease? The Grease Plate Special? Grease cut in strips and deep-fried in more grease?"

And so we slipped away, unnoticed, a little drunk, a little nauseated from cheap off-Broadway cocktail-party snacks, and we made for the 42nd Street subway station. Soon we were bound for Brooklyn where our Manhattan lives seemed a little larger and the world outside of it very much quieter and slower, and soon there was Sal's, open all night, a blue fluorescent glow, Edward Hopperish, on a now dark commercial street of warehouses. On the subway Emma pulled out her spiral notebook and began scribbling. I said let me see, she said no. We moved automatically to our booth at Sal's; on that hot night the cold Formica tabletop felt good on our arms, and the waitress brought us a small pitcher of lukewarm water.

Emma after a moment, a scribble or two, tore off a sheet of paper and handed it to me. "That theater party clinched it for me," she said. "Ten words, listed there, are now officially banned from usage. All people caught using them will be taken summarily into custody, suspension of habeas corpus if necessary. This is Emma's Great Reformation—no . . . Emma's New Order, I like that better."

EMMA'S BANNED WORDS

1. vision
2. craft
3. work

Work, I asked?

"Yes, as in 'I have my work,' or 'I enjoyed watching his work in that production.' Actors are just jerking around up there, it's not work, you know that."

4. medium
5. art

"Art" is a pretty useful word though, I pointed out.

"It's just banned from possessive uses: as in 'my art' or 'the key to the actor's art, his craft . . .' Like that."

6. stagecraft

Yeah, I admitted, that *did* have to go.

7. demand
8. piece

Emma demonstrated in a high, hollow actress's voice: "Well I felt acutely burdened by the *demands* of that role, it was a difficult *piece,* a hard *piece* of work, it took all that I had to give, all my art, my *craft* . . ."

9. joy

"Actors should never discuss their joy in the role, the joy of their craft—I tell you Gil, there was much JOY at the party tonight."

10. love

"As in 'I felt this support, this approval coming from the audience that could only be described . . . yes, as Love . . .' As in 'What I Did for Love.' As in 'The only way to describe what goes on between the actor and his audience is . . . love . . .' "

I laughed. I've heard people talk that way all my life.

"Of course I will expand the list for all the professions. Like in writing, there's nothing worse to my ears than the word *text*—god, I hate that. And in the music industry when they talk about *product,* as in someone's shitty disco record was 'good product.' Hate that too." Coffee was brought to the table. "Emma's New Order," she repeated, pointing a prophetic finger. "I promise you, the world is in for a rough time if I come to power. Heads will roll."

I ordered the breakfast special which I could (and can) eat at any hour of the day; Emma went for a chocolate shake and a plate of french fries which she doused in steak sauce.

"I'm not writing, Gil," she said, munching. "I make fun of your theater life because I'm jealous: you have an artistic life. Lisa's got her painting. If I'm not going to have sex, I damn sure have to be writing, don't you see? Something has to justify my existence."

I could take care of the sex end of the problem, I said.

"No you couldn't," she said smiling, "it would take ten analysts ten years to make headway. Want some fries?"

Not all gooped up, no.

"This is even better when you stir mayonnaise up in the steak sauce. I do that in the apartment when no one is around to comment on it. Sometimes I have fries with Thousand Island dressing. Do you still love me?"

After those admissions, how could I?

"I mean, so many neurotic women are writing novels now," she went on, "I could name you half a dozen. All they do is write about how frigid and screwed-up they are and the critics are even tolerating this junk, awarding this self-indulgent trash all the great prizes. I mean I should be writing—this is my era. Self-involved, neuro. I'm hopeless. Writer's block."

Maybe if you had sex again it would help, I said.

"Nah, forget the sex. It's a distraction. Besides, I've passed my one-year mark now. I'm going for the record."

I sloshed around my buttered toast in the runny egg and Emma pointed out that some sensibilities would rate that an equal atrocity with the Thousand Island fries.

"So I was thinking and I thought of something," she said.

Yes?

"I'm going to write a pulp novel, one of those soft-core romance deals. I was thumbing through *Publishers Weekly*—you should see the advances those women are getting on those things. And *anyone* could write one." She corrected that: "No, anyone who had read a lot in the genre could write one. Their roots are in good novels, the Brontës, Jane Austen, magazine serials of the past. It's the new boom in publishing. See? There are two whole bandwagons I could be on. They'll ask one day why, why Emma, couldn't you turn a buck in the '70s which were designed specifically around your literary talents?" At the bottom of all this, she seemed truly distraught.

"*Love Once Was Here,*" she said in a minute.

Beg your pardon . . .

"*Love Once Was Here.* No, not quite. I'm working on my title. Here it is, here it is: *What We Had Was Love.* Oh god, that's swank. That's the one. I see the TV rights being negotiated already for this baby." She nudged me and I looked up from my egg. "Help me write it. I mean by asking about it, checking up on me, giving me lectures, telling me how I'll be nothing, forgotten, be as an unmarked grave, men shall walk over me and not realize . . . where is that quote from?"

I said sure, I'd help lend moral support.

"I'm coming up on twenty-three, and do you know what that means?"

What.

"Two years left."

Emma never told any of us her birthday—to this day I do not know, though I gathered it was in the fall sometime. She refused to acknowledge it, celebrate it, deal with it, for contemplation of aging gave her Death Obsession or a Mortality Crisis (concepts utilized enough that they became abbreviated DO and MC around the apartment). At twenty-three she had two years left until twenty-five, and twenty-five was the age Keats was when he died. There was a fragment of a poem in her journal, now that I think about it . . .

COUNTDOWN TO KEATS

Immortality or bust—
I've got a year and a few months before his mark,

when I consider how my light, etc.
Laforgue's still a year beyond (minor, thank god)
Shelley almost four, Byron way down the road.
I have my nightingales too, you know,
but frankly I'm not measuring up.
Some drawbacks, John: Grecian things do not
move us in this age,
but then again, no TB and that's a plus.
You, John, are the first to confront the mediocre,
the gauge of true gift,
the one who puts the poets in their place,
and I had hoped to improve my song
within your span.

. . . which I took to mean that she was using Keats's checkout time as her own gauge for success; this poem, as the others, was crossed out with an expletive written on top of it. With each passing death-date of a great writer, she said, it was one more nail in her coffin. I remember her distinctly, looking down at her plate, nothing to say in defense against her own accusations, trailing a french fry around a plate of steak sauce and grease.

Keats didn't have to temp every afternoon and work at Baldo's, I pointed out.

"That's a point," she said, now smiling again, smiling for the rest of that evening, making plans for the New Order, smiling (it seems at a distance) for the rest of the summer, which may well have been the summer I was waiting for all my life—you say the word summer and I think of that one. Gee, it seems horribly fragile to look back at it: you're aware that if you moved this straw or said those words or did any number of things someone eventually got around to, that you could have ended it all much sooner. I can't quite retrieve the young man with all that faith—where did he get that energy? Didn't he know the odds against being an actor—or Emma being a poet, or Lisa being a painter? How did he have so much faith in the world? No, it wasn't all stupidity and it wasn't all innocence and youth. I think New York was in there too, egging us on.

1976

"IT is the Bicentennial of This Great Land,' " Emma read, as we sat around two weeks before July 4th. " 'And the tall ships will sail up the Hudson River as an unmatched spectacle, thousands will take the oath of citizenship on Ellis Island, Lady Liberty will herself be aglow, and in the evening the city promises the world's biggest fireworks display.' " With that she put down the *Daily News* which had listed a rundown of events. "All this means people from all over This Great Land will arrive here, particularly from the Heartland of This Great Land—"

"This land is your land, this land is my land," Lisa sang.

"—and that means there is only one place *this* girl can be while all the hoopla is going on: out of town. The *News* says some *six* million people will line the harbor, three million down the block at the Promenade. Do I wanna be around while three million people cut through our front yard to see this shuck?"

But I wanted to see the tall ships.

Emma raised a finger. "You won't be able to see anything. The *News* said people are camping out already to get a space. Think of it, six million people, pushing, shoving and sweating . . ."

Okay, so the city will be a circus.

(Emma's New Order had grown in magnitude—her notebook was full of violations and regulations concerning what had to be destroyed; a one-person bad-taste gestapo. The Bicentennial was going to be an orgy of objectionable American behavior:

"Has-been celebrities trying to revive their careers by telling the world what America means to them. Street-performers and buskers—"

"Heeyyy Mister Tambourine Man," Lisa broke in, imitating our Carmine Street friend.

"—and folkies singing self-righteous, outdated protest songs and MIMES—good God, it'll be a field day for mimes, Mime City, Mime-o-rama, they'll be pulling on ropes, running up against invisible walls. And crafts. Little statue of liberties and red-white-and-blue kitsch, all kinds of Americana." She paused, noticing that she hadn't moved us. "I hate junk like this. You're expected to go out and have Fun *en masse*, merely because everyone else has turned out too."

So, got any better ideas?

Emma raised an eyebrow. "Welllll . . . Lisa. Darling. If you must go out with . . . this *person*, this boyfriend—"

"He's not really my boyfriend, Em," Lisa said, already defensive. "He's just someone I go out with."

"Someone you go out with and have carnal knowledge of—"

"Emma," Lisa whined.

"He puts his *thing* inside you—"

Lisa threw a pillow from her chair at Emma.

"Well doesn't he?" Emma ducked as a second pillow went forth. "I am being stoned, persecuted for speaking the truth! You won't even let us meet him." Emma turned to me, pouting. "She's ashamed of us, Gil . . . (sniff, sniff) She won't let us meet her banker Wall Street friends . . ." Lisa got up, ready to leave the room, refusing to listen. "Look at you, Lisa, you are consumed with self-hatred!"

Emma hadn't let a day go by without prying, prodding, provoking and pestering Lisa about the subject of Tom, who was handsome (Emma: "One demerit . . ."), who was rich ("Two demerits . . ."), who worked in an investment banking firm on Wall Street ("Fifteen demerits . . .") and who, from all reports, was one of those average all-around athletic American jock successful-in-high-school class-president types and A Real Nice Guy (which frankly *I* didn't like, and let's just say he wasn't going to fare well in the New Order).

"As I was saying," Emma continued, purring, "if you insist on having this Tom in your life to the exclusion of your friends—"

"Ooooh, you're so bad," huffed Lisa. "Gil, have I *once* ignored either of you? Do I still do things with both of you?"

"As I was saying," Emma continued, "that if you insist on having this man in your life, he might as well be of some use to the rest of us, your friends here in the commune. Your friends less rich and monied and privileged."

"I'm going to the bedroom," Lisa said, crossing her arms.

"He has a beachhouse," Emma said, speeding up before Lisa walked out, "or rather his filthy-rich bourgeois capitalist oppressor parents do, right? The three of us would have a blast down there."

Lisa shook her head disbelievingly. "And of course, Tom could come as well."

"Tom? Well if you think he'd want to go. Hasn't he seen enough of his beachhouse at this point?"

Lisa marched off, mumbling something; she and her magazine retreated to the bedroom and we heard the slam of the door. It *would* be fun, I yelled in the direction of the door, to go to the beach, escape the city. We heard: "*Not a chance,* people!"

"She's thinking about it," said Emma.

And sure enough, the next day Lisa sat us down and informed us of the plan:

"As it is Tom's beachhouse, or his parents', rather—"

"The filthy-rich bourgeois capitalist-scum parents," Emma added in a whisper.

"—as it is the Davidsons' beachhouse," Lisa continued, ignoring all interruptions, "we must treat the property with respect and behave in such a way as to remain unobtrusive to the neighbors and local residents, some of whom live on the Jersey Shore year-round. And as for the behavior I expect of my dearest friends," she continued, pacing the apartment as if this were a military briefing, "need I say that I expect my friends, my *dearest,* closest friends and compatriots, colleagues in a mutual struggle for New York survival, not to embarrass the shit out of me, not to mortify or humiliate me, not to tell stories of past experiences or to proffer information of an untoward or unattractive nature to said host of the beachhouse, one Tom Davidson. Am I understood clearly on this point?"

I nodded and so did Emma, who raised her hand for a question.

"Ms. Brandford, does that include the remarks you were making concerning penis size the other night?"

Lisa folded her arms. "I think some of us here have an attitude problem," she said, resuming her pace, "and I think some people should realize with the snap of my fingers, my merest whim, this weekend comes to a crashing halt and you will be forced out on the streets for your entertainment."

Where you will be seized upon by mimes, I said.

"And you will be forced to buy crafts," Lisa added.

So Emma got in the spirit of things. Cooperative and helpful—could she bring potato chips and snacks? Buy some of the beer? She was *too* nice, too helpful. I felt like I was in an old western and things had gotten too quiet out there . . .

"You wanna know my theory?" Emma asked, slipping into my room after midnight. "I've been listening to her on the telephone with Tom. She's just Miss Wisconsin prep-school cheerleader Sweet Little Lisa, and I think Tom would be shocked to discover her friends are on the lunatic fringe. Just wait until he gets a load of us."

When I was in the bathroom brushing my teeth, Lisa pulled me aside, looking for an ally. "I think you'll really like Tom," she said, as I put off spitting in front of her. "He's not exactly East Village material, but he's stable and I think that's what I like about him, his stability, since everything is so unstable in my life. Anyway, it'll be the four of us," she added, patting my behind, "a couples' weekend," she chirped. First Sign of Someone Entering a Serious Relationship: the desire to see all unattached friends encoupled as well. "Who knows," she whispered, leaving the bathroom, "you and Emma might find yourselves alone on a dune." I spit out my toothpaste.

June 28th. Countdown to the Bicentennial . . .

I got home from the theater to find Janet (the smart-looking black woman journalist on the *Womynpaper*) and Mandy (now Janet's lover) and Emma sitting on the floor near the TV, not watching it, a soap opera blaring out, a six-pack nearly consumed, an array of junkfood nearby, the haze of chain-smoking above them.

"You know us," said Mandy, with a schoolmistress tone, "Janet and I have tried to discourage heterosexuality in all its forms . . ."

"With all of us down there together," Janet added, "Old Tom the Stockbroker won't know what hit him. We'll be especially counterculture."

Then they saw me and switched subjects.

"Nothing's up," Emma said, all innocence, when questioned later, "I just think as long as we have a whole house for the weekend, Janet and Mandy ought to come down too. All our friends together."

I see, I said. An interracial lesbian couple to spice up the Big Weekend.

"I'm sure if Tom is a decent human being, he won't give it a second thought. I've already suggested to Lisa that they come down, and she's not going to refuse because it will mean Tom is narrow-minded and uncool. Or at least that's how I put it to her."

Somehow in the next two days *Susan* got herself invited.

"You know, girls," she said, "men can't deal with women with hairy legs. I'm not going to shave my legs just to wear a bathing suit just so men can be more comfortable, you know? Like, I got on the subway yesterday in short shorts. I did. It was hot, you know? And every man on that train looked at my legs. They couldn't deal with my hairy legs." Or someone who weighed a ton in hot pants, take your pick. Lisa, throughout the burgeoning of the guest list, fell into a worse mood. By Thursday, July 1st, she was barely speaking to us. Emma decided to cheer her up.

"Hey Lisa, get a load of this!" Emma barged into the living room wrapped in a sheet, modeling a 75¢ Statue of Liberty Styrofoam crown with points going off in all directions. She held up her cigarette lighter: "Give me your tired, your poor, your huddled wretched teeming masses yearning to huddle and teem and retch . . . What is that old thing? Teeming refuse, huddled masses, wretched shores—no, teeming shores, wretched huddled refuse retching to be free! Well Lady Liberty got what she wanted, this city is full of refuse. Teeming, teeming on the shore . . ."

Lisa wasn't laughing. "I'd say wretched masses describes the upcoming beach weekend, all right," she said. "This whole beach thing has gotten out of control."

The night before, around 1 a.m., we had begun to pack, having sworn to do it days earlier.

"I think I'll take my journal," said Emma. "I could write some marine poems, something vagarious, wistful by the sea . . ."

"The day you write *one* word in that book will be a red-letter day in history. Excuse me, wait, let me GET MY CAMERA," Lisa went on, still in a bad mood.

Emma didn't say anything for a while; Lisa slapped a few things into an overnight bag and then left the room, soon out of earshot. I was waiting.

"For that remark, of course," Emma said lightly, "she will *die*."

Emma's writer's block hadn't let up really. *What We Had Was Love* was a chapter and a half off the ground, nothing serious had been started, no poems in ages, and yet the collection of ratty spiral notebooks and pads was no more. She now bought fine leather-bound, embossed journals, bought small hardcover notepads in quantities, purse-sized in case the muse struck on the subway, and she even got a fountain pen, a series of quills, a blotter, two kinds of ink and some bonded stationery ("You don't think this is affected, do you?" she asked at the time). She also said, "Walter Benjamin said that if you're going to write you have to surround yourself with nice things, not second-rate junk—good paper, good pens and ink, quality items—it makes the work look important, finishable." Emma had the process, the Zen, the preparation and ceremony of writing down to a science. I think of her now in the chic Brooklyn Heights café, papers spread out, her notebooks opened, her third cup of espresso beside her, a look of concentration, of seriousness on her face, waiting perhaps for . . . for, I'm not sure. Maybe someone to come up and go, "Oh my god, you're . . . you're a writer, aren't you? I can just tell," and she would smile, demur a little, and say "Yes, yes I am a writer." Except that whole year she never *wrote* anything.

But back to the beach trip: The morning arrived and there were some serious political maneuvers staged to see who got to ride in whose car. Lisa would go with Tom in Tom's air-conditioned Impala ("What twenty-seven-year-old so-called young person drives a goddam Impala?" Emma wanted to know). No one wanted to ride with Susan. But Susan had a car. Janet could use her sister's car but she would have to go to Queens to get it.

"Oh by the way, everybody," announced Susan as we gathered in front of the walk-up waiting for Tom to show himself, "this is Chris." Chris was a twenty-five-year-old gay man, skinny, the uniform mustache, dressed like a teenager, very friendly. No one told Susan she could bring a guest. Emma gave me a sidewise glance, smiling.

Lisa said to me quietly, resigned to events, "We wanted to leave the circus in the city and now we've got one of our own at the beach. Lesbian journalist and black mistress; Susan the Fag Hag and her Attendant Boy; Emma, Bitch Goddess of Four Continents . . ." She pressed my arm: "Try to make friends with Tom so he'll have a good time, okay? You are now my only hope. I may walk into the sea, never to be recovered . . ."

The best thing she could do—I told Lisa—was to live it up and think of it all as madcap, bohemian, your wild youth. Appeal to Tom's sense of Modernity.

"What if I'm as modern as Tom gets?" she asked.

I said I'd try to make friends and I meant it, as it's rare that anyone ever appeals to me on any human level, let alone *needs* me to do anything, so I decided to be Mr. Helpful.

July 4th, the country is two hundred years old, and Tom was right on time with his refrigerator-cool Impala. Lisa got in the front, Emma and I scrambled into the back. There was small talk and then there was more small talk; Lisa was decidedly nervous.

"You know, Tom," Emma said, running her hands along the velour, "I don't know how you can keep this big a car in the city. Gas is almost $2 a gallon now, what with the Arabs—what does this baby get? Seven miles to the gallon."

"Eight I think," said Tom. "I'm not going to let the Arabs tell me what I can and can't drive, you know? I believe that you can afford anything you want to, if you work hard enough."

Emma leaned into me to whisper: "And you can really afford anything you want if your dad's a millionaire. Bet he gives a lot to charity, this guy."

How much do you give to charity, Emma?

"Don't change the topic."

Lisa sensed an ebb in conversation. "Well you guys," she said, "do you want to go to Jersey by way of the Verrazano Bridge? We can see the tall ships sail in."

I said I wanted to see the tall ships. Tom pointed out that we could glimpse the carrier President Ford was on.

"No, the excitement might be too much for me," said Emma. "I might *come*."

Lisa turned around to smile the first in a series of BETTER WATCH IT smiles, as we turned toward the Holland Tunnel. It looked as if the entire United States was coming into the city going the other direction.

Tom tried to make conversation. "Sure glad we're heading out of the city. Look at the crowds coming in."

"Yes," said Lisa, "look at them all. All those cars."

"Isn't it odd they don't charge you to go out of the city?" Tom asked. "You pay going in but not out."

"I hear they're going to raise the toll soon," Lisa added.

Emma again leaned into me: "Gee, hand me my journal—let me get this scintillating discourse on paper . . ."

We stopped behind a line of traffic in the middle of the Tunnel. There was silence, then Tom pointed out the line of blue tiles that represented the New York–New Jersey state line. There were two tubes for the Holland but three for the Lincoln Tunnel. Did we know that the Statue of Liberty was actually on the New Jersey side of the line, but New York claimed the island? Well it was true. And then there was more silence.

"I hate the Holland Tunnel," said Emma, stirring. "I mean, think about it: we're *under* a river. Beyond us and these shoddy looking tiles is the Hudson River, full of toxic waste and filth and slime, waiting to rush in. It'll happen one day."

Tom informed us that the tunnel was under the rock under the river.

"Well that makes me feel *a lot* better," said Emma. "We can be crushed by the rocks then drowned, flailing about, thousands of us in putrid mud. And what about the blowers, the big fans that suck all the carbon monoxide out. One of these days they're going to break and we're all going to asphyxiate down here. It would be a simple thing for those fans to break. I wonder how long it would take . . . probably under a minute for us all to suffocate."

No one comforted Emma. Eventually the traffic inched forward and we emerged from the Tunnel of Death, went through a series of split-second-decision-requiring intersections, and then we were sailing at full-speed down the New Jersey Turnpike.

"So," said Tom, trying again, "I met Janet and Mandy one night when I dropped Lisa off at your place. How does everyone know each other?"

Before Lisa could answer, Emma said, "Oh, we met them when we went dyke bar-hopping one night."

"Really?" said Tom. "So they're, uh, lesbians?"

"Yes," said Emma, "they are."

Tom didn't seem fazed. "I've always wondered what they did."

"They perform cunnilingus on each other, as a rule. Although some lesbians use—"

No, no, no, Tom broke in, laughing. He had meant what Janet and Mandy did for a living, careerlike not lesbianlike. Lisa followed with convulsive laughter, Tom kept laughing, and Emma joined in so she wouldn't seem embarrassed, which she was. Many miles and suburbs went by before Emma spoke again, and then only in distress:

"I'm car-zee-ated," she announced, as we swung around the exit ramp of the Garden State Parkway.

What?

"Carseated. It's when you have nausea in a car. 'Carzha.' You can have buszha, subwayzha, planezha, taxizha—"

New Yorkzha, I suggested.

"Yes, there are metaphysical connotations, too: like Lifezha, Sexzha, both of which I have all the time."

Polite laughter. Emma moved close to whisper.

"Okay, so Tom isn't a complete piece of shit, but notice our friend Lisa, huh? She acts differently around him. She's not one of us anymore . . . she's gone over to the other side—"

Emma—

"No, and that's not all. She waits to see if he laughs before laughing at us, did you catch that? He matters more than we do. This is the great fault of most women, I'll have you know, they get a boyfriend and then the friends go *out* the window . . ."

I told Emma she was being premature, at least wait and see how the weekend goes. Lisa was nervous having us all together.

"I'll seduce Tom in the dunes—I'll make the sacrifice to put an end to this. Or you can seduce Lisa in the dunes. Or we could really put an end to it and you could seduce *Tom* in the dunes. We both could seduce Lisa, we could share her—"

In the dunes, I clarified.

"In the middle of the Garden State Parkway for all I care. We have got to save her. How DARE she go and have sex—successful, all-American, no-nonsense, healthy, functional normal-people sex without consulting us first? We'll tell her when she can go have sex and when she can't and if so with whom."

Then there was Highway 9, and the strip, a world of beachtown junk and souvenir places and stores called Kwik-Pik and

EZ-Stop and Stop 'N Get It! filled with cheap beach things. We passed a shack with a hand-painted placard advertising LIVE BAIT.

"Worms. There's a nice thought for you. Someone sitting there selling cans of squirming, squiggling worms. *Teeming* worms." No takers on Emma's worm gambit. "Some human being goes out and collects those worms," Emma went on, beating a dead . . . horse. "What did you do with your one life on the earth? 'Uh, I filled cans with worms . . .' "

Every filling station–Kwik Snak junkfood store advertised SLUSHEES and FRE-ZEES and ICEES and SNO-BALLS.

"The finer question," said Emma, "what Henry James would have been eager to define, is the precise difference between the Slushee and the Icee. I think the Icee and the Sno-Ball are indistinguishable to the naked eye, both are finely chopped ice covered in some chemical-toilet blue flavoring that turns your mouth blue and your urine green. I think the Sno-Ball was really the forerunner of the Slushee, the Slushpuppy, the Fre-zee and the Coolee, which demonstrates a finer ice-slush technology, a more difficult-to-attain consistency."

No one was listening to Emma. She again elbowed me, leaning in to whisper, "This is a tough crowd. This knocked 'em dead in Peoria. Don't I pay you to laugh at everything I say?"

I'm laughing, already, I'm laughing.

"There was a moment, a brief moment that I *almost* had mercy, let my guard fall, almost forgot the sanctity of my mission. This Tom has to go. When she doesn't laugh at everything I say then we're dealing with a New Lisa. Look at her . . . holding hands with him. In his Impala. She's turning into Pat Nixon before our very eyes." And then, as the inspiration hit, she said to the front seat: "I'd really like a Slushee now."

Emma wanted to stop because she was nauseated and there's something about a big car's backseat that is nauseating with that car-smell air conditioning and so I said I'd like to stop too. Lisa sort of wanted a diet drink. Emma wanted a Slushee. Tom didn't want to stop anywhere because he wanted to get down to the beachhouse and open it up before Susan and the others arrived. Emma requested a Slushee again. So Tom spotted a

SLUSHEE sign at Eddie's Convenience Mart but he couldn't get over in time so we had to go up the road and make a U-turn (which took forever because of all the traffic going the other way), drove back to Eddie's and tried to make a left turn into the parking lot (which took forever because of all the traffic coming from *that* way), but after the traffic subsided we turned into the gravel parking lot of Eddie's Convenience Mart: For All Your Beach Needs.

"I have many beach needs," said Emma, bursting forth from the Nausea Car, "and we may be here a while."

Eddie's Convenience Mart had aisle after aisle of junk, a tanning oil section, a beach inflatable-toy section, a pulp beach trash-novel section, a fishing lure corner, two freezers full of Frozen Confections, two refrigerators full of drinks. Lisa got a diet drink, Tom got some tanning oil, I got a candy bar and a blue Slushee only because Emma said she was getting one but then changed her mind and said she would vomit if she had to get back in the Impala with a Slushee, but she did buy an inflatable porpoise, an issue of *Soap Opera Digest*, the steamiest romance novel she could find in ten minutes of browsing, and a postcard of Eddie's Convenience Mart with a picture of Eddie in the parking lot, a fat man in Bermuda shorts, raising his hands in a gesture of welcome. At the cash register Emma asked if Eddie was around and she was told Eddie was dead and the store had new owners and Emma asked why they didn't change the name and they said that they kept the name as a tribute to Eddie.

"Eddie's gone to that big Slushee-stirrer in the sky," she said as we left.

"You know," Tom began, feeling philosophical on the way to the car, "sometimes I think the Good Life is something like this. I think, hey, why don't you drop the rat race, the hustle and the worry—"

"The bustle," said Emma, finishing up his cliché.

"Yeah, the hustle and the bustle of Wall Street," he went on, and I didn't hear the rest of it, but it was the usual: quit this very profitable I-make-more-money-in-an-hour-than-you-do-in-a-month type of job and go away and do something simple and menial and I guess people are sincere when they say it, but somehow that makes it even worse. And Tom was still going on about it in the car: ". . . and I mean what more do you really need? A roof over your head, right? Eddie must have a very uncomplicated, relaxing life."

"Yes, very relaxed at the moment," Emma added.

"And sometimes I envy that. Knowing the local fishermen. The local kids who come down for things—"

"Like Slushees," Emma said, still being helpful.

"Yes, I can sometimes see all that. You know, when I retire."

"Tom's Convenience Mart."

Lisa said nothing, her arms crossed in the front seat. She knew us too well and she knew we thought Tom was generating bullshit, and that Emma, in her way, was laughing at him.

Emma prodded me again as we got back on Highway 9, the car noises covering her whispers. "Something very interesting happened in the course of Eddie's Convenience Mart, something very subtle."

So subtle I didn't know what it was, in fact.

"On the way down we were trying to make him like us—or rather I was, you've just been sitting here like a pile of nothing. But the whole I-wanna-give-it-all-up, that Big Bad Wall Street crap was his way of reaching out to us . . ." Emma poked my arm, she was giddy with her theory. "He's trying to show us there's a touch of the Old Bohemian in him, and of course, there's not. We'll have him wrapped around our finger by weekend's end."

Emma, I protested, your scheming is going to hurt Lisa.

"These are the times that try men's souls, Gil," she said. "We're losing her to the other side, the establishment." Then after a minute: "How dare she. Doesn't she have any consideration for my feelings? Having healthy, uncomplicated, unneurotic sex in front of me, just right in my face—it's like she's saying Here Emma, look at me, this is how normal functional people behave."

Emma, for god's sake—

"La Rochefoucauld knew: One finds something not altogether unfortunate in the misfortunes of one's good friends."

Emma, you start behaving yourself right now. I am part of no conspiracies. If you want to wreck the weekend, it'll be your doing and I'll be just as mad at you as Lisa.

"Okay, okay," she said, flopping back in the seat.

From Highway 9 we went on this county route and then turned and turned and turned again (Emma groaning with each turn, commenting on her imminent illness), and then turned finally into a driveway, two ruts through the mixture of soil and sand, and there we were: Tom's Beachhouse. It was two stories, a big gray box with lots of screened-in windows, a porch to the side and another second-story porch facing the ocean, steps that led down the dunes and the spiky grass to the strip of beach; there were clotheslines with towels hanging limply, rusting lawn chairs on the decks, a barbecue. All people on the Jersey Shore name their beachhouses and the Davidsons had named theirs Dunecrest and there was a sign on a pole supporting a gaslight (which was really electric) and someone had written DUNECREST in cursive with a wood-burning set across the sign.

"Dooooooncrest," intoned Emma. "The new CBS afternoon soap. Six people. One beachhouse. The passions, the turmoils, the sexual inadequacy and impotence . . ."

Lisa, getting the coolers from the trunk, flashed Emma another death-ray look.

"I think it's a beautiful name," said Tom. "Very poetic."

"Yes," said Emma, taking her embossed journal in hand, "maybe I'll write a poem called that. 'Dunecrest' by Emma Gennaro." Lisa rolled her eyes, and turned to stomp into the house.

"If you do write something, show it to me," said Tom, smiling and genuine. "Lisa says you're a poet and are going to be famous one day. She thinks you're very talented." And then Tom went to help Lisa with all the stuff she was carrying.

Aren't you a little *tiny* bit ashamed, I asked Emma. Lisa was Emma's biggest fan, Tom admires Emma, everyone loves Emma and what is Emma doing? Plotting their annihilation. But Emma wasn't listening to me. She stared out at the sea.

"I bet Tom has a small penis," she said blandly. "I bet if you had the stopwatch on him, he doesn't clock ten minutes."

Susan's car pulled into the lot: "The Dykemobile is here!" screamed Susan. Chris bounced out of the car and told how on the way they had made him an Honorary Dyke, and how Susan got lost with Tom's excellent directions. We all trudged toward the house with our stuff.

Susan fought to share a room with Chris, and no one put a stop to it. Emma and I got to share a bed. I made a joke about sleeping next to her, snuggling up as it got colder, ha ha ha.

"I'm coming up on my two-year celibacy mark and the support group is throwing a party for me and I'm not going to mess up my record for the likes of you. Nothing personal, you understand."

Now I had honestly put aside all thoughts of Emma—really I had. But that was before I had to spend a four-day weekend in a bed beside her, both of us laughing and drunk and conspiratorial each night. If it hadn't been for the bed, I would have been my normal indifferent self concerning having sex with Emma. No, really. If you go two years and turn down all offers and go to support groups and walk down the street virtually wearing a sign I AM CELIBATE, then I take you at your word. Emma unpacked and I watched her throw a garment on the bed.

"Don't look so strange. That's my nightgown."

Circa 1896, Grandma's flannels from the mountain cabin.

"I'll have you know in certain southern portions of Indiana that would be considered lonjureee. I might get cold."

How could anyone be cold in a bed with ME?

(Too bad I can't put in a little picture of her expression in response to that remark.) "Freeman, I am celibate as the Risen Christ. *Noli me tangere*—got that?" And then she went out the bedroom door, only to lean back in to coo, "Unless, you big stud, you get me drunk," followed by her best dumb-cheerleader giggle as she walked away.

Drinks are on me, Emma.

I went out to the porch and looked out at the sea on this

beautiful day. Emma noiselessly joined me sitting on the steps that led down to the beach and we both stared out into the void; the others ran down to the beach to throw the Frisbee back and forth or stick a foot in the water.

"The day is nice," said Emma.

Yes. The sky is very blue.

"What is this, Hemingway dialogue?"

Ernest and I are both from Oak Park, Emma.

"I've tried not to hold it against you." She moved to the step below me so she could have more room. "Good stuff, huh? The Atlantic Ocean. You know, you get used to craning your neck in New York, everything, elevators, walk-ups, skyscrapers, is vertical, and then suddenly—WOW: horizontality to the max. Makes you feel like a speck, completely nonexistent." Then Emma turned up to look at me. "I'd like to expand this thought into a full-fledged neurotic comment, but it's too much work at the beach." She turned back and we both stared catatonically ahead, looking at the waves.

Thinking profound thoughts, Emma?

"Yes. I was thinking about dinner."

Susan padded up to the house and yelled up to us on the porch to get down on the beach and have Fun like everyone else. Susan was wearing this vast lemon-yellow one-piece bathing suit that made her look like a parade float. One giant arm held a cigarette, the other a daiquiri, and you had to fix your eyes to these neutral objects while talking to Susan lest you stare at the mottled flesh, the unshaven legs that were her pride, the anatomy unashamedly there.

"She looks like a buoy," said Emma, after Susan padded back to the beach. "I wish I was that unself-conscious. I'm the ugliest thing here."

Susan might edge you out, Em.

"No one counts Susan when you talk about human beings. Mandy and Janet have hard athletic bodies—the good thing about being a dyke, I guess: softball. Janet is magazine perfect—look at her catch that Frisbee there . . . geez. Lisa, of course, is the winner of the Miss America Swimsuit Competition."

Lisa was engaged in a clumsy game of catch with Tom. Tom was tan and muscular and all-American and had one of those perfectly chiseled bodies you could eat off of, and he was one of those guys who lived for an excuse to take off his shirt. He was throwing the ball gently to Lisa, who would drop it on any account, and he kept trying to throw it to her softer and gentler and it would still end up in the grass, her flitting after it, giggling. Tom would occasionally run and tickle Lisa and kiss her and make her squeal which balanced out the condescending looks and rolling eyes when she dropped his simple, easy "girl's" throws.

"I hate Tom," Emma said, watching the same spectacle.

Patience, tolerance, I urged.

"No it's no use. And what happened to our Lisa, huh? Where is that adorably neurotic screwed-up Midwestern mess from Milwaukee we've come to know and love? What is this frolic-on-the-beach-with-the-jock-boyfriend shit?"

Exasperated, Emma got up and retreated to the bedroom to change. We had at last surrendered to the notion that we had to make an appearance on the beach. I changed first in the small bathroom next door to our bedroom: khaki shorts and a loud Hawaiian shirt that was too big, and flip-flops. I heard much banging around of suitcases and grumblings and cursings from Emma in the bedroom.

What's the problem, Emma? (I ask through the closed door.)

"I'm tall for a girl, right? My breasts are gross. They aren't so big but I will give them this: they are in proportion to my frame."

Yeah, so?

The suitcase slammed shut again. "So what is it with these thighs—I'm renting myself out to Cellulite as a Before picture. My legs are Ionic columns . . ." Pause. "I meant Doric."

Would you come out? You look great.

"You haven't seen my thighs. They're going to let Apollo astronauts use my fat thighs for simulated moon surface." Some more noise within. "That's it, forget it—I'm not wearing this."

Finally the door opens. It is Emma, serene, unflustered. She is in a billowy black blouse, black capri slacks (Liz Taylor, circa 1963), sandals, only her ankles and hands exposed. She put on a big pair of dark sunglasses, and said as she led the way outside, "You didn't really think I was going to expose my wretched body, did you? Let's get real here . . ."

It occurred to me as I walked down to the beach, and for some reason not before, that I was the Whitest Person in America. I've never been "in shape" in my life. My chest hasn't changed since I was fourteen and it would have been nice to have some hair on it or some sun on it or something to recommend it, but I was determined to set an example for Emma, so off went the Hawaiian shirt—

"Oooh blinded by the light, baby!"

"Gimme those sunglasses—I can't see, I'm blind . . ." Janet and Mandy fumbled around like St. Paul after his vision, falling to the sand, rolling about.

"It's so white, so bright, so clean and fresh!"

"The George Wallace Poster Child, don'tcha know?"

All right, I *won't* take off my shirt. I put it back on and then everyone said they'd stop kidding me and then I took it back off and they didn't stop kidding me, so I turned over on my back and tried to have the patience to lie there and get a tan. Attention moved to Emma:

"Emma," Janet asked, "why are you all dressed in black on this hot beach, girl?"

"I'm in mourning for my life."

Janet and Mandy looked at each other blankly.

"Chekhov," Emma added. "You didn't seriously think the Emma Body was to be revealed in public, did you? I'm sitting over here next to Gil who is also the Whitest Person in America."

"Don'tcha want a tan?" asked Mandy.

Emma winced, showing a polite disdain. "Give me one good reason to turn yourself a different color."

Janet and Mandy shrugged and ran back to their Frisbee, then altered course for the surf. They ran headlong into a wave, shrieking shrilly as the water washed between their legs and splashed up their fronts.

"Look at them," said Emma, all emotion drained from her voice as she reclined back, listless, against an ice chest. "That's a sewer they're swimming in. Tons of New York garbage, toxic waste, chemicals, the backwash of the Great Metropolis. And feces: human feces, fish feces, *Susan's* feces. Living things are out there too, you know—eels, sea worms, man-of-wars and slime and all kinds of living GOO, and when they're not shitting they're looking for something to slime up against—ucccck. Sharks, barracudas, swordfishes—"

There are not swordfishes, I said, looking up at her.

"Yes there are, I've seen them on sale at Peterson's fish market, so I'm sure they're out there, waiting . . . waiting. Biding their time: waiting for Emma. Manta rays too, hammerhead sharks and things with tentacles and sucker-pods and mouths that go like this—" Emma demonstrated a grouper's expression from behind her sunglasses, which made me laugh. "Are you seriously gonna lie out here?"

Yes, I was one with the shore.

"It's too hot," she said, getting to her feet lazily, wiping the sand away. "There are mosquitoes and you're gonna turn pink you're so white."

White for life, I resigned and got up.

"Come inside with Doctor Emma, Doctor of Blenderology—I'm going to show these people how to make a blender drink and I'm going to get everyone drunk and things will get out of hand and squalid and disgusting and Lisa and Tom will discover they're not right for each other, Tom will walk into the sea *Star is Born*-like and leave a will bequesting this beachhouse to the three of us." At this moment, a hundred yards away, they were sitting together under an umbrella, leaning against each other affectionately. "To the blender, troops!" ordered Emma, pulling me behind her.

Emma's Secret of Blenderology was remarkably simple: put a little pretty-colored liqueur/fruit juice in a blender, add half a bottle of vodka or gin or tequila—something clear—and put in some ice, then blend to Slushee consistency.

A big cumulus cloud wandered in front of the sun, so the gang moved indoors and sat around waiting on new blender creations.

"Let's play a game or something," said Susan.

Yeah, said everyone.

"I know," she said, brightening, "how about Truth or Dare?"

No, said everyone.

"What's wrong with Truth or Dare?" asked Chris.

"Uh, how about Who Am I?" proposed Mandy. That was where one player thought of a famous person, living or dead, and everyone took turns guessing by asking yes-or-no questions.

"I've got someone, I've got someone!" said Susan, settling into a big beanbag chair, which she nearly obscured. "A great person!"

All right.

"Is this person a man?" asked Tom.

"God no," said Susan.

"Is this person a lesbian separatist feminist writer published in the last five years?" asked Emma.

"Well, uh, yes," said Susan, irritated at the speed of play.

"Lotta challenge to this game," said Mandy.

Having gotten that far though, having guessed ten or more feminist writers, even Janet and Mandy gave up.

"It's Kristin Howell Kroppett," said Susan, laughing, throwing her hands up. "C'mon you guys—she wrote *Rape of My Thoughts: Daily Coping in a World With Men.* She's very famous—"

"Her own mother hasn't heard of her," mumbled Janet.

"Let's try another game," said Lisa.

"Truth or Dare is always fun," said Susan. "I remember—"

Everyone again: NO TRUTH OR DARE.

Somehow it was decided that we all had to write personal ads, like the ones in the back pages of the *Village Voice.*

"Looking for well-hung Chicano twins for hot oil and whipped cream S & M parties—," began Mandy, when Susan cut her off, having mysteriously become in charge of the game.

"*No,* honey," she insisted, "we must do it for real. We'll learn a lot about each other this way. So few people can articulate their needs these days."

"I need another drink," said Emma, articulating. As Lisa went to bring the pitcher of some brown-looking cocktail in, everyone scribbled, balled up false takes, grumbled. Doing it seriously is difficult, so no one did.

"Swinging hot-looking single white sex-machine coming off

eons of celibacy looking for middle-aged dwarves into bondage and discipline for women's prison scenario—"

"Emma, please!" Susan cried, with an exasperated gesture. "You have to take this seriously now . . ."

More scribbling. Tom read his:

> SWM, 27, attractive, interested in most everything, stuck on Wall St., seeks culture, variety and good times through SW, 21–25, intelligent, artistic, committed, well-read, tall and attractive would be nice too.

"You could probably cut some words out of that and save money," Tom pointed out, clearing his throat.

(That's odd, I thought, Lisa isn't tall.)

"Here I am, Tom," said Lisa, pursing her lips, Marilyn Monroe-like, "I'll put my response in the mail today. I'll learn to stand on tiptoes."

Susan read Lisa's aloud:

> SWF, 24, pretty good looks, some smarts, starving artist in the Village, looking for Mr. Perfect, a smart, successful, hunk, initials T.D. if possible, must have Jersey Shore beachhouse—

"All right, all right," Susan said putting it down, "we get the point, Brandford." I noticed Emma, out of Lisa's line of sight, filling her cheeks with pretend vomit.

Susan read Janet's clever lesbian ad reverently, Mandy gave up and said she couldn't do it, Chris's was sappy ("Some day he'll come along? The Man I Love? If you love Gershwin, showtunes, opera . . ." etc.), and then Susan solemnly read mine.

> SWM, 22, lonely in the big city, struggling actor in career and in life. Waiting for someone I don't have to act with, someone caring and understanding—

"Gil, this is wonderful," said Susan, interrupting herself. She read on:

> —someone not after the shallow '70s self-involved cheap thrills relationship, a seeker of something permanent and deep, soul-baring, giving. I have much to give to such a woman; all I ask is she be open and kind, liberal and willing to be vulnerable and honest at all levels for a true union of hearts and intellect. Big tits a must.

"WON'T ANYONE take this seriously?" Susan stormed, as the rest of us laughed. Too late, though. The cloud had passed and Mandy and Janet headed back for the surf, Tom took his shirt off again and Lisa bounced off the sofa to give him a hug.

"Back to the blender, soldier," Emma said, nudging me.

That afternoon, like those of the days following, took forever to complete, operating in the Beach Time Warp where one walks to town, gets a popsicle, walks back, ducking into the air-conditioned supermarket to look at magazines you don't buy, comes back to the house, talks with someone, goes out to the beach, walks up the shore then turns around and walks down the shore past the house and down to the infinitely far pier, wades, climbs a dune, finds a shell, throws away the shell, sits on the porch and then asks someone what time it is to discover an hour has gone by and it's *just* three-something and the day, like the sea, stretches before one, time given to you to waste . . . one falls into an automatic plod from point to point, conscious life ceases, only thoughts that don't require energy are sustained and those not for long. More booze, a soft dehumidified potato chip, a cookie out of a bag someone else brought, someone's low-tar-and-nicotine cigarette—sneak one for later —the body's needs are few.

"There are going to be fireworks tonight," I heard Janet say, as I lay on a deck chair on the porch facing the sea. "Asbury Park and some in Sea Girt too and we'll be able to see them from here."

Under the spell of Emma's Brooklyn Bombers, Multiple Orgasms and Spanish Flies (I'm sure she was making the same drink over and over, inventing names for it), I drifted in and out of afternoon sleep on the porch, letting fragments of conversations waft up from the beach . . .

Chris: "Then I was with Michael but John, who didn't know I was alive on the Planet Earth, starts getting interested after all this time—and I've always wanted him, Susan—you know my type . . ."

Mandy: "No that's the thing about the Chicago Cubs—I couldn't be faithful if they won the pennant, you know? They have to lose, they have to fuck it up right at the end and disappoint everyone because that's Chicago. One day they'll win something by accident and it's not going to be the same. And the White Sox—good god, don't talk to me about the White Sox . . ."

Tom: "Well no, Lisa, that's what's so interesting about what they call risk arbitrage—one day all of Wall Street is going to be virtually a casino, a place to stake a bet on futures and numbers and rises and falls—nothing to do with investment or corporate soundness. And this computer boom they're predicting is going to blow the lid off of trading as we know it . . ."

Emma from the kitchen: "Now it's obvious that Ronald Reagan is going to wrest this summer's convention from Jerry Ford, take the nomination, become president, and destroy the world, right? And I got to thinking. If Reagan had been a successful movie star, he'd be showing up on TV movies now and not headed to the White House one day. Originally he was going to be in *Casablanca*, then the part of Rick went to Bogart. If Reagan had been in *Casablanca* his career would have succeeded and he never would have turned to politics. Now here's the big Question for the late twentieth century: if you had a choice between having *Casablanca*—the greatest Hollywood-style film ever made—the way it is today OR keeping Reagan out of the White House and maybe saving the world from nuclear destruction . . . which would you choose to have? You laugh, Janet, but I stay up nights working on that one . . ."

For the next hour I was quasi asleep, drifting in and out of insensibility, waking up finally when I heard the sound of my own name, mentioned by Chris:

"But has anyone seen him onstage? Is he any good?" And rather than hear a chorus of YES, I heard Mandy go "Sssssshhhhhh! He's right out there in that chair."

Well? No one *had* see me onstage. I hadn't *been* onstage yet, which I think is a pretty good excuse. What have I done this past year? If I seem slow in remembering, it's because it was so boring. Monica at the theater and I keep reading new play submissions. I kissed her at the Christmas party and began to maul her drunkenly and she said she had a boyfriend now and put me off. She didn't exactly push me away, though. There must have been about five good minutes of kissing in there before she remembered what's-his-name. I was stage manager twice, once for *Kitty Korner* in the fall (whewwww, did that ever bomb) and this spring I managed *Signora* which was fun because we had a good actress as this rich divorcée in Amalfi seducing her own son—

"But Mandy, a name is a political statement!" Susan was under the porch. "As a lesbian you have a duty to change your name to 'ManDie.' "

Where was I? Oh yeah, my career. I'm everyone's favorite nice guy at the Venice. Gil do this, Gil do that. Stage managing is fun but it's not acting, is it? Well hell, there are no parts for me. I can't play Signora, now can I? This fall there's lots I could do. I'm going to audition for everything. And if the Venice doesn't cast me, I'll audition at other theaters, though they don't like for you to do that. Maybe I'll go to . . . (Contemplation of life/career/work sent me right back to sleep.)

An hour later:

"Wake up, sweetie pie," Emma said in my ear, tapping my already red shoulder. "You're gonna burn, better come inside."

I got up and felt half-drunk and queasy. It seemed about fourish. The light had begun that late-in-the-day slant. Janet and Mandy saw me stir and yelled from the beach to come down and play Frisbee. "Come on down!" yelled Tom. "We'll show these girls how to play a little Frisbee." Maybe later, I yelled back. (Yeah, like an hour after my funeral.)

"I used to be good with people," said Emma as I joined her in the kitchen.

When was that?

"No, I used to be able to talk and make conversation and get on with my fellow man . . ." Emma was distracted by the mess she had made of the kitchen. "I tried talking to everyone today. I bored them, they bored me. I tried my Panties Theory out on Janet to no avail."

Panties theory?

"You know, that little girls' panties are the key emblem of twentieth-century literature? *Ulysses* and *Finnegans Wake* by Joyce, Caddy's drawers in Faulkner's *The Sound and the Fury*, Nabokov's *Lolita*—all of them, panties-obsessed. It's clearly impossible to write a great novel without using little girls' panties."

Moby-Dick?

Emma put her hand on her hip. "Gil, I think it's perfectly obvious that Melville is implying that the whale is wearing a pair of little girls' panties. Ahab doesn't want to kill the whale, he just wants it to rise out of the water in order to *see* its panties."

And Janet didn't go for the theory?

"Intellectual discussions went out in the '60s, Gil. There's only you and there's only me. You never look at me strangely when I talk about panties. What do you want to drink?"

Nothing ever again.

"I have new thoughts on all subjects," said Emma, again presiding over the disaster area/kitchen that looked like an explosion of ice crumbs, peels, fruit bits, empty booze bottles and multicolored liquids had occurred there. "And I've reached a revolutionary conclusion."

Yes? I said, yawning.

"Tom can't help being boring and average and rich and tan. And in his limited Republican WASP little way he is sort of sweet. It's Lisa that's the problem. I now hate Lisa."

No you don't. (I poured myself a glass of straight orange juice.)

"I've been watching everything from my kitchen window here," said Emma. "Susan went in the water. Tidal waves along the Eastern Seaboard, sea levels are rising around the world. She went swimming and Russian trawlers started following her;

long-haired activists in rowboats interposed themselves between the two: 'Don't kill this one! Put those harpoons away!' "

So you've been sitting here all afternoon thinking up these rotten jokes, huh?

"Nothing else to do. That's why I woke you up. I'd gone two hours without savaging anyone and I couldn't take it anymore. And I've been contemplating my life. Looking at Lisa and Tom, seeing them close and affectionate and intimate . . . and it just came to me, it was borne in on me that I will NEVER live a life like that, there will never be anybody for whom *I'm* like that. I am one human being incapable of walking hand in hand with someone on a beach. Now why is that?"

I wish I knew, Emma.

"Well work on it and when you figure it out—why normal life violates me, reviles me, assaults me, repels me—let me know, willya?"

Emma got bored with the blender as people took her making fresh rounds of drinks for granted. She deserted her post and Lisa took over. Lisa was going to make a red, white, and blue drink. She'd seen it done somewhere. Coconut liqueur on the bottom since it was thickest, grenadine syrup and vodka next because it was second-thickest, and blue curaçao on top. It all fell in on itself and made a purple sludge and it tasted awful but Lisa kept making them, trying the red, white, and blue in different orders, arrangements, and proportions. This became known as the Purple Sludge and, once acquiring the taste, we found ourselves begging Lisa to make them all weekend long.

Tom went to get steaks. Later it came out Susan was a vegetarian, Chris was sort-of, Mandy and Janet didn't want steak, I wasn't hungry as I was full of potato chips which I ate mindlessly in the kitchen with Emma. But Tom bought these steaks. And they had to be cooked on the barbecue and Tom and Lisa shooed everyone away from the barbecue—not that anyone volunteered to help in the first place—and played Suburban Couple On The Patio and between them they made four trips to the store for 1) paper towels, paper salad bowls, plastic cutlery (which wasn't a huge success because we couldn't cut Tom's well-done steaks with plastic knives), 2) beer, because everyone was sick of candy tropical blender drinks and Purple Sludge, 3) some more beer because it wasn't enough and we drank it all waiting for these steaks to get done, 4) fixings for potato salad, a three-bean salad and a pudding dessert, all of which Lisa was inspired to get when the steaks were nearly done so the meal could be put off another twenty minutes. ("Potato salad and pudding," sneered Emma to me privately. "Already she's thinking like a school cafeteria dietitian. Watch her make us eat everything on our plate.")

Lisa was furiously working in the kitchen, doing five things at once. I offered help.

"No, no, I'm fine Gil," she said, dumping a ton of mayonnaise into the potato salad. "I know Emma has been trashing me out all day and don't pretend she hasn't."

I pretended she hadn't.

"I mean, I expect that out of Emma, to complain and make fun of everything and she can get away with it as long as she's funny and makes fun of herself as well. Be Entertaining—that's all we ever ask of her, right? But sometimes . . ."

Sometimes what?

"Sometimes it's not unreasonable to expect her to behave and not act terribly to everyone." She took a quick look at me. "This is obviously falling on deaf ears. You think everything she does is perfect."

Not true, I said, although at that time it was virtually true.

"Well all I'm saying is that it's not doing any of us any good to wallow in our neuroses and be Fashionable New York Neurotics and become complete bitches, okay? There comes a time to grow up, too."

Oh no. Lisa no. Don't talk *growing up*. We were doing such a good job of not growing up—don't be like that . . . My heart sank when she said that. Not that she didn't have a point.

"She's out of control," Lisa went on, washing some of the dusty plates in the beachhouse so there would be something to eat on. "She's getting worse every day. Pretentious, she's more pretentious. For someone who hates sex, is screwed up by it, hates anyone else to have it, she certainly is setting a world record for talking about it. Every other word out of her mouth is *penis* or *clitoris* these days, or *come*. Would you like a Diet Cola, Emma? 'Oh yes, I'd *come* for one.' Did you like that movie, Emma? 'Oh I loved it—I *came* all the way through it. It gave me a *wide-on*.' A wide-on? Think about that. The woman is obsessed."

That's just Emma, I said.

"Emma on overdrive. Hyper-Emma, Super-Emma. And you're getting weirder just like her."

I wasn't weirder, I protested.

"Why is she trying to ruin the weekend? Break Tom and me up?"

She's not, I lied.

"Not born yesterday Gil honey. I know what's happening. Here"—she threw me a limp rag—"dry some dishes."

I dried some dishes. Then I said that Emma was not trying to break them up, she was worried that Lisa was going to move out for Tom and leave us and it was because Emma was jealous and possessive of Lisa that she acted odd. But how seriously could you take Emma's schemings?

"I'm just DATING this guy for christ's sake! Three lousy weeks, it is not love, it is not Ozzie and Harriet here. Geeeeeez. Normal people let their friends date other people and don't go insane at the idea that they're going to find some happiness when they're not around. What? I can't have a life out of that apartment?"

Well . . .

"I mean, I'm tired of psychoses and oh-my-miserable-sexlife and oh-I'm-so-frigid and all this CULT of our own neuroses—I've got to get out every once in a while, okay? This weekend is a disaster."

Everyone was having fun, I assured her.

"Everyone but meeeeee," she sang.

Dinnertime.

We all sat down to eat Tom's steaks. Conversation was meaningless and occasionally fun with Emma playing her usual trick of listening overly carefully to what everyone said.

Tom: "There's nothing worse than a bad cut of beef."

Emma: "Well, nuclear war . . ."

Susan informed us how meat was bad for us, how barbaric it was to eat it, how proud she was to be a vegetarian. ("That must be why she wants to sleep with Chris," Janet whispered to me.) Tom commented a number of times about how good the steaks were. Lisa said the best steaks she ever had were in the West because meat was even better in the West, Texas and all, and even the roadside interstate Mr. T-Bone and Steak House and Jiffy Sizzlin' chain steakhouse steaks were better than the best thing you could get in New York as a rule.

"What really interests me," Emma said, enjoying herself, "is steak sauce. Which brands people like best—you'd be surprised how people disagree."

Tom nodded and told how his father and mother would nearly come to blows over steak sauce, and Emma continued to draw him out on the subject of steak sauce, and Emma mentioned how she put steak sauce on everything and how many many things you could put steak sauce on, steak sauce steak sauce steak sauce. Lisa sat there with her arms crossed, glaring at Emma.

Dinner ended eventually, after dessert which was a big bowl of cement-thick chocolate pudding made from a mix which no one could finish a tiny bowl of so we had the pudding around all weekend and never did finish the whole thing. Lisa ended up having to wash all the dishes.

"C'mon, Emma, help me wash up."

"I don't want to. I'd rather shoot myself than wash dishes."

Janet volunteered to help.

"NO," said Lisa seriously. "Emma. Emma and I have to have a little talk."

So we all slunk away leaving them to talk. Janet and I walked down to the beach, Mandy was wading in already up to her waist. There was one clean unsandy towel and it was Janet's but Mandy was going to use it so there was a tug of war which made Mandy fall in and so she pulled Janet in soon after her and I retreated to high ground.

You're not supposed to go in until an hour after you eat, I said.

"Mandy rose from the foam," said Mandy, narrating her own

departure from the surf, "her body glistening in the soft evening light, her body tan and shimmering. The cold water streamed down her bountiful bosom . . ." (Mandy was sort of flat-chested) ". . . rivulets tracing the outline of her spectacular form. Janet looked on in envy—"

"I did what?"

"—in envy, as this vulnerable feminine vision found her way to the beachhouse."

Janet added to the trash-novel narration: "Mandy turned to see Janet emerge from the surf . . . her body gleaming, her breasts taut but supple, her nipples erect . . ." Mandy turned and feigned a yawn. "Mandy," Janet continued, "was beside herself with lust—she had to have Janet, press her seething undulating body close to hers . . ."

"Now we're talkin'," said Mandy.

They went up the shore and took a high, private path along the dunes. I walked around for a few minutes and then spotted Emma emerging from the beachhouse coming down to the shore.

Don't tell me, I yelled, turning her head, you are actually going to put a foot in the water.

"Now that no one's looking, I thought I could sneak down here and have a Private Vagary. You're interrupting my Private Vagary."

I took a step back.

"Lisa and I, while I—kind soul that I was—helped her wash the dishes, had *words*."

Which words, I asked.

"She said I was being *evil*—that was her word: *evil*."

Well you are being evil, and I'm glad she told you. What else did Lisa say?

"Just nastiness to me. She was curt and officious—and I can't stand it when she gets curt and officious—and she called me a bitch—"

Oh she did not.

"Well, she meant to call me a bitch. It was a high-class Lisa way of calling me a bitch. I got so flustered—I mean, she was talking about moving out, leaving us for good—"

I don't believe that, I said.

"Well it sounded as if she was about to and would threaten to do so at any moment. Anyway, I got all flustered and ran into the bathroom to pull myself together and I walked in on Tom, urinating."

A bit awkward.

And then Emma arched an eyebrow, her mouth drawn close to a tight smile. "Ah," she said, raising a finger, "it however did confirm the Small Penis Theory proposed earlier in the afternoon. He must sneak something extra into bed is all I can figure."

I'm walking away, I'm not listening . . .

"Gil, this is what the Warren Commission referred to as the Second Penis Theory!" She followed behind me as I walked resolutely down the beach. "You're laughing, I can tell you're laughing. No use walking away, I know you're laughing."

I think we ought to wait until the Warren Commission finds the smoking gun.

Emma (in a rare moment of physicality) caught up with me, and put an arm around my shoulder. "Now you see? That's why I retain you. You always pick up on my allusions."

Which wasn't true.

"Lisa never does know what I'm talking about. If she wasn't so busy having sex with all the men in New York she might be able to have read more than one book in her life—"

EMMA.

"You always have to explain the jokes to her. Gil, she's averaging out before our very eyes, she's going normal on us—"

Emma, this is crap—

"Well all I'm saying is keep your ear to the ground for a new roommate. If she dumps us, we can have a replacement ready—"

Emma, what is WRONG with you? Lisa has dated this guy for no time at all, she's not moving out unless you drive her out by acting so weird—hey, what happens if *I* want to date someone? What if I want a social life outside the Sacred Apartment?

Emma stopped walking, put her hand to her head. We were

about to receive a dose of Italian-American fury: "WHAT? You're not planning on stepping out of line are you? Who've you got in mind? Oh, yeah, that goddam Monica—are you *seeing* her?"

It's none of your busi——

"Monica? the weasel-woman with . . . with hair that goes, ullllcch, Gil, NO. Tell me right now. Are you seeing her?"

I said I wouldn't tell her given her tone. Then I said no, I wasn't seeing Monica.

"We're two very strange people, Gil," she said seriously, "and as no one else is really like us, we have to stick with each other. I'm not kidding: I mean the rest of our lives. You don't think I'm serious, you're smiling. Half the times I'm serious these days you think I'm joking."

Did she mean that? Was that a declaration of love?

"I can't break in a new person at this age. I'm beyond changing."

I had to give that a thought or two: the rest of our lives.

Emma seemed subdued. "I hate it when my mouth just keeps going. Forget I said anything."

Emma, I said, can we deal with everything later? Right now, for Lisa, our friend, who loves you, who you love too—

"Yes yes yes, I know," she said, chastened.

—just watch the mouth and BEHAVE, okay?

Emma smiled, nodding. She really hates being criticized, it brings her to the verge of tears. She can say five hundred bad things about herself—that's all right. But if someone else implies them, her eyes get watery and her face gets red and voice weak. And she was that way now. "Right," she said, "new leaf. Watch me, Gil. I'm going back to the house and have fun with Lisa. Tell her I think Tom is a hunk, a Greek god."

And you're not going to break anyone up or seduce anyone in the dunes?

Emma looked at me simply. "Gil, there's only one man I would cash in my celibacy for. Elvis Presley, circa 1956."

Tricky to arrange at this point.

"Well, I'll agree, my standards are high. Can't be sleeping with just *everybody*."

And I walked along the beach, thinking things over, and wondering if the things I was thinking about were even worth thinking over. There were times with Emma where it came to me clearly: NO MORE EMMA, you don't need this, you don't behave right around her, it's not so much being in love as just being in a big mess, an interesting mess, but a mess. On the other hand, sometimes . . . What We Had Was Love . . .

"Gil!" It was Tom, I discovered, as I turned around. He was running to catch up with me. Oh yeah, that's right, I'd promised Lisa that I would make friends, make sure he had a good time. "Gil wait up!" he called, catching up with me. "I wanted to walk up the beach too and then I recognized you up ahead, that crazy Hawaiian shirt."

Yeah, crazy me and my crazy shirt.

"Thought you were going to come down and play catch with the girls," Tom said laughing.

Well I passed on that.

"Did you play baseball? You look like you might have played baseball in school. Right build."

No, didn't do anything that involved coordination. Just was in the theater.

"Oh yeah," said Tom, absolving me, "I had lots of friends in the theater in high school. I actually got to be an extra in our high-school musical pageant," he said laughing again. "Not quite ready for Broadway like you."

Tom was going down bad with the baseball opening, but the Gil ready-for-Broadway was sending him up the charts. Nice guy, this Tom, a man of taste . . . We made small talk—no, make that electron-microscopically small talk, as we walked toward this pier ahead of us, one of those elusive horizon beach piers you never really catch up to. We gave up as we hit the beachfront of a little town called Shoretown, which, true to its name, was indistinguishable from any other city on the shore. There was a bar. Did I want a beer? Tom asked. Yeah, why not—two guys sneaking off for a beer, a macho Man's Beer, while the women cleaned up back at the house. I felt the decades rolling back the longer I stayed with Tom, it was rapidly approaching the Eisenhower era.

"Here we are," said Tom setting down two long-necked Budweisers, as he turned his chair around backward to sit in. Why do people sit in chairs like that? "Lisa tells me you and Emma are *an item*." Well, Tom wasn't wasting any time, getting right down to business. Perhaps this was what he wanted to talk about all along . . .

I said we weren't an item, really.

"Lisa thinks you two will end up together one day."

Does she have any evidence for this? Did Emma tell her this?

"Don't know," he said, shrugging, pausing for a sip. "She just said she had a hunch. What's it like living with two hot-looking chicks, eh?"

Hot-looking wasn't the word I'd have used for Emma and Lisa, I thought. In fact *hot-looking*, like *chicks*, is not a word I would use EVER. Hmmm, it occurred to me I hadn't had Men-with-Beer-in-a-Bar talk since college, and I didn't like it then much either. CHICKS?

"Must be something, Lisa and Emma running around in their panties and stuff. Guess you just get used to it."

A panty man. Joyce, Faulkner and Tom Davidson.

"You don't have to be secretive with me. If you've scored with them, you can tell me. I think you're amazingly lucky—I wish I was that lucky."

Scored with them. Gil, Lisa and Emma, zero at the half, game called off due to lack of interest. I said, yeah, I was lucky.

"So it's really platonic, huh? Nothing funny going on."

Yeah, Tom, I said, don't you have any purely female friends?

Laughter. "Not that I wouldn't want to go to bed with!" And more laughter, a long take on the beer that finishes off the bottle.

I didn't say I *didn't* want to go to bed with them.

"If you're getting somewhere with Emma, more power to you, man."

You like Emma, do you Tom?

"The great thing about going out with Lisa was getting to meet Emma, I think. I'm thinking of asking her out."

WHOA HORSES. Now let's get this straight—

"No, I mean, *after* Lisa and I call it quits, don't want to offend her. Look there's nothing serious between Lisa and myself; we've just been going out three weeks, it's not as if we're engaged or anything, is it?"

Well no. I guess dating Emma would be all right once Lisa and he go their separate ways . . . *dating* Emma? Does he know what he's dealing with? How inconceivable it is that she would "date" anybody, how impossible it would be to . . . Ooooh. Wait. Hold it. What if she DOES go out with Tom? And they, you know, DO THINGS. No, no, no, no, no, we're gonna nip this in the bud here:

I said it's unlikely she'd date anybody.

"Oh hey, that's why I am asking you. Like, I'm not a thief, if you've got designs on her I don't wanna step in and mess things up, that's why I'm asking. But she doesn't go out much?"

She's a lesbian, I said.

"No, really? Oh no. Really?" He shook his head. "That makes sense, all the dyke friends at the house. Shit."

Yeah, I went on, I think she's hung up on Lisa actually.

"No kidding? Shit. Hey," he said, laughing, getting up to get us some more beers (he had all the money, he was paying), "wouldn't mind watching those two, you know—hehhehheh, you know?"

You're a crudbomb, Tom. No I didn't say that, just thought it. Never insult the man buying your beers (Poor in New York, Lesson 23). Actually, I'm not much less of a crudbomb. What if he tells Lisa I said Emma was a lesbian, after Lisa no less. I've got to get to Lisa first and tell her . . . no, she'll be hurt to find out he's after Emma. I gotta tell someone. Mandy will back me on this . . .

8:20 p.m. The violet sky, dim beach light, the soft lapping sound of twilit waters (yeah, with dreck like that, *I* should be writing "Dunecrest.") We get back to the house to a chorus of Where have you boys been, you two go out on the town? A night out with the boys? Boys will be boys. I went through the beachhouse trying to find Mandy, passing a room with Susan talking to Janet (". . . it's important as a lesbian like myself to create an actualizing sphere about myself, to achieve positive reinforcement within the womanspace . . .") which I steered clear of. Mandy was out on the porch.

"Hey Gil, what's up?"

Could we go for a walk?

I told her what I had said to Tom.

"Perfectly understandable lie," she said sympathetically. "But I think Emma's sincere about her celibacy—she won't go out with Tom, or sleep with him . . ." She trailed off, thinking about it. "He is a bit of a hunk, isn't he?"

I faltered. Would that matter to Emma? She always says she can't stand vain, hunky athletic jock types . . .

"Maybe it's because she can never get them interested in her," Mandy said slowly. "One thing comes back to me from those celibacy meetings . . . nah, it's just crap."

Tell me now.

"Well she was saying she might give up her celibacy as long as it was thoroughly unimportant, a trifle, a guy she couldn't respect, just something physical and cheap—"

EMMA said that?

"Well she was just talking, thinking aloud . . ."

No. No.

"Oh Gil, don't worry, she's not going to sleep with Tom. It'd kill Lisa to see her boyfriend act like such a jerk."

Yeah, but Emma's trying to break those two up. Maybe she'd lead him on, thinking she was doing Lisa a favor, then . . . then, really follow through. And start to enjoy it. And Tom spending money on her. And *Emma* will move out, Lisa won't speak to her—Emma and Tom will get married and live on Long Island—

Mandy slapped my arm: "You're getting carried away." Mandy was staring out to the sea oddly.

What is it? Something more?

Mandy went on, preoccupied. "It's odd you should say Emma was a lesbian. Ironic. I mean, Janet and I were talking about this—well, fighting actually—about this today, whether Emma had lesbian tendencies. You know I thought *I* wanted a celibate lifestyle and then discovered *I* was just lying to myself about *my* lesbian tendencies. Then Janet and I disagreed over some other stuff."

About Emma's maybe being a lesbian?

"No, about whether we should sleep with her if she is. Or try to seduce her. I mean, I'm an old-fashioned kind of dyke, a one-woman woman. Lots of women are into bringing in a third, sharing lovers—there's this whole ethos of lesbians not being jealous of one another, not competitive like men. Rivalry is phallocentric. Panlesbianism is vulvacentric, all encompassing, no jealousies, lots of sharing."

Do you go for that?

"I think it's bullshit," she said heatedly. "Janet however thinks like that. She wanted us to try to get Emma to have a threesome with us, and I said—perhaps a little jealously, I'll admit—that she just wanted to sleep with Emma, and she said of course she did and what was wrong with wanting to sleep with women, and I said not when you're with me sugar. And it was a fight. She thinks I'm immature and haven't been 'out' long enough, that I'm still uptight. What do you think?"

Nothing wrong with being loyal, I said.

We walked back to the house, walked up the stairs, went out on the upper porch and saw Tom and Janet coming back from the other direction.

Mandy grimaced. "What are those two up to?"

I had a horrible suspicion: sharing facts.

Mandy whispered, "Quiet, I can almost hear them."

When they got closer, we could hear them laughing about something. "Thanks Janet," said Tom, "you cleared up a lot for me." Janet told Tom he'd cleared up a lot for her too. Mandy scowled.

9:10 p.m. Emma and Chris and Susan go for a walk to town to get sparklers and illegal fireworks if they can dig them up. Lisa has come back from the store to make new blender drinks, most of her brand-new recipes resembling Purple Sludge.

"Gil, hand me the blueberries," said Lisa, stationed at the whirring blender, not able to take her hand away from the top lest what she was making spray all over the place. "Tom said that you two had a nice little talk, man to man. What did you boys talk about?"

Uh, baseball?

"Oh you did not! Don't fool me for a minute, Gilbert Freeman."

Then what did we talk about then?

"Me, I suspect." She winked, acknowledging the immodesty. She turned off the blender and put in the frozen blueberries. "I've got too much goo in here . . ." She poured some into another bowl for later pulverizing. "You probably gossiped about me which would only be natural. I just hope you said nice things, that's all."

All kinds of nice things.

"I'm in a better mood about this weekend. Emma likes Tom and I'm so happy. I thought she was making fun of him all night, but I see she really, really likes him."

I didn't have a pleasant look on my face.

"She says he's a Greek god. And . . ." Lisa started giggling. "I went and told Tom she said that about him . . ."

Bet Tom liked that.

"Well he *is* a Greek god, isn't he?"

(The man could not be the God of Kitty Litter, Lisa.)

"And you know what else?" Then she started laughing that kind of yuck laugh someone laughs when their lover does some silly crazy wacky adorable thing. "He said he was becoming liberated by all this countercultural company. He said he wouldn't mind it if I had a lesbian affair. Get that! Wouldn't be jealous or anything if I had an affair with a woman—I think that's remarkably liberal. He said," more laughter, "that he thinks Emma and I should hook up and we all ought to be a fun *threesome*—he's just crazy! Imagine Emma and Tom and I in a threesome! He's crazy!"

Tom, you're public restroom filth. I swear before God you will NOT sleep with Emma—you got Lisa, I lost that one to you, but there is no way you will get Emma. She is mine all mine, and if she sleeps with anybody it will be me—

"Gil, can I see you a minute?" Mandy said, poking her head into the kitchen.

We got out of earshot. What was it?

"Janet told me what Tom told her and we're in trouble now."

Mandy spoke seriously, as if responsible for a military mission. "Can anyone hear us? Let's go to the porch again . . ."

We went to the porch:

". . . Tom was asking Janet about lesbianism and whether it meant a woman couldn't enjoy sex with a man because of it. Janet, who thinks life is her weekly column in the *Womynpaper*, who has no shame, who looks at every woman as a—"

Go on, go on.

"Sorry. Tom told Janet you said Emma was gay, and Tom then asked Janet if he should make a pass at Emma anyway. Janet, very kindly, said don't waste your time and at this very moment is running into town after Emma, fixing to work her evil charms."

Well tell Janet Tom was wrong and that I lied and made it all up . . .

"I did tell her."

And?

"She said I was jealous and was making *that* up to keep her from going to find Emma. When I get my hands on her . . . Oh god, look. Here they all come."

9:45. Chris and Susan and Janet and Emma return with fireworks.

I drifted by the living room.

"Oh Chris you don't think I will, but you're wrong," Susan was saying. "I dare you to skinny-dip too—I'm going to do it, just you watch. I bet Gil will go with me . . ."

I drifted away from the living room.

"Gil, come here," said Emma, putting a sparkler into my hand, leading me back outside, down to the shoreline. "You'll never guess who wants to sleep with me."

Janet—I was about to say, but then caught myself. If I knew about Janet it meant that I knew etc. etc. and all that would lead to my initial lie. Who, I asked?

"Chris."

WHAT?

"He's been gay all his life. And he wanted to sleep with a woman because all his friends were women and—oh it was very sweet, you had to hear his reasons. Women were beautiful and he was an assistant designer of women's clothes and he understood so much about them except them sexually and he thought perhaps we could have a small fling, just once, to see what it's like."

If he wants a woman, why not Susan?

Emma looked at me.

All right, all right, dumb question. But what did Susan have to say about Chris's fling idea?

"She supports him. Remember she can't overtly chase him because she's still going around pretending to be a lesbian separatist, creating something-or-other within her own womanspace, you have to hear her newest thinking. She came along on the fireworks expedition to support Chris in asking me, help him tell me."

What are you going to do? I asked Emma.

"Politely refuse of course. He's a long way off from Elvis. Tom, after all, has at least got Elvis's body, he looks a little like him around the eyebrows too—"

WAS SHE GOING TO SLEEP WITH TOM?

"What is your problem, Gil?" she cried, stepping back, then smiling. "Don't be so worried I'm going to have sex—it's a big deal after not having it for two years, so I'm not going to have it lightly. When I have it, it'll be with someone I can deal with—"

WHEN? The vocabulary up to this point has been IF, and NEVER AGAIN.

"Well that's ridiculous, isn't it? I mean eventually one day, inevitably, *sometime* I'm going to have to have it again. Just not now, not until I'm ready."

Back to the beachhouse I stormed, frantic. Whadya bet Emma was going to be ready TONIGHT? Oh, all this comes from flaunting Monica (whom I'm not even doing anything with) in her face. Ah, I reap the reward here! Oh boy, here comes Susan from the house.

"What are you up to, Gil baby?" Susan toddled over, a Purple Sludge in her hand. "Did you get some fireworks?"

Yeah I got some.

"What's wrong? Is Emma down there? I'm going to have a talk with that girl I've been meaning to have. It's obvious, isn't it? She's a lesbian. Bound to be. And I got confirmation on this from Janet who thinks so too, *knows* so."

Yeah I think so too, I said happily. Why don't you go down there and pursue this topic, Susan, as only two women can do? Take her away from the house, far far far far away and have a long long long long talk and show her what her true feelings are. You alone, Susan, could do this—she listens to you, she trusts you—

"She does?" Susan brightened.

Oh yeah. If you put it to her in the right way, gently, take your time, maybe she'll see the light. Go, go to her now . . .

I went back up to the house.

In the living room Chris and Janet and Tom and Mandy were sorting out fireworks, lining up the most impressive for last. Lisa was wholly occupied making drinks, drinking most of what she made, getting drunk and being silly.

"Where is that Emma?" Janet asked, hand on hip. "She just slips away on us."

"Yeah I was going to take a walk with her," said Tom.

"Uh-uh Tom, I got dibs on her first," Janet laughed.

Mandy formed a gun with her hand and pantomimed blowing Janet away without Janet realizing it. I went into the kitchen to talk to Lisa.

"I'm sooooo drunk, Gil," she said, sloshing her current red drink onto the floor. "Here have one of these."

I accepted it, tasted it, spat it out into the sink.

"Don't like it?"

What the hell is this?

"I didn't think the ketchup would work. But we're out of mixers. I thought if I put enough sugar in it it would be like a Bloody Mary."

WELL I GUESS YOU WERE WRONG.

"Yeah, guess so. Gil," she began again, walking over to hang on me affectionately. "Guess what. I'm drunk."

Coulda fooled me. Did she want to be put to bed?

"No, not before the fireworks at Asbury Park. Gotta set off the fireworks and all, don't we? Where's Emma?"

With Susan.

"If you were going to have a homosexual affair with someone of your own sex . . . who would the person of your own sex be? That's the question." She propped herself against a kitchen cabinet. She apparently expected an answer.

Uh, Jim Morrison in 1967.

"No, like now, like alive."

No idea, I don't have many male friends.

"I think I'd be a lesbian with Emma. Does that shock you? The idea of like lesbians and all?"

No actually, after tonight, I think the WHOLE WORLD is a lesbian—all the women, all the men, I'm a lesbian, my mother's a lesbian, you name it, they're lesbian.

Mandy came in, still a frown on her face. "What's all this about lesbians?"

"We're just having a discussion about sleeping with women, I mean women doing it with . . . I mean—"

"Yeah I know what lesbians do, Leese. Let's get you to a couch and let you lie down. Before you fall down."

Mandy led Lisa away to a sofa in a dark room, Lisa whining the whole way about fireworks, missing the fireworks. I went out to the porch.

10:45. Fifteen minutes until the fireworks.

Mandy came out and shared her newest tactic with me: "I think *I* better seduce Emma."

I begged her pardon.

"No, I think it has to be done. I'll show Janet how it feels to have your girlfriend run around and want to sleep with everything. If *anyone* is going to be lesbian with Emma, it better be me . . ."

Come one come all! The more the merrier!

If you had known, Emma, the intrigues, the drama, the Byzantine plotting and scheming all for you, all to sleep with, to win the affection of, to woo and court and seduce and make love to YOU YOU YOU, would that have satisfied you? Would it have satisfied you that everyone on the Planet Earth wanted to make love to you? With all the suffering and all the self-induced misery, I'm just curious if it might have made a difference if we all had had one Big Bicentennial Orgy with you—would it have gotten through your head, Emma? That people loved and cared about you?

"I'm going to kill you Gilbert Freeman," said Emma, barging up the porch steps, hands out ready to throttle me.

What did I do? (Better question: Which of the many things I've done did you find out about?)

"You sicced Susan on me. Do you know what it is like fighting her off, her propositioning me, crying, every hysterical trick in her book, trying to get me to neck with her on the dunes? There was less fighting on the sands of Iwo Jima, for christ's sake. And when I asked what had gotten into her she said YOU, you Gilbert Freeman, had put her up to this."

Nonsense, Emma. You believe everything Susan says?

"Can I have a sip of your drink?"

Emma borrowed my glass and finished it off.

"You're looking tense, Gil. Is something going on in the house?" Emma looked at her watch. "Almost eleven. Just enough time for that walk I promised Tom—"

DON'T DO IT.

"Why not?"

He wants to sleep with you, throw Lisa over for you. He told me so.

Emma smiled. "You're kidding."

What do you expect? You run around telling him he's a Greek god—

"What do you *want*? A few hours ago you were begging me to go up and be nice to him. I told Lisa he was a Greek god. He's not a Greek god, Gil. Body's not bad but—"

You're going to sleep with him, aren't you?

Emma was laughing now. "What are you so worried about? Why Gil, you must be drunk—why are you so upset about . . ." And then she started laughing, and I felt she was laughing entirely at me, which she was. "Gil, you're not . . . you're *jealous*, aren't you?"

NO. ABSOLUTELY NOT.

"Yes you are. Or perhaps it won't bother you if I sleep with Tom?"

DO AND YOU'RE A DEAD WOMAN.

Emma was giggling now. "Gil, you are so drunk! This is a scream! If I think he's vile for Lisa, why would I accept him for myself?"

Elvis's eyebrows.

Emma was still laughing, shaking her head. "You're too much. I'm sure he doesn't want to anyway."

I said: Look, I don't care if you have sex all the time and don't have it with me, but if you're not going to have sex at all and then have it with . . . with TOMS, then I object. I think I should be included.

Emma smiled at me as if I was a twelve-year-old and consequently I felt like a twelve-year-old. "Look," she said in turn, "it's the thought that counts right? Actual sex means viscosities, and you know how I feel about viscosities—"

We know, we know.

"So accept the fact that in an ideal world we would sleep together. You can tell anyone you like we have already, if that's what you want."

But I wanted more than that. Or did I? As I thought about this, a giant red firework burst to the north over Asbury Park—the display was beginning.

"I promise you," Emma continued, "you wouldn't want to make love to me now. You'd hate every minute of it."

Really? I said, if I made love to her now I might see fireworks. Gil, always with the jokes.

"Fireworks!" yelled Chris. "It's time! Everybody out on the porch!"

Tom ran out with a box of matches, fireworks of our own and a bunch of small American flags he got in town. Mandy and Chris and Janet absently waved them, cheering facetiously, but soon got caught up in the fireworks, giant red explosions, then giant violet-blue explosions, and then blindingly white explosions, accompanied by lots of gold frilly twinkly things fluttering down in between.

Everyone but Lisa was out on the porch and Chris suggested drunkenly we sing the National Anthem.

"The National Anthem sucks," said Emma. "No one can sing it anyway. Let's do 'God Bless America.' "

And it was so uncool to sing "God Bless America" in 1976 that suddenly it seemed that it might be cool to do it, and we sang it—archly at first, overdoing the vibrato, sending it up—but by the second rendition of the one and only verse, we were singing normally and it would have been hard to say whether we meant it or not.

Lisa stumbled out to join us. "Fireworks," she said blearily.

"Come lean against me, hon," Tom said and she went beside him and held his hand, teenage couple-style.

Mandy flitted about pouring more sludge into people's glasses. Janet had put two American flags down her low cut swimsuit, a flag for each breast. Chris had a good tenor and led us in "God Bless America" again.

We stood on the balcony, craning our necks, occasionally looking beside us to see each other illuminated in greens, blues, infernal reds. Lisa dropped her glass and picked it up, stumbling. "This is my for-all-time favorite holiday ever," she said.

"I want more," said Emma quietly.

And to our surprise, there *were* more—from the other direction. Just as the Asbury Park fireworks ended at 11:30, the Sea Girt fireworks began and we jumped for joy as if we were in kindergarten. I was drunk. Emma was getting drunk. Everyone was drunk. In the lulls between firework displays, we sang, louder and sillier than before, waving our flags. The people in the beachhouse next door came out on their porch and raised their glasses to us and then *they* started singing; this middle-aged crew, leathery tanned women, doctors with a paunch, shirtless in ludicrous Bermuda shorts, waving a cocktail glass at us, rich drunk people our parents' age looking over at the young folks having a good time. Who could complain to the police about us? Young people singing "God Bless America" at the top of their lungs. And finally the last of the Sea Girt fireworks finished, in an identical blur of red, white and blue. And there we were, suddenly aware we were there saying nothing.

"That's what *I* like about America," said Susan, taking a deep drag of her cigarette. "Lots of free entertainment."

And the weekend was off and running. To draw out a chart of the complications would look like one of those flowcharts for a giant bureaucracy. Considering how much time we discussed who was sleeping with, wanted to sleep with, couldn't sleep with, hated to sleep with whom, nobody really *slept with anybody*. What a lot of talk.

Final memory of the 4th: Lisa drunk, screaming out, completely happy, "Hey everybody raise their hands who likes living in the USA."

Groans all around. Tom raises his though. Susan sneers, "Well, since *Roe* vs. *Wade*, the place is not the most backward of the planet's peoples." Emma—I was waiting for it, the inevitable savage comment—merely put her hand up. "Nyeh, I guess so. Compared to Russia and all. Hey guys, the evening's young. Any of you people up for a moonlit walk on the beach?"

1977

YOU want to know what my major accomplishment was in 1977? I washed the dishes. Me and Lisa, every evening. Sometimes she'd do the suds and the washing, sometimes she did the drying and the putting away. A good place to talk, the sink.

"So you're guaranteed three parts onstage this year, huh?" Lisa asked distractedly, swirling the dishes around.

That was what Dewey Dennis (that jerk) promised me. I'd made a big lunge for stardom during the fall and got in two crowd scenes. But no spoken lines yet. It doesn't count as your debut until you say something. I auditioned for three other theaters' spring seasons as well: *Mama's Home*, about a terminally ill patient back to make peace with her family before she dies. There's a role in it for a twenty-five-year-old rebellious son. I would have been perfect for that. There was also *Folks These Days Got No Time For de Blues*—did you catch it at the Tribeca Rep? There was a white Southern aristocratic son who had to throw an old black man off his land, and I'd have been great as the bastard son. How about *Dalliances*, British spinsterish librarian meets American grad student for summer term of discovery and revelation? We could fill out this book with plays I auditioned for.

"Well you can't lose hope," said Lisa, a little hollowly. "Look at my painting, for example. Am I in a gallery yet? Has the Whitney Biennial called? Leo Castelli? Maybe they called when I was out. Don't know what you're worried about. You got onstage in that *Billy Can You Hear Me?* thing . . ."

Which was about autistic adults. I was an extra. Not much dialogue, but my name in the program.

"We'll hit the big time eventually."

Emma these days was fond of pronouncing: "We're all goddam NOWHERE. The abyss!" Typical of Emma, this was overstatement. Lisa wasn't nowhere—she was drawing for another marketing agency—and I wasn't nowhere either—I was working full time, on the books, in an off-Broadway theater. What it was was a *holding pattern*. It wasn't success but it wasn't failure—like the doldrums, no winds blew, no current moved, not a ship in sight. It is easier to be absolutely nowhere ("The philistines! The world's against me!" someone like Emma can rage) than to be in the dreaded holding pattern. Because to get out of the holding pattern, you have to risk losing your place and having to go back to square one. Lisa tried to explain this to Emma one night and there was still fallout from that argument. Dishwashing continued:

"Emma's crazy, I'm telling you," said Lisa. "She needs an analyst or a psychiatrist or a good spanking, which I'm about ready to give her."

Well, I said, it's been a rough year for us all, and Emma's in a high-strung period, lots of problems, and we ought to be sympathetic—

"NO. No. I'm through being sympathetic for *her* problems, which are without end, Gil, face it. Does she trouble herself over our needs? I'm depressed as shit lately too. We never sit down and go on and on and on about poor *Lisa's* bad day, Lisa's problems."

Did Lisa want us to?

"No, not really. I just would like some mention, some *token* concern."

Lisa, I am here. Talk to me.

She stopped washing dishes. "I can't tell you this."

What? Yes you can.

She stood there, thinking for a minute. "Well I'll tell you this. I was feeling utterly rotten about a day or two ago—I mean, if there had been a bottle of sleeping pills we might have been in trouble."

I had noticed.

"So there I am on the subway, right?" Lisa mechanically washed a dish, over and over. "And there I am . . ." And she paused again. "And I just started crying, tears rolling down my face. And I tried to straighten up but then I sort of saw myself crying on a subway and being miserable, and that made me cry more. So I turned away and got up and walked to another car with less people and damn if I didn't start bawling again. I was hopeless."

What was it?

She turned from me to look in the dishwater. "Oh I don't know—things. Haven't you just ever felt like crying?"

Lately, every other day.

"Well the next thing I know, this woman, this old motherly Jewish woman sits down beside me and touches my shoulder. And I say it's all right, and I apologized, but she was one of these good souls, you know? One of those Real People, and she said, honey, get off at Rockefeller Center next stop and I'll get you a coffee—what you need dearie is a coffee. I mean this woman was . . . was so good."

Yeah.

"Which made me cry even more, that here I was, nothing really wrong with my life, bawling my eyes out and that some other human being had come to my rescue on the goddam subway and that made me even more pathetic to myself. So the tears went on and on. I can't believe I'm telling you this."

I took the dish from her, the one she had been washing forever, and began drying it repeatedly. The cleanest dish in the world.

"And so she bought me a coffee at this cookie stand and she

made me take a sip and told me a nice girl like you, life will get better, I was young, I was pretty, my life was ahead of me, nothing could be too bad. I felt so ashamed for all this attention, so I told her . . ." She lifted a sudsy hand to her brow, a gesture of disbelief. ". . . so I told her I had just had an abortion."

You told her that?

"I had to justify why I was carrying on so. She told me now now, dearie, you young people's lives move too fast, but it was over now and I'd be all right. I just sat there and let this woman mother me for a half hour and then I *insisted* she go on her way—I cannot tell you how embarrassed I was. I mean, I needed the cry, needed the attention—I don't really regret it, I just . . ."

Yeah, I know.

"Please put that silly dish in the cupboard," she said, and we moved to new subjects.

We were all so unhappy that year. You know what it was? I have a friend who says every three to four years you re-examine why you are in New York, and all you can see are the bad points and these New York Crises are cyclical. Every three to four years you question your sanity, your being there. I think we were simultaneously re-examining ourselves, wondering why we were putting up with that awful city. And god was it hot. That was the hottest summer there ever was—check the almanac and see—and I remember seeing the Coca-Cola sign in Times Square read 109 degrees. Crazy. And the city got proportionately crazier with each rising degree.

"It is hot in ways it has never been hot before," said Emma, adjusting the giant thirty-inch windowsill-sized fan to blow exclusively on herself. "I bow down before The Fan, I will serve it as my master," she said, offering up her arms for the breeze. "I am in an ecstasy, a religious transport—"

"Your time is almost up," Lisa said, looking with a dead seriousness at the watch.

"But can't we share it, Lisa? Friends like us, you and I together, Emma who loves you—"

"You'll die first. I want my ten minutes of unalloyed Fan and I will not be deprived."

Fan-politics and who got The Fan and for how long and ways

and means of dividing and alloting time before The Fan continued through June until Emma returned home with a revelation.

"Guess what, gang," Emma said, expecting us to snap to attention. "We're going on a little trip outside."

Riiight, I said.

"Oh you're gonna be sorry when I tell you the wonders mine eyes have seen," Emma went on like a TV evangelist. "I've just seen the prototype of the new subway car—a clean, new shiny chrome subway car on the F line."

Lisa: "Go throw yourself under it."

"Ah, these fools, ye of little faith, the lukewarm I shall spew out—"

"I am anything but lukewarm, Emma. I'm boiling, I am fricasseed, I am on a spit."

"All right," said Emma, making for the door. "I will go ride the F train by myself . . . the *air-conditioned* F train."

Now we'd have stolen pensioners' checks and sold drugs to children to get cool at that point, so we followed her zombie-like to the Carroll Street station and waited for this alleged F train to pass back through. Many trains passed by, none of them shining F prototypes, all of them dirty and hot and disgusting. The metal columns and steel beams of the subway platform were hot to the touch. The air was its usual mixture of vermin, urine, the smoke from burning trash lying against the third rail. Tension was high.

"You have two more trains, Emma," said Lisa calmly, "until the slaughter begins."

Three trains later it arrived . . . the stylish pink glowing F logo coming into focus through the darkness. Once inside the new train we had a Subway High—it was cool, ice-cool, no, even COLD in fact, it was like airport lounge and Holiday Inn motel-room cold, dry and crisp and restoring, resuscitating. We sat and watched Brooklyner after Brooklyner stumble in, first noticing the cleanliness, then the look would transform, there would be a glow in the eyes; it was cold, wonderfully beautifully cold; there was a look of peace . . .

And so this got to be a common procedure on weekends

through that miserable summer. The train to Coney Island was fun and elevated over Brooklyn so you got to see things, and at Coney, which on occasion had a breeze and lots of greasy junkfood and plenty of interest, we would get out . . . but only sometimes. Riding back we would get out at Hoyt-Schermerhorn and run across the platform for another prototype train to come back and take us away again. In that interim we'd get all hot again and we'd debate if Hoyt-Schermerhorn was the coolest station to wait at, and after that we debated how to pronounce Hoyt-Schermerhorn. We could have ridden, and did a few times, to Flushing which was the other end of the line, but that took us to Manhattan which meant it would get crowded with hot people, and plus it was all underground which made it dull—we wanted to be above Brooklyn, looking down into streets and neighborhoods and softball games and this vast cemetery that the train passes over and into streets called Avenue X (Emma suggested a best-seller: "He went to college and now he's back to improve his old Brooklyn neighborhood; his first stop the blackboard jungle, the public school in the toughest part of Brooklyn—Avenue X . . . he fights them, they fight back, but soon they come to love him . . ."). We listened to Brooklyners talk and we heard one girl get on with her friend and they were talking about boys and she said he was never any good and his family wasn't any good but one should expect that because he lives on Avenue V and nothing good ever came from Avenue V, and we had to wonder how so much information could be compressed into "Avenue V" and how that could be so different from "Avenue W."

"Creative, weren't they, these street-namers," Emma said. "Numbers and letters. And when it gets too high in the numbers, they start over again with avenues or boulevards, so you can have 23rd Street, 23rd Road, 23rd Avenue, 23rd Boulevard. They go out of their way to make you anonymous in New York—they've got it down to a psychology."

One of these times we got off in Coney Island, which is a bit of a downer all by itself, a faded resort that had its height in the 1890s, now a collection of burnt-down roller coasters, towers and scaffoldings and amusement park machinery standing deserted and overgrown, a ghost town of a past generation's good times, now squalid (which is part of its cult charm, I guess) and dirty; the barkers are old and used up and the fortune tellers are toothless crones (Emma figured that they weren't very good fortune tellers or they never would have allowed themselves to stay in this profitless, touristless wasteland), all the paint is peeling, the painted clowns and balloons are rusty, tattered streamers, abandoned bathhouses and ballrooms, all turn-of-the-century baroque, once gilded and once very very fine.

"We could do the disco bump cars," said Lisa. "It's air conditioned in there."

Naaahhhh.

"How about the New York Aquarium?" Lisa tried again.

"I feel sorry for the whales," Emma said, kicking the trash beneath her on the sidewalk. "All those dirty yucky fish in dirty water, dead things floating about. Don't have the money anyway."

Ferris wheel?

"Last time I went up in that I had a serious mortality crisis," Emma said. "Ditto for the Cyclone."

It was hot and I suggested we head back to the subway station and catch another F train.

"This place usually does it for me," Emma said, looking around, "but today it's depressing the shit out of me."

Lisa and I felt the same thing.

"This is a Despair Park, not an amusement park," Emma said, knowing it wasn't a funny joke. We stopped before a boarded-up hotel. "That makes me sad," Emma continued. "Honeymoon Hotel. Look how nice it must have been. I bet if you got in there you'd find some fine furnishings, ceilings, railings."

Lisa added, "Think how much *life* was lived here, how many girls got pregnant under the Boardwalk and had to marry their children's daddy, and how many servicemen came here for a last weekend before going off and . . ." She shrugged.

"Dying," Emma said, finishing her thought.

"Will we be more depressed if we get drunk?" Lisa asked.

The Sands Bar and Grill. A beach motif—fishtanks, a starfish or two above the liquor shelf, a fishing net which had fallen in a heap atop a high cabinet. Old men smoked and looked into their drinks in the corner, the barman was totally indifferent to our being there, figuring one look and we'd turn around and go.

"This place is gonna cheer me up loads," Emma said, selecting a table.

Lisa got the barman's attention and ordered three Jack Daniel's.

"We're going to get not a little drunk, I see," Emma said when Lisa arrived at the table with the booze.

A worn-looking woman emerged from behind a curtain of aquamarine beads, noticing there were people in her bar for a change. She went to the till and got some coins, went to the jukebox and put some quarters in, making some selections. A big band number, before our time, came on, something sad with a saxophone, almost upbeat enough for one of those stately slowdances.

"Wasn't that sweet?" Lisa said, watching the woman then go behind the bar and straighten up, run the rag along the bar.

"She expected more out of life," Emma suggested as we drank. "Here she is in the Sands Bar and Grill, spiffing it up for the only customers this month."

"Well she might be happy, you never know," Lisa said.

But we *did* know: the woman was miserable.

"Can only afford one more after this, you guys," Lisa said, and I said much the same. "Gotta get back to town," Lisa added.

"Another date with Bob?" Emma asked. She was resigned to Lisa's dating by this time.

"Well I said I'd call."

"There are phones here in Coney Island."

Stand him up, I suggest. Stay with us this evening.

"Okay," she said, not needing much convincing. "It's been crummy between us anyhow. I'm about done with him."

"Well at least someone's there willing to . . ." Emma grappled for words. "To . . . do normal things for you, touch you, molest your body."

"Our sexlife sucks, if that's any consolation to you," Lisa said, after a sip.

"I like to hear that. Makes me believe I'm not missing anything."

More drinking, more silence.

"I'm still poor," Lisa reminded us.

Emma said she had money as she just had cashed her temp-work check and she said if necessary she'd spend it all on getting us drunk. "Easy to live this way," she added, with only the minorest inflection of exaggerated drama, "when you're not going to live very much longer."

"Oh not that again. Cut that out," Lisa said.

I told Emma she was too young to die.

"It's never too young to die," she said. "The headaches aren't going away, in fact, they're getting worse. Every time I bend down, every time I run to catch the train, every little bit of stress and BANG my head is in a vice. Look, I'm being calm about this. Not hysterical, considering I have an inoperable brain tumor."

I insisted Emma did not have an inoperable brain tumor.

"Maybe an operable one? One of those operations where you don't come back with any identity, have to learn the alphabet over again, talk baby talk for five years. That's gonna go down well in the apartment, I can just see it."

Lisa shook her head. "I'm not changing diapers, I just wanted you to note that right now."

"Go ahead, laugh, laugh, it's not your chronic headaches."

I suggested some possibilities: sinus infection, migraines, stress, eyestrain, overwork, overworry . . .

"Brain cancer, brain tumors, a number of mental illnesses."

"Have it your way," said Lisa, waving Emma aside. "I'm not going to humor you. Go see a doctor."

"On what money? On that nonexistent medical plan we temporary workers get? On the US's nonexistent national health insurance? Spend money that I could be drinking with? Oh I guess I could go to a ghetto hospital. Between the gunshot victims and rape victims and stabbing victims they might fit in a CAT scan. I'm just going to die quietly, in my room. Young poet dead at twenty-four, one year before Keats, just like Keats, except I didn't write any poetry—a minor difference."

Round three. Emma bought.

Something by Peggy Lee played on the jukebox, something even sadder and more lost to another era than the others.

"This is ridiculous," said Lisa, slapping the table. "If we came into a bar like this in Carroll Gardens, full of oldies on the jukebox, a bar all to ourselves, on some day when we weren't in a mood to get depressed, we would run around saying what a FIND it was, what a cool bar it was, a little piece of yesterday. So let's stop pretending this bar is the end of the world."

Another song came on, something called "Moonglow," Emma informed us, a classic slowdance number. One of the old men got up and lumbered toward our table. Unemployed, his face said, a drinking man, once a worker with leathery hands, a creased lived-in face, gentle to women, you could tell, and with men, the kind who would have been in a few fights. "Wouldya like to dance with me, sister?" he said to Lisa, then turning the next second to Emma.

"Yes," said Emma, surprising us. "But just one dance."

This was maybe the strangest thing—among an encyclopedia of strange things—I have ever seen Emma do. Both Lisa and I, after a quick perplexed exchange of looks, watched Emma and the man dance together slowly, the man rocking a bit, Emma following unsurely, standing at a full step back from him.

"I didn't know Emma could dance," said Lisa simply.

See? Just when you thought you had her pegged, Emma would surprise you. I'd heard her before watch some horrible old out-of-date song-and-dance man on a variety show and say "Oh I feel so sorry for that man, what a bomb his act was . . . but one time that brought the house down. He still says the jokes with dignity . . ." And she'd offer to give herself to this man, just like she'd do for the hotdogmobile man. Outside her temp office was a man who sold hotdogs in a little funny car which had a dome and the body was the shape of a hotdog. Emma would come home despondent over the hotdog man condemned to live in the hotdogmobile, with a recording of tinkly whiny music he had to listen to all day. "God, and I'm so sick of the hotdogs he makes . . ." Well, don't buy them then. "You gotta buy 'em, no one else does," she'd say for herself. "It's so sad. I come up and he goes, 'Ooooh here's the pretty little miss, and she can have her hotdog annnnyway she wants it, yessirree.' " And then there was a guy with one leg who vended windup dancing poodles at Rockefeller Center, spread out on a flattened cardboard box. Emma would imitate him: " 'Get your poodles, pretty poodles, look at 'em dance, the dancin' poodles, arf arf, look at 'em, dancin' poodles . . .' " Degradation. I don't think Emma felt she had anything in common with youth. She could be moved by the sadness of old men, old mislived lives, goodhearted failures, something to do with her father maybe. I'm not going to keep speculating, instead I'll focus on that memory of Emma and the old fisherman—I have a sense he was a fisherman—shuffling to this dusky saxophone music, Emma's face soft and kind in the blue light from the jukebox and the aquariums, attempting a brief gesture of beauty amid the full ashtrays and the stale smell of spilt beer.

The music ended. Emma bowed her head a little, the old man nodded to her, a thank you.

"He said I reminded him of his wife," Emma said, a bit red in the face, now that she was back with us. She scooted beside Lisa under the table and finished off the drink she'd left behind.

Lisa patted Emma's knee, smiling. "Dead? Divorced?"

"Didn't ask."

We all sighed, listening to the next number play on the jukebox. "That was sweet, Em," Lisa added.

Then we heard the patter of rain outside, first scattered, then clattering down furiously, a summer thunderstorm.

Maybe it'll cool down, I said.

Suddenly the other old man was up, the first old man trying to restrain him, bring him back to the table. The second old man wanted a dance too. He was very drunk, toothless, crude, wore clothes he must have slept in, lived in for months.

"No thank you," said Lisa uneasily.

"Whatsa mattuh, uh? You don't like me? *She* danced with *him*. You can't dance with me, sugar pie? Huh sugar pie? Hehehehehehehe . . ."

Let's go, I said.

"Hold it hold it," the man said, tottering, "I adn't had my dance with the girlie yet. Want my dance with the girlie. C'mon . . ." He put his hand on Lisa's arm too firmly; she shook him away.

"Barney!" called the woman behind the bar, coming to intervene. "I'll dance with you, Barney, dance with me," she said. "Here. Here. C'mon, take my hand—"

"I wanna dance with the girlie—"

"No no, here I am. I'm dancing. You're not dancing with me. Ah, therrre we go . . ."

We got up and left, stood under the awning for a moment, charted a course for the subway stop, ran through the rain and rode home, where we didn't want to be, where it was still hot, where we were wet and sticky from dirty city rain, where we were half-sobered from a half-drunk and felt mildly sick and restless, where we still were depressed.

Lisa decided enough was enough, and the next week she formulated a plan of action to keep us from turning all our weekends into the Manic-Depressive Ward. I would work on a new audition piece, she would work on a new painting and try to place it in a gallery, Emma would work on new poetry and give a reading at the Coffeehouse on Bleecker. As it turned out I didn't need to audition for anything, as a Dream Role came along and fell in my lap.

A Children's Theater reprisal for the millionth time of *Peter Cottontail*. Arnie Schmeen, Jr., approached me, hand on my back, him and me, old buddies. Schmeen had *just* the role for me: Papa Bunny.

No way, I said. Politely, of course.

"It means an extra $60 a week—two performances at $30 apiece."

All right, I'll do it.

Papa Bunny, in a bunny suit, white pancake, a little ball of cotton on the end of my nose, and I had to hop around and say lines like *C'mon little Bun Buns, let's hippity hoppity awaaaaaay over to the carrot patch for dinner! Hippity hoppity hippity hoppity . . .* And then I jumped up and down with both feet with a lot of eight- and nine-year-olds in tow behind me (students of the Children's Theater Consortium). I told no one. NO ONE. Not Mom, not Dad, not friends. This WAS NOT my New York Stage Debut, do you understand? I could deal with my own Private Hell—I got by for two weeks undetected—as long as nobody knew about it. Emma and Lisa somehow (was it you, God?) found out.

I'm not sure how they found out but I suspect Monica or someone called from the theater and said that a Saturday matinee had been canceled due to lack of interest, or something like that, and Emma made conversation and asked what I was doing in it, dressing? working props? and Monica or whoever went, why no, he's Papa Bunny! And anyway with that piece of knowledge they decided to drop in one afternoon and see me on the big stage. I picture Emma going, "Well we have to go down and see him; it's his New York stage debut, right?" and Lisa would have reservations, saying, "Gee, I don't know, he obviously didn't tell us because he was embarrassed." And Emma would say, "Embarrassed in front of us? Nonsense . . ."

And so, once upon a time, it is Saturday afternoon and the kids in the audience are wild and throwing things and talking throughout our speeches and me and Mama Bunny are rolling our eyes and it is all we can do to get through the act, and the little kids playing the Bunny Children (the Bun Buns, as the script calls them) are upset because no one is listening to them and Benny Bunny gives his little speech only to have a wadded up program thrown at him, anyway it is just the End of Civilization As We Know It, and there I am going *Now Bun Buns follow me*, and hopping about in time to this xylophone music and there, out of the corner of my eye, are Lisa and Emma, not knowing whether to laugh or put their heads in their hands for SHAME, and they see I spotted them so now they can't get away quietly and unnoticed, they have to stick it out.

So there I am backstage after it's over, staring at myself in the makeup mirror, listening to Julie (Mama Bunny) rant about what a thankless job this turned out to be, and then in the mirror I see the door crack and two heads, Lisa's and Emma's, peek through, and they say a sheepish "Hiiiii, Gil, it's us," with a little nervous laughter.

Come on in, I say.

"We just had to come see you," said Lisa.

"It was your New York debut, Gil, we couldn't not come," Emma said quickly, although underscoring that *this* was my New York debut fell with a Big Thud and everyone grew quiet in the dressing room.

If I had wanted them to come I would have invited them, I said simply enough, not a note of recrimination.

"Yeah well," sighed Lisa, "you know us."

"You know, it's all gonna get better from here," Emma said, bending down to kiss my cheek, still white with bunny makeup. "You look cute in the bunny suit—god, I'd give anything for a picture. I mean, c'mon Gil, laugh a little. This is, like, a typical struggling episode; you'll look back on this and laugh."

I am a grown man out there in front of people who think I'm stupid in a bunny suit and I agree with them, I said, and I added that if Emma had even warned me I could have found a better show, a better time for them to see this thing . . .

Lisa patted me on the shoulder. "We'll see you when you get home, okay? We'll go out and do something."

I noticed some crumpled paper Lisa was carrying and asked her what it was.

She faltered. "Oh, well, now, yeah this uh," she laughed as she unwrapped this bundle, "is some flowers—we just thought, you know, debut and all, we'd get you some flowers." She put them down on the table. They were very pretty.

"We're goin' now," said Emma, and they left all smiles, all plastic oh-god-this-was-a-mistake smiles. And I went to the bathroom, after saying a normal goodbye to the kids, after talking a little more with Julie, after putting up my suit, scrubbing my face clean of makeup, and I cried, feeling like such a NOTHING, a nothing that was not merely aware of being nothing, but rather a nothing that had been kicked around and degraded *on top of* being nothing. And it was one of those cries where after you were done you didn't feel any better, just tired of crying. I did not go straight home but went to movies and stayed out until 2 a.m. so I could come home and the girls would be in their beds already and I wouldn't have to talk to them, and they must have known I was doing that because they didn't wait up.

Whereas I was forgiven for not telling them I was onstage, Emma was not forgiven when she gave a reading at the Coffeehouse on Bleecker and Thompson and didn't invite us or tell any of us, and we only found out because Lisa passed by there and Emma's name was on the chalkboard as one of the poetry readers the *previous* night.

"It's no different from what Gil did," said Emma, when confronted, trying to defend herself.

"Not telling us in your case is very different," snapped Lisa. "Gil was in a bunny suit reading someone's else lines, but you were reading your own poetry. What's more you told us you hadn't written anything new."

"Well I hadn't," said Emma, "it's all old stuff. I didn't want you to come see me back up there doing old stuff."

I didn't believe that, I said, digging in, avenging myself. I'd seen her working on new stuff. She just didn't want to share it.

"Are your poems about us?" asked Lisa coyly. "Trashing out your friends who love you at the Coffeehouse in verse?"

Emma took this badly and left the room.

We all were artistically frustrated and frazzled that summer, getting on one another's nerves something awful. Of course, if it had been this sour all the time we wouldn't have stayed together as long as we did. I remember, thinking in no particular order, the time Lisa came home with spiky hair, a T-shirt on under a leather jacket, black capri pants, spiked heels.

"What happened to you?" said Emma, wide-eyed.

"I'm punk," said Lisa.

Punk?

"Yeah, you know, like the Ramones and Sex Pistols and New York Dolls and all that. I'm counterculture. Hey guys, I'm a rebel."

"No you're not," said Emma.

"I'm working on it, I'm working on it," said Lisa, a hint of a smile. "You guys gotta support me on this, okay? I mean, I'm getting *nowhere* artistically, right? I walk in in my knit sweaters and plaid skirts, Miss College Coed, with my portfolio and before I show them a single slide the gallery owner says, sorry, we have no openings for a secretary. I don't look like an artist. I go through *Art News*—I don't look like them, they don't look like me. Until now."

Emma loved it. "Is your work going to turn angry, spiteful, revolutionary?"

Lisa nodded blandly. "I'm consumed with rage. Angst."

That's a start, I said.

"You gotta do something vile, *épater les bourgeois*," Emma mused.

"Paint a lot of sexual things," Lisa said, considering it.

Something dirty, I suggest.

"Yeah," Lisa went on, "I could do lots of vulvae and labiae and clitorides—"

"*Very* good," applauded Emma.

"Hey, I did Latin."

"Dead end though," said Emma a moment later. "Georgia O'Keeffe and Louise Bourgeois. They've sort of done the female sexual symbol to death. What's good and punk? Self-destructive. You could do like that guy did in Paris that carved off his penis in public."

Lisa considered it. "I don't have a penis."

"Use Gil's."

I discouraged this.

"Maybe I can rage against crap culture," said Lisa. "You know, happy faces and I FOUND IT religious stickers and Keep on Truckin' and CB shit."

"Nyehhh," said Emma, "Pop Art, Lichtenstein, Rauschenberg, Warhol, they parody pop culture. Pop culture parodies itself."

"I could do nudes," said Lisa, going through the kitchen to get a beer. She eventually passed the can around. "Why don't you pose for me, Emma? Come on. No joking. I'll do your portrait."

"If you get famous everyone will see me nude. Through the centuries."

"You'd be a great subject."

"They'll say you were imitating Bosch."

"I'll make you a Botticelli."

"I'm a terminal Rubens."

Lisa beseeched me as well but neither of us would strip for her. "Philistines!" she cried. "You're standing in the way of Art!"

But it wasn't long after that, after a brief spell of getting along, that Emma had her big disaster, the Night of the Living Dead, she called it. Lisa walked by the Coffeehouse and Emma's name was posted for that night's poetry reading, and so Emma was duly confronted again.

"All right, all right," Emma said, "but if you come you better cheer a lot." It was to be an evening mostly of oldies but of a few new ones she was eager to try out on the crowd—perhaps this would begin a new phase in her writing. "Yes," she'd say, "I am leaving my Worthless Phase and beginning my Mildly Tolerable Period."

And so we went down to the Coffeehouse to get an anonymous middle table where we could seem like the crowd when we cheered and not just Emma's friends up front. I never told Emma this at the time, but although I loved to hear her read, I HATED going down to the Coffeehouse and hearing other people read their pretentious trash—like the guy on before Emma. Talk about insufferable. His name was Trigger Rothberg (give me a break, already), in his late forties and he got up there looking weary and time-worn (instead of a talentless clerk which is what I suspect he was) and he would bring up an ashtray and a bottle of whiskey and a scotch glass, and go through an elaborate ritual of pouring some, and then bumming a smoke from the audience:

"Anybody got one for me? Filterless? You, sweetie—thanks," he'd go on as he accepted the cigarette, lit it up. "We poets never pay for our own smoke, heh-heh . . ."

Oh get outa here.

"Some of you know me, others of you don't," he'd begin,

assuming a wise, old-man-of-the-road pose; he'd name-drop Kerouac and jazz artists and laugh, chuckle, oh yeah, there was the time—heh-heh, did he tell this one? He had an old crony in the crowd who'd yell for him to tell it anyway, and he'd tell how he and Ginsberg were "pushing boo one night up in Harlem, he and I . . ." He was at a party with Marilyn Monroe, Joe DiMaggio was there, and there were tales of hanging out with people on "that goddam blacklist." After enough of this he'd shake his head, shake his head and chuckle again, oh he'd seen so much. He'd begin to read: "And they told him/You can't come in here boy 'cause you're black/and the Man is like that sometimes . . . And they told us in '56 that it didn't make no difference/But we knew/It made a difference . . . The Man is like that sometimes . . ."

Lisa pantomimed gagging herself, leaning over to whisper, "Gil, Emma'll have a clear shot with this guy leading off."

But trouble broke out. He went on too long and someone told him to sit down, and he told them they were too young to appreciate the '50s, and then the boy told him he was an old fart talking shit and, what's more, shit nobody cared about. The old fart's crony stuck up for him, and finally the master of ceremonies, a skinny Jewish guy named Joel who ran the Coffeehouse, emerged and made conciliatory remarks—"Another night, Trigger," he said, patting him on the back, "come back next week and read again"—and then we all clapped for him just to get him off the stage.

Emma was introduced. She came out, adjusted the microphone beside the table where she opened up her notebooks. She read a few youthful reminiscences, a poem about New York, and then a long self-analyzing poem . . .

> I might work as a character in
>   someone else's book;
> I try to be quotable for you,
>   in case you turn out to be the author.
> I can make an exit quick,
>   in any event.

I'm good on paper.
I'm even good in theory,
    but theory isn't fact:
So much of my life waiting to be disproven,
    a future of mixed results.

I should run from poetry,
    mine but yours also,
For there I am most naked—

"Yeah, let's see your tits, honey!" yelled the now-drunk crony of the pretentious guy who went before. He and Trigger were finishing off Trigger's bottle of whiskey and decided to make a scene, show that two old men still could get something going . . .

Everyone glared at him, ssshhhed him. I fired him a deadly look, Lisa pointed a threatening finger at him.

Emma began again:

I should run from poetry—

"Good idea!" yelled the drunk, he and Trigger greasily laughing until they started coughing.

I got up and took the crony's arm—this is the most macho thing I ever did in my life, so listen up—and told him one more word and he was DEAD.

"If you're gonna be a pig, go do it somewhere else," Lisa hissed audibly; others in the audience added yeahs and grunts of disapproval.

Emma got no further than that line again.

"You people like this shit?" said Trigger's drunk buddy, standing. "That's not poetry, that's not . . . that's just shit . . ."

Trigger tried to calm his friend down now, probably sensing his Coffeehouse career was at an end if this went on.

Joel got up and reprimanded the men, asked them to leave.

"That ain't poetry," the crony went on, as Trigger tried to escort him, fumblingly, out the door. His friend knocked over his beer, the glass rolled off the table and broke on the sawdust floor. "Hey sister, write about something somebody cares about . . . 1951, Senator Joseph McCarthy came out of this great land and did a number on you people—"

Everyone groaned, some yelled shut up, get out.

"Not everybody was alive," Emma said darkly from the stage, into the microphone, "in 1951."

Trigger and his friend were now at the door. "And another thing, sister—that's a shitty poem, a shitty shitty shitty poem . . ." He said "shitty" as loudly as he could, doubling over and almost falling over. Trigger led him outside, ushering him back to his apartment, he said, for the rest of the whiskey. They finally left and all was quiet.

"I can't apologize enough," said Joel. "Please Emma, go on and finish."

But Emma was deep in thought rereading her poem.

"Emma?" Joel said, tapping her shoulder gently.

Emma looked up slowly. "This isn't a very good poem, is it?"

Mild laughter all about, thinking she was joking.

"No, it's not very good," she said quietly. She then gathered her papers together, put them neatly into her notebook and began to leave the stage, shaking her head.

Lisa and I looked at each other, then Lisa put her head in her hands, looking down.

Joel said, "Well, okay, uh sure, another time Emma. That was great, sorry about the ruckus. A big hand for Emma Gennaro."

And there was enthusiastic sympathy applause.

"Why'd she freak out there?" Lisa said to me.

Well, we both knew how sensitive she was.

"But those guys are *nothing*. Drunken bums."

I know that, she knows that, you know that—who could say why she bolted?

Emma must have left through a back door. So we got up as the next poet was reading her first poem (". . . you put stars in my heart for safe-keeping/the light within, sister mine . . .") and slipped out and looked around hoping to find Emma, and then after ten minutes went home. Emma wasn't home either.

"Boy that was a bad night," she said when she came back home at 11 p.m., standing in the doorway.

Where had she gone? We had worried.

"I just walked around the Village, went to a movie. Thanks for coming down, guys." Emma went to her bedroom and shut the door.

"Wanna come out and talk?" Lisa yelled.

No answer.

You were great, I yelled also. No one could foresee the drunks. She better not be taking the drunk assholes personally. Her stuff was great, everyone loved it, next week they want her back . . .

No answer still.

"Come on, Emma," Lisa pursued, "the evening's young still; we can go out and get plastered."

Emma's bedroom door opened slowly and she stood there looking pale and unhappy. "Look," she said, "I don't care about the drunks, or the Coffeehouse. But it occurred to me up there reading that my poem wasn't very good, no one in the audience (except you two) woulda known a good poem if they heard it, and that the Coffeehouse was just a place for losers and poseurs and I couldn't sit up there another minute and go on with the charade."

Sure sure, that made sense to us, we said.

"Now I gotta figure out if my being a poet is part of an even bigger charade," she said. "And I think I'd better sleep on it. Good night." And she went back inside, closing the door behind her.

And it was downhill from there.

Lisa and I were sitting around, equidistant from The Fan, the morning warming up to its usual inferno. I read the paper, she read her paperback, Emma was still asleep. Lisa turned on the radio and it was Elvis singing "Until It's Time for You to Go."

"Whadya know? WNBC not playing the latest disco crap," she said.

I told her about my possibility of a role in the newest Venice production. In atonement for the Bunny Suit I did get noticed for being "a trouper" so maybe it wasn't so bad I was Papa

Bunny. The new play was a family drama by a playwright who showed up to rehearsals every night and tried to align the actors' performances with His Conception, which was probably his real life. Lots of screaming and yelling, cursing, all kinds of novel cursing and torment, someone discovering their homosexuality—'70s off-Broadway theater in a nutshell.

"Do you get to play the fag son?" Lisa asked.

No, the intolerant football-hero brother. This and the high-school original musical made for the second football hero I played. Explain that one.

Then the radio announcer spoke, all somber: *Yes, until it's time for him to go. Too soon, Elvis, too soon. We'll be playing Elvis throughout today, in tribute to the King. Dead at forty-two, today in Memphis . . .*

Oh shit.

"*No*," said Lisa putting down her book. "*Elvis?* There's one you never thought would die. How did it happen?" she asked me, though she knew I knew only as much as she did.

The disc jockey later filled it in, a drug-induced heart failure apparently.

"The King of Rock 'n Roll," Lisa said. "God I grew up on all those crummy Elvis movies, had a crush on him and everything."

And then we looked at each other with the exact same thought: WHO IS GOING TO TELL EMMA? Lisa considered aloud:

"Oh we can't tell her. Let her go out and read it on a headline or something. I couldn't bear to watch it. Damn, and she was just recovering from the Coffeehouse debacle."

You had to know that Emma was a *philosophical* Elvis fan, not a screaming polyester-clad middle-aged woman Elvis fan, or a trendy nostalgia Elvis fan, but someone who felt rock 'n roll had been in decline since the Beatles and maybe everything fresh or new or important the genre had to say had been said between 1955 and 1965 or so. Elvis wasn't just a pop hero, he was a symbol.

Emma, one time: "Look, it's like Tennessee Williams not writing like he did when he was younger, or Orson Welles not making a good film for the last twenty years—the second you stumble, reveal yourself to be human, BANG the vultures are all over you. Just like Elvis. 'He's not what he was,' they say. Throw him on the American scrapheap, make him a laughing stock. Make the bastard *pay* for trying to add a little entertainment to our miserable lives. How dare he be human!"

The only time I ever saw Emma really flustered concerned Elvis.

"Oh Elvis was a thief," Susan once argued, a year earlier, at one of her parties. "I mean, I've read this everywhere. He stole it all from black people. Black people invented rock 'n roll."

"That's somewhat true, of course, but Elvis—"

"Well he's fat and used up now," Susan insisted, never knowing when to quit. "He's a wreck, doing Vegas, all bloated and I can't see how anyone can still like him . . ."

Emma was furious with her. "Elvis created a myth—the Rock 'n Roll Hero. And now he's got to live out the rest of his life in this persona, like John Wayne, like Mae West, like our damned dying-in-the-gutter poets, like Hemingway and Fitzgerald, like anyone who tries to do anything creative in America, you stick with your legend until it kills you. There's the irony—someone like Elvis isn't living out *his* American Dream anymore, he's living out *ours*."

Do our dreams in America become public property? I wonder. Did I want to be an actor because of my love of the theater, the challenges of its art, the qualities it would demand of me? Or was it that, like Elvis and "rock 'n roll" and Emma and "poetry," I was chasing words too—words with a lot of dolled-up cultural American myth attached to them, perhaps, but just words. Was I in New York for the right reason? What is artistic struggle all about? Why did God create Man? Why did the record company put "Don't Be Cruel" on the flip side of "Hound Dog" and make half as much money as they could have? We'll be coming back to some of these mysteries, so don't go away.

Yeah, Emma got good and depressed over Elvis. And everyone else who died that year—Bing Crosby, Groucho Marx, John Wayne, 1977 was a big year for death. Of course, for variety, there was Emma the Failure:

"I'll never be a poet. It's just not going to happen. If it was going to happen something would have happened by now. It's not the rest of the world against me—I could deal with that; it would be confirmation of talent. It's *me*. I can't write, and when I do write it's shit. Ever since the Coffeehouse—"

"Emma," insisted Lisa, "*forget* the Coffeehouse, those stupid old drunks. You're gonna let them determine your fate?"

Emma shrugged, "No, I guess not . . ."

"You're the next Virginia Woolf," Lisa said absently.

"Who went mad and killed herself," Emma reminded.

Uh, Emily Dickinson, I said, knowing Emma loved Emily Dickinson.

"Who went unpublished, virtually, in her lifetime."

(We knew better than to mention Sylvia Plath.)

"Emma don't be like this, keep the faith," Lisa pursued. "You'll be . . . I don't know, the modern George Eliot."

"She was ugly," Emma muttered, retreating to her bedroom.

And then the San Gennaro festival. A chance for Emma to make her annual extended joke of her blood liquefying. That year she didn't want to go.

"Nawwww," she said, refusing to leave her bed. "There'll be young attractive Italian-Americans fondling and kissing each other, and being young and happy, and BLECCCH."

"All right then," tried Lisa, "let's go somewhere else for your holy day, somewhere out of this lousy apartment. The Adirondacks, go hiking, walk on trails, bask in nature. Waterfalls. Animal life."

"No, I hate nature," Emma said, utterly sincere. "I love New York—it's all pavement and concrete and steel and asphalt and there's no nature, no life forms. Trees. I hate trees. They remind me of life going on, the cycle, death—natural things: disease, cancer, tumors. I don't want to be reminded of biology."

And the headaches got worse too. We would hear Emma groaning from the bedroom; we'd knock discreetly after a while. She'd be doubled up on the bed, looking drawn, miserable. See a doctor, see a doctor, we'd *beg*. No, no, just let her die . . .

Lisa retreated from Apartment Life. She and Bob went out a lot, got back late. Lisa would come in at 1 a.m. and Emma's light was still on so she would visit and Emma would prop herself up in the bed (which she hadn't left all day) and smile weakly, part Camille, part *Song of Bernadette*, the brave invalid, and they'd talk for a while.

"She's gotten benedictory, Gil," Lisa would tell me. "It's as if she's issuing her last words. 'Be happy with Bob. Maybe you two should settle down . . .' I mean, Emma, sending me forth into a man's arms. She *is* sick."

There was also Connie. Behind Emma's back, previously, Monica and I had had a little drunk after-the-party affair that lasted precisely and exactly four dates before we mutually intervened, both of us having satisfied our curiosity and gotten sex out of our systems for a while, and I had told *no one* about it. A year earlier I might have flaunted it to make Emma and Lisa jealous and get reactions out of them and induce commentary and feel very sexual and someone-who-has-affairs-all-the-time-ish but the current mood made me more practical. I just did it, enjoyed it, and quit doing it when I quit enjoying it and there was barely a ripple in the surface of my social life, even Monica and I parted friends. But Connie. Connie was another matter.

I got the part of the football-hero brother, with a whopping total of two scenes, 46 lines, and a dinner scene where I sat there and ate through twenty minutes of other people's dialogue (macaroni and cheese Tues., Thurs., and Sun.; hamburger casserole Wed., Fri., and Sat.). And one night this woman, dressed oh-so-sharply, came backstage with her escort (I assumed a boyfriend) and her name was Connie.

"I don't know anyone in the cast," she whispered to me amid other backstage conversation, out-of-town relatives of the star generating kudos, the parts they really really liked, etc. "In fact I've never been backstage anywhere before." She extended her hand. "Connie Mohr. And you're Gilbert Freeman?"

Had we met before?

She winked. "Your name's in the program, sweetheart. I wanted to come back and say I liked you." She pretend-punched me in the shoulder. "Real macho. Like every football jock I ever met."

Hey thanks. My first FAN.

"Ha, you have lots of fans, I bet," she said. "Not everyone has enough gall to barge backstage and ingratiate themselves. That's what I'm doing. Ingratiating myself."

She introduced her escort, who worked on Wall Street with her in the bond-trading department, he was looking for a future in commodity trading, Chicago branch, blah, blah, blah. She didn't seem to be very proprietary about him, she didn't seem even to care he was there. Nah, I thought, they can't be together because she was—could it be?—flirting with *me*.

"How long have you been doing this?"

A two-sentence version of my life story prepared for such questions.

"You're just twenty-three? Oh goodness, a child. I'm—well, never you mind, we'll talk age another time." But she couldn't have been any older than twenty-nine, thirty—no way. "So Mr. Twenty-three, you got your whole career ahead of you. Glad I met you now! After you get a Tony you won't remember your lowly fans who made you what you are."

Could we get this woman packaged and sold in economy-size buy-one-get-another-free containers? I'll buy stock in the company.

"Here's my card." She gave me a sleek business card. The investment firm was Golam Brothers, Cohn & Schwartz . . . which I'd heard of. She was one slick number, wasn't she? Couldn't get over how well she dressed (later I asked her, throwing tact aside; Brooks Brothers suits at $800 apiece, silk blouses, $150 shoes, her briefcase was $500 and Italian . . . around the house it was T-shirt and jeans, but at work you had to dress the part—they were judging you, the bastards, by your clothes, and she didn't slave six years at Harvard to have these New York Jews look down their nose at her, nosirree. Oh, that wasn't anti-Semitic, as she was a Boston Jew. Or rather, it was acceptable anti-Semitism, coming from a Jew . . . I think.

She was blond and blue-eyed, a solid compact figure, more attractive than she was beautiful. ("I got these New York Jew-boys running after me night and day, Gil," she would one day tell me. "The Blond Jewish Girl—great to take home to mother.

You get the blond shiksa and keep kosher at the same time—let's talk Most Popular Girl in the Office, right? I turn 'em all down. Some of these poor mama's boys, thirty-year-old virgins I swear. Except for circle jerks up at some Catskill Jewish summer camp over some pair of tits in a porno magazine, they've had nil for a sexlife—and they feel guilty about THAT." How did she do it? Seem so elegant, so world-wise and at the same time talk absolute *filth*? I loved it.) Her address on the business card was P.O. Box something-or-other, on the Upper East Side. ("It's important to have an Upper East Side address," she said over lunch the first time we went out, "because they look at addresses on Wall Street. Guess where I live? Jersey. Won't *do* to have Jersey as an address for Wall Street purposes. I've got the psychology, the mental game of working the Street down to an art form and I ought to write a how-to book. After I'm up the ladder, of course. Be glad you're not in that crazy phoney world downtown, Gil." Phoney compared to the theater? She couldn't have meant that. I've never met anyone who loved that wheeling-and-dealing, cat-and-mouse, buy-and-sell-their-own-mothers kind of world more.

"Gotta go," she said, pressing my hand. "I know nothing about the theater and now I want to know more. Don't suppose . . ." She hesitated, looking up vulnerably at me, widening the eyes, biting the lip charmingly. ". . . Don't suppose you'd consider having lunch with me one day. My treat. Someplace nice. On the company, so don't feel guilty—you should see what I can do with an expense report."

I'd love it. I gave her my phone number.

"Don't lose my card now," she said, turning, smiling. "I just had these printed up. I'm giving them out to people *on the street*, for christ's sakes. I just love handing out my card. You should see me on a commuter flight to Boston—I'm slinging those cards out like a blackjack dealer, up and down the aisles. Connie can WORK a plane, believe me." Another clasp of my hand. "I'm looking forward to lunch. Don't forget me now. Seeya, kid." And out she went, with her patient escort in tow. Was Mr. Escort one of the thirty-year-old virgins she had following her around? Never saw him again (or for that matter many of Connie's male friends I met, and there was a reason for that but let's not get ahead of the story).

Lisa was happy about Connie for me, Emma was not.

"Great," Emma said. "Dissension in the ranks. What is the appeal for you guys about slimy capitalist con-artists on Wall Street? All those people should be prosecuted for peacetime crimes. They have nothing better to do than finance apartheid, war after war, Republican after Republican, and they never pay taxes. Usury. Money-lending. Read Ezra Pound."

Pound was a Nazi-sympathizing Fascist who should have been shot for treason, said Lisa impatiently.

"A few personality defects, I'll admit," Emma said.

When Connie called to "finalize" our lunch date, Emma answered, put the phone down rudely, came into my room and said, "It's the Jewess."

Racism doesn't become you, Emma.

"I'm not anti-Semitic, Gil. I'm anti-Connie. I'd make fun of whomever you'd go out with, traitor that you are. Loyalty to Emma *one inch* deep. Go ahead: Send me over the edge, commit me to Bellevue. Let me say just two words to you before you sleep with her and I want you to think about it when you press your naked bodies against one another, when you feel the heat of another human being against your *burning* erogenous zones . . ."

Yes?

"Premature ejaculation."

Emma didn't want to meet Connie, see Connie, hear about Connie, take phone messages for Connie. Fortunately for Emma (not so for me), Connie and I had two lunches and then she seemed to drop out of sight, no explanation . . . me, affairless, as usual. Whatever she thought she liked maybe she didn't like, or maybe something she wanted wasn't there—take your pick of depressing theories I was contemplating.

I guess I'm not the type of guy a real woman wants, I told Lisa, while we were washing dishes. (You're thinking: Is that all you two did, wash dishes all summer? It was our only time to talk, the clattering and banging of pots covering our intrigues. Emma couldn't be trusted to do dishes—coffee cups reminded her of T. S. Eliot lines, the kitchen knife was a viable means of suicide, it was an exercise—like, she said, her life—in futility. They would just get dirty again.) I think I must appear too immature or something, I went on. Too wimpy. Monica always kept asking, 'Are you gay? Are you sure you're not gay?' Maybe I am gay—

Lisa put down a pot with a clang: "I *hate* this kind of talk, Gil," she said rather passionately. "Just because Emma's a sinking ship doesn't mean we have to follow her down. She's got us all spooked. If you're gay, you're gay, but not because Emma keeps telling you you're sexually inadequate with women. She makes me feel like some kind of slut, that I'm promiscuous because I date a handful, *one or two* guys a year—this is ridiculous. Her craziness is rubbing off on us. And that's why I'm moving out when the lease is up."

Oh no. Really?

"Really. It's not fun anymore, it's not productive, I am not going to be responsible for someone who needs to be in the hands of an analyst; I'm tired of feeling guilty for having fun in front of Emma."

But move out? Well, you said that last year, Lisa, when you were going out with, um . . .

"Yeah, what's-his-name. But this is different and I've made up my mind." Then she turned to me, putting a sudsy hand on my arm. "This has nothing to do with *you*, Gil, and no matter what we're going to keep getting together and doing things and remain friends always. C'mon, you don't think things are a barrel of laughs around here anymore, do you?"

No, but . . .

"I'm going to move in with Bob."

I thought you two didn't get along so well.

"Well enough. He makes a good salary too, he lives better than we do. I want to stay at home and paint sometimes, not scrap for money every day. Besides I want to try him out and see if we could be married."

MARRIED?

"Yes," she said, looking into the suds absently. "For kids. I would like to have a kid. And if art doesn't work out and I have to work at marketing companies or advertising agencies or whatever, I would want to have the kid about now, raise him for a while and then join the workforce rather than interrupt any progress I might make, go through a maternity-leave hassle, lose my place in the company."

Lisa was just twenty-five. All of this seemed remarkably mature and cold and deliberate.

"I'm twenty-five going on the-rest-of-my-life," she answered, "and I'm tired of not having any stability. My life's just bumbling from spot to spot at the moment."

These are reasons for marrying, I said, but not good ones. Did she love Bob?

"What? Do you expect TV-movie, romance-novel love? I was madly in love with Joey Feingold in high school—I bet if I saw him today I'd still go ga-ga, get weak in the knees. But we don't marry Joey Feingold. That's schoolgirl stuff, swept away, knight in shining armor, it's crap, late Victorian crap that grew up alongside the cult of the virgin bride, a bill of goods, Gil. My feminist seminars taught me one thing, not to expect a man to answer all your problems, be everything to you. I'm looking for security, comfort, companionship . . ."

And as she went on I stopped listening. There was the fact: we as a threesome were through. And another fact: Lisa and I as a twosome were through. Married people NEVER did right by their friends (make that: DO right, I've still never seen evidence to the contrary; the only couples a single can deal with are couples you met already encoupled). And Emma and I were through too. We couldn't make it without a stable third like Lisa who balanced our asininities with sense and practicality. Yes, the Apartment's Point of No Return.

And with this in mind, I threw myself on the company of my theater friends. I would hang out with them, my co-workers, my fellow artistes (ha ha), I would make my lot in life at my place beside them . . . I had a core crowd, of course, developed by this time at the Venice—people dropped in and out of it, but it was down to this handful: Julie (Mama Bunny) who was sweet but real offendable and sensitive so you had to watch what you said around her. She had a boyfriend so we didn't see her much socially. There was Monica (who actually had become a real Ack-tress, fairly insufferable after two large roles placed her far and away ahead of her contemporaries, her résumé gaining respectability by the season, and she fell into wild-and-crazy theater stories and could be real tiresome), Tim (a techie-for-life, intelligent-looking with glasses, soft-spoken, sweet but a bit of a bore), Donna (an overweight black woman full of talent and noise and life who either cheered us up or wore us out, was always "on," one of those dynamic theater-types no one ever gets to know really), Crandell (handsome actor who got more roles than me and then had gotten old somehow, fell out of favor, too limited perhaps, a little too cardboard, so when he was drunk he was bitter, but otherwise a nice guy). These were my friends.

Emma got quieter. Slept most of the day. Watched TV incessantly while she was up. Lisa avoided the apartment like the plague, out every night with Bob.

"She's moving out for Bob," Emma said, staring at the TV one night when I walked nearby. "She told me."

I know. I guess we'll all end up going our separate ways.

I had thought Emma would beg me to stay with her, not desert her, I expected it. But she didn't. She just kept watching the TV.

Nobody loved me—that was damn obvious. Connie should have, but she didn't. Lisa should have, Emma—of all people—should have but no one thought of these things. It would have been hard to say on some nights who was worse off, me or Emma. Emma was born to be depressed, I was not. I was a generally happy person who was very unhappy. Each night as I lay awake, looking at the ceiling, every breath would become a sigh, it would creep over me again, my loneliness, my meaning nothing to anybody. I would be so loyal to someone, so good to them, I would make them laugh all the time and forgive them anything and as for sex, if they wanted sex, if they'd just have it with me, I would make sure they didn't get *out of bed* all day, I would RUIN them for other people, I would show them what passion was put on this earth for, and all this was just centimeters below the surface, it was just waiting there to be released and I did not understand, I did not comprehend, I did not perceive WHY it should be no one wanted to take this from me, to make even a token pass over these qualities.

And so I'd sit there in the apartment and could not watch TV or talk to Emma or listen to the radio or read because all these things were awful, and there was the newspaper but I always read the newspaper at the theater and I found myself reading things over again until I threw the paper aside, so I thought, well, go get something to eat, go take a walk, go breathe air, move, do something, go into town, it's a nice night, so I went to the Village and poked around, made my way to Baldo's for a slice of pizza. I ordered and got a slice and I saw my reflection in the glass window and there I was eating a slice of pizza and I saw myself chewing automatically like a cow or some subhuman something and I thought: why bother putting food in your mouth and living another day? Which was odd, as I don't think things like that, I am a happy American person. And as I ate the crusts I looked back to the window and decided I had a double chin now and I was getting older, not on death's doorstep, but older, and looking it for once, and there I was chewing bland flavorless pizza looking fat and washed out in the fluorescent light of Baldo's window reflection and I was all alone while everyone else in the world was out on a date or laughing or dancing or having fun or experiencing love in some form somewhere—wait, focus on the thought: making love somewhere, in each other's arms, touching, another human being's face and lips just THAT far away before you kissed them, and this wasn't some special occasion but what some people, MOST people did every night, and there I was fat and older chewing on a pizza all alone, and instead of a simple *I am very lonely*, which would have sufficed, the mind burst through some kind of previously untried barrier and it told me: *I have been lonely all my life*.

You should always ignore it when you hear *I have been lonely all my life* because that's crap, of course you haven't, and it's just a mood, a bad day, a nasty stretch of life and it will go away one of these days. But what staying power *I have been lonely all my life* has once it gets into your head. I left the pizza place and passed old people, old New York old people, this middle-aged gay guy . . . yes, I said, like them: *I have been lonely all my life.* Oh what nonsense. Go home and go to bed. But going home in the early evening meant passing our landlady Mrs. Dellafini, the widow, and I avoided her because she might talk to me and bore me, bore me about her cat, the cat who was her only friend . . . and I thought, see? There are a lot of us, and like Mrs. Dellafini *I have been lonely all my life.*

I went and sat in Father Demo Square and could not stop finding depressing things to think about. From out of the blue I thought: Emma will one day break her celibacy streak with someone. It's bound to happen one day, isn't it? She said so that time at the beach. And you, Gil, won't be the guy she breaks it with. Okay. Fine. Right. I am going to go away and make my own life anyway. A theater life. Why, I bet Monica and Tim and Donna and the crew are at McKinley's Bar on 44th right now. It's their night to work and they'll be there. I should go to them. No, I'm in a shit mood. Do you want to sit here and sink deeper into your shit mood? No, I'll call McKinley's and tell them I'm coming. I called McKinley's and they were there and I told them I was coming.

I went down to the subway. Lots of lonely people on the subway, I noticed. Lonely lonely people. *I have been lonely*—

NO. STOP THINKING THAT.

And so I get to McKinley's and as I go in I hear them scream and welcome me and usher me back to Our Regular Booth, and I regret this already. I do not like my friends.

"Gil, Gil, you're just in time," said Monica, waving me over to sit beside her. "I was just telling them this—you know the story . . ."

I knew all her stories. She told these stories we all had heard and stranger yet, these stories we were all *there* for the real-live source of, so when she embellished and exaggerated and turned her co-star's flub or messed-up line into an onstage twenty-minute ordeal (which we all knew it wasn't) why didn't we all speak up and go: Monica, this is crap. Back to reality, please? No, we could not have done that any more than we could have said Tim, you'll spend your whole life as a techie being taken for granted, and it's not as if you're that good, and maybe that explains why you'll be a lifetime Venice Theater wash-up. And Donna, you're so busy inventing what you think we want to hear about your make-believe social life that you don't have time to consider that you don't really *have* a social life, or a lover, or a chance of getting one anytime soon. And as for you Crandell—

NO. CUT THIS OUT.

"Gil? Earth to Gil?" Monica laughed her chipmunk laugh. "Earth to Gil?" Did she think that was clever? "Wake up, boy, are you listening?"

Yes Monica, yes Monica.

"And anyway, you know Fuskins, what an old turd he is, so there we are and he flubs the line, he says . . ."

I look at my friends whom I can't stand tonight. Donna is laughing at Monica, bated breath, waiting to tell her own story, the story she is making up right now, watch her eyes, she'll outdo Monica, just watch . . . Tim is bored. Why doesn't he say he's bored? This little circle is his whole life, isn't it? God, I don't want to be in that position. Or am I soon to be in that position? *I have been lonely all my—*

ORDER A DRINK NOW.

"Is something wrong, babe?" Monica was irritated because I usually back her up, set her up, push her stories through. Why do I do that? I don't like her at all, and my not liking her at all is exacerbated by the fact that I slept with her and now I'm stuck being nice to her. Not that I wouldn't sleep with her tonight. Maybe I should sleep with her tonight. Would she?

In this spot here: an hour, two hours, two and a half hours of boring theater talk, recycled gossip, tales told for Time No. 78.

Tim had to be going. Donna too, with the usual show of her travails of riding to Harlem on the subway, men men men, animals, she'd be lucky to get to her apartment without getting raped, at least that's what she was hoping for, ha ha ha . . . Why are you making light of rape, Donna—has it gotten to that? You wouldn't like to be raped, you really shouldn't talk like that and be even more pathetic than you are. There was this story they told about Deanne Potter in my high-school class: that Deanne Potter was this really fat and ugly girl (although her face was sort of pretty, you could see it attached to a thinner girl) and she had bad acne and an abusive mother, no father, and that she would go down to Scoville Park and sleep on park benches hoping to be raped by somebody . . . could that have been true? AND WHY THINK OF IT NOW? What was with me tonight?

It was me and Monica and Crandell now.

"Well," said Crandell, nodding knowledgeably, squinting like a fireman assessing a burning building, "it's down to the three of us. Yep, we stick together, you gotta give us that. I can see it, Gil will run the theater one day, Monica will get all the leading female roles, and I'll get the male ones—we'll run the place. If we can just *hold out.*" He nodded again, dramatically. "If we can make it, against the odds—show those bastards."

What kind of two-bit scene are you playing here, Crandell? What is this soap opera? Why does it get that way with you at this level of drinking, at this time of night? (I'm thinking this, not saying it, of course.)

I will walk Monica home. Monica thinks this is strange, she can walk home by herself, but great, great, she'll like the company. Away we go to the Upper West Side, up Ninth Avenue.

Talk, talk, talk.

"No Gil, we haven't seen a lot of each other," she said at some point. "We used to talk an awful lot, didn't we?"

Not only talk, I say, nudging her with my elbow, heh-heh.

And then she laughs, a weren't-we-once-foolhardy-and-young kind of laugh. She's playing some kind of scene here too. But then, so am I.

"I was telling Paul the other day about you, about how you forgot that time to put out the ashtray for Garner Fuskins . . ."

Paul?

". . . and how we were hiding you—here Gil, get under this, get under that, in this closet, in that closet—do you remember? My god, I thought, we *all* thought, he was going to kill you . . ."

Paul?

"And then he found you and nearly throttled you and I thought, my god, he's going to kill Gilbert, I have to help and I had this scene I was going to play, I was going to run up to him and pretend we had just gotten engaged and that someone had filled in for you even though your name was on the assignment sheet—"

PAUL? I finally ask.

"The guy I'm living with."

And so back to Brooklyn, back to Brooklyn and the subway the other lonely people were on tonight, all the people who could say *I have been lonely all my life*, except I could say more than that, I could say *I WILL be lonely all my life*. If you can help it you should never get to *I have been lonely all my life,* and having decided that, you should NEVER let it slip even lower to *I WILL be lonely all my life*. Or else, you'll be as depressed as me in 1977 and you wouldn't want that.

"Where the hell have you been?" asked Lisa in a pinched whisper when I got back, the second I got in the door.

Out.

"You don't know what I went through tonight here with Emma."

I thought Lisa was on her usual Bob-date and Emma was out watching a movie or sulking or with Mandy. But no.

"We were at the hospital, that's where. Emma thought she was having a heart attack, she couldn't breathe and was gasping for air and I thought it would pass—"

Where was Emma now?

"In her bedroom sleeping, with twenty milligrams of Valium in her. She was passing out so I called an ambulance."

How were we going to pay for an ambulance? Good god.

"And we went to Brooklyn General and they told her it was some kind of panic attack, nervous breakdown stuff, and she wasn't having a heart attack."

Well thank goodness.

Lisa flopped down in a chair. "And while we were there I talked to a doctor and told her she was all strung out because of her imaginary brain tumor and he made us an appointment with a neurologist, for a CAT scan."

Neither of us said anything.

Then Lisa looked up with a half-smile. "So. How was *your* night?"

The hospital called confirming the appointment at an East Side clinic, a week from the next Friday. We braced ourselves.

"I'm getting a CAT scan tomorrow," Emma announced the day before, cheerily. "No big deal. I'm not nervous. They just put your head in a vice and inject things and . . . and the thought of it makes me want to die beforehand. Why am I doing this? To hear the wonderful news that I'm going to die of a brain tumor, lose my mind. You guys, wanna go for a pizza? We can get mushroom and onion in anticipation of the *vegetable* I'm going to become . . ."

Black Friday, the day of Emma's CAT scan, was rainy and we couldn't get a cab to show up and Emma paced around the apartment nervously, not speaking to us except to say something disparaging and defeatist. The cab arrived and Lisa and I waited in a sterile white modern hospital waiting room at Lenox Hill for the whole thing to be done with.

"What if there's something?" Lisa said, tossing a year-old *Time* magazine back on the coffee table.

There won't be, I said. Her symptoms are six weeks old and most of them are self-induced and hysterical and she read a book about brain tumors and she told them all the right things to get them to give her a CAT scan.

Emma emerged, white as a corpse, clutching a handbag with an unsure hand. We went out for coffee, heard about it, assured her nothing was wrong, that everything would be all right, while Emma just looked into her coffee and said, "No, no. I know in my heart I have a brain tumor—from the moment I thought of it I knew that's what it was." And this went on for a week, then a phone call came for her to come back and talk to a Dr. Shears at Lenox Hill. She asked if her friends could come with her and Dr. Shears said yes.

No one got any sleep the night before the appointment. Lisa took a day off work—she told her boss the story and no one is so heartless not to let someone accompany a friend to the brain-tumor doctor—and I called in sick. We waited and I prepared myself internally for the worst. How would I deal with this? Would we stay with her, care for her? Send her back to her parents she couldn't abide with the suburban Catholicism and her Aunt Leonie's miracle-working priests? But what a burden it would be . . . and yet we had a duty toward her. Somewhere in this gray inner discussion was a sense of unfulfilled love to make it all the more poignant. When I play Romeo, I told myself, trying to compensate, at least I can associate the experience of losing Emma, the one I loved, the one—it came to me right there—who was the Love of My Life, whatever that would be worth to anybody—

"Would you please come this way? Dr. Shears will see you now." The receptionist, cold from years of ushering people in to hear the worst, took us into another office mechanically. Emma sat in a big chair between us; Lisa held her hand. Dr. Shears came in with a folder marked Gennaro. Dr. Shears was a light-skinned black woman, cigarette pinched in her lips, a look of permanent harassment on her face. She coughed, put the cigarette out, only to fish through her white robe for the pack and bring out another cigarette, and then she took her chair, looking through Emma's folder, a look of annoyance on her face.

"Gennaro?" she said. Emma cleared her throat to identify herself. "Yes, well," said Dr. Shears, "you're perfectly fine except for being a selfish little girl who's wasting my time and somebody's money."

Emma blanched, beginning to say something—

"No, now girl, I get about thirty-five patients a week for CAT scans, right?" Dr. Shears talked through the cigarette. "And I'd say a good half of 'em are some other illness or stress problem, and one or two have some possibility of a tumor, but I get at least 40% people like you, people convinced they have a brain tumor so much you might think they actually want one. Now I've seen your type, several times a week so don't you lay one on me—you told me you had a *half-year* history of headaches and fainting and dizziness and insomnia and all kinds of stuff and I am inclined to believe, looking at this report, that you are one more New York girl who needed an analyst and not a CAT scan. This city's full of sick people who need time on my CAT scanner and you took up some of it. Which I don't appreciate."

Emma couldn't speak, she started to say something, when Dr. Shears got up.

"Come on with me, girl. We're gonna go down the hall and take you on a little tour."

Wordlessly we followed.

Dr. Shears put an arm around Emma, changing tone, softening. "Now baby I'm not trying to hurt you, but you can't go and do this kind of thing every week now, hm? I just want to show you some'n and you can go on home with your friends, okay sugah?"

We walked down the white ammonia-scented hallways, everything terrifyingly sterile, ultra-hospital, fluorescent and sanitary. Dr. Shears stopped before a room, the door next to a big glass observation window, the curtains pulled shut. She opened the door and we went in. It was dark, the curtains were closed to the outside window too.

"Light hurts Mrs. Gonzalez's eyes," she whispered to us, "that is, the days she can see."

Mrs. Gonzalez lay in a bed before us, a not yet middle-aged woman, staring into the void, briefly stirring as Dr. Shears approached her side; then she stared about strangely, some other-than-human energy seeming to motivate her, make her head dart about.

"Hello Señora Gonzalez," said Dr. Shears sweetly, taking the woman's hand. The woman seemed panicked. "No," Dr. Shears went on, "no, honey, there there, it's me. It's all right, it's all right." Then Dr. Shears looked up at us. "She can't hear us because last week she went deaf, but I believe people have a sense of what's going on around them, so positive thoughts now, don't say nothing you wouldn't want her to hear." Mrs. Gonzalez began to say something incomprehensible, words, sort of, and a name over and over.

"Mrs. Gonzalez has two lovely children who come to see their Mommy every other day, Miss Gennaro. Mrs. Gonzalez came to us a month and a half ago." Dr. Shears motioned for Emma to come over by Mrs. Gonzalez's side. "Come on . . ." I noticed the straps holding Mrs. Gonzalez to the bed. "Miss Gennaro you come on and hold Mrs. Gonzalez's hand. Touchin' is important."

Emma, in utter misery, did as she was told.

Then we went back to the office.

"About eight weeks ago Mrs. Gonzalez came to us and she sat in the chair you're sittin' in Miss Gennaro," said Dr. Shears, lighting another cigarette, "and I had to tell her her thirty-eight-year-old life was at an end because she had a tumor a mere half-inch into inoperable territory, and that meant slowly losing her mind, her vision, her identity and having her children and husband watch it all, and there ain't a damn thing I can do about it." Dr. Shears looked seriously at Emma. "But I sure as hell can get your folder off my desk. Now don't you go down to Columbia or Sloane-Kettering and pull this routine again—you go home with your friends and get yourself an analyst or a boyfriend or whatever and get your life straightened out and get your *healthy* life on track, and be damn happy you ain't gonna be Mrs. Gonzalez this year." Emma looked at her folded hands in her lap. "Now there are some forms you gotta put your name on and Miss Driscol will bring 'em to you." Dr. Shears said it was nice to meet us both (Lisa and me), shook our hands, ushered us out and gave us a card of an East Side analyst, saying, "I got a hefty supply line going from the brain-tumor clinic to the psychiatrist's couch; I oughta get a commission." Then she laughed this light musical laugh and went back somehow to her uneneviable work.

Lisa and I stood there a moment. Lisa said slowly, "I feel so sorry for Mrs. Gonzalez. I feel we degraded her being in there and I feel . . . degraded myself somehow. My life should not have had this episode."

I'm sure Emma feels like shit now, I said, and we shouldn't add anything to that.

"There is no humor in this," Lisa said. "I can't redeem this in any way."

And we took a silent ride home in a cab, through the drizzle. Emma got out of the cab first, and stammered that she was going to set up an appointment with the analyst and fill the Valium prescription the hospital had given her on the heart-attack night and she might go to a movie and just be by herself for a while and we said sure.

"God I hate hospitals," Lisa said as we entered our apartment, all gray and cool for a change. "First time since this June that I've been to a . . ." She checked herself. "I'll make some tea."

Been to a what? A hospital? Was Lisa sick too? Lisa gave me a look that inquired whether I picked up on what she almost said, and I gave her a quizzical look back saying, yes, what is it you want to tell me? "I'll make the tea," she said again.

Were you in a hospital, Lisa? I asked.

Silence.

You don't have to tell me, I added. No one goes for any good reason to a hospital and I wasn't in a mood to hear anything bad anymore.

I heard her fill the kettle in the kitchen with water, turn on the stove; she came in and set down two teacups:

"I had an abortion, Gil. Remember when I told you I cried on the subway and told the lady I had an abortion? Well I *had* had an abortion."

This was shaping up to be a HAPPY HAPPY DAY.

"Bob's fault," she added, then shaking her head: "I mean, both our faults really. But it was Bob."

This hasn't made it into the etiquette books yet, has it? Upon Hearing of One's Close Friend's Abortion. I said I was sorry.

"Well I wasn't sorry to have it," she said matter-of-factly.

The kettle whistled. Time out.

"Don't tell Emma, not that you would. I've never told anyone, especially Bob."

I won't tell a soul, I said.

"I'm telling you because seeing Mrs. Gonzalez—I mean, that, *that* is tragedy, not my little abortion, you know? I'd been down about it, depressed and all—not that being depressed around this apartment would stand out."

Tension-releasing laughter.

"I'm glad I'm talking about it," she went on, pouring our tea, sitting in the chair (her overcoat still not off, mine neither), cupping her hands around the warm mug. "I knew from the second Bob and I took a chance that it was risky and I should have . . . I don't know. Anyway, I missed a period, went to a female clinic, the one I went to for endometriosis down in the Village a few years back, great supportive lesbian nurses, female doctors. And I said I might get hysterical, which wasn't true—I just wanted it over with and I didn't want to *feel* anything because I'm a coward and I wanted *plenty* of drugs, so I told them I might get hysterical and they . . . and they gave me plenty of drugs. I was like punchy through the whole thing—like at the dentist, I made jokes and stuff. I saw them come at me with the, you know, hose-thing and, ha, I thought, shit Lisa, you coulda done this at home yourself with the Hoover and saved $250, you know?"

I said I was glad it wasn't too horrible.

"No there was just one moment, uh, like right when I think it came out. I mean I wanted this out. If I feel even a tinge of guilt, even a passing thought of what this fetus might have been, it instantly comes to me: did you want to have this kid, out of wedlock, ruin your life? Its life? I mean there was no doubt."

No none at all, I said.

"No doubt at all. I was just there going come on, get this out, get this thing over with, before I start thinking about this thing as a . . . as a child or something, before I start thinking about being a mother, before I know whether it's a boy or a girl, while it's a thing."

Yes.

"So there I was, in the stirrups and all"—here Lisa's voice turned thick, having kept up the patter long as she could—". . . I thought I want this thing out, out, out, and then it *came* out, and all I could think then was . . . my god. It's out. That was the end of that."

I didn't know, had no idea, she was very brave—

"Oh it's not that big a deal—or rather, it's as big a deal as you want to make it. And these days, it . . . I couldn't afford one more big deal, you know? And—well, yes, there was one hysterical side effect, that whole business about marrying Bob. I mean, most women get married when they're pregnant, right?

Not *after* they're not pregnant anymore. I was thinking in reverse, trying to erase it or something. You can marry Bob, I told myself, but that won't make it a miscarriage—well, just, forget I ever said that. Marry Bob," she said smiling, between sips of tea. "He is SO bad in bed. Who'da thought that clown coulda pulled back the bow and let one rip like that?" And she laughed, shaking her head, amazed at her own life in her own words, and I laughed too. Then after the laughter died down: "Oh mercy. Mercy mercy. I'm gonna go it alone for a while. Single woman on her own. I'm looking forward to that."

We were never as close, Lisa and I, as that moment. I miss being that close to her. In a way I am still close to her, I am close in memory, and you would think being close and enjoying being close would prevent two people from drifting apart, but you'd be wrong.

And that was it for the Apartment, a phase of life come to a fairly dismal end, like all happiness, beaten down into the ground, squeezed like a dishrag (appropriate image for that year) till every drop is wrung out and there's nothing left. Good riddance to that year. A lot of nights, I seem to recall, where it seemed I had been lonely all my life.

But prosperity was just around the corner. Sort of.

1978

SO let's join Gil the next spring. Put that apartment behind him—let's watch him cut a swath through that wild singles New York groovin' social scene, let's see him take that New York Theater World by storm!

Hey Dew, I call out to Dewey Dennis. Can we have a talk?

"Sure Gil, I've been meaning to talk to you . . ." And up we go to his office, his office with the poster of the cat hanging from a trapeze, the poster of him in *Midsummer Night's Dream* as Lysander in a toga, from a production back in his college days 150 years ago. He obviously kept the poster to remind people that he once took off his shirt in front of an audience and they didn't laugh. One was tempted to picture him in his potbelly now wearing that toga—

"So you understand where I'm coming from, don't you, Gil?"

(Dewey is talking at me, so I tune in.) Yessir, I say. I was curious about the Shaw festival this coming summer. It seems to me I should be part of the repertory company. There are a lot of young male roles, and frankly sir, I've done an awful lot of spear-carrying around here this year.

Dewey clears his throat. Uh-oh, something tells me. Now you've done it, boy . . .

"You know, Gil," said Dewey, leaning back in his chair, putting his arms behind his head, "I'm not the kind of guy who pulls his punches. I like to tell it straight."

Yessir. Keep those clichés a comin'. (I didn't say that out loud.)

". . . but I think it's best to put it straight out, lay it on the line, you know? I don't think you have a future with the Venice Theater." A pause. Was I supposed to say something?

". . . And I think you know that we *like* you, respect you as a professional—and you're a professional, Gil, no one thinks other than that, Schmeen, Sr., Schmeen, Jr.—you're top of the line, make no mistake about that."

Nixon always said "make no mistake about that."

". . . But face it, be a realist here. We don't need that many young teen, young adult roles. You look a little young for us here. We got boys coming out our ears here. Don't take this wrong, Gil, you are good, real good, *damn good,* and no one's saying you're not. You've got a future somewhere, I know it."

Somewhere, but not the Venice, he was telling me.

"I'm sorry to have to be the one to tell you this, but you did ask what your prospects were here and I thought it was fair to tell you, not hand you some line of bull."

That was rough. But you know . . . not *that* rough.

I had been restless for some time—I knew I should be moving on. You see, I didn't respect Dewey Dennis or the Venice Theater enough to get upset. I wanted to say fine, Dewey, just fine, I'll leave and go on to better things than here and in some small way you must envy me for leaving this BACKWATER, this nothing place—and admit it, Dew, you know this is nowhere, and even if I go do regional theater in Illinois I'm not here which is nowhere and in a way you're doing me a Big Favor. I'd say that mental response is about 60% how I felt, and 40% how I wish I'd felt, but more true than not true.

So I get home and tell Daniel, my new roommate (he also works at the Venice).

"Oh gee man, that's tough," said Daniel, about to open a box of some instant dinner.

I don't need the place, I said.

"Yeah, you oughta go . . . you oughta go, like, someplace else."

Good idea, Daniel.

I'd always rather callously ignored Daniel—and the next thing I know he comes over and gives me a heartfelt hug: "Hope like you're not too upset."

What a SWEET guy. How does he survive in this town? Why hasn't the theater world eaten him alive? I'll tell you about Daniel. He had this cockroach-infested flat in Hell's Kitchen. Hell's Kitchen used to be dangerous and full of ethnic flavor, now it's just dangerous. Life was getting normal again though, living with a guy, a bland guy, a guy whose idea of a good time was planning lighting-board designs for famous plays. I liked him, a techie devoted to his craft, a life small and contained and lived in such a way that it would not spill over into mine.

"Oh god, macaroni and cheese again," he'd say from the hot plate near the sink which was the extent of our kitchen. "I'm so sick of macaroni and cheese."

He was not the best conversationalist in the world. He had a girlfriend, but once I took a look at her I didn't feel envious. She wasn't ugly (her name was Lucy), she was just bland like he was and they were bland together, sitting in our living room in front of his black-and-white set watching the entire evening's fare, from 7 p.m. to the news, Lucy and Daniel hand in hand. Somewhere in the middle of the news, Daniel would look at Lucy and Lucy would look at Daniel and one of them would say, "Well, I guess I/you had better be getting back," and then Daniel would accompany Lucy home on the subway to Long Island City, which was in Queens and therefore this was an hour-long process.

I enjoyed his hour out of the house. I could call Lisa (now living on the Upper West Side, on the fringe of Harlem, in a run-down but interesting neighborhood) and I could call Emma, who had slept on Janet's sofa for a month before moving in with one of Janet's weirder friends, Jasmine, and they lived in Williamsburgh, Brooklyn, in a fifth-floor walk-up in a Puerto Rican neighborhood that from all reports was the bottom rung of New York housing. I thought, of course, I'd keep up with both of them frequently, but it was more like once a month. Everyone got very busy. Lisa had let her hair grow out and got a six-month stint at another marketing agency, she'd met this guy named Jim (surprise, surprise, a new boyfriend) and she was doing all right. Emma cut her hair (which I thought was a *big* fashion mistake), but Jasmine was real counterculture and druggy and was big into punk music and sang with this band on weekends and Emma was enjoying fitting in with that. Fine. Everyone has his or her life, I have mine.

Except mine was a little bit more boring than theirs. Daniel set the pace, I'm afraid. His hour out of the house was a relief because we were always passing and bumping into one another there in that small place. New York City is often thought to be such a lonely city and there's a lot to say on that subject, but there is much more to say on the subject that New York City is a city in which you *can't* be alone, in which you'd *pay* to be alone, from the morning crowded subways, to the elevators up the skyscrapers, and the crowded offices and cubicles and bank lines and post-office lines and lunch-counter lines and movie lines and sheer rubbing shoulders with the eleven million who use Manhattan every day, what you wouldn't give to be ALONE with no other people, to talk like a madman to yourself or sing with the radio or eat cereal from the box while you lie about the sofa with nothing on watching inexcusably bad TV, or whatever. Just ridding yourself of the throng for a little while. I had one hour, one measly hour.

Daniel had been living there alone but he had needed more money when the rent went up and decided to put up an ad at the Venice and I answered it and there we were. It seemed like *his* place, and I never shook feeling like a guest—particularly as there was not drawer space for me and I used my suitcase as a clothes cabinet. Felt like a traveling salesman. We had a

1940s refrigerator which filled up in an instant (if we'd defrosted it we could have fit more in there, but . . .) and so I bought lots of cookies and dry foods and breads and ate a lot of hotdogs from the street vendors and never cooked anything for myself. Daniel would, however, cook for himself and sometimes for Lucy and they would sit in the living room and you'd hear the clink of forks on plates as they ate silently, bland food, bland people. They'd wash the dishes (it certainly was nice being away from the sink after the apartment with Emma and Lisa) and they'd make quiet sink-talk and then it was TV again. I am not this dull, I told myself with some frequency.

One night Daniel asked how long I would be gone when I was going to see a movie and I said two hours or so, and then I figured out he wanted to sleep with Lucy in the apartment and I should disappear . . . so I said sure, I'll stay out four hours, which I did. When you have to spend four hours doing nothing you are really aware of the time. I could kill four hours—bookstores, movies, diners, just sitting, having a drink somewhere with the paper—by myself *easy* when I did it under my own volition, but that night just went on and on. Everywhere I went I was bored. Couples populated the world. I was feeling blue and lonely and in need of companionship. Internal dialogue:

Hey go to McKinley's and see Monica and Tim and Donna and Crandell . . . Nah, they're boring, you just saw them the other night, not to mention every day at lunch.

Hey, go and see Lisa. Nah, she's dating someone and if you just dropped in she'd be making love or something and, no, just no.

Emma? Williamsburgh is years away and you'd have to hang out with Jasmine and her band friends and smoke drugs strong enough to kill you. (That was unfair, I'd only met her once—a real space case, she seemed.) I'm doing fine without Emma, anyway. I'm glad she cut her hair and looks uglier; she's looking all anemic and run-down too. Well, maybe the analysts she's going to will help. Any more social options?

Go out and pick up a stranger and take them home. And do what? And go where? A disco? With spinning disco balls and neon and lighted floors and cheap Californian-looking sleaze-monsters wearing open shirts and medallions and white disco suits, dancing to vacuous music thump thump thump? Not my scene, man. This was the Golden Age of the Singles Bar and I was not part of it, me, in the prime of my youth.

There were a lot of suggestions that never failed to play in my head and I never failed to reject them. Try to get back with Monica . . . naaaah. Ask out Catherine, the pretty new actress at work who flirted with you two months ago . . . naaaah. Get out Connie's business card and call her at work and have lunch or dinner and pick up where you left off . . . naaaaah—wait a minute. Maybe Connie dropped out of sight because you didn't pursue her. Could be, but then she always made all the aggressive, initiating moves. Yeah, it wasn't my place to insist on seeing her—she was richer, classier . . . no those are dumb reasons for letting things fade. But where would I take her? A pizza stand, on my capital of $5 spree money?

I kept thinking about it. Daniel and Lucy were watching cop shows in the living room, I was lying on my bed reading the same page of a book over and over. Call Connie. Do it boy. What if she turns me down, makes some kind of excuse, gee, she can't make it this week . . . Well then at least you tried.

So the next day I called down at Golam Brothers and after ten reconnections I dug her up in Bond Research. What was she doing there, I asked.

"Dying, that's what. A major career setback. Gil, I thought you weren't at all interested in me—"

Connie that was nonsense, I just couldn't call you up, take you out on a date for a decent evening compared to—

"What is this? Courtly love? The middle ages? Gil, guys don't have to pick up the bill anymore. I'll pick up the bill . . . oooh, something's up, gotta go. Dinner my place on Friday? I'm a great cook—"

Sure, sure—over in Jersey?

"I'm on the East Side now, babe. Lexington and 85th," and she gave me her address and apartment number. Eight o'clock.

Well. And that was that.

Night of the Big Date: I shower and wash everything there is to wash just in case. My nice jacket which is J. C. Penney's and synthetic, but what can I do? Tie is not wide enough, stupid colors too—I only have two ties and one was stained. The collar of my white shirt is permanently gray, my socks have small holes in them and these shoes are unpolishable and worn out. Well the jeans were all right. I WAS INADEQUATE IN EVERY WAY. No, no, calm down—no pre-date panic. How old am I? Good god, twenty-fucking-five and here I am utterly inexperienced at dates. Does she expect me to stay over? Should I make a pass?

Will I be late? No, too early. I walk around the block three times. I bought wine, two bottles of Liebfraumilch. That was baby sophomore-in-college wine, wasn't it? Well it was five dollars a bottle which was a lot for me but I probably bought shit. Too late now. I rang the bell.

Up the stairs, down the hall, knock on the door. Pause.

Connie looked like one-hundred-thousand-million bucks. I was a pile of dung, but then we've gone over this ground before.

"A little vermouth perhaps?" she said, sweeping through her apartment, as I was escorted in and looked around. "Sit, sit . . ." It was a decorated apartment. I'd never been in a decorated New York apartment.

Nice decorations, I said, as if her place were a Christmas tree—oh so very very *clever*, how DO I do it?

"Did it myself, and spent the whole of this year's salary already. But I want to entertain a lot. Like tonight. Vermouth with a twist of lime?"

Sure.

"Here you go," she said, handing me the vermouth. I would have drunk drain unclogger if she had handed it to me. Come to think of it, my first vermouth, I think I *was* drinking drain unclogger.

"Vermouths are in this year. Campari's big in the cafés of Europe these days. Are you a Pernod fan?"

Pernod. Opera composer? Impressionist? French poet? Sure, I said, hoping it didn't taste like the vermouth.

"Good, we can have some of that next."

News for Gil: it tastes *worse* than vermouth. But I drank that dutifully too.

"An hors d'oeuvre?"

Yes I was starved. (Don't guess Connie has made peanut-butter crackers—a hunch tells me . . .)

Connie runs to the kitchen, a sleek modern Kitchen of the '70s, functional, full of amazing gadgets and food processors and tools. I haven't been making eye contact with the hostess; I am shy and stupid things are coming forth from my mouth. But I take a chance to observe her here: hair longer than last time, great silk patterned dress and a stylish apron on around it . . . Why did she need an apron? Surely Connie never spills anything. She was messing with some sauce on the stovetop—what a graceful way to move, her wrist and the tinkling bracelets, she brings the spoon to her lips to sample the sauce . . . a pause, she judges, she winces, she grabs something from the spice rack and pours it into her palm, then taking a pinch sprinkles it into the pot. Deadly serious business this sauce. I thought under the impetus of vermouth and Pernod: pay that kind of attention TO ME.

"Hmmm," she said seriously.

I decided to make jokes about my complete lack of class. If the sauce doesn't work out, I said, we can just use ketchup.

"Gee," she said playing along, "ketchup on TV dinners? Is that done?"

The dinner table was all set up—napkins finer than any single article of clothes I owned, plates featured in dishwashing detergent ads (I could see myself in them), flowers. The woman had flowers on the table. The plates matched the tablecloth design (cloth was beige, there was a brown fine stripe on the china); wineglasses and water glasses and several pieces of silverware. I did not deserve to eat there. While I am preoccupied with the dinner table I discover that Connie has been talking at me for a while about her career:

". . . and as we didn't get along and he's Chicago and I'm Harvard it was inevitable that I transfer out of that department. Well fine, but there's nothing opening up. Bond Research was taking the best deal; I'll get out of it after making my mark. I realized, in a way, that's good, good being in the unglamour departments, because you can shine. Sales is thankless right? And yet in Sales, if you're good, you have made money for the company—they're not going to ignore that. Over in Investment you can bust your butt and no one knows who did what good thing, you never get credit for what you do. How's the Venice?"

Wake up Gil, your turn . . . Well I told her about my depressing little talk with Dewey Dennis, where he said I didn't have a future there.

"And you're still there? You really need an agent. Have you auditioned anywhere yet?"

Well uh, I will when I get some time off—

"*Take* the time off. Tell Dennis what's-his-name if he isn't going to cast you, you need time to audition; and if he wants you to clear out, he'll let you look for work on company time. Don't be too conscientious here. Don't let 'em take advantage of you."

The truth was I was lazy and scared. I didn't confess this, though.

Dinner was served.

"You like the duck?"

It was the World's Best Duck.

"Now you're just saying that. Really?"

You know it, Connie, and I know it—it was the World's Best Duck.

"You marinate it in this game consommé for three days—well, okay, I thought of it Wednesday, two days in this case. Then you baste it in Armagnac. The orange is squeezed freshly over it."

It was liquid duck, it fell apart on the palate, dissolved into an explosion of sensations, rare almost-tastes, suggestions, depths . . . Where'd she learn to cook like this? Her mother?

"Ha. Mom was doing well to open a can of beans. I picked this up in France. I lived there two summers, in between Harvard. Paid for it myself—worth every penny."

France, huh?

"I love France," she went on, barely able to consume her food for all her elaborate hand gestures. "I belong there." She nodded toward the posters around the room. "Those posters," she said between bites, "they're all from art galleries, special showings while I was in Paris. There's only Paris and New York. Have you been to Europe?"

No, but I wanted to go one day, I said. (Gee really? The Art of Conversation is dead tonight . . .)

"French cuisine is the finest in the world. Italian is right behind it, but Italy's hot, right? A bowl of pasta, a heavy Tuscan soup, then a main course—pow, you're out for the afternoon, asleep in an hour, sluggish all day. You get up from a meal in Lyons"—she kissed her fingertips, Frenchlike—"filled, satisfied, enriched in every way. It's perfectly geared to the climate, the life, which is what cuisine is about, isn't it?"

Yeah. Right.

"There's not a wine region in France where the cuisine isn't tailored to the character of the wine . . ."

And on and on she went while I sat there fascinated. This is the way to live, I said to myself, this is the way to be. Not "Oh my, all my problems, blah blah blah." There was knowledge out there, knowledge about art, literature, cooking, travel, and some people gave their minds to it, and others sat around, whined and watched a lot of TV. Not mentioning any names here.

"Oh I could go on all night about this," she broke off. "Don't get me onto the subject of France. I'm uncorkable. Speaking of that—would you do the honors?" She cocked an eye toward my second bottle of wine (I bet I bought shit wine; I bet she knew it was shit and was just being nice; I felt inadequate for the 500th time that evening). I got the corkscrew and tried as suavely as possible to open it—please Connie, keep talking, don't watch me foul this up . . .

"I like the French attitudes about sex and male-female relationships. We're *so* off the track in the United States. This equality thing."

SHE of all people, not a feminist?

"No not at all. Mind you, I'll get everything *I* want. I don't have much in common with most women anyway, in that I never would get in a position where a man could stop me from doing what I wanted to do no matter what age I was born in. You act like you're subservient and you get treated that way."

Yeah, I said, devil's advocate (me the big feminist here, ha ha), and I said that in Paris, say, of the last century she would have had to have been a courtesan to gain power, money, influence.

"I know, I know—that'da made things a lot simpler for poor Connie, huh? I'd have *killed* to live back then. Oh Gil, you tool a man around for a month, you get a necklace; a year, opera tickets and great dinner; two years, a flat—and for what? Putting out for a Frenchman. Now *that* was what I call a deal. Connie's on Wall Street, she knows a good deal when she hears one. Of course, today, sex with men is *out,* a good feminist is a lesbian these days, if you read what the leaders say."

I wonder what Janet and Connie would say to each other. Would there be bloodshed? Would they understand each other?

"Most feminists who take this hard-line, political lesbianism stuff couldn't get laid if they had to," Connie continued.

Bloodshed.

"All the things women traditionally are good at, have done for centuries—courtesans, mothers, raising the children, high priestesses, you name it—that's out now. The object is to go out into the business world and be as shallow and stupid and conniving and empty as your male counterpart, dress like a nun, sue the company for fifty million if someone pinches your behind at the water cooler, no sex, no femaleness, no fun." She sighed. "I hate all the actors now," she said, changing tacks.

WHAT?

Connie smiled, blushed a little for letting her thought slip out like that. "No, no, not you, I mean film actors. All the sensitive and caring and sharing and supportive men of the '70s, men who cry, men who share in the child rearing, men who give up their careers for their wives' careers. No thank you. I don't like that at all." She pointed her fork at me, raising an eyebrow. "I don't trust it. I don't believe it. When men stop acting like bastards something's up. I can deal with a man acting like a typical man, I can outthink him, predict him. I can't deal with the Mr. Sensitives, the '70s househusbands on *Donahue*—no way. And I'm so sick of gay men in this town, give me a break from that too."

Lot of gays in the theater, I say, not exactly making headlines 'round the world with that observation.

"Yeah well, put 'em all in one place so they can meet each other and not get Connie all hot and bothered for nothing. I hate the '70s." She took a sip of wine, then sneered: "No style, no class, no flair. This city's idea of a good time is dressing up in polyester and dancing to noise. *This*, supposedly, qualifies as fashion."

Yeah, but the decade's been pretty peaceful. As someone who missed being eligible for Vietnam, let me tell you how much I appreciate that.

"Carter," she went on, rolling her eyes. "President Jimmy Carter—what a joke. That guy's gonna let the Shah fall because that one-term governor from white-trash land, that *peanut farmer* has had it occur to him that some people in the world aren't very nice sometimes."

Could be worse, I said. Governor Reagan, Moral Majority in tow, is waiting in the wings.

"Whadya mean *worse*? Worse than Carter addressing the nation in his jeans and sweaters? Worse than Rosalyn and her expensive-and-still-tacky pantsuits? You know, maybe as a neighbor in the building here, I wouldn't mind him, but as a president?" She smiled at me, sensing we were not aligned politically. But she minced no words: "I voted for Reagan in the primary and I was prepared to hang with Gerald Ford, but Carter getting elected is something I still can't believe. Mencken said the only thing to come out of Georgia worth a damn was Coca-Cola and I think he may have been right."

A Republican, huh? You know, this was the first time (save for born-again religious farm kids at Southwestern Illinois) that I ever had met someone young *claiming* to be Republican, proud of it, ready to take on all arguments about it.

"Reagan will knock Jimmy back to his sunday school class come the '80 elections, just you watch."

Reagan? Mr. B Movies?

"Yeah, Mr. B Movies," she said, getting up to clear away our plates. "He's the most persuasive, slickest packaging of a conservative agenda this century; the interests he represents are going to turn back Johnson's Great Society bullshit. But I don't want to talk politics, please." She took my plate.

Emma, my friend Emma, I mentioned, had a theory that Reagan was the Antichrist.

"I'm not much on Christs or Antichrists, but if he's going to cut my taxes, pour tons into the military-industrial complex and whip the economy into shape, I'll vote for him. I would sleep with Milton Friedman, so there. You mention your friend Emma a lot."

Didn't mean to, I said.

"Where does she work? What does she do?"

She wants to be a poet. She works for temp agencies, odd jobs.

"Has she published? Does she have an agent?"

No.

"Is she any good?"

I think so, but she's a bit shy with her stuff.

Connie put the dishes in the sink, muttering, "No one ever got anywhere being that. Shy, I mean."

No, I guess not.

Connie ran some water in the sink. In a moment she came back to the table with two brandy glasses. "Crème caramelles in a second. A little pre-dessert brandy?"

Sure. Pile it on, I can get used to living like this.

"This Emma," she said as she poured, "she's someone you're involved with at the moment?"

(Hmm, not wasting any time, is she?) Uh, well, I said, she was my roommate last year.

"So you've broken up?"

Why am I lying? Why am I trying to make Connie think Emma and I had an affair? That's a dumb question: for sexual credit, of course. But what I want to tell Connie is that I'm wildly attracted to her but that my social life to date has defeated me and I'm scared to make a move. Maybe if I hadn't met Emma—no, forget Emma, she has nothing to do with this evening.

"She was always rude to me on the phone, this Emma girl. Got the impression that she resented my being your friend." Connie resumed her place, after placing the crème caramelles before us.

Yes, I told her, Emma did resent her.

Connie continued eating, a trace of a smile between bites. "Whatever for? Could it be . . ."

Yes?

"Just a thought."

Silence for a minute—a minute in which I knew what she meant and she knew that I knew what she meant.

"Let's go in the living room," she said, rising.

I sat down on the plush sofa. She sat beside me, an inch away.

"Something wrong?" she asked, nestling in.

No, why do you ask?

"Oh it's just you seemed to jump a bit—the body language is all wrong, kid. Nervous about something?"

No, I said, nothing at all. (Calm down, I told myself, get realistic here . . .)

"What kind of music do you like?"

I told her I liked anything, that I would like to know what *she* liked, actually. She got up and slapped in a tape cassette of some classical piano music, very tinkly and romantic . . . no wait, here comes an orchestra, so that makes this a . . . a symphony? No, no, what's the word—Emma knew about classical music, why didn't anything rub off? Sonata. That's it. Nice sonata, I said.

Connie smiled, "It's a concerto actually—"

SHIT. CONCERTO, that's what I meant . . .

"I made this tape myself," she went on, leaning into me, a pressure ever so slight. I adjusted myself so I could be more leaned against. "It's sort of a favorites tape, I got five slow movements from Romantic piano concertos and put them back to back—this is Rachmaninoff's First, Chopin's First is next, then Brahms's Second—it took me ages to follow it, and now it's my favorite. Beethoven's Third and, the killer, Ravel's slow movement. I die every time I hear that one. I used to have a lover who put that on and I think of him everytime I hear it . . . You must have music like that."

Gee, what to say . . . Like, there's this Elton John song I slow-danced to with Karen Schmitt at the high-school prom but that wasn't going to cut it beside Chopin. Quick, what classical music did I know? William Tell Overture. Beethoven's duh-duh-duh-DUH Fifth Symphony. Flight of the Bumblebee. Yeah, that's it, I always think of my old lovers when I hear the Flight of the Bumblebee. I'm hopeless. I said there was lots of reminiscent music for me too, but I couldn't think of anything that really got to me.

"Mid-period Beatles slays me too," she said. "I can't even put them on anymore, nostalgia overwhelms me. I'm back at my high-school prom with Davie Epstein, in Brookline, Massachusetts. I'd gotten my Harvard acceptance and he was going to stay in Brookline and work in his Dad's real-estate office. Oh god."

Why didn't I say what I had to say about Karen Schmitt? Connie wasn't a snob, she wouldn't have sneered at me for not knowing classical music. She's sharing her thoughts with me and I'm being *worthless* here . . . I said that I envied her having specific memories like she had to the Beatles. The Beatles for me broke up when I was in tenth grade which doesn't mean I didn't remember them but they were my older brother's property, if you see what I mean.

"All that seems a long time ago," she said blankly.

Were you a campus protester?

"You kidding?" Connie smiled, and laughed a little, knocking her hair back. "Miss Reactionary here? I thought the governor shoulda turned the teargas on 'em, Ronnie Reagan-like."

We both laughed because she was obviously joking. At least, I think she was joking. Maybe she wasn't.

"Ever been in a demonstration, Gil? I have. It's just a mob enjoying itself. 'Let's go take the administration building!' And everyone goes yeahhhhh and then everyone runs to see how far they can get—it's a blast. I got caught in the one at Columbia when I was down here seeing my boyfriend. No one's honest enough to admit they were fun—they were all the most serious business in the world, all of them meaningful and pure, not a trace of levity, just a holy purpose. If you've ever been in one you know how it's just a mob getting out of hand, getting off on itself."

Yeah but they were protesting the Vietnam War which was worth making a little noise about, tearing up a little property over. If she had been a guy she would have had to go fight—

"College deferment."

Didn't she find that a little hypocritical?

"I'm just a realist, Gil. I'm not saying college deferment was fair, it wasn't. Lower-class whites and blacks fought Vietnam because they went to crummy schools, couldn't get into college given their environments. But that's how life's always worked. But we're talking politics again."

Yes, but I was learning a lot talking politics with her because it was becoming obvious I was falling for a very civilized Fascist. Hey, I'm thinking to myself, maybe Emma is right, you aren't this kind of person—you're not her class, you're not her type. What kind of future is remotely possible here? None. What's worse is that I don't have enough sophistication to argue with her, she would win every argument even though I was right. Nah, this is doomed. Maybe I should just get up and tell her I'll call again and just go away. There, I felt better already, the burden of having to sleep with her is off my shoulders and other parts of my body. I can relax. I can walk out of here a free man—

"I think you should stay here tonight," she said, putting a hand on my leg. "What do you say?"

I say nothing.

"You've been nervous all night, kid. If you were sitting over there worried about making a move or whether you should or not, or whether I liked you or . . . or whatever you were thinking, I think you should know it's all right . . ."

What was I going to say? Guess I'll know when I hear myself say it.

". . . and from the moment when I came backstage to see you

after the play, I think I knew where I wanted to take this relationship . . ."

It was like in those out-of-body experiences, where you look down and see yourself. I wished I was out of my particular body, come to think of it. I was just SO not ready for this.

". . . so you tell me, what do *you* think?"

After a minute, I said: gee, we've just gotten to know each other and all—

"If you want to," she said, moving closer, homing in—the heart is racing now—"then don't hestitate to tell me. No need to be nervous around me." She was an inch from my face. Great perfume, I notice. Figures.

Uh, I said, uh well, I don't know that I'm ready yet . . .

Connie smiled, undeterred. "You know," she said quietly, slowly, and very sexually, "that Emma girl's got you spooked, hasn't she? You are *this* far from falling in love with me, but she's got you afraid to step out of line."

I nodded. God, I was being vulnerable. I always thought it would be this miserable to be vulnerable and wimpy before a beautiful woman . . . but you know, vulnerability can take you a lonnnnng way. I don't think I'd ever realized that. It was beginning to dawn on me then that my virginlike fear and trembling might have had its appeal. Maybe I should play it out, keep up the act. Of course, then again, *what* act?

"Now," she said, her voice gravelly, her face very close to mine, kissing territory, "I think you should just consider stepping out of line. Hm? Think that's a good idea?" She put her hand behind my hair on my neck, slipping a finger between my neck and the collar.

You may be disappointed, I said.

"Ooooh no, no," she smiled, her lips fuller suddenly, that perfume having the intended effect. "I'm never disappointed. I always have a good time. In fact, let me tell you what. We don't have to do anything you don't want to, for starters. In time, I think we could think of many, many things to do." She scooted herself over to lean across my lap; her arm lowered to my back, the other hand came up to play with that dopey disco-age puffed-up haircut we guys thought looked so cool at the time. You oughta see my résumé picture. You oughta see the photos I have of myself—I look like Farrah Fawcett, feathered hair. YUCK. But I guess you don't care about my hair. I guess you want me to get on with this Sex Scene.

"Nooo, don't worry about a thing, kid. Ole Connie doesn't ever have a bad time. Because she's not after a quickie, a one-night stand, she's after a night of intimacy, of talking . . ." She tightened her grip on me. I felt it incumbent on me to slip my own hand up to her back. ". . . of telling stories, of getting to know one another—what better place than . . ." She nodded toward the door to the left of us.

The bedroom? I ask. (Boy, I'm really Einstein tonight . . .)

"Uh-huh," she said, slowly nodding. "Silk sheets. Cost this girl a fortune. Ever spent the night against silk sheets?"

I'd settle for *clean* sheets given how often I do laundry.

"Well then, I think for educational purposes you should stay over. Silk sheets and all."

I said that it had occurred to me that I was out of my depth. This was her last chance to opt out. She reassured me:

"Hey kid, I never slum it. I only go for class."

Class, me?

"No, I mean it, you're one classy dude—"

(Note to readers: cut the woman a break for "one classy dude," this was 1978. Those were important words for me and I'm sorry they were in '70s lingo.)

"—and you gotta drop those deadbeats."

You mean Emma.

She kissed me lightly; I could feel her breath on my lips a moment before she touched them with her own. "Uh-hm, I mean Emma. Cut her off." Another kiss. "Give her a little room, hm?" And another kiss. Okay, okay, I'm warming up here. "Let her know that there are other people in the world, people who are . . ." Pause. Come on, finish the sentence, Connie. ". . . willing to spend all night, I mean every single minute, I mean not wasting *a second*, making love to you." She moved in for the kill now, pinning me to the sofa, taking my head in her hands. "Would you like that?"

I said I thought I could fit it in my schedule.

"I know you'd like to, because it's been a while since the woman you love has been doing what she should have been doing . . ."

I began to protest, to keep up my Emma-affair story.

"No, you can't fool Constance, don't even try."

No, I said, it indeed *had* been a while . . .

"That's a shame," she said, loosening my tie. "A real shame. All that time, you could have been over here with me, getting the works, right? Hm?" She smiled as she bent forward to kiss me more significantly. I mean, I know I'm sitting there being kissed and I should be falling into the experience romance-novel-like, but I was sitting there being strangely objective, thinking: Wow, this woman can kiss. She can cook, she can set up a pretty good seduction too. I'm being made here—putty in her hands. Should this disturb me? Well, even if it should it's not. I guess at some point I have to kick in and do my part too. Kiss back in other words, get the ball rolling. But wait.

Connie hopped up. "Be back," she said, walking toward the bedroom. "Don't go away now." The door closed behind her. Sex preparations. God, this was of such a different echelon from the Monica grope-and-pounce lecheries. This is real movie sex, I said to myself. This could be filmed. Well, *she* could be filmed. God knows what will become of me in there, in the Bedroom. Odd. I used to have serious postcoital tristesse back in my fumbling college encounters—it was always disillusioning, empty-making, sort of a big letdown. Now I'm having precoital tristesse. Stop thinking, I tell myself—can't you ever go on automatic?

Do you remember the guy waaaay back there talking about sex for the Average Middle-Class Heterosexual American Male in his early twenties? WELL, HE'S BACK! And he has decided on a similar list for the Average Middle-Class Heterosexual American Male in his *mid*-twenties. One doesn't look for types anymore, the women are irrelevant really, but one's *relationships* fall into a number of categories:

1. The Transition Woman.

The woman, like Connie for me, who takes you from post-adolescent sex (backseat fumblings, stopwatch sex, grope search and destroy . . .) to adult sex (silk sheets, lots of seemingly profound talk in bed, foreplay, glasses of brandy). You feel older, wiser, newer, better afterward. And you almost invariably have the right perspective on it, and nearly never fall in love with her.

2. The Placemarker.

These can go on for years. You love them. They are nice. They love you (usually very much) but you know out there somewhere is someone better. This woman is so cheated on, it's not funny—she doesn't know *half* of what goes on behind her back. Most long-term girlfriends are like this. On occasion this woman moves in, but usually the guy will insist on separate accommodations for the sake of noncommitment.

3. The Maybe-Wife.

Yeah, you'll give it a shot, commitment, fidelity, sincerity, loyalty . . . but it will still seem something is missing. Some marry this woman, the first long-term well-working relationship after college. Looks good on paper. But I think it's fair to say there's a lot of growing up left to do yet and those sacrifices you make for the Maybe-Wife (or real-life wife) will eat at you around twenty-eight or twenty-nine ("I coulda been halfway up the ladder by now if I hadn't stayed in Podunk while you finished beautician school . . ." etc.) and she will get the blame for much she shouldn't. In fact, every time the guy misses being free for a moment—a spare baseball ticket he can't accept, a night out with the boys he can't participate in, the single ex-roommate wanting to do the town while he has to drag his feet—the Maybe-Wife is going to get the abuse for it. In time, the Maybe-Wife, once so important, so viable, will be shuttled to Placemarker status whereupon she will be in danger of replacement. I never went for a Maybe-Wife. All my theater friends had these heavydeep'n real relationships going on, lots of fighting, lots of tears, lots of compromises.

4. The Quality Item.

Ah, she's still around, not as present or as possible as before, but she's got staying power. You'll throw it all over, every concern, every contingency, for this one. Because you have asked yourself this question a lot lately: why am I in the middle of the prime of my life without having had my true and lasting and endlessly perfect love? (Yeah, there's another one of these lists before the book ends—thought I'd warn you.)

ANYWAY, there I was with the Transition Woman.

Her bedroom was worth everything—she could have been a lot less than she was and I would have stayed for the plush soft carpet, the new silk sheets, the sheer ease and comfort and quiet and *coolness* which her air conditioner provided. I could stay there, lying beside her, my arm across her waist, forever. She was right: the night did seem to stretch out before us. It was eleven or so according to the glowing digital clock.

"Plenty of time for an encore," she said.

If I'm up to it.

"You will be," she said, nestling closer. "You wanted that a lot, kid. Been a while?"

About a hundred years.

"I love it when a man is hungry. You know he means it."

While I'm contemplating the C-grade dialogue, her hand moves lower.

"That's the spirit," she said, rolling about to lie on top of me. She brushed the hair out of my eyes. "Let's tell dirty stories, hm? Like your first time?"

Oh god.

"I'm not kidding. Tell me yours and I'll tell you mine."

It was fairly horrendous.

"Not half as bad as mine, I promise."

I made the story short and sweet: Karen Schmitt, seventeen, last year of high school, senior picnic, drifted away from the class for a walk in the woods in which everyone whooped and yelled and figured we were both going to neck and hold hands and we surprised everyone and ourselves. Never saw her after I went off to Southwestern Illinois. Whole thing lasted five minutes tops. I've always wondered . . .

"Wondered what?"

Just sort of what happened to her, and whether she's doing all right.

Connie squeezed me closer. "She's probably kicking herself for not holding onto you a little tighter, letting go of a good thing."

Doubt that.

Yeah yeah, I know I know, she was laying it on thick, pumping me up, making me feel like I had a Place in the Universe, not to mention her life. I could reinterpret the whole thing, of course, and examine every statement and reduce it to motives and bedroom talk and insincerity and role playing, but please don't make me do that. Let me cut my best deal with my memories —so few seem this warm and worth remembering.

"Davie Epstein was my first. After the prom I told you about. I had . . . gee, I shouldn't confess what a little snob I was, but I had this long-running schoolgirl fantasy that I was going to lose it with some upper-class WASP Harrrrrvad boy. I had the whole thing planned out, the lines, the look, the right dress. No one was going to know I was a middle-class girl from Brookline."

I didn't assume she was middle class.

"My father managed a watch and jewelry store. You could put the whole thing in this bedroom."

Would never have guessed. I picked her for a close friend of the Rockefellers.

"Brookline, Massachusetts?"

I'd never been. Her folks must be proud of her.

"Not really. We don't get along very well, but there are many people to blame for that, my sister, my brother. A long story and I'll tell you sometime. Anyway. I had this fantasy. This blond achingly beautiful Ivy League prep-school boy, played by Robert Redford right? He was going to come along and find me irresistible—I look WASP don't I? This wasn't out of the question. So here was Davie, Davie who stayed to work in his father's office, who didn't go to college, who didn't want me to go to Harvard, who figured correctly it would mean the end of our relationship if I went (and he was right), this Davie was all over me prom night. And so when he drove me home he got real fresh and I said no, and he said why not, and I said I was a good girl and . . . and, some shit, I was waiting until I was married or something. But he kept asking."

Did he get violent?

She didn't say anything for a while. "No. Not at all. He seemed defeated. He said that this was the last time together, I was going off to Harvard, we were through, he would have nothing, I would have everything. That kind of thing. He said . . ."

In the dark I couldn't tell what she thought of her own story.

". . . well, he said, he wanted to make love because that was all he had, and that he wanted to have a memory of me, something real since I was going away from him forever. He was a realist, that Davie."

I didn't say anything.

"So, I thought about it and I said yeah, okay, and I stretched out in the backseat in this silly prom dress all pulled up. And he got out and undid his pants and entered me but it didn't last or get anywhere, he couldn't come or anything. And I just sat there with all this taffeta and dress material pulled up around me waiting for something to happen, to me, to him, just something."

Poor guy.

Connie laughed ironically. "Our last date."

Yeah.

"And to boot, his first poke was a goodie. I got blood all over my prom dress and I lived in fear of my mother seeing it. Oh what a mess, what a mess. Not an auspicious start."

Few people's ever are, really. At least I think that's right.

"I wonder sometimes too," she went on, rolling off me (it was getting hot), "what old Davie is up to. He's married now, I know that. Sometimes I have this fantasy. When I go home to Brookline, picking up the phone and saying, hey Davie, kid, let's take another crack at it, let's turn an awful memory into a good time." She held my arm firmly. "Do you think you can make up for the past, Gil? If I went back and we did it up right this time, wouldn't that make up for it? Wouldn't it kill the bad part of the story? Change everything?"

Why don't you do it?

"Well. You know how impossible that would be. Why don't you look up Karen Schmitt?" Then she laughed. "Go for ten minutes this time."

I laughed too. No, it would be impossible.

"But poor Davie. We should be allowed in the world to go and clean up our messes, you know? I want to go back and tell Janie Johns in second grade I didn't mean it when I said she was ugly. I should pick up the phone, call her, get it over with—she'd think I was an ass and maybe wouldn't remember, but if she did . . . Connie's a sentimental old thing, isn't she?"

Was this an example, I asked, of Jewish Guilt?

She laughed. "Yep, I think so. It's how we fill our evenings."

More dirty talk.

"Tell me," she picked up later, "about Emma in bed."

I said: oh what an evil question.

"That's half the fun, babe—talking about other lovers."

Do you want me to talk about you?

"Don't I stand up to scrutiny?"

Yes yes, that is true.

"So come on, spill the beans."

I should have given up the game here, right? Told her Emma was an obsession, but we never slept together. Been honest. Forthright. Sincere with this wonderful no-nonsense woman. I thought about it. Naaaaahhhhh . . . I told her Emma was miserable, a fraction as adept and passionate as Connie. Well, that's what she was after wasn't she?

"Oh you're just piling it on, Gil. I don't believe a word."

Emma was totally cold, no kidding, I said. F-R-I-G-I-D. These last few months, I said, we hadn't slept together at all. (Well *that* was true.)

"Poor Gil. You're not badly in love with her, are you?"

I'm over her completely, I said.

And you know, when I said that, it was TRUE. Sometimes saying something makes it official. Then again, sometimes saying something you think you feel makes you realize the opposite is true. After Connie and I made love a second time, and I spent more time seeing to her enjoyment, she collapsed beside me whispering, "Gil, I want you back here every night, 9:30 p.m. on the dot. Whoa baby . . ." Then she kissed my cheek. "Love ya, kid." And I said, I love you too. And *that* was one of those times where saying something made it suddenly not true. I said it and the words echoed in the air-conditioned bedroom and they hung in the room as we went to sleep and the next morning as she made a first-class breakfast I remembered I had said them. Would they catch up with me? Oh my, poor young Gilbert, didn't he know he had nothing to worry about? He was just one in a line of suitors and lovers and new adventures for Connie. Those words made no more impression than if I had mentioned the weather.

But those other words. About Emma, when I said I was over her, those were true. I didn't need to see her again. Never again. I ought to write her off. No that's all silly. Be her friend, see her once in a while, sit there smugly when she asks you about Connie.

"What are you looking so goddam smug for," Emma asked eventually. I had called her temp agency and we had arranged to meet for a lunch at a slice-of-pizza place near Times Square. "You've gotten back with Connie, I know that. Every weekend, sex with the Capitalist America poster child. Does she write you a check or does she issue a money order? Do you have a stock option?"

You're jealous Emma. Connie is class, there's no taking away from that—bitch away as you will. I care about Connie very much.

Emma poured parmesan cheese over her slice, then peppers, then oregano. "From what you've told me," she began, enunciating every word, "she will toss you aside when she's through with you."

So? Everybody eventually gets tired of everybody (like me getting tired of Emma, I wanted to say). I'm having a good time now, the meals are great, I'm living like a king, hitting the good restaurants, nights at the theater, feeling good about myself.

"It's the sex, isn't it? You surprise me Gil. I expected more out of you." She sighed facetiously, barely summoning the energy to seem resentful. "I know someone perfect for you."

Yeah?

"Jasmine. No, no kidding, you two would hit it off."

If we didn't get arrested for drug possession first.

"Hey don't knock my roommate, she's cool. Didn't *sell out* like some roommates I could mention." Pause. "Did I tell you I was thinking about getting a tattoo?"

Fortunately that plan wasn't realized. Abuse and all, I liked seeing Emma. It was obvious she was happier now, having a good time. Jasmine's weekend band was called Kill the Rich. I got two passes to their next gig in the mail from Emma, and a follow-up phone call:

"You *know* you want to come to CBGBs tonight. You *know* you don't want to go back to those imperialist arms. Those silk sheets, Gil . . ."

What about 'em, Emma?

"Made by Taiwan slave-laborers. Her salary bonus? Due to investment in apartheid. Bet she buys her fruit straight from American companies in El Salvador." She did her idea of how Connie talked: " 'This El Salvador? Could you kill a few laborers, spray a few villages with poisons, send out a few death squads and get some bananas, huh?' "

Are you quite through?

"Next time she takes you up to Montauk—how was that by the way?"

Great, of course.

"Next time she takes you up to Montauk, just think how her money is connected to torturers in South America—electric cattle prods on testicles, Gil! CIA!"

Bye-bye, Emma—

"Workers unite! Revolution forever!"

CLICK. I guess you hang around a group called Kill the Rich long enough and you end up talking that way too.

Sometimes I thought Emma was right, Connie and I weren't long for the world. But then we'd have a week when I'd see her every night. Like all affairs, it had its mild ups and downs . . .

"Honey, you just never run out of steam do you? Connie's had a long day at the commodity bureau and she's not quite ready for gymnastics this early in the evening. Why don't *you* take me out for a change? A nice big dinner?"

And other times, I couldn't have scripted a more perfect affair.

"Some more claret? Of course, you'll have some. So you're sure you can get the weekend off? Good, that's good because I think we need a little sojourn to Quebec City. I'll speak the French, you sit there and tell me how well I speak it."

You got it.

"We'll take the night train, get a private compartment." She looked up from over the glass of claret she held with both hands. "Ever done it on a train? Romantic, let me tell you. In France one time . . ."

Another story, another facet of Connie, one more reason to utterly ignore my career—who needed a fulfilling job, the audition hassles, the pain of finding work at another theater? Naw, I'll just play this out until it ends and enjoy it while I can. Throw myself into work and finding a new theater when we go our separate ways . . . do you suppose, I'd ask myself, that this might just go on forever? Could it work? Like both of us moving in together, living in sin? What a couple we'd be—the oddness of our romance made for . . . well, more romance.

"I'm having a party, kid," Connie announced. "Full of Wall Street types, guys at work, bores, but some nice ones in the crowd too. Very important strategy—show yourself as the woman who can cook, entertain, work a full day, pull it off without a thought . . ."

Give that woman our toughest account! She's a marvel!

"You've got it, Gil. So, I want you to come. Suit and tie—well, a sport jacket. And not that ratty thing you call a sport jacket. I swear I'm going to dress you head to toe one day, when I make a million and have it to burn."

I approached and hugged her, tickling her a bit. I'd rather she *un*dressed me.

"Ha, not tonight, please."

She had said that last night.

"Like I'm just saving you from my period and all kinds of nastiness down there at the moment."

I didn't care.

"Trust me. When Connie's female problems clear up, we'll

make up for lost time. But first my party. Why don't you bring a theater friend or two."

Yuck. I see them all the time.

"I want to bohemianize the party a bit, liven it up."

I say as a joke: how about Emma? That would liven it up.

"Why *not* Emma? There's an idea . . ."

Remember folks, I ASKED FOR IT.

If I told Emma to come she wouldn't. If I told her not to come, she would insist. If I kept the invitation secret, and she found out (Connie mails her one, phones her up) then she'd come and be mad. What to do? I opt, next time I see her, for: Connie's having a party. Full of business types. Want to come?

"Was I invited?" Emma looked astonished.

Yes.

"Let me get this one straight," she said, crossing her arms. "She invited me to her respectable cocktail party? I think I know what she's up to. Compare and contrast. Watch Emma stumble around and feel out of place, show how little class she has."

Yep that was probably it, but I said: nonsense. She just wants to meet you, after all the millions of stories I've told, good things I've said about you.

"Uh-huh. Whatever you say. Tell her I'll be there."

I decided to spend the day with Emma, hoping she'd change her mind. We went back to Brooklyn Heights to find Sal's Diner again. Sal and the waitress welcomed us back, asked us why we didn't come around all the time, where'd we been, huh? It'd been about a year since I'd seen Sal's—it was a bit sad-making, for we used to eat there every other night. Sal's was eternal; they would be grinding away for their paycheck long after we'd packed our bags, the waitress would be wearing that checkered top and wiping tables with that rag twenty years from now.

"Ran into the worst snob the other day at work," Emma began. "He asked me if I was BBQ."

BBQ?

"Stands for Booklyn, Bronx or Queens. There's a secretary at United Agencies where I'm temping. Loud, nasal accent, named Shirley, wears tight sweaters, dresses two years out of style. This guy at the watercooler watches her walk by and says, 'Very, *very* BBQ.' I wanted to put his head in the cooler."

I told Emma how when I tell people I live in Hell's Kitchen, way down toward the river on 45th Street, I get looks of sympathy.

"I'm getting fed up with the rich in this town. They're the ones who've made the rents so impossible, and then look down their noses at the people who had to flee to the goddam slums just to stay here."

Yes, she'll meet plenty of these types at Connie's party.

"God, I miss this part of Brooklyn," said Emma. "I want our old house again with Mrs. Dellafini. I want my windowseat back—it's the last time I wrote anything good . . ." She looked at me directly. "Whadya think? The three of us again?"

Lisa wouldn't go for it, I have my doubts, and you know good and well you drove us crazy (not to mention yourself crazy) and it would all happen all over again—

"Just indulging in a little nostalgia, that's all," she said, looking down in her coffee. "I'm having a blast with our band anyway. Last night, Cock, he's the bass player—"

Our band? I interrupted.

Emma rolled her eyes, laughing. "Oops, that was a slip, delusions of grandeur. Jasmine's band. But I get to read poetry in the break. People love it. I mean, I change my tone a bit. For that crowd you can make it up as you go along—as long as you say 'fuck' and 'shit' a lot, sound like Bukowski." She did some impromptu punk poetry: "Life is like a turd/a fucking turd . . ."

A little quieter, please.

"It's great, they love me. I'd probably sell more this way than if I try being a poet the respectable way."

Yeah, but it's not great poetry is it?

"I don't see you on Broadway this season, so I wouldn't criticize." (That was a sharp remark I wish she hadn't said.) "You told me after that jerk guy said you had no future at the Venice that you'd be gone by the summer, and here it is nearly fall and you're still there. 'Can I get your coffee, Mr. Schmeen?' "

I'm looking for new work, I said stiffly.

She pointed her coffee spoon at me. "No you're not. You know what you're doing? Having sex. All the time. Day and night. *I'm*, at least, still in the ball game here, still trying to get somewhere . . ."

I changed the subject. You were telling me about Cock.

"Cock the bass player, yes. You know why he's called Cock?"

Why?

Emma smiled and rubbed her hands together. "Jasmine used to go out with him but said she had trouble walking the next day. She's trying to set us up. Figures if the celibacy goes by the boards, it might as well go out in style."

I change the subject again. What's all this about you in some new group therapy thing?

"I go to this group on Fridays," she told me eagerly, "since the Celibacy Support Organization folded—I'm the last original member. Anyway, this new group is about twelve to fifteen, and we sit around trying to make ourselves happy. Naturally, I'm near-suicidal coming out of there every Friday night. I see these *losers* who are sitting there thinking the same thing of me. One man cries every session, he can't tell his children he loves them, he can't show affection, blah blah blah, he has all this self-loathing. I sit there thinking, thank god I'm not the WRECK you are. But next month the session shifts to me and my life and I'm sure I'll cry and carry on just like he does. It's a performance in a way."

If you think that, I said, why not quit, save your time.

"It's great fun. I have nothing better to do than wallow in my problems for an hour each week. When I do it with them I don't end up doing it with you and Lisa. It's a financial arrangement. I'm paying to dump all this shit on strangers so my friends won't get it."

But if you know all that, realize what you do is shit, then why not—

"Listen, stop being logical."

I change the subject again. What time do you wanna meet for Connie's party?

"I want to make sure my tattoo's dry in time for it. Shall we say, six o'clock, 86th Street subway station, under Gimbels, corner of Lexington."

I stared at her, looked in her eyes. Emma, I said, you *will* behave yourself, right?

"Me? Make trouble?"

Yes and you know what I mean. I care about Connie a lot and this is the first decent relationship—

"What about our relationship? Isn't it decent?"

Too decent, I said; rated G for general audiences.

"I never thought a little sex could turn your head so."

Well, it's been *very* little lately.

Emma pointed a fry at me to make her point. "Ha, I knew it. The passion has died. She's looking for new stud material."

If she is and I get dumped, I guess you'll be happy, I said. You'd rather see me miserable and alone, isn't that right?

Emma looked taken aback, and decided to ease up: "All right, all right."

D day. I have never wanted less to go to a party.

Emma was, predictably, acting up. "Yeah well maybe this *was* a bad idea. I can't even stand this neighborhood . . ." We were walking from the subway to Connie's East Side apartment. "I don't think I'm ever going to be able to like Connie. Are you going to act all coupley, Gil? Stand in corners with her? Say 'I dunno, what do *you* think darling?' "

You know I'm not like that, Emma.

"I don't like the thought of you two together, to be honest."

Emma, please.

"I might drop things on her carpet on purpose."

I pause walking. Emma stops too. I tell her to go ahead and right here, two hundred yards from the apartment, get it ALL out of her system. Everything nasty she had to say.

"You mean it?"

I started her off: Connie is a selfish, New Right, capitalist Wall Street type, self-absorbed—

"Callous, materialistic pretentious Ivy League cow, who's not as good-looking as she thinks she is."

Since you've never met her, Emma, I think you'll find her every bit as good-looking as she thinks she is.

"She's not even a little bit ugly?"

We walked in silence for a while.

"My analyst is talking about a masturbation therapy."

Good, as I didn't want to talk about it.

"He thinks I should experiment more, get in touch with my Sexual Self, play with myself more."

Fine. Can we not talk about it one hundred yards from Connie's door?

"Aren't you interested?"

Enraptured. But let's see if we can not talk about your playing with yourself at this particular party.

"I was thinking of discussing with the party *their* masturbation lives. Bet a lot of them do it in the office, lunch breaks, coffee breaks, under the desk. While looking at the Standards & Poors. 'Oh god, oh god, IBM is up three-and-a-quarter, oh oh oh—"

Would you cut it out? We rode up the elevator to the 17th floor. The door opened; we could hear the party.

"Then again. I haven't touched myself for years. I mean most celibates in the support group jerk off two and three times a day, there's a lot of pent-up frustration. Me? Never touch myself. I disgust myself. Imagine, pawing for a half hour at your vagina every day till biology reduces you to an animal state—"

ENOUGH. Please, Emma.

"You know, I think one night back in Brooklyn I think I heard you doing it. No, really, the bed was going eeh-uh eeh-uh—"

Emma for god's sake.

We rang the bell, Connie opened it. "So, Gil," she said kissing my cheek, then stepping back so Emma and I could behold her glory, and her *Vogue*-cover looks. "This must be Emma."

"Good guess."

And in we went.

"I hate everyone here," Emma whispered to me, after two minutes.

I made an exasperated sigh, telling her that I had TOLD HER she wouldn't like it.

"Wonder what the average salary is here?"

I left her at the refreshment table, not concerned for the moment with Emma's socialist critique.

I met Doug in Municipals. Did I know that federal tax-free investment in nuclear power was the ticket? Washington State and its five-plant Great Northwest complex—that was the place to put my money. Minimum investment $10,000—think of it, *tax*-free. Yeah, well next $10,000 that comes my way, buddy . . .

I met Sylvia in corporate research. Aren't people boring who talk business, she said, and I agreed. She hated to talk business—that's the way it was at work, all day long, business business business. But she did like to gossip. Like that man there, who did A, B and C, and that woman there, who only went to Rutgers and doesn't know beans about market expansion, *but* she did this-and-that and so-and-so, *and* made a play for the man who doesn't know she's alive, him right there . . .

I met Maury. What about them Yankees? Mark his words, it was gonna be the Yanks in the pennant race, Boston's gonna fade. He had box seats, sometime we ought to go together—*box* seats. Five hundred a season for box seats, writes it off on the company but don't tell anyone, our little secret. What did I think of the Orioles?

Emma drifted back over, a plate full of cocktail food. "There is not an interesting person at this party. Susan's parties are better than this, at least there's something to ridicule. These people are bores, Gil."

Be more open-minded, Emma. Why, I have met *many* fascinating people here—you're too close-minded.

"You're a lost cause, Gil," she said, munching. "I'll give your bitch-girlfriend one thing, she can cook. This goose-liver mousse is *the word made flesh,* God on a piece of toast. You eat like this all the time?"

Yes, actually. I was going to mingle some more.

"Suit yourself."

Connie approached. "How's it goin', kid?"

Fine, her party was a smash, many compliments all around. People, of course, wondered what *I* was doing here.

"Let 'em wonder. It unnerves them to think I might have a life outside of Golam Brothers, Cohn & Schwartz, because they don't. How's Emma doing?"

She's a big girl, she could take care of herself.

Connie arched an eyebrow. "One wonders."

I drifted toward the refreshment table and got stuck in a conversation with Saul, who I assumed worked at Golam Brothers.

"Christ, no," he said immediately. "I'm just . . . I'm just a friend of Connie's. An old friend."

Suddenly, I knew all. He was an old boyfriend. Wait, Connie didn't have boyfriends—she had lovers. An old lover.

"How long have you known the Con?" he asked. "You're not Golam Brothers either, I take it."

I rehashed a polished version of Connie and myself.

"Sounds like the Con," he said, laughing slightly.

All smiles: what sounded like the Con?

"Her sexual credo, variety is the spice of life. Next month it'll be an artist, next month a politician, I think she's got a checklist."

I was getting brave, what the hell. I asked if he was a checkmark, and if so, what category.

"Yes. Writer. Journalist mainly, for the *Worker's Guardian.*"

But that's, uh—

"You got it. Communist weekly. I was Connie's token Marxist."

He looked like a Marxist; baggy clothes, small intellectual's round glasses, beard, dark thinning hair, about thirty.

"I'm sorry, I've had a little to drink. I'm not offending you or telling you anything you didn't know, am I?"

NO no no.

"She does use 'em and toss 'em aside, that girl. She's something else."

I knew, as one knows all World Truths That Are Irrefutable, that I was not long for this romance, that she was slumming, that this was my brief shining moment. I also felt momentarily displaced, and then a trifle lonely (lonely in the future tense, soon I would be back on my own again), and then sort of smug and happy that I was going to escape some day free and clear, no theatrics, no little-girl dramas, no adolescent "I thought we were going to have true love forever" scenes, that HEY, YOU ARE NOW IN THE MODERN WORLD and this is how adults behave. Affairs, brief encounters, ships that pass in the night. I could hardly wait until the next woman.

And then I heard Emma's voice cut through the crowd: "Oh I always vote for entertainment value. Nixon, and then Carter. I mean how could that miss, a peanut farmer with a booze-loving brother, Bible-toting sister, one of those steely Southern women pushing him along like Lady Macbeth, Mama on the front porch down home callin' the shots. I mean, this was sure-fire entertainment, and I voted Democratic fast as I could."

"I don't think that's very responsible," someone said.

"Or particularly amusing," someone else said.

I needed a drink so I went to get one and when I came back Emma was in high gear: "Well a little nuclear war wouldn't hurt us too bad—I'm sort of in the mood for it, looking forward to it finally happening almost."

"Be serious," said a woman impatiently.

"Oh I'm quite serious," said Emma.

"Well then that's stupid and so are you."

A bit flustered she went on. "No, I mean I foresee a time in a post-nuclearwar world in which . . . in which a new romanticism, a new literature—"

"We should have a nuclear war for literature's sake?" said the woman, shaking her head. "Look, we're trying to have a serious conversation here about arms control, Salt I versus Salt II, and you interrupted so why don't you spare us this, okay dear?"

Emma retreated to the other side of the room. Emma, I wanted to tell her, your routine is . . . routine. It's not gonna work here.

Connie approached again. "What's with Emma? Not exactly the Most Popular Girl. Got enough to eat there, kid? Good, good."

I met Saul, I said.

She gave it a flicker of thought. "That's nice. Did you all have a good talk?"

Well, we just small-talked.

Connie flashed me a look. "Saul never small-talks." And then she went back to see to someone's empty wineglass.

I was feeling two-drinks happy. Where was Saul? I wouldn't mind talking to him again, getting a little background on Connie, not that that was playing fair exactly. But why not?

"No the band has no management yet," I heard Emma's voice say, "but we're doing a series of tape projects. Our bass player, Cock, has this *in* at Alternative Audio and they put out bootlegs of Fucked-Up Youth, Squirming Fetus, those bands—"

"But aren't bootlegs illegal?" the woman beside Emma on the sofa asked.

"Oh yeah. But so is dealing in blackmarket barbiturates, but the band does that too for money. We're doing this tour with Up Your Ass—actually, they've got a new lead singer from London so they're changing the name to Up Your Bum . . ."

Emma, I'm coming to GET YOU.

"Have you heard their new single, 'Vomit Choke'? It's about going to sleep on a full stomach and shooting up heroin—you're just *asking* to drown in your own vomit that way—"

"Excuse me, I think I need another drink," said the woman, as she hurriedly went in search of wine on the other side of the room.

"Hello, Gil," said Emma, looking at her plate of hors d'oeuvres, avoiding my eyes. "Ellen here was just telling me about new pension-plan tax-dodge schemes and she asked about my plan and I said my line of work was irregular and she asked more about it and I told her, so get that look off your face."

Would you please try to be sociable?

"I need human beings to work with, Gil—this is a tough crowd."

It's not a crowd, it's a cocktail party given by my . . . my girlfriend.

"Did you know that Jasmine does phone sex? You know where middle-aged men call up and a girl talks dirty to them? You get thirty bucks a throw—it's a respectable business Gil, all the major credit cards are accepted."

My arms are crossed. My expression is unpleasant.

"Anyway, I asked Ellen what tax breaks Jasmine was eligible for, being self-employed. She said, after much throat clearing, that our phone bill was deductible as a business expense. If we incorporate—"

Emma I think you should leave the party.

Her eyes met mine. She stood up and stared intently at me, lips pursed, and that right eyebrow raised. She said quietly, "You're asking me to leave?" And she said that in an intense tone, suggesting ominous consequences.

Do what you want, I said, and walked away.

I found myself drawn into a discussion of the health spa in the atrium of the Golam Brothers Building on Beaver Street, how some middle-management type who hogged the whirlpool shouldn't even have been admitted to the executive club, how the heated towels were hotter last year, how the staff was more courteous before J. P. had his heart attack, how there was this new masseuse named Kira with the greatest body in the world and how this visiting bond salesman in from Chicago chased her around the saunas while the men yelled "Get the goods, Bob! Get the goods!" (All right Emma, nearly a decade on, in print, before the world, you were right, these people weren't my people, they were phoneys and bores, and I should have come clean at the time.)

Emma's voice from across the room, again: "*Of course,* Carter was right to give back the Panama Canal, and the Brits should give back Hong Kong when the lease runs out, Gibraltar on general principle, and the Soviets Eastern Europe—colonialism is dead. Until we prove that to the third world we'll never be able to get along with them or be able to depend on them for support."

"Panama can no more run that canal," said a man, "which we built, which we manage, oversee for security reasons, than they can run their own banana republic. The terms of our treaty were no worse, no more corrupt than other agreements of that period—"

"Which is to say pretty corrupt," Emma interjected.

"I like Senator Hayakawa's remark," said a woman with a nasal voice, "that we stole it fair and square."

"Well, you *would* like it," said Emma, "because it's the slick kind of obscurantist Republican doublespeak that appeals to conservatives and the American business community alike. Let's laugh away all our Latin American atrocities, all our South American imperialism, inept meddling from Teddy Roosevelt to the CIA and Allende—"

"Hold on hold on," said the woman defensively. "Don't put words in my mouth—"

"You name the goon and we put him there—Somoza, Papa Doc and Pinochet and D'Aubisson—a real rogue's gallery, all best friends of the United States."

The man broke in. "And you would rather have, I take it, Castro, or local versions of Castro, all over Latin America, from Tierra del Fuego to the Rio Grande one day? I'd rather have Battista, given what Cuba represents today."

"You wouldn't rather have Battista," said Emma, exuding distaste, "if you were a poor Cuban slave laborer, with a starving family on a bourgeois sugar plantation in 1958, and Cuba would *be* in our sphere of influence if hysterical Fascist generals hadn't drawn up that half-baked invasion and that half-brained John Kennedy hadn't agreed to it . . ."

Strangers were gathering. She'd done it now, defiled the name of America's patron saint, JFK, the Light still shone from his face through the '70s . . .

"What was that about Kennedy?" said a bearded man.

Emma don't do it . . . don't do it . . .

"I think he was the lousiest president in the twentieth century after Harding is what I think. For one thing, how can you make a historical judgment on two and a half years, and another thing, if you do, how can you overlook wiretapping Martin Luther King, trying to assassinate world leaders, Castro among them, a two-bit doomed-to-fail mission to Cuba, let us not forget ladies and gentleman the Vietnam War—*that* little costly number, though I suspect the economic boom justified it for most of the people in this room—"

Wooooo boy.

"—and let us not forget that during the Cuban Missile Crisis he put the nuclear missiles on alert, making him the first president since that war criminal Truman to consider firing the damn things."

Connie approached scowling. She said coolly, "I want to thank you personally for bringing this acquaintance to my attention. How can I repay you?"

What could I say? Well, I began, she has a point about the CIA and American involvement in South—

"This is a cocktail party," Connie continued in a level, deadly tone, "and not the UN, and maybe you and your Brooklyn crowd don't get asked to many of them, but they are generally civilized affairs where people mingle and are nice to one another—"

I know, I know, I know—no need to be sarcastic, Connie, I'll retrieve Emma at once.

"What *is* your problem?" Emma said icily as we moved to the foyer of Connie's apartment. "A little too loud for you?"

Yes and you know it.

"I embarrass you in front of all your young-banker friends?"

I don't give a damn about them, but I care about Connie—

"She's the phoniest piece of business here!"

Sssssh—damn you, Emma, keep your voice down—

"She must think she's Madame de Staël, whirling about, playing Hostesse. These people are *losers*—her social circle is *nothing*. I don't doubt there are some interesting people on Wall Street but they're not here. Let's judge her by her own terms—"

We're not judging Connie one way or the other—

"No, let's judge her by her own standards. There's not an executive here, it's all middle management, assistant to the assistants. The big boys down there must know what she is, one more whiny little grasping Radcliffe nouveau-riche slut in a Brooks Brothers suit—hey, how do you bet she got her job at Schmolem Brothers or wherever? Huh?"

(I'll give Emma this: she could put together a string of insults where there was *nothing* left standing . . . what a pro.)

Emma, I said at this point, just LEAVE, go home, go away—

"I'm just hitting my stride, Gil—"

Keep your voice down. Let's move this to the hall.

(We moved it to the hall.)

"I bet this Connie number was on her knees in the *interview*—"

Emma, that's enough! I am FURIOUS with you!

"She's gonna dump you like yesterday's devalued pork futures, Freeman, and you're gonna have to come crawling back to me—"

You are the most selfish person I have ever met. I don't think you're my friend—I think you just pretend to be my friend; I don't think you know anything about friendship—

"Bullshit Gil, it is because I am your friend I am saying come away from these stupid shallow phoney—"

My life is not going to be lived like your life, Gennaro! It is going to be FUN, it is going to have ALL kinds of people in it, I'm not going to condemn everything that moves, and I don't want to be neurotic and work up a virtual CULT of my problems like you do—

"Well I *got* some problems, okay? That's *me*, that's the way I am—I'm doing real well to be as good as I am given how messed up my life is—"

WHY is it messed up? It's not messed up, except for what you do to drag yourself down: you're smart, you're talented, you're pretty—

"I'm not pretty."

I'm tired of it Emma. You don't need friends, you need a cassette tape—get Jasmine to make you one, over and over it can play back to you: Yes, Emma you are smart, yes, Emma you are pretty, yes Emma—

"I'm mad at you too, Gil," she said, and I saw her eyes fighting Emma-when-criticized tears, and her cheeks redden. "I thought you and Lisa were going to go the distance with me and both of you are becoming bourgeois bores—she is not going to be a painter and . . ."

And I'm not going to be an actor, is that it?

"You tell me! How many times have you auditioned in the last six months. You're still nowheresville in the goddam Venice Theater after they've thrown you out the door—oh of course, how could I be so foolish? I know what you're doing! You're putting your dick in somebody—that's reeeeeeal important, that's a life's work! There's a committed artist for you—"

Connie cleared her throat. She was now in the hallway too, standing in the door.

"Emma. Emma Gennaro," Connie said, walking slowly toward us. "Gee that name's familiar. Weren't you on the bombing raid over Hiroshima in '45?"

"It's a pleasure to bomb at your party, Con."

"Well sweetie, it's the last one you'll have the pleasure of trying to ruin. Why don't you just move along home now so I can have Gil back? There are some people dying to meet him back inside."

"Really Con? What happens when they find out Gil has no liquid assets to invest?"

Connie managed an annoyed smile. "Coming Gil?"

Emma poked my arm: "Or would you rather go to Sal's?"

No, I said quietly, I don't want to go to Sal's, goodbye.

Emma just stared at me, mercilessly.

I'll call you sometime, I said.

"Don't bother," said Emma, turning. And as she walked away in a shaken voice she said: "Don't bother calling me ever again."

Connie and I watched her disappear. Connie turned to me, not a hint of curiosity about what had transpired. "Dramatic girl, Gil. Be glad you're done with that."

We went back to the party. Class act, that Connie. She knew she had triumphed so she didn't rub anything in, prove sarcastic, remind or recriminate over Emma, she never mentioned her again, that is, the rest of that evening, which was the next to last time I ever saw her. We had one more very bitter lunch after that, but that concerned something else.

"Connie's unforgettable," said Saul, sitting beside me on the sofa. It was late in the party, down to fifteen or so, everyone had broken off into quiet conversation, dark corners (Connie had lit candles all around, put some soft jazz on, the kind of jazz that has never been listened to, only talked to or screwed to) and we sat there going through Saul's pack of Gauloises which were just about to kill me.

I said, In her way, Con is a health freak as I began coughing. Instant lung cancer, those cigs.

"Yes, that's a relatively new development. The jogs around the reservoir in Central Park, the vitamin program, the sauna and workout room at Golam Brothers." Saul laughed darkly. "You met her almost a year ago, huh?"

Yeah. After that play where I was the football hero. She said I looked good in the football uniform. We had lunch a time or two and then she dropped out of sight and then I called her up and . . . well, here we are.

"She had a bad year last year," Saul said, studying me. "She probably told you about it."

Well no. Bad year? Thought Connie never had a bad year.

Saul looked intensely at me. "She told you, didn't she?"

Told me? Told me what? I thought: no, she's not got some fatal cancer or something, I hope. Am I the last love of her life? Has she got six months to live?

Saul, after my silence, looked up to the ceiling. "No, she didn't tell you. That's a shame too, I thought she might have started dealing with that. I see not."

My mind was full to capacity. What is it? I asked. She's not ill, is she?

Saul turned solemn, but not too solemn. "Well yes."

Tell me.

He cleared his throat, a half smile, a shake of his head. "No, nothing serious, just inconvenient, and you shouldn't be alarmed because you may not have got it, and there's no reason necessarily that you will get it like I did. I mean herpes, genital herpes, is only passed when the sores are extant and otherwise you might never know . . ."

Connie was watching us while embroiled in another conversation, looking over at us, smiling when I caught her eye, not confident, wondering what we were talking about. As for me, I just sat there (Saul got up to get me a drink), thinking absolutely nothing—experiencing a true mental void. And when the thought-machine began to crank up again all it could think was:

Oh my. Oh my. Oh no.

MIDDLE

I'm interrupting this narrative for a progress report . . . Mother is six months pregnant, and Gil the Father spent yesterday driving out from Chicago to his childhood home in Oak Park, dragging a crib down from our attic, accidentally scraping paint off the living room walls at my mother's and breaking off a leg of said crib. T minus three months and counting.

I'm currently still stuffed from this meal I went to last night. I'm at this big family do, the Mandlikovs, with Sophie (you'll meet her in a bit). God, when Russian-Americans get together to eat they do it unto the death—the kind of food from Eastern Europe that makes cement in the stomach, cheeses meeting cabbages meeting minced meats meeting creams. I crawl to the sofa to fall asleep while the family has its reunion around me, and as I fall asleep I hear Sophie's half-brother Steve going on about New York:

". . . It's a cesspool. What did you say, John? Ha ha, I think a nuclear bomb is the only answer."

I turn over and tune him out. (That guy gets on my nerves . . .)

Later on, he's at it again:

"I don't know why anyone would live anywhere else but Chicago. L.A. is a mess with the crime and the gangs, and New York saw its day in the '50s . . ."

Uh, no. There's that certain breed of Chicagoan that just can't accept the fact Chicago *might* not be Paradise on Earth.

"We've certainly got the art of New York—"

(Geez, not even close.)

"—we have a finer symphony orchestra. And theater. Now we have a theater scene that, though not as big, certainly matches in quality the dying New York theater scene, now in its death throes. There's not a playwright in the country that wouldn't rather open here—"

I get into it: That's just not right, Steve. New York is still the theater capital of America. Look I was in New York theater for ten years there—there's no comparison.

Steve blanches. "But I read an article in the *Tribune* . . ."

I duck out of this one. I go back to the dining room to pick at leftovers. The women are all in one room, some are sewing, some are trading recipes, these matriarchs comparing their children's futures. There's this little crepe thing filled with cottage cheese and spices—don't know what it's called—and I'm running one of these decadently through a pile of sour cream—

"Mr. Freeman?"

I turn and it's someone's kid, but I've forgotten who.

"I'm Steve Mandlikov, and I was wondering if you'd talk to me a minute." Out goes his hand. Firm handshake that seemed to commit him to liking you. Good-looking boy, healthy and fresh and clean the way Midwestern teenage guys can be. Hey waita minute, this is Steve the Asshole's kid, Steve, Jr.

"You see, I'm thinking about being an actor. And Aunt Sophie said I should talk to you because you were in New York, in the theater. Were you really on Broadway?"

Yeah. (Oh boy. I see myself here—a vision of Gil, twenty years back.) Let's sit down and talk about it.

"You heard of Forensics?"

Carving up dead people?

"No, like speech and debate tournaments? Well, I won the dramatic monologue state championship this year for Illinois . . ." He paused because people are usually impressed at that point. "And I'm going to the national tournament in Seattle. So I'm not a no-talent if you were thinking hey this kid's probably a . . . a no-talent."

Forensic tournaments? Sounds like this generation's attempt at *The Parson Comes to Dinner*, Steve, Jr., this time in the role of Little Jimmy. There's theater in Chicago, I suggest, a healthy growing small scene—

"Nyeh, it's all in New York. I'm moving there after college."

What do your folks think?

"Dead set against it."

Steve, Sr., in the next room: "They can't even make pizza in New York as good as we do in Chicago . . ."

(Yeah, Steve, Jr., I'm thinking, you deserve your escape from the Midwestern Mafia. I could sit here and discourage you, I could say it's all a racket, I could say it's magic and love and all that stuff, I could make you want to get on the next bus, and I could scare the hell out of you. But instead I'm going to give you Joyce Jennings's phone number, and Jerry Gardiner's agency number.) You tell 'em I sent you.

"Gee thanks, Mr. Freeman. Can I ask a question?"

Sure.

"Do you miss it?"

Every day.

And then when I was about to leave Sophie corners me, and after discussing my expectant fatherhood, she asks:

"Heard you tell Steve, Jr., you missed New York every day. You're not thinking of going back now, are you? It's a little late now, Daddy-to-be."

Nostalgia's no crime. Nothing serious. I'm writing this dumb book to get New York out of my system.

"Just wondered. You lit into Steve with the passion of a New Yorker."

(Oh yeah. After the second feeding, that jerk got onto New York pizza again. I'm sorry. Chicago is nice, but New York is better—pizza is all we need look at to prove this. In Chicago it's bread, a big pan of greasy fried bread with a bit of goop on top. I want my thin, limp, triangular slice of pizza for $1 with the orange grease lying in pools atop the rubbery cheese, all forming one brilliant gestalt—I picked that up from Sophie the sociologist—and I'm sick of Chicagoans who haven't been ten miles from the Loop running down New York. Chicago pizza isn't proper pizza, it's pizza-flavored QUICHE!)

"I'm not sure you've got New York and a few other things behind you."

Yeah, but I'm working on it.

"Want to go down to the lakeshore? Walk off the blintzes?"

And that's where we went. And the night was overcast and the clouds caught the city's faint orange glow in a way that seems peculiar to Chicago. And there was the lake which also had the vague glow of city lights and we sat and listened to it contentedly lap the shore. No, it's not the Atlantic Ocean, it's not Coney Island or Far Rockaway, but it's grown on me, it grows on me more and more every year.

Back to the story.

1979

MY answering machine: *Hello. This is Gil Freeman and I'm not home. If you are calling about a temporary job, a part, or anything that may mean money for me, PLEASE, I'm begging you, leave your name and number and I will get right back to you as soon as possible. Thanks a lot.* BEEP!

I couldn't have been poorer. One hopes that one's accommodations continually improve but mine were going down, down, down . . . from the luxury of a Village sublet with money in my pocket to run-down Brooklyn to Hell's Kitchen and now Alphabet City, the Lower East Side, *lower* being the operative word. I lived on Avenue A (hence Alphabet City) and as a rule, you should never live anywhere in New York designated by letters; this holds true citywide. Avenue A was slumland: heroin addicts in alleyways, homeless everywhere, bums up from the Bowery (which is nearby) for a change of scenery, the leftover druggy hippie-types mingling with the Puerto Ricans driven down from the West Side when that neighborhood gentrified and the PRs got summarily evicted. The last place in New York (to answer the question you might be asking) that you could rent a place for $200 or so a month.

I lived in a virtual prison cell. It was a one-room "studio," with a dripping sink, a rickety table that held my hotplate, a rusted icebox underneath; there was a bookcase I made from bricks and planks, beyond which was my mattress on the floor, far as possible from the dripping sink. My clothes when they were clean were kept in the suitcase near the slit-in-the-wall window; when they were dirty, they were piled at the foot of the bed. Didn't do much formal entertaining in this phase of my life. With each move I was steadily decreasing my living space—if the progression kept up, I'd be living in a bus station locker soon.

I checked out this tiny real-estate-page ad that led me to Avenue A and this grocery. I went up the block, I went down the block, but no, I had the address right and this place was a grocery. RUIZ CARIBBEAN FOODSTORE . . . and in smaller, hand-painted letters underneath: SNACKS • FOOD TO GO • COLD BEER. A short, plump, balding man (with a few strands of side hair combed across his shiny head) met me with a smiling if not somewhat distressed expression, peering out the store window. He ran out to the street to escort me into his shop: "You here for the apartament?"

I was led inside.

"Back here, through the store, eh?" I followed him as we wound through the narrow aisles of the store . . . junkfood of all varieties, chips, pretzels, bag after bag of cookies, corn chips and tortilla-things; canned vegetables, followed by pet food and baby diaper products, a cooler with the Cold Beer, a greasy cardboard box filled with plantains. (C'mon confess it: How many fellow Midwesterners have purchased plantains thinking them bananas? Ever bitten into a plantain expectantly awaiting a sumptuously sweet banana? Yummmm . . .) All the shelves were yellow—the paint was cracking and peeling—and an ancient layer of dust coated everything; the aisles themselves were so narrow that you had to sidle through them or else sweep everything onto the floor with your coat. Señor Ruiz and I went through the store, out the back door and into an outdoor court enclosed by fences topped with cut glass shards and barbed wire; beyond this "garden area" (there was a tiny plot of dirty grass and a spindly tree growing up from it) there was the Ruiz's house and they were renting out the ground-floor room.

"See plenty of space! Plenty of space!" said Señor Ruiz as he swung the door open. He had to be kidding—maybe in San Juan this qualified as plenty of space. "You gotta sink. You gotta, eh, room here for you bed. You gotta window . . ." A small frosted-glass window that made all the light look gray. "You gotta ploog for you electric things, here." Señor Ruiz held these luxuries as major selling points, it was obvious. "For the toilet you come out of the apartament . . ." I followed him back out into the courtyard, and followed him through a second door. ". . . and you and my family can share thees toilet here. It has a bath and that is the toilet bowl."

Let me get this straight: I have to cut through the store, across the courtyard, one key for the store, one key for the apartment, and one more key for the family entrance and the bathroom?

"Only three keys. Only three keys."

Don't know about this . . .

"It ees cheap, very cheap for you."

How cheap.

"Soo cheap, my wife she say, Raul, Raul why do you—"

How cheap.

"I say $300 a month."

I'm sorry, señor, I think I better look elsewhere.

"No I make mistake: $250."

I don't think so. How about $150?

Señor Ruiz was distressed again, his eyes filled with emotion, his voice thickened . . . "No, no, we need the money. I rent from my own house, you leeve with my family, you go through my store. If I do not need no money, I no do thees, you know?"

I sort of followed that. How about $175? (One seventy-five was my limit actually; Gil's Rule of Rent: never accept a monthly rent more than a week's take-home pay.)

We haggled.

I realize now poor Señor Ruiz was really in a tight spot. He had fixed up (so to speak) their ground-floor room to rent and then realized that the tenant had to cut through the store every night. If that was 3 a.m., the Ruizes could never be sure that the tenant wasn't swiping food off the shelves of the store. So he had to rent it to someone he could trust, or at least convince himself was honest. I've always had an honest face.

We agreed on $195 a month. No contract.

"We make a deal, we shake our hands, eh? You name? Ah, yes, come for a cup of coffee, we talk some more . . ."

Best coffee I ever had in my life was the coffee I got at Ruiz's Foodstore. Some Caribbean blend.

"Heel, I want you to meet my wife . . ." Heel. He could never accept that *Gil* had a hard *G*. I corrected him for a while but that got him onto "Jill" and "Heel" was preferable. Friends (not that I had many after leaving the Venice, being on the outs with Emma, rarely seeing the Yuppie Lisa) liked calling me Heel as well.

"Nie to meetoo," said Señora Ruiz, a tremendous Hispanic woman, equal in bulk to her husband. Her command of English couldn't really have been called a command.

There were three kids. A young, shrill daughter named Manuela who put on too much makeup and wore these midriffs and tube tops so one was always confronted with her chunky, huge fourteen-year-old breasts. "You no wear that outside ona street!" Señor Ruiz would yell from behind the cash register when Manuela would try to slip by. (Since all egress went by the Ruizes' cash register and by Señor Ruiz, he was sort of the Colossus of Rhodes, the sentry, no one entered or received permission to go but through him.)

There was Rickie (a lot of Puerto Rican guys, even in Puerto Rico, I'm told, go by American nicknames). Rickie was fifteen and trouble and continually breaking his mother's heart and running in gangs, showing no respect here, no respect there—most fights upstairs (in high-volume Spanish) were over Rickie. I had one major contact with Rickie. I bought a six-pack of beer once and he saw me, followed me to my room, knocked on my door, came in and acted like my room was his property.

"You. You actor, huh?"

Trying to be.

"You famous?"

No.

"You gonna give me a beer?"

What about what your parents would say?

"Fuck my parents."

I gave him a beer. He looked through my records.

"Ain't got nothin' here but shit."

Sorry. What did he like?

"Heavy metal, man. Judas Priest, Iron Maiden, Kees."

I don't have any Kiss. How about the Rolling Stones, which was as heavy as I got.

"Fuck the Rollin' Stones, man."

But I put on the cassette of the album, the one with the song with the line: "There're some Porta Rican girls just dyyyyyin' to meetchoo!" and he liked it after all.

"Shit man, can I borrow thees?"

He was going to sit out on the street with his friends and his $180 box radio (jambox, ghetto blaster, boombox . . . no one ever did settle on a name for those big radios) and blast it over and over. I lent my tape to him and that's the last I ever saw of it. A minor concession, I figured—if I ever got in a hassle on the street he and his pals might come to the rescue.

And finally there was Johnnie, called Juan by his Mama. Johnnie was the oldest at sixteen and he was quiet, almost as if he was subdued, yelled into submission by his noisy family. He grew up in San Juan and moved with his family to New York when he was seven. He seemed to remember Puerto Rico with very little affection. Johnnie would come down about once a week to look through my books.

"You sure read a lot of books," he said.

Oh not at all, not compared to some people. Half the shelf was stuff Emma gave me.

"Emma. She you lady?" he asked, smiling.

No. Not anymore.

"Yeah, yeah," he nodded wisely, "women. Ahh. What can you do?"

I appreciated adolescent sympathy, the sincerest around.

For this, I conspired to give him a beer from the rusted icebox.

"My Mama hate to see us with beer, you know? That's why Rickie ees *so* estupid. I do everything I wanna do but I no get caught. Rickie he so estupid he alllways get caught, and then they have a beeg fight, Mama Papa and Rickie. I am smart. He is not smart."

That's how it looked to me too. I lent Johnnie some books. He picked up *Gravity's Rainbow*—I talked him out of that one, not being able to finish it myself. Take *1984*, I said, and *Catcher in the Rye* and an anthology of modern poetry.

"I'm gonna be a great writer too, man," he told me.

One day when I was walking home Johnnie was hanging out untypically with Rickie's streetcrowd. One boy started making fun of me ("Hey you actorfaggot, hey . . . hey turn around . . .") and I heard Johnnie join in just to be cool in front of his crowd, and he was too embarrassed, I think, to come around to see me again. He left the pile of books outside my door one night, returned. And I should have found him and said I understood why he joined in and I'm ten years older and I don't care it didn't bother me and he and I should still be friends but I didn't. I just hope he didn't feel too guilty and get a little messed up by it, because he was a sensitive kid who shouldn't have had to grow up on Avenue A.

One day on my answering machine: BEEP! *Hey Gil, Lisa. Gotta talk to you about something—you haven't been home in the history of the world. Could you pick me up some jalapeño sauce? Hola. Qué tal? Como estás, amigo? Ha ha, just kidding. There's something big I have to talk to you about—it's so exciting! Call me, call me, call me.* CLICK.

Next message: *Gil Freeman? Yeah, uh, this is Tony Woodward down at the Chelsea New Generation Playhouse . . .*

MY GOD could it be—a successful audition for me???

I've spared you the details of my latest get-out-there-Gil-and-audition drive—there's only so much rejection you can read about and only so much I can write about. Most people went into auditions hoping to land a role. I used to think that way too. Expectations lower, however, and my current goal was to not be asked to finish early. You see, you start your audition piece and the terror of every actor is to be interrupted in mid-piece with "Thank you, thank you very much for coming down. We've seen enough and we appreciate your time." GOD THE TERROR OF THAT. Better a life of continual rejection than to be cut off in midaudition. A fate worse than anything—although no actor, I suppose, has *not* had that happen at one time or another. It may have nothing to do with you, actually—they may have found the right actor already, or decided justly and correctly from looking at you that you weren't right for the ninety-year-old man. But still, nothing was worse: that was my goal, to make it to the end of the audition piece.

I projected NICE, the good-natured NICE Midwestern sensitive actor, when I went into these things—no cockiness, no swagger, no gimmicks (you see, sometimes, these actors come in and they've memorized a passage from the director's autobiography or they pull some stunt to get attention, get remembered—it is always embarrassing). No, I was the NICE one, the one they couldn't cut off in midaudition piece. But I was not nice. I would have stabbed, killed, strangled with my bare hands ANYONE who was between me and that part, gladly, ruthlessly, with sadistic glee.

After Connie and I (ha ha) broke up, I auditioned for every theater in the Western World, that is, on Manhattan Island—no place was too low to consider. But I had come to accept the fact that nobody wanted me in a stock company; I was too . . . uh, stock, too average, I seemed to get the feeling. All right. Forget financial security—that would have been too easy, wouldn't it? I would audition for individual roles all over town. Get a copy of *Backstage* each week, sit down, circle the relevant roles . . . ACTOR, MALE 25–30, Drama of a Brooklyn family . . . Yeah, I'd think, hit 'em in the audition with Biff in *Death of a Salesman*. ACTOR, MALE 25–30, Drama of an alcoholic wanderer . . . Hit them with the tuberculose son in *Long Day's Journey into Night* or Tom's opening in *The Glass Menagerie* (if you could get through Tom nodding wisely, saying "In Spain, there was Guernica . . ." without laughing, you deserved the part). Retarded son? Do *Flowers for Algernon*. Jocks? *That Cham-*

pionship Season or Brick in *Cat on a Hot Tin Roof*. Homosexuals? *The Shadow Box,* hot off the press; *Boys in the Band* was in disfavor, like *The Children's Hour,* too much emoting about how sick and dirty and unhappy you were, while the gay director and lesbian casting agent sat out there grimacing. ANYWAY, for each and every stereotype there was a perfect piece. Unfortunately all the other actors in New York knew them too. Nothing like being about to go on with the fifteenth Mangiacavallo in *The Rose Tattoo* of the day (the word was out they needed a nutty Italian immigrant) and hearing the director scream "Oh good god, not another *Rose Tattoo*—jeeezus christ!" Such experiences did not inspire confidence. But see, Emma? I still had it in me to get out there and court humiliation—your faith was justified. If I'd been on speaking terms with her, I'm sure she'd have approved.

But lo. April of 1979 I got a major role. A three-person family drama at the Chelsea New Generation Playhouse. The Chelsea New Generation Playhouse was probably representative in 1969 of a New Generation but ten years had made it just one more hand-to-mouth struggling theater, off the beaten track (walking distance from nowhere), desperate for hits (they'd had two in one season, both of which went to Broadway, so now they had Hit Fever and wanted every production to win a Pulitzer).

The name of the show was *Bermuda Triangle,* a drama about three people, mother, son and father, fighting it out realizing they love each other while on a vacation none of them wants to take in Bermuda. It starts off funny then gets bittersweet and in my opinion falls completely apart at the end. The son is urging his mother to get a divorce because he is fighting this Oedipal battle and hates his father and cares less for his mother's happiness than that his father have his world shattered. The father is tired of his wife, blames her for turning the son against him. The mother has a drinking problem brought on by father and son squabbling. There were worse things on off-Broadway, I promise you. This play was the work of Christopher Smalley. Smalley had had a well-received debut with *Bad Memories,* which must have been directly autobiographical, about him and his father. He was big on fathers and sons fighting it out and was convinced families worked like that, that people fought it out until they fell in each other's arms and said how much they loved each other. I always wanted to say: Don't you know people go through their lives NOT saying anything, not fighting anything important out, squabbling over how the roast was cooked and not who loved who when and because of what Freudian reason etc.? I hated this kind of drama. Rather, I hate it *now*—I was damn glad to be immersed in it then.

Our director was Brent Malverne and how he got to be a director God only knows. No wait a second, I think I know how: he was so dominating, so loud, so brash, so full of hyper-energy and ideas and bubbling, overflowing sentiments that people mistook this for genius . . . "Gilbert, darling, no, no, no. Listen to me: I want to see that RAGE, that ANGER, give it to me, give it to me from here, right *here*!" He clutched his bowels. "Make me feel it, talk to me, work for me, kid!" It's just Act One, I said—shouldn't we save the fireworks until Act Three? "Your sense of drama is pure Elizabethan, Gilbert. This is 1979—full blast, all the way through. We want to drain the audience, drag it through the mire, the experience. A sensory overload; it's the only way to communicate to a numbed, a battered audience these days. Saturate them in emotion, in EXCESS—yes, that's right, excess, no restraint at all. I don't want one inhibition, is that understood people? Full throttle."

"Brent," said Bonnie McHenry, who played Mom, "that's nonsense. People are going to get up and walk out if we scream and carry on for three acts of this dreck."

I *loved* Bonnie. She was tall and statuesque, one of those women who looked like a gracious, slightly faded forty from the audience, but looked like fifty and hell on closer inspection, cigarette lips, a cackle that it took *eons* of smoking to produce, this kind of sunlamp tan which made the skin leathery and tough. She had made her career, as a young woman, in the bitch Noel Coward roles (always the interloper, the climber, the rotten older sister) and she could be brittle and refined without a thought. That's why it was funny to see that in real life she was as vulgar and guttermouthed as a Championship Wrestling fan—god, every other word out of her mouth was unprintable. She was tough. She was unforgiving.

Every once in a while, Bonnie would let up, take a breath and wind down and show herself to be vulnerable, almost childlike and optimistic inside. But watch out: Underneath that she was hard and tough again, this single woman, husbandless, childless, independent for a thirty-year, three-decades-the-hard-way career. I thought she hated me at first. Once I was bleating my lines, getting whiny, and she—not the director—cut me off in rehearsal, setting me straight: "Gil, you gotta be sympathetic or no one's gonna hang with you for this whole crappy play—stop the whining and the nagging and . . . and the *acting*. Just say the lines; save the scenery-chewing for Act Three." I was sure she thought I was a second-rate amateur, beneath her standards. I was just being sensitive though. One time backstage she hugged me, ambushed me, cackling, "Ah, you're not put off by Bonnie McHenry, are ya kid? Nahhh, you're doing fine, just fine. We'll do the bar after this, okay? You and me and not . . . you-know."

I knew who she meant by you-know. Tucker K. Broome, our co-star. Neither of us had come out and said it, but he stunk, he was awful, wrong for the role, and an unprofessional drunk to boot. We were united in this—I was so happy to be on Bonnie's side.

Tucker K. Broome (one of that generation of actors who insisted on middle initials) was familiar to people on a number of '60s situation comedies—he was Colonel Whackum on *Company B*, the blustering bank manager on *Blank Check*, and the foreman of the flip flop (you know, those rubber beach sandals) assembly line on *Flip Flop* (this set up one reviewer's shred under the headline: FLOP FLOP). I could devote the next three pages to things I didn't like about that man (who is dead now, so libel suits are not a threat).

He was pretentious ("I remember one time Thornton Wilder took me on his knee and he said to me . . ."), he overrated everything about himself. "I remember one time on *Flip Flop*, I told the director—"

"Don't hand us goddam *Flip Flop*," interrupted Bonnie. "This is theater, not can-I-have-a-second-take TV, fella—not to mention second-rate TV."

He was insecure, he stormed out of rehearsal at a moment's notice, and as things got closer to the opening, he drank more and more. He tried to mask his drinking by regularly using this extract of menthol, some alcoholic stuff (not crème de menthe) that looked to be eating away his tongue and mouth—completely disgusting. So as not to give his co-stars a blast of his lunchtime martinis (not that he cared about our comfort, but whether he'd be fired), he'd dab his tongue with this vial of greenish fluid, then grimace like a Cheshire cat and suck in air through his teeth to mix up the mint with his breath, and then his co-stars would get a blast of MENTHOL in the face instead of Manhattans.

"Shoooeee," said Bonnie one rehearsal. "Good god, Tucker, I'd rather have the scotch than that shit."

Righteous indignation, the man indistinguishable from the ham he's been the last thirty years: "Scotch? Scotch, my dear woman? Whatever do you mean?"

"I mean I'm sick of that goddam mint, and it's turning your teeth green."

Brent the director steps in: "Children, children, please can we get on with it?"

In a doddering explosion of affronted dignity: "I won't work with this woman—I can't Malverne, I cannot!" And he would rage out of the rehearsal to drink some more, at a bar down the street.

"Bonnie, love, must you antagonize Tucker every rehearsal?"

"Brent, you don't have to face Lysol-breath every night—you get up here and see if your eyes don't water when he's yelling and bellowing away."

Three weeks until we opened.

"I'm contemplating some new blocking . . ." Brent said, sitting in the musty theater, third row, lying across several seats Cleopatra-like. "When you go to change from your Bermuda shirt and swimsuit into your lounging clothes, Gil, I think you should change onstage. I envision you changing, slipping out of your wet bathing suit, and Doris [the mother played by Bonnie] turning and furtively staring at her son's undressing, seeing him as a young man who has come of age, vital, potent."

I am not showing my ass to a New York Theater audience, Brent. NO WAY.

"Gil, I can't believe you're so shy. It's a wonderful idea."

I'm not taking my pants down, particularly as it serves no purpose.

"This is 1979, Gilbert darling. Up the road in *Equus* there was a young actor doing frontal nude scenes every night for hours out there, showing his prick to the world."

Good. Now that he's through up there showing his prick to the world let him come down here in Chelsea and show his ass to the world, but *I'm* not doing it.

Bonnie, slightly laughing, spoke up: "Brent, it's a crap idea —it sucks. It's just gratuitous. The New York audience is more sophisticated than that—our play isn't a bit better because Gil shows his ass. What's next? I change onstage and show my tits while Gil looks on?"

Brent hopped up excitedly. "Yes, yes! A balance, an incestuous subtext lurking beneath the script. That's brilliant Bonnie! Gil's bottom in Act One, your tits in Act Two!"

Bonnie was laughing, shaking her head. "Brent, I'm forty-nine. I'm not showing my tits and Gil's not showing his bottom. Why don't you see if Tucker will pull out his dick in Act Three?"

Brent: "It is a thought—"

Tucker, quiet through all this, burst in, "She's insulting me again, Malverne. She never lets up. I can't work with her!"

"Oh shut up, Tucker," said Bonnie. "What are you complaining about? Afraid you'll have to show your dick?"

"I thought this was a professional company performing a drama, not *Oh, Calcutta!* when I signed on. I've got a career in family-oriented TV at stake, Malverne. And as for your suggestion, Miss McHenry, let me say that . . ." Blah blah blah.

Bonnie had to have the last word: "What are you going on about, Tucker? Two nights ago you got mad when I said you didn't have a dick, and now I'm giving you credit for having one—you're never satisfied."

Brent: "Children, children—"

Once more I passionately insisted on not stripping onstage.

"Gilbert darling," Brent pleaded, "think it over."

Bonnie cackled, "Aw Brent, you just want to see Gilbert's ass night after night, don't you?" More cackling, as she thought about her (probably true) theory.

Brent: "What are you implying?"

"You see how abusive and insulting she is, Malverne," Tucker said, scanning the situation for a pretext to abort the rehearsal and find a bar. "I can't take this amateurish display another minute!"

I continued to fight for my right to remain clothed; Bonnie kept cackling and firing off insults at Tucker and Brent; Brent took half an hour resenting the implications of Bonnie's statements, Tucker jumped ship for the barroom; and Smalley the playwright came back from supper to find things in an uproar and, mercifully, put his foot down at the nude scenes.

Two weeks until we opened.

Everyone was nervous—Bonnie mumbled about being able to sniff a bomb a month in advance, Tucker was understandably worried about being replaced, Gary (the producer who hired me) and Brent were at each other's throats. I, however, was just happy to be in a bomb—even THAT was so far beyond my expectations. Bombs away! What did I care?

I liked my routine. Leave the house by eleven or so, walk crosstown by way of 14th Street, a doughnut stand, the newspaper/magazine store (read the headlines, read the tabloids, peek at *Backstage,* the *Village Voice,* pay for nothing), then maybe to Rosalita's, where you could get a hearty Cuban breakfast (fruit salads, beans on the plate with runny egg . . . I'm getting hungry thinking about her ladling whatever she felt like making onto your plate, the breakfast special—and the Coffee That Would Wake the Dead . . .); and then onward to the theater, pop in and see who was there, duck out for a drink with a stagehand or actor, watch *All My Children* in the costume room, involve myself in violent discussions over who should do what and why so-and-so can't run her life, etc. The Village was right there so I could wander and browse through bookstores, record stores, hang out at old places (though many had changed ownership or gone bust, alas), old bars, old coffeehouses—a completely lazy existence. You could do all this when unemployed too, but you felt guilty about it: I should be out looking for work. But not when you'd been cast and were working every night—this was the life, this was the feeling, strolling about New York all day, goofing off, and waiting for that friend to run into you. What am I up to? Ah, the usual. Acting. Yeah I'm in a production in Chelsea—not bad, might go over, not getting my hopes up. Oh yes, definitely come see me, check it out—if it's no trouble. God, what happiness.

Answering machine: BEEP! *Gil, this is Lisa, remember me, your oldest friend in New York? Guess who I ran into. Jasmine Dahl, the girl who lived with Emma? She told me to tell you that her independent record is out this month and to look for it and buy it, and there's one of Emma's poems on the back cover, AND she also told me to tell you that Emma wants to get back with you and I wish you would, Gil, because*—CLICK. The message ran over the allotted time.

Next message: BEEP! *It's me, Lisa again. I want to say that God should personally damn this machine to hell, I* hate *these things. The playwright of your new play had this interview in the* Voice *and everyone in town is talking about this play you're in and Jim and I are coming for opening night, and we'll seeya there. I got gossip—you would never BELIEVE in a million years what Emma is doing for money now—and I have NEWS, Gil, big major all-star news but I gotta tell you in person*—CLICK.

Oh Lisa, Lisa, Lisa. Do you think I haven't figured out that you and Jim-at-the-advertising-agency are getting married? I have nothing in common with you any longer, darling. I said this aloud in a room all by myself.

Next message: BEEP! *Uh, hi Gil, remember me? Betsy at the . . . you know, our group. You don't come much anymore and I don't either really. But I enjoyed our talk, you know? You wanna get together maybe for coffee, talk some more? I thought I could talk to you real well, I mean . . . God, I hate these machines. Please call me back* . . . And then she gave her phone number.

I stood there for a minute. Betsy. Who was Betsy? Which one was she? Some of the women in that support group—she was correct, I never went to those meetings anymore—weren't half-bad-looking. Was she one of them? Why not call her? Go ahead. You don't have to commit yourself to anything. Coffee between rehearsals—when she finds out you're in a play she'll understand your saying "Gee, Betsy I'm so busy right now . . ." and if she's pretty and nice and you can deal with her, you can go out with her.

Betsy and I met at the Village Herpes Victims Support Group which met on Wednesdays in the Public Health Center, where several groups, fifty or more, met during the week helping people like myself cope with the trauma of herpes. You're probably wondering: Why hasn't he mentioned his herpes before now? and now mentioning it, why isn't he his usual neurotic self? Well. I didn't mention it right off because herpes is not my life—I am not a virus. And I'm not neurotic about it and in a sense . . . well, you may not believe this, but the thought of getting herpes, the suspense was worse in a way than finally getting it. Well, I thought, don't have to worry about *that* anymore. Also, what a drag, the whole New York singles scene: the dating, the pantomime of openness and sexual revolution and modernity, the phone number game and follow-ups, the back-at-my-place-for-coffees, the whole routine of getting to know everything about the other person in a night so you could sleep with them and not feel sleazy, which led to so much performance, so much pretense and lies and CHARADES. I'm an actor, I can spot bad acting—take my word for it.

With herpes, it was obvious to me: MY SEX LIFE WAS OVER. I was finished sexually. No sense even trying because you'll have to break the news one of these days, or lie, and having been lied to I would not lie to anyone else. I was celibate and single for life and I was capable of wearing that mantle, really. I had my work. I had the theater. If I got famous by throwing myself into my work, I would be desirable to thousands (like rock stars, movie stars) and no one would give a damn if they caught bubonic plague from me. I had my craft, my art, my *oeuvre,* my artistry. I had masturbation.

"So glad, Gil, you called me—I mean *so* glad," said Betsy, as she swept into our arranged meeting place, a diner on Seventh Avenue and Christopher.

Looking forward to it, I said. I looked at Betsy up and down: one of the pretty ones—one of the very pretty ones. Perhaps today I wouldn't think so—Betsy was one of those early-'80s emaciated, always-on-a-diet women, skinny to the detriment of her breasts and behind, two areas guys generally don't mind encountering flesh. Women got convinced in the late '70s that the more they looked like guys, the better—how slender could they be? Yuck. I mean, I'll take anything, but given my choice I'd like some *meat on the bones,* you know? Women never believe this, I think. Well anyway, back to Betsy: she could wear those outfits models could wear, very chic, fashionable, Madison Avenue-ish. Not my type at all. Maybe, MAYBE we could get along.

"My friends call me Bitsy," she laughed.

Maybe not.

"You know," she said, slipping her coat off after having sat down in the booth, "I found that group was stifling too, you know? Why did you leave it?"

Tired of dwelling on herpes herpes herpes all the time, I said. I look at the whole thing as like a bad case of the flu, you have to warn people you have it before getting too far—in fact, you have to get callous about it, bored with telling people. The worst rejection in the world would be: You degenerate filth, get out of here, I never want to see you again! And that was highly unlikely, whereas: You creep! Why didn't you tell me, you bastard! would be far worse, wouldn't it? With those thoughts in mind, I could proceed with my life.

"Oh that's so reasonable, that really is," she said, as the waitress set down big slick menus in front of us. "That is so reasonable and smart—I wish I could think like that but I can't. I just think about herpes *all* the time, you know?"

Well at first that's natural.

"It's been eight months. What are you going to have?"

Breakfast.

She laughed at this; crazy me! Breakfast at 3 p.m. "Oh, you're an actor, right? Late-night rehearsals and all. I have a friend in the theater. Let's see if you know her . . ."

I didn't.

"Where does it get you?"

What?

"The herpes. I get it so bad around my bottom. Like when I have an interview or am nervous or anything. Oh it's awful."

Let's not talk sores and bottoms, okay?

"Sure, sure. I'll have breakfast too."

Two breakfast specials. What else did we talk about? Small things, jobs, bosses, my opening (which I underplayed). Betsy was in publishing, book publishing at Marcus & Windom. They published good things and they also published at lot of trash best-sellers. She hoped to be a book editor one day. Publishing pays no salaries—starting salaries of $11,000, can you believe it? With a masters in English no less.

You oughta check out theater salaries, I said.

"Yes, but think how much more exciting the theater is than publishing."

Not if you do it for a while, I said.

"Yeah, things get boring," she said, sighing.

A pause in the conversation. We really had nothing to talk about. She came up with the other conversation ploy, before reverting to the only subject I ever remember her talking about:

"I don't feel I can be sexual anymore. I can't imagine being free in bed. You know, my boyfriend and I, Roger, broke up over this."

I thought Roger gave her herpes.

"Well he did," she said, looking into her plate, twirling her hair nervously, "but after I got it I couldn't sleep with him anymore. I mean, yes, we did sleep together, but I wasn't, I don't know, interested. I need to start afresh, you know?"

Hmmm, did this mean me? How many people in that group has she called and gone out with? Let's get to the heart of the issue: Are you, Gil, going to sleep with this woman? Yeah I think I'd like that. She's neurotic, nervous about everything, barely picked at her food—I generally don't get along with people who can't drink when they drink, eat when they eat, and she's as good as told you she doesn't make love when she makes love these days. Pre-herpes this is a bad move; post-herpes we're not so choosy.

"What you thinking about?" She looked up as if she feared I was going to reject her in astounding new ways.

Did she want to meet me after the theater for a drink?

There I did it. And having once done it, I felt all right about it. What do you know, I said to myself all through the night's rehearsal, there may indeed be sex after herpes . . .

"Gilbert darling," yelled Brent, in a particularly absent period of my performance. "Are you awake? You're dropping your cues—you should be hanging on Bonnie's every word; your mother is accusing you of wrecking her marriage. Attention must be paid, darling—now get with it."

"Isn't it time to go home?" mumbled Tucker, checking his watch.

"There'll still be a place at Butner's Bar and Grill, Tucker, no need to rush," said Bonnie, suppressing that cackle.

"I swear, Miss McHenry—"

Brent cut this short: "That's enough kiddies. We're all tired and the play is tired—"

"What do you mean by that?" asked Smalley, sitting in the back row.

"I mean the performances are tired tonight; we're sick of the material and it's dragging. Why do you have to be so goddam sensitive, Christopher, about everything?"

Smalley bristled. "Who's being sensitive? You just said my play was tired."

Brent exhaled and put his hand on his hip. "What I *said* and what you knew I meant was that we were all tired of the play—"

"No what you *said* was . . ."

The Sensitivity Wars raged for another ten minutes.

"I don't care what either of you said," snapped Bonnie, "this shit is a waste of time. We've got the play down pat and we need an audience at this point."

"I think Bonnie is right," said Tucker, stepping forward into an upstage table, knocking over a vase—he fumbled trying to catch it, he grasped, almost, no . . . SMASH.

"Oh just *fine*!" said Brent, committing his ultimate assertive act, hurling his clipboard to the floor. "I oughta make you pay for that out of your own pocket, Tucker. That's the third time you've done that. What are you going to do opening night? Move around like a rhinoceros?"

"I don't think I have to take this!" Tucker yelled.

And there we went again, Tucker storming off. Our all-night rehearsal over at 9:30.

"Brent," called Bonnie.

"What is it now?"

"What possessed you to hire that old drunk? He's going to louse up the play—he's getting worse nightly. And who does he think he is? Olivier? God, his delivery is so arch. And the mintbreath—Brent, that's killing us up here. I'm gonna pass out."

Smalley joined in: "She's right Malverne. He's not been right for the part from the start; I'm looking for Willy Loman here not Sir Ralph Richardson. My character sold real estate, for god's sake. He's a self-made American businessman—"

Brent was on the defensive: "Didn't you watch *Flip Flop*? He was a line foreman in a flip flop factory. Who would have thought he had so little fire left in him? He did *Death of a Salesman* in regional theater—"

"My goddam Uncle Herbert did goddam *Death of a Salesman* in regional theater," Bonnie shot back. "Tucker's used up, *through*. He's gonna die the Big Death here next week, believe me."

"You have to stop undermining him—"

"Brent, honeychild, listen to Bonnie," Bonnie said, pointing an accusing finger at him. "I have seen them fold before and it happens just like this. I've worked with every drunk in the business. They either get better the more they drink, or they get worse and worse. Have you looked into replacing him with the understudy?"

Brent was sputtering: "But he's . . . he's a draw, Bonnie. He was a star at one time; people will expect him—"

"A STAR? Tucker Broome, a star? He did shit TV, has had a shit career, was never any good at one thing he ever appeared in. *Flip Flop*, for christ's sake—*Flip Flop!* You cast a man on the basis of goddam *Flip Flop?*"

"I think you fucked up," said Smalley accusingly.

"Oh now just a minute! Just a minute! We're all tired and we're losing our professionalism . . . " Brent couldn't defend himself though.

They were right. Tucker was a disaster. He was folding. Bonnie and I were going to die with him. The play would be a flop. The playwright—who needed a hit—would be finished. Brent would go on working at the Chelsea . . . but with an expensive flop to his credit. He too must have been scared. How did I feel appearing in a disaster? Well, used to it by this time. I'd been backstage or onstage for a number of fiascoes—I was getting pretty fiascoproof at this point. Young people, someone told me . . . yes, it was Joyce Jennings: Young people can walk away from flops; it's not as easy for the over-forties. The argument raged on. I looked at Bonnie shake her head, light up a cigarette, the language turned bluer, the blame being heaped entirely on Brent's casting decision. The techie crew (and I can *read* the techie crew, I can tell you what they're thinking like a mind-reader) had that look of: Boy, are they EVER in a bomb now. I started laughing. Well, I wanted to live like this, didn't I? Hell, at this point, why not drop my pants? It's all so hilarious—adults getting up to make a fool of themselves in front of people dumb enough to pay to watch.

And it didn't matter anyway because I was having SEX THAT NIGHT.

Betsy met me outside the theater at eleven (even though rehearsals ended this evening at ten and Bonnie and I had finished up at the bar.)

"How'd it go?" Betsy chirped.

It's going to be the worst bomb in a long time for off-Broadway. A spectacular bust, as opposed to ignominious silent disgrace.

"Oh I'm sure it'll be all right. Shall we get a drink?"

Yeah let's have about sixty-five.

We went to a place in the Village where you could get a $3 pitcher. This was a two-pitcher seduction, really. Drunk but not so drunk as to—euphemize, euphemize—hinder performance. You know, this situation was just about perfect: I didn't care how bad the evening went. I didn't care what became of Betsy. That was awful, retract that! No, it's true though—I'm sorry. We all run across dispensable human beings from time to time, let's admit it. Yeah, I said to myself, shoveling peanuts into my mouth, watching her nervously ramble on, twirling her hair compulsively, she is just what we needed on the verge of Theatric Disaster.

"The play's not going well?" she asked, conscious of boring me.

Well all right. Well not really. Well, actually, it will be a disaster and it's too late to replace a major character.

"That's a shame. Well, it'll just make you look better, huh?"

Now she had a point there . . .

"I've had enough beer. How about you?"

I put another handful of peanuts into my mouth, shrugging. If she didn't want to drink any more that was fine.

"I was thinking about a whiskey actually," she corrected, half-smiling. "We can hold our booze, you know, in publishing."

I went up to get two whiskeys.

"I was anorexic for a while," she said, when I came back. I put the drink in front of her and she greedily took it. "I'm not back to normal yet, digestively."

Sorry about that.

"It was just the herpes thing," she said, twirling a new strand of hair. "I had anorexia and bulimia when I was a teenager. I had to be hospitalized one time. They said if I kept throwing up I would strain my heart muscles. I wasn't getting any nutrition. I still couldn't shake the anorexia. It's a control thing, you know."

Control? Starving yourself?

"Yes. You can get to where you know if you've put on a

quarter of a pound." She pinched her elbows as a demonstration. "I could tell around here, if I'd eaten enough to gain weight. You get such control of your body—it's very seductive."

Yeah but you may die, and it looks so ugly.

"Yeah, really ugly," she said, looking into her whiskey glass, contemplating some former self-image. "I have a picture of when I was eighty-seven pounds if you can believe that—"

Oh I didn't need to see that, if she didn't want to show me.

"No, I want to show you." She went through her purse.

(I really didn't want to see, but . . .)

She handed me the photo: "It's important I show you that. I look like something out of Dachau, huh? All pale and blue—ullllch. I have to show that so I don't go back that way. I almost did when I came down with herpes."

Betsy, it's just not such a big damn deal. Inconvenient and life-adjusting yes, but it's not leprosy or cancer or deadly or even harmful and all kinds of reports of all kinds of incurable sexual diseases were starting to surface, so, you know, herpes might be the least of our worries.

"They said they'd have a cure anyway," she said confidently, "by, probably, next year, 1981 or so. They're right on the edge of finding it. So I read. I read everything I can get my hands on."

I did too when herpes material came across my path, but I never went out of my way to search for it.

"You know, I'd really like to ask you back to my place," she began, a nervous laugh, testing my eyes. "But uh my roommate Ginger is there. She's always there. I'd give anything for her not to be there one night."

Oh. Well. My place isn't too far—

"I'd like to see your place."

No you wouldn't, I said. Avenue A and Alphabet City—it's very dangerous and by the time we got there and I accompanied you out it would be so late . . .

A staredown. Who'll blink first? She goes:

"Perhaps, like, I could stay over?"

HOMEWARD BOUND.

As we walked down Avenue A from the crosstown bus stop on 14th Street, the street was packed with gangs and drugged-

dlers and streetpeople. One punk I recognized (he hung around Ruiz's store) passed by and sent up a flurry of noises and whistles: "Oooooh mama! Ey, ey, you wanna give me a piece, actorboy? Aiaiaiaiaia . . ."

Betsy got prim as she walked briskly alongside me: "A lot of scum out on the street tonight. Name me one neighborhood the Puerto Ricans have improved in the United States of America."

Now now. I live under a very nice Puerto Rican family, I said.

Another catcall from a stoop: "Hey mama, blond mama—ey you wanna present? Ey? I give you some'n to remember me by, ey? Ahaha!"

Betsy: "Macho trash culture—these people are the lowest."

We got to Ruiz's Caribbean Foodstore.

"You live in a foodstore?" asked Betsy.

I gave the instructions: Betsy, you're my cousin. The señora's a staunch Catholic and I don't want a lecture, okay? Be nice to the store-people, they're my landlords. I never bring anybody here so it's not clean; the place is a hole but all I can afford, and I like it and don't need to hear about what a pit it is. She nodded without conviction. She was prepared for the worst—I'm virtually positive she'd never been to Alphabet City before. No doubt, I was dispensable too for her. We had come to my place to dispense with each other.

"*Buenas noches*, Heel," said a tired Señor Ruiz behind the cash register. "Ah!" he brightened, "you have a lovely friend."

Señor Ruiz, I introduced, this is my cousin Elizabeth.

"Isabela!" He took her hand politely. I went to the beer cabinet to get two quart bottles, some milk for tomorrow, some eggs. I could do omelettes. Nah, maybe not. We'll go out for breakfast—

"She ain't no cousin," hissed Rickie, loitering in the aisle.

Señor Ruiz heard that: "If Heel say she his cousin, then she his cousin! EY?"

I winked at Rickie who had been silenced. "She still no yo' cousin," he whispered to me.

Back to My Place.

"What an apartment, what a neighborhood," she said, shaking her head.

I warned her, didn't I?

"This is all the space you have!" she cried in horror, as I opened the door, kicked underwear into a corner, threw a sheet over some piles of clothes and smelly socks—all in one sweep of the room.

How 'bout some more beer?

She looked as if she needed it. "Sure," she said.

I checked my phone messages. The first one went: BEEP! *Uhhhh* . . . CLICK (the caller hanging up). My god was that Emma? It sounded like her uhhhh. Surely . . . Naaah, I'm hearing things.

"What is it?" asked Betsy.

I thought it was someone I recognized, I said. Moving on, next message: BEEP! *Gil, damn you, you are not in existence anymore. I'm going to catch up with you, you know, at the opening. Jim and I have tickets virtually on the front row and don't tell her I told you but Emma thinks she'll be there too. You two have to make it up—I mean it. Oh, damn you! Fuck this machine!* CLICK.

"Emma?" asked Betsy, smiling, curious.

(Wonder what Emma would think of Betsy? Probably would be unprintable. Emma's probably playing out her fantasies of rockband groupie with Cock right now, celibacy a distant memory. WHO CARES, Gil—she's past history, remember?) I told Betsy Emma was no one of any importance.

"Was she the one?"

One who what?

"Gave you herpes?"

No. She's the one I can never now sleep with because of the herpes. But it didn't look like it was going that way anyway; and I don't care anymore etc.

Betsy looked down at the bed. My dirty sheet atop a mattress on the floor, all scruffy and fuzzy with lint in a disordered heap. "You need a housekeeper, Gil," she said laughing.

Gee, I said, acknowledging all, the maid usually comes in on Friday; Betsy *just* hit the wrong day.

Laughter. She drank her beer, I drank mine.

When I first touched her, she melted and was eagerly all over me, hurried sloppy kisses, pained anticipatory sighs—I thought she was going to pull my hair out as she took my head in her hands. Then I put a hand on her thigh intending to move upward and *click*, she froze up as if the power had gone off. She scooted back. I touched her again and she scooted further back, a little grunt as if to say: no, not there. I guess she wanted to keep things above the neckline.

Through kisses, I asked if something was wrong.

"No," she breathed, "no, no . . ."

So I touched her again and she seemed to relent—not happy about it, it seemed, but she perhaps conceded that lovemaking was likely to involve anatomy in that general vicinity. She was doing nothing with her hands as I undressed her. In fact as I was trying to undo her dress she didn't help at all. I sort of like a little SUPPORT at this point, you know? I don't want to take someone's clothes off. I mean, there I was pulling on her boots. Lady, give me some help, for christ's sake . . . I've seen this routine back in college, actually—it's like the girl is saying: I don't participate in this, YOU do all the work and therefore I won't feel guilty in the morning or if something goes wrong it's *your* fault; if I lie still enough and do as little as possible, I might be able to persuade myself we didn't even HAVE sex last night . . .

She moved her hands chastity belt-like to her waist and I kept tugging on her boot. She laughed a little private laugh. A smile passed across my face, a desire to laugh. That must have been because I suddenly saw myself with this immobile WASP beauty tugging to get her boots off while she went into some trance during which she could allow someone to have sex with her. God I wanted to laugh. What if I left and went to get some beer about here? No, stop thinking like this—you're going to start laughing, I thought. What if I said: gee, I guess NO ORAL SEX FOR ME TONIGHT . . . cut it out, cut it out—

"Is something wrong, Gil?" she asked.

NO nothing. Just having a little trouble with the boot. She surrendered and helped me take off her boot, then the other boot, then she went back to lying there, her arms tightly guarding her body, hands clasped over her waist, apparently wanting to remain in her sweater and jacket. This must be what morticians go through, I thought, dressing and undressing a corpse. Well, to hell with the skirt. I'm not taking it off alone. I'll work on the jacket and sweater.

"Yes," she said simply as I slipped off her jacket. As I went for the sweater, she resisted. "Could . . . could I—it's cold in here a bit . . . could I keep it on for a while?"

It's eighty degrees in my room, for god's sake. Okay, okay, shyness is a rare commodity these days—charming in its way. Not VERY charming, but as I said: we are not expecting perfection in the post-herpes phase of living.

Hmmm, some more foreplay, I guess. If we have some more foreplay perhaps she'll tear her clothes off, become a creature of passion. Yeah, and I've got some swamp land in Florida I bought sometime after I purchased the Brooklyn Bridge. C'mon Gil, a positive attitude. Tactic Two: I lie beside her, holding her warmly, a fond embrace, not sexual but close, tender, the sensitive male, supportive, intimate . . .

"Something wrong?" she asked meekly in a mid-sex whisper.

No, I said. What? This wasn't doing anything for her? Well, we were doing all right with the kissing portion of our program, so back to that we went. She was ALIVE again, kissing kissing and more kissing. All right, another go at the big game; my hand slips down her side to her waist and the belt of her skirt. ICE STATION ZEBRA again . . . all motion stops. Well now. We seem to be darting from yes to no here. How about something in between, Betz, we got a wide range to land in.

Oh hell. Undo the woman's skirt. Some resistance but at least it's not France in 1946 like a minute ago. I decided to guide her hand to my jeans. Any interest? Perhaps she'll keep her hand there . . . She moved her hand back after a dimension check to its official position, clasped with the other hand above the pelvis. All right, no interest in that particular part of my anatomy, I see. Not a big draw lately. I got an idea. I'll take off MY clothes and maybe you'll feel left out. Here we go . . . shirt is off, girl. Guess what's next? My jeans. Unbutton them . . . no slow down, don't rush, let her think about it. Jeans to the floor. We'll keep on the underpants, a fresh clean pair brought out for this occasion. And now I slip beside her under the covers. HEEEEEEEERE's Gil.

"Gil," she said.

Yes?

"Don't you want to make love to me?"

Well yes darling, but it seemed you were resisting me.

"I'm just a little shy with someone new, that's all."

No need to be shy with me, I said. (I should have added: because we'll likely never see each other again so what the hell? But I did not add that, bad bad boy . . .)

She started fumbling with her skirt. Great, we're on our little way now . . . Her skirt hit the floor. We both lay there. I guess it's up to me to start things off here. We were on safe ground with the kissing, as I recall. This time we'll see where the wandering hands gets us.

Now what does our audience at home think? This lovemaking experience ends with what comment from Betsy (multiple choice):

a) "Gee, that was the best sex I ever had, Gil. You're a master, a craftsman, I was a block of marble, you were the sculptor."

b) "I never really knew until this moment what it was to be a woman . . . I'll never be frigid and neurotic and withholding again after this night . . . "

c) "God, wait till I tell all my friends! They'll be wanting some of this too! You *stud* you!"

d) "Gil can you get me a taxi, do you think? And uh . . . well, like, next time I promise to be more into it okay? I'm just, you know, not back to normal yet. It'll be more fun next time, I promise."

Some people might have gotten depressed. But not me. I got to have SEX WITH SOMEONE, post-herpes, got it out of my system for a while, solved the moral qualms, and didn't get emotionally involved with a woman who wouldn't take her sweater off. A kiss on the cheek, put her in the taxi and BUENAS NOCHES, señorita. And then—I *love* this feeling—back to one's own private bedroom, no lump of flesh staying over, heating up your bed, stealing covers, taking space, seeing you look like crap the next morning . . . alone again! Post-coital aloneness—*can't beat it*. I walked into my room and saw I had forgotten to put the milk and eggs away in my icebox. I thought: more eggs for me tomorrow this way. A four-egg omelette and not a two-egg omelette; more Cocoa Krispies for me, a second bowl . . .

Now okay. It's obvious Betsy and I aren't meant for each other. But she sort of got under my skin, that woman. No, can't say she ever became important to me (or me to her), and I can't say it was all because of the good sex (because we had—look this up in the almanac, too—the world's consistently worst sex). Betsy was like a Big Mac. You're not always in the mood for gourmet food, sometimes you want something easy and convenient and happily trivial. I'm not defending myself very well. All I know is that I wasn't alone for two years with herpes in New York. Some people end up alone, I didn't.

Besides, as Emma once said: In sex, it's the thought that counts. Someone wanted to have it with me and that was more important than the end result, the final byproduct, etc. After a while, even Betsy got a kick out of coming down to Alphabet City. I could visualize her going on at the office about this bohemian on Avenue A. My god, her yuppie master's-in-English friends would shriek, not there! It's so dangerous! Ah the adventure of romance, what those durn fool crazy lovers won't do . . . She even got to like fried plantains and black beans on rice which I'd cook on my hotplate, following recipes that were on the cans. The more I think about living with the Ruizes, the more memories keep flooding back, and the more I miss them:

I see Señor Ruiz watching soccer games on the Spanish station on his little black-and-white TV behind the counter, ignoring the customers, making incorrect change half-distracted. On Thursday nights, invariably, Iris Chacon's show came on (lots of rumba, lots of salsa, lots of tongue-rolling *rrrrrrrrrr*s and *yeeeeha*! noises and Iris in the tightest clothes imaginable, shaking and gyrating). I remember coming in to find Senõra Ruiz all perfumed, dolled in a tight black frock, a flower in her hair (for some reason, some occasion—an anniversary?) dancing with Senõr Ruiz behind the counter, both of them too big to salsa up and down the aisles without bumping things to the floor. He'd take her and spin her about nonetheless and this girlish years-younger laughter would just spill out of her. She tried to fight him off as I came in the door—"No, no, es Heel, Heel . . ."—but he was not to be put off, hugging her, tickling her a bit, making her squeal and giggle, kissing her neck. On Fridays it was some teenybopper Latin American show that reduced Manuela to screaming frenzies, ridiculed by her brothers who had no interest in the newest teen-idol group of sweet androgynous Puerto Rican boys. They would taunt her, pulling out the plug in the middle of the show and running, leaving her in hysterics while the set took another five minutes to warm up.

I came in another evening to find Señor Ruiz listening to the news. I went to get my usual can of pork 'n beans. When you live in a store you have to be careful about your shopping. Once I got a can of pork 'n beans from another store and Señor Ruiz was the incarnation of despair: "Why you go there? We got beans here, Heel—see?" No, I said, those were red beans and white beans and South American black beans but not pork 'n beans. Señor Ruiz took my can and examined it and said he'd get some pork 'n beans in too. The next week there were three cans of pork 'n beans and I bought one. The next week six, then nine . . . apparently, he thought I was good for three cans a week. There's only so much pork 'n beans I want to eat, but because he ordered them and they were piling up I kept buying them. To this day I can't eat another bite of pork 'n beans. ANYWAY, I was getting my weekly two cans of pork 'n beans and Señor Ruiz was watching the news.

"Hmm, mmmm, mmmm," he said, shaking his head. "This ees a bad bad theeng for our country, Heel."

What is?

"The Communists all over the place in Central America. We know what happened in Cuba with Castro. The communists are trouble, *trouble*. I am not a Communist, Heel."

No, Señor Ruiz.

"Thees man, thees Carter—no ees a good president."

The TV was showing pictures of the Sandinistas celebrating their victory of the deposed tyrant Somoza. I pointed out to Señor Ruiz that Somoza was a worse man, a bad man, a dictator.

"Bah," he waved me aside, "you still no want the Communists down there. They no give up until they in the United States. I am not a Communist, Heel. I am an American."

I NEVER like to hear someone rag on and on about how left-wing and lazy the Hispanic people are in America. Yeah, okay, some are but there is a sizable percentage of Latin American macho voters for whom a Ronald Reagan is still short of the mark. Somewhere mixed up with gratitude for being in America (and always the lowest parts of it too—the love Señor Ruiz felt for Alphabet City!) is a sense that Americans don't do enough to look out for themselves, don't play tough enough. You'd expect socialism to rise from the filthy streets of Manhattan but it never has and I don't think it ever will. They don't have any interest in changing the game plan; they want to play the capitalist game, have been looking forward to the fruits of it, and having come prepared to scrape out an existence they are not going to subsidize anybody they don't have to. Slum-dwelling right-wingers are a phenomenon NO ONE writes about in America; people are absolutely convinced they don't exist. But *you* go live in a slum and ask around, you may see this too.

I was in the store when Rickie got five dollars from his father. This was something to do with a good report card.

"Now you go give half to your mama, right now—go," he urged Rickie with a mild push. Rickie went up and did as he was told.

As I was there, looking on, Señor Ruiz spoke to me next, explaining the division of spoils: "When I give them money, when they get money from work, when their *abuela* send them money I say go, go give some of it to your mama. She save it for you one day. I don't care what they give, as long as they give something. One dollar is not much but you give 20¢, 30¢ to your mother. You do this out of respect. You never too good to give some of it to your mother, yes? They always do, they always give. If I find they get money and no give some to their mother, they know I keel them so they always do."

Nice idea, I said.

"I do it too, to my mother. I pay the rent, I pay the beels, I do all the work . . ." I repressed a smile because Señora Ruiz worked round the clock, on hands and knees, cleaning, cooking, fretting, fussing while all Señor Ruiz did was sit behind the cash register. ". . . but I not so beeg in the world, I not so rich, I not got so bad a memory that I cannot give some of my money to *my* mother, back in San Juan. When you get too beeg to give to your mother—when you think you so so beeg—then you nothin'. You nothin'. I tell my kids always respect to your mother. You got no respect to your mother then you got no respect for nothin'."

Perhaps that's so.

"You have parents, Heel?"

The question caught me off guard.

"You have a mother living, a papa esomewhere? I never hear you talk about them. They musta be proud of you in the city, no?"

Yes, I said. (I didn't think of myself as having parents anymore really; maybe at Christmas and Thanksgiving . . .)

"You have brothers, eseesters?"

Two brothers, one older, one younger.

"You must mees them everyday, yes?"

Yes I miss them, I said. (To myself: Yes, I miss them once or twice a year, Christmas and Thanskgiving.)

"They come to see you sometime?"

Yeah, maybe soon, I said.

I could not explain to Señor Ruiz how unimportant we all were to each other. Oh yeah we loved each other (for want of anything else to call it) and all that, but we didn't hang on each other, invest much hope or any of our dreams in each other. We were a family, an average American family. How could I explain our independence without saddening Señor Ruiz—I could hear him going on . . . "No Heel, you must go back to Illinois and be with your family; the family is everything. You got nothin' if you don't have your family." Well. I have nothing to say on the subject of my family. Let's move on.

Opening Night. The bright lights, the neon glow, the limos

and wonderfully dressed people . . . (all that was uptown on Broadway, actually—down in Chelsea we did well to have patrons spend the money on a taxi).

"Good god almighty," screamed Brent, running around backstage like a madman, shrill and out of control, "thirty minutes! I'm not going to survive this—I'm not! Bonnie—you're beautiful, you're beautiful, you're going to be great tonight!"

"Yeah I know, get outa my face while I put on my makeup willya?"

"Gil, Gil, Gil," Brent flitted over to me, rambling, "I feel it, I sense a great night—a night to remember!"

If Tucker doesn't show up, I said, it WILL be a night to remember.

"He'll be here, I'm sure. Tucker, dependable Tucker—he's a drunk, yes, but he wouldn't not show up, would he? He's a professional . . ." Brent kept talking hoping someone would agree with him.

"He's an asshole," said Smalley, nervously pacing back and forth like the caged cats at the Bronx Zoo. "He's out getting tanked, preparing to ruin my career." He turned to Brent. "After he drags my career into the sewer, I'm taking you with me Malverne."

Twenty minutes to showtime . . . no Tucker K. Broome.

"I'm getting worried now, if I do say so," said Bonnie who wouldn't have sounded the alarm unless necessary. "What about Don? Can we use the understudy?"

"We'll have to," said Smalley. "He's looking over the script now, and he's got his makeup on."

I asked Don how it was going.

Don, crumpled over his script at the makeup table, looked up with an unconfident look. "Well, considering . . . I guess I've got it down. No, I'm not confident, but I'm all right. I think." He dived back into his script.

Smalley threw up his hands, doubling the pace of his pacing: "Great! Great! He doesn't know the lines!"

"Chris, get outa here—let him concentrate," said Bonnie escorting everyone out the door.

We exchanged anxious looks.

Suddenly there was a commotion, a banging of doors, the sound of yells and curses. Broome had arrived tipsy. No, not tipsy: drunk.

The door opened and Brent walked Tucker to a chair, lecturing him: "Look at you, Tucker! Tucker I am APPALLED, I really am—I don't know how to express my indignation—"

"Shut up Brent. Lemme handle this," Bonnie said, taking charge.

"Helllo Bonnnie," said Tucker, slurring his speech.

"Can you go on Tucker?"

"The show MUSH go on!"

Bonnie sized up the situation and went to her makeup case and pulled out a bottle of pills. Amphetamines. I got her a glass of water.

"Take these," Bonnie said, forcing Tucker to take the glass, putting the pills into his palm. "Now, Tucker, take them." Bonnie looked up at me: "Don't ask about the uppers, Gil. There's lots of medicine in Aunt Bonnie's kit, right?"

The stage manager said people were still milling and he could hold curtain until 8:30. Tucker was coming to, sort of.

"I'm a professional," he mumbled. "I can go on with flu, I can go on no matter what. Last year I went on with cancer. The doctor said set back, retire, get off the stage—to hell with 'em. Cancer. I went on with cancer—I'm a professional . . ."

Cancer. Bonnie and I exchanged educated looks.

"Do you know what it's like to go on with cancer?" Tucker asked, before turning to look at himself in the mirror.

"Forget it, Tucker," said Bonnie, "the question is: Can you go on in a minute?"

Soon, he was dabbing makeup on his face, reviving slightly. Bonnie told me to be prepared to cover. If he dropped a line one of us would pick it up—confidence, have confidence. I was confident. The blood was pumping—I was up, I was ready. Scared to death, but ready.

Act One . . .

DORIS

What do you want from the boy, Morgan? You always pick on him unmercifully. Didn't he live up to your little plan for him?

MORGAN

[Tucker swayed a bit, unsure of his line:] Yes he . . . I don't know. I don't know what to . . .

DORIS

[her body projected confidence, her eyes which I caught said P-A-N-I-C; she covered for him:] You don't know, do you? You don't know what you want. You wanted to mold him in your own image, go into business—

MORGAN

[who was reminded of his line, picking it up:] . . . Yes, yes, go into business and make something of himself. I did want that. Was that so bad? Was I so wrong to . . . [fading again] so wrong to . . .

DORIS

So wrong to shape him, push him somewhere he didn't belong? Yes, you were.

And then the drugs took effect. Tucker, as if a switch had been thrown, came to, picked up his lines, began to come alive, but he was still short on motor control. He bumbled into desks, fumbled with doorknobs, took out his gold pocketwatch and couldn't open it during his speech.

Intermission. Backstage:

"I've got it now, I've got it now, I'm rolling," said Tucker, clutching a cup of coffee. Brent was pushing cup after cup on him; Smalley was pacing more frantically than ever, not convinced. "No really," said Tucker, chuckling. "A bit shaky there, yes, a bit shaky for a moment, but I'm hot now, I'm *hot*."

"The drugs have kicked in," Bonnie said, sighing a measure of relief. "It'll be hyper-Tucker for a while."

The stage manager tried to calm us: "I was out in the lobby.

Everyone is enjoying it; no one thinks anything's wrong. They're saying Tucker plays a great drunk. The problem is—"

"I know the problem," snapped Bonnie. "It's MY character that's supposed to be the drinker. Gil, we'll have to alter the script a little—how can we explain this away?"

"*No script alterations*," stammered Smalley. "You've butchered this play of mine enough."

"Five minutes," said the stage manager.

Tucker was speed-king all of a sudden: "I'm fine, I'm bright, I'm alert. You want to hear my lines: 'Doris, I've had enough of this drama. It's a time in my life that I—' "

"Okay, okay, you're peaking," said Bonnie, "now try to keep with it and don't let it slip away from you."

"Look I'm shaking," said Tucker, holding up his hand. "I'm shaking . . . if I could just have a drink to calm me."

But Tucker wasn't just "all right," he was STUPENDOUS. He went out and gave the performance of his career. In fact, with uppers coursing through his veins he delivered every line with a freshness, a precision and dynamism never seen in rehearsals. The audience was on the edge of their seats—he was a marvel to watch, his theater sense never better.

DORIS

We're not a family anymore, damn it. You're tearing us apart—you and your goddam expectations. How can you stand there and be so nonchalant?

MORGAN

You can't move me anymore, Doris. You've lost the power to do that. Maybe a long time ago before you threw me over for our son. Maybe . . . [Tucker was stretching out on the sofa, but as he sat down he toddled against the end table sending a vase to the floor; the one he kept knocking over in rehearsals].

DORIS

[ad-libbing:] Oh fine, just fine. Now we'll have to pay for that too. Just like we . . . have to pay for so many things you've broken. [She looked unsurely at Tucker stretching out on the sofa.] An afternoon nap, dear? The excitement too much for you?

MORGAN

Ullllhh . . . [Tucker groaned something as he lay down—no . . . could it be? He was *falling asleep* onstage? Passing out? Shit, just ten lines before the end of the act!]

DORIS

[looking beseechingly at me:] Well, that's typical—tune us all out; roll over and go to sleep.

CHARLES

Yes, Dad, that's just typical [I wasn't adding anything—but we were stuck for lines . . .]

DORIS

[thinking quickly:] He's drunk again. He tries to pawn it off on me as if I have the problem but it's him, all him.

CHARLES

Yes, I've been trying to tell you, Mother.

Pause. Dead Air. What now? Bonnie said the last line of the act:

DORIS

There are many things, Morgan, I have to tell you.
You'll have to face the truth.

Lights dim, curtain falls. Applause.

Bonnie turned to me, saying, "I think he's out cold."

Brent came running behind the curtain hugging us, kissing us: "Oh brilliant, just brilliant! I've never seen Tucker so brilliant—he was brilliant, wasn't he brilliant? I mean, brilliant!"

Smalley was right behind him: "He never did it so well in rehearsal. Who'd have thought he could have pulled it back like that?"

"I sent Don home. Obviously the crisis has passed!" cried Brent.

Bonnie and I looked at each other.

"You idiots," snarled Bonnie. "Didn't you watch the last minute? He's out, out cold." She nodded to the sofa where Tucker was prostrate.

The four of us scooped him up with the help of two stagehands and took him to the dressing room. Someone turned on the shower and let it run cold. We took off his suit coat and put him under it, but he numbly stirred and seemed to sink back into his reverie.

Brent was in hysterics: "My god, he's passed out for good! What are we going to do, my god, my god . . ."

Bonnie was calm to the core. "Brent, Brent, take it easy. We've got ten minutes to think of something." Then Bonnie looked at me, as if to say, Gil, YOU think of something.

Smalley had a burst of violence, pinning Brent to the wall, holding him up by his collar: "Malverne, it's YOU who are through! Why did you cast him? Why? Why? *Flip Flop?* You threw my play into the trash can, finished me on Broadway because this man was in *Flip Flop* fifteen years ago? Huh?"

Brent yelled to be put down. Smalley dropped him to the floor, then stormed around a minute, cursing this, cursing that, finally sweeping Bonnie's makeup things to the floor in a rage.

"Hey fella, that's my makeup!" Bonnie marched over and took Smalley (appreciably shorter than she was) and sat him down roughly in the chair. "Now calm down and think. How do we get our hands on that understudy?"

Brent was sniveling on the floor. "Oh god, it's my fault—I sent Don home in the middle of Act Two . . ."

"That's right," snapped Smalley, "everything is your fault!"

"We could send a police car," said Brent, shrinking into himself, "and say it was an emergency, speed him back here."

Bonnie crossed her arms. "But he may not have gone home. It could take a half hour. No. We're going to have to work around Tucker in Act Three—"

Smalley was on his feet again: "NONSENSE. That's not the play! We cancel, we go out and cancel."

"And your play sinks into nothingness, Smalley. Closing on opening night," Bonnie added.

Now it was Smalley who started to simper. "I'm ruined, ruined! You Malverne! You'll die, DIE for this. I have Mafia connections!"

The stage manager stepped in: "Five minutes, folks." The manager looked about the room, seeing Tucker in the shower. "Oh shit," he said, as Bonnie drove him from the room, closing the door on him.

"Gil," said Bonnie, her mind working steadily, a gleam in her eye. "Let's say Daddy died offstage, drunk—was hit by a tourist bus. We'll do the third act, as if . . . God, how do we get around the final fight scene?"

As I thought aloud, Smalley stood to go:

"Well, I'm going out to go out and get totally drunk. I'm going to turn a bottle of scotch upright and drink every drop. Writers are supposed to die in the gutter in America and that's what I intend to do right now. Good evening."

Bonnie winced. "No, Chris stay here and help us—"

Smalley laughed a brief but maniacal laugh. "No, no thanks. I'm not driving the nails into my own coffin. I'm walking out of here, good night." And he began to walk, we restrained him, he shook us free.

"Just as well, Gil," Bonnie said, biting a fingernail. "Now let's think fast."

"Bonnie," whined Brent, still huddled on the floor simpering, "you don't really suppose he has Mafia connections do you?"

Bonnie lost her cool and hurled a box of tissues at him: "Oh shut up, Brent, *I* have Mafia connections and after his Mafia connections break your legs, mine will be back to break your arms." Brent laughed uneasily and used the tissues to blow his nose.

I had been giving Bonnie's suggestion a thought: Yeah, what if Dad got hit by a tourist bus—

"That makes sense with the play, Bermuda and all, right?"

Yes, and we could pretend, in our grief, Dad was still around. One or the other of us taking his lines, as if he were there. It would be as if . . . as if we were haunted by his presence, creating dialogue for him because—

"Because we could not accept that he had died. Died a drunk. Which would cover for all of Tucker's bumblings." She grabbed my hand and led me out of the dressing room to the side of the stage. The stage manager asked if he should signal the foyer and get people back to their seats.

"Yes, do it now," she said. Then she turned to me and looked me squarely in the eye: "We have got to go out and do this cold before we talk ourselves out of it."

What about the final fight scene where we fall into each other's arms and say how much we love each other?

"We'll do it without him . . . But shit, how do we resolve the business about the watch he was going to give you?"

I ran back to the dressing room, took the gold watch from Tucker's pocket, and came back: We can say, Bonnie, that he with his dying words left it to me.

"Nah, nah, too hokey even for a Christopher Smalley play. No, better yet, they found it, the police, returned it and you can brood over it, make up some lines . . . but how do we end this thing?" Bonnie clutched the stage manager's arm: "Look when I say . . . when I say 'The weather is clouding up, it's time to go home,' you hit the lights, end of the play, okay?"

The stage manager nodded nervously, adding, "I'd say you've got about three minutes."

Bonnie and I looked at each other, panic in both our eyes. "Good god," she muttered. "All the critics out there tonight too." Then she laughed darkly, looking at the floor shaking her head. "What a night. This'll figure in my memoirs, I promise."

My heart was racing, adrenaline instead of blood in my body. Could this work?

Bonnie put a hand on my shoulder. "Yeah, it'll work. I was in a *Showboat* in '59 when the captain had a heart attack before his last scene, dropped dead backstage. Understudy couldn't go in because he had been used for another character. So we sent out a chorus-extra to sit there with the other player and they talked about 'Boy, if the captain were here, he'd look out and say . . . etcetera.' No one caught it, but a few critics—and the director convinced them at a party afterward that this version was the original Ferber version. We dressed the old stagehand who worked the door as the captain for the ensemble scene at the end and then kept putting other singers and dancers in front of him—this old coot even took the guy's curtain call—"

"Thirty seconds," said the stage manager, as the lights in the theater darkened for our entrance.

"Here we go, kid," said Bonnie, kissing my cheek. "Even if the worst happens, it's only theater, right?"

And we were on.

We made up something like this:

DORIS

I can't believe he's . . . he's gone. That policeman he just . . . I just can't believe it.

CHARLES

I still can't believe it.

DORIS

No, I can't believe it either.

Bonnie privately rolled her eyes at me, telepathically transmitting: C'mon kid, let's get brave, open this up a bit . . .

CHARLES

Don't think me bad, Mother. But I had been waiting for something like this to happen for years. In a sense it had to end this way.

DORIS

[indignant:] What do you mean by that?

CHARLES

You knew he was drinking himself to death anyway—you said as much yourself—

DORIS

I never said anything of the sort. Just what are you saying?

CHARLES

I'm saying, we should have seen this coming, that one day the old fool would just . . . would just walk out in front of a bus, drunken, stumbling—

DORIS

Don't talk that way about him! You shouldn't say such things now that he's . . . that he's . . . What are you trying to do to me?

I swear, Bonnie—I was griping to myself—if you don't stop ending your ad-libs on a question for me to answer, I'm going to wring your neck . . .

CHARLES

[I laugh darkly, like a madman:] I mean, in a way it's merciful that he stepped, the old fool, in front of a bus —a tourist bus! Here in Bermuda! A tourist bus in Bermuda! What a fitting end for that rotten man—

DORIS

DON'T say this, no, no! [working up to hysterics]

CHARLES

It's true Mother. You knew he was a goner with his drinking—he was dragging you down with him—

DORIS

It's not true!

CHARLES

He was turning you into an alcoholic so you could both go together. What do you think all that nonsense about his watch was? He was a dying man . . . he wanted to make his peace with me but . . . but no one had won our little war yet—there couldn't have been any peace.

Bonnie turned to me, gave me an approving wink—I'd explained the watch and matched Smalley's dialogue perfectly.

To cut a long long, eternally lasting stage moment short, we got more inspired as we went along, explaining all the loose ends, inventing stuff ten times better than the original. I, for instance, hurled Father's watch to the ground after brooding over it, cursing my father, saying I didn't want it, refused it. Later, toward the end, after we both had staged numerous hysterics, I knelt down before the watch and tried to reassemble it . . .

CHARLES

[tears running down my face, sniveling:] No, no, I'll put it back together Mama, I'll do it, I'll get it fixed. You heard him didn't you? Daddy said he was going to give it to me—you heard him right? He said he was going to get it engraved . . . to his son Charles . . . [sobs] I'm sorry Daddy, I didn't mean to break your watch—I . . . [more sobs, I'm stalling for time here] Uh . . . [some more tears, wipe your nose, laugh a little bit] . . . See it's almost like it was, huh Mother? See? You can almost hear it ticking . . . [oh shit, I'm doing a Timex commercial, change tacks:] . . . no, no, I've broken it. It's too late, too late for me . . .

DORIS

[running to me, kneeling beside me:] No honey, we'll get it fixed, we will . . . [She kissed my cheek and whispered into my ear at high speed, "How do we end this damn thing?"]

The watch business went over *great*—I heard shuffling and quiet sniffing. The audience was in the palm of our hands. God, could you believe it? We were having fun suddenly, taking our play where we wanted it to go . . . Bonnie went over to the broken vase, racing me to it, lest I get to the material first:

DORIS

[picking up the pieces:] We have to piece things together, don't we Charles? We have to go on. Like this vase . . . [uh oh, I could tell she just put herself out on a limb there] We're all broken up now, and uh . . . we need to come together . . . [she's suffering—should I run help?] . . . we'll have to fix this like we have to fix our lives. [I'll help her.]

CHARLES

[putting a hand on her shoulder:] Forget that Mother. It belongs to the hotel. [She must have forgotten this wasn't our home, the way she was talking about the vase, so I thought I'd remind her.] It doesn't matter. Leave it alone.

DORIS

[thinking fast, saves it:] But the flowers. Whenever a vase breaks, it's the flowers you worry about. They need to be put in water and cared for, just because . . . just because the pretty world they were in is broken and gone . . . [Very nice, Bonnie!] I'm like these flowers, in a way, Charles . . . [Oh crap, Bonnie, leave it alone! You had it, now you're messing it up!] . . . and you too. Can we go on together? You and I?

But there was panic in Bonnie's eyes. What was wrong? She was distressed—she was signaling something to me. What?

DORIS

I just wish somehow this nightmare would end . . . this evening somehow would be over with. Finished . . .

Good Lord, she's forgotten her cue to the stage manager to end the play! No problem, I'll say the line, which was . . . What the hell was that line? It's gone out of my head completely. Over the river and through the woods . . . As the sun sinks slowly into the west . . . And so ends another day . . . shit, what was it?

DORIS

Can you, darling, end this nightmare for me? Can you figure out a way to make all this awfulness go away? [Her eyes were flashing that special onstage SOS only other actors can pick up.]

Oops, for the first time we were drowning. The audience was stirring, and we were losing them. No, how unfair! We'd been so astoundingly brilliantly divinely inspired up until now (well, I mean considering we only had to be as good as Smalley). This was pathetic: Bonnie was now breaking down and crying, for want of anything else to do.

CHARLES

What is it Mother?

DORIS

Nothing, no, I can't tell you . . .

Oh this stinks, this really stinks. More audience restlessness. Actors can sense the mood out beyond the footlights like you wouldn't believe, telepathically. We were floundering. Wait. What was Bonnie doing now? She was . . . she was unbuttoning her blouse. What was she up to now? Wait . . . I think I know what she's up to . . .

DORIS

Do you remember how it used to be between us? [Her eyes, her body seemed to shrug, seemed to say "I'm desperate, I gotta do something."] When it was you and me and . . . and he wasn't around . . .

CHARLES

Mother what are you doing? Please tell me.

DORIS

Don't worry I just want to hold you . . . hold you like I used to hold you . . . [She had taken off her blouse and was stalling about lowering her bra straps; the audience was certainly back in the palm of our hands now . . .] Come to me, dear. [Her eyes said: Oh shit, why not? as she lowered her straps.] Come to me, darling. Come to Mother.

CHARLES

Mother, no, what are you doing?

DORIS

We'll go away together . . . [She exposed her breasts and reached out for my hand. She drew me closer—I decided to get into it, tremulously touching her breast like a child, nestling myself there like a big baby.] We'll go home together, away from all this awful brightness and sun and heat—and and

CHARLES

[mumbling from her bosom; we were fishing for the line —on the tips of our tongues!] Yes yes, the weather, it's the weather isn't it? I mean, the weather is so depressing and we should go home.

DORIS

Yes, it's time to go home! The weather is bad and it's time to go home!

No response.

CHARLES

Yes it's clouding up.

DORIS

Clouding up and time, time my darling to go home home *home* . . .

That did it. The stage manager ordered the lights to dim, the curtain to fall. And as they did Doris finished up—

DORIS

We'll go back home and make new lives. Back to Ohio.

Blackness, darkness all around. The pause. THUNDEROUS APPLAUSE!!

Bonnie and I ran backstage to SCREAMS, to SCREECHES of excitement and praise and adoration from the backstage crew: "You did it! You did it! Damn you, you fucking did it!" It was like the end of a soccer match, we were fallen upon from all sides, hugging, embracing—Brent cut through the crowd and piled on too. "I don't believe it," he said, tears in his eyes. "You were marvelous, superb!"

Bonnie and I pulled ourselves apart and looked at each other, our eyes immediately overflowing with tears, nervous-release crying.

"We did it, didn't we, baby?" she sniffed. Then we hugged each other tight enough to do damage to internal organs. Then we started reliving it, comparing notes:

"Did you get my last line? 'Back to Ohio.' What kinda goddam asshole last line was that! Back to goddam Ohio! It just came out of my mouth!"

What about me and the watch? What about her showing her tits?

"Well I had to do something—they were getting ready to *get up and leave* out there! And hey, it's not as if they're bad tits, right?"

No Bonnie honey, they are the best pair of tits I have ever seen in my life!

The stage manager interrupted: "What about curtain calls?"

Brent: "Can't do one without Tucker—the audience will wonder why he doesn't come out. Let it go—turn up the house lights." Brent threw himself into Bonnie's bosom (she had been fiddling to get her bra back on for two minutes). "Bonnie, you were superb—you . . . you showed your tits, god bless you!"

"Yeah," she said triumphantly, "I showed my tits!"

"You showed your beautiful tits!" Brent repeated, hugging Bonnie, jumping up and down with her in their embrace.

Bonnie was handed a scotch and soda which she downed in one. "Well what the hell? After you suggested it, I sorta thought I might like to do it after all—so I got my chance, right?"

"You've got to write down *everything*," said Brent, "everything that you did tonight so you can vaguely imitate it tomorrow, okay? We'll go on with Don, strike Tucker from the program, have them reprinted—"

"Hey everybody!" Bonnie yelled to everyone backstage, her mind far from tomorrow night: "Brent's taking the whole crew out for drinks and we're hanging out all night until tomorrow's reviews, okay?"

Cheers and whoops all around.

"You're gonna need $500 minimum so I hope you got some money in the bank," Bonnie told Brent, giving him a half-friendly poke. And then she turned to me, in the relative quiet, as everybody milled about, reliving bits and pieces, preparing for the drunk ahead of us. "Gil, that was classic. Even if they shred this thing, even if we bomb–*we* know what we did. I remember you telling me about not being able to get an agent. After tonight my agent is your agent—I'll get Odessa to sign you on. Wouldya like that?"

YES I WOULD LIKE THAT.

Tucker was roused, sopping wet, and stumbled forth from the dressing room. Brent cried, "Hank, guard the door. Let no one backstage until we get Tucker out of the way."

I went to take a shower and when I got back, Bonnie (looking like a million) was ready to party. Brent flew by, a new man—the stage manager, Gary the producer, everyone was waiting on me. What a night it was going to be! That is Pure Joy, you know, post-theatrical partying, after a coup, after a success. The drinking, the dancing, the late-night breakfast across from Sandy's Newsstand waiting for the newspapers to be dumped in bales there, five a.m. There's a glow, a shared spirit not unlike criminals who've robbed the Vatican must feel, conspiracy, inclusion. Emma would cite me as a violator of the New Order, but Love too. Emma.

Hank stopped me in the hall. "Oh Gil, I'm sorry. Some people were here for you, Jim and um . . ."

Jim and Lisa.

"Yeah, I'm sorry. I thought you'd gone on to the bar. They left some flowers outside."

Damn. Well, that's all right Hank. Hey, was there anyone named Emma out there waiting to see me?

"Don't think so." Hank smiled a wide smile at me. "That was great out there tonight—really something. You know they'll be talking about that for years here. You were great."

Well, it happens. Miracles can occur.

We *just* got by in the reviews—the *News* liked the play and not the actors (except for "the subtle genius of Broome's stagecraft," wouldn't you know), the *Voice* quibbled but generally found it Smalley's best work, the *Post* praised Bonnie and said Bill Freeman was someone to watch (not spell his name right, but watch, definitely watch) and *all of them* liked Bonnie's tits.

"You laugh but these tits are gonna keep this old bomb running till Christmas," she cackled before we all stumbled home at six-thirty a.m., tired beyond description.

And speaking of miracles, major and minor, when I got home and fell toward my bed/pile of dirty laundry, I thought to reach over half-asleep already for my answering machine:

BEEP! *All right, all right, this is Emma. I saw you last night, you were brilliant, I am jealous because you have talent, because you are God and I, I as you know, I am a piece of shit, I am dung, I am lower than the low . . . this is an apology. Although we were both a little—NO, scratch that: it was me, all me, all my fault, I am shit, dung, refuse, rubbish, ORDURE—I am ordure, Gil. I am . . . New Jersey. I stand out on a corner and I violate the sanitation laws—people rush up to me with their poop-scoops. This is an homage to you Gil, I'm doing your lousy one-liners. Dross? You want to talk dross? Detritus? Scrim? Crill? Slag? I'm in the Outer Darkness, Gil—that's where I'm calling from, you oughta see the rates. You wanna hear gnashing of teeth? Here: gnassssh gnassssh gnassssh . . . Remember in* Suddenly Last Summer *where Katharine Hepburn says most people's lives are trails of debris, except she doesn't say duh-BREE, she says* DEB-*ry. Well I'm* DEB-*ry.* (Emma's Hepburn imitation:) *Yez, poooooor Emmah, she was olways* DEB-*ry* DEB-*ry* DEB-*ry*—CLICK. (That must have been the record for talk on my answering machine; she could always talk fast.)

Next message: BEEP! *That ends the abasement-and-humbling portion of our evening's entertainment, but before we bring on Guido Fozzuli and his Dancing Poodles with the Dancing Lasers and Dancing Waters, let us have a word from Miss Emma Gennaro*! [Emma made this kssssh noise into the receiver to sound like the applause of millions.] *Thank you, thank you, oh* *please—that's too kind. Yes, I'm back and I'm here to speak to you tonight about a serious subject: Gil Freeman. He has been struck with that crippler of young adults, Life Without Emma. Only you can help. Send all your money to me. And when you've done that, I urge you, I beg of you, to make Gil pick up that phone—go ahead, you know you ought to—pick up that phone and call Emma. You know in your heart that it's the right thing to do. And now back to Guido Fozzuli and lasers shooting the dancing poodles, or the poodles making dancing water, or—*CLICK.

That voice. Some voices speak to you from outside your body and some speak to you from inside, and my imaginary Emma Voice, the one I heard in my head, the one that said all the intolerant, insensitive, hilarious and 100% honest things, the voice I heard in my head when something happened she should have been there for, THAT voice had gone off the mark a bit, wasn't quite what she really sounded like, and hearing the real Emma I realized that time—just eleven months—had deprived me of so much. I played the tape over and over again, saying to myself yes, yes, that's what I missed. That's what I can't do without any longer.

1980

IN September I made my TV debut, in a commercial for the Garden State Assurance Trust, a local insurance company. At Emma's and Janet's new East Village apartment, we gathered to watch this command performance.

Emma turned on the TV:

It was Ronald Reagan: *It's time to look back for that which made America great, its integrity, its goodness—*

AAAAIIII! Janet, Emma, myself and my theater friend Kevin screamed in unison: TURN IT OFF!

"Damn election year," muttered Emma. "You can't get either Ron or Jimmy off the TV—there've been ads for one or the other every five minutes."

"Ronnie Ray-gun, the Black Man's Friend," said Janet scowling. "And he's probably gonna get in too."

"What kind of choice is this election? It's gotta be the worst ever," mused Emma.

Nixon or pro-Vietnam Humphrey?

"Yeah, that was bad."

Pro-Vietnam Johnson or pro-Vietnam Goldwater?

"Forget I said anything," Emma shrugged. "It's always bad, isn't it?"

Janet brought everyone a beer. "The world's being run by old men, Gil. Brezhnev is a hundred 'n eighty and may or may not be dead, the Ayatollah is in his hundred 'n eighties too, and Reagan is in his hundred 'n seventies. Those old men who keep hangin' on, the kind who never die."

Try the TV again, Emma.

Emma turned back to the channel my commercial would be on.

Americans will never cower before a foreign government, will never negotiate with terrorists . . . America will not be held hostage . . .

"Of course true to my doctrine," said Emma, "of voting for entertainment value, I'll vote for Uncle Ronnie."

"You may get your way on World War Three," said Janet.

Emma's buzzer sounded. We figured it was Jasmine.

Janet and I kept watching Reagan: *The Great Society has failed. No one believes anymore that the welfare system of the United States is healthy. Fraud, welfare, swindling is now accepted in the cities of America. In Newark, New Jersey, a welfare queen there took the government for $270,000, masquerading under fifteen different names . . .*

Janet dipped into black-stereotype-speak: "Now Ronnie chile, you talkin' bout my Aunt Sadie now! We gots us some Ripple on that money and played the horses and got us a Cadillac with a fuzzy pink interyuh . . ."

"Well," said Kevin, camping it up. "He's got a good-looking son, that ballet dancer. Although Ford still had the best-looking presidential kids of all time—Steven Ford, you remember?"

Dream on, Kevin.

"Gil," he said, hopping out of the chair, "can we talk a moment in the kitchen?"

Sure. Kevin and I went to the kitchen. Kevin worked with me at the Soho Center for Experimental Theater. He was the gay lover of Nicholas who owned the place. Emma always described Kevin as a Muppet. He was twenty-four or so, big bushy blond punked-out hair, he sort of bounced about with floppy gestures, and the expressions on his bright, blond face were exactly what he felt: Kevin ecstatic, Kevin moping, Kevin cross—not an ounce of deviousness or guile in him, apparently.

"Will *you* ask Slut Doll to do the theater project?" he asked, once we were in the kitchen. "I mean, I'm no good with things like that . . ."

Yeah okay. But will Nicholas mind *my* asking her?

"He won't care, as long as she does the music and the sound effects for the show. Lately I screw up everything I touch at the theater—"

Kevin, you worry too much.

"Nicholas is going to dump me *any* day."

Is that so bad? You fight all the time.

"Where'm I gonna live?"

Emma from the living room: "HEY GILLLL . . . you got one minute to get in here."

Kevin and I went back into the living room and Slut Doll, née Jasmine Dahl, had arrived and was talking to Janet and Emma. "Hi Gil," she moaned in her monotone.

Jasmine, actually, was the incarnation of monotone. She dressed one way—in black—she looked one way (always frizzed-out jet-black hair, horror-movie white face makeup with her eyes darkly outlined) and she talked in this amazing monotonous drawl that allowed no emotions or highs or lows, with lots of West Coast Southern Cal you-know-like-man kind-of interjections. She was capable—and mind you, she was intelligent—of going on for years about the blandest thing—

"You know it's like I need eight hours of sleep but I only get about five, you know? I'm like missing three hours of sleep. Because I need about eight hours or I'm not really, you know, I'm not really awake?"

And other times she was quite striking with her ideas:

"My next album is going to be called *Pre-Impact Terror*, Gil. Remember that plane crash a few weeks ago at O'Hare? Everyone like dies? Well, one of the relatives sued whatever-it-was airlines for $50 million; $25 million for death and damages and another $25 million on their loved one's behalf for the pre-impact terror they experienced. I mean like you know, that's *art. Pre-Impact Terror.* Life is a series of pre-impact terrors, right? You get it? There's also the sexual connotations . . ."

Yeah, I'd worked that out, Jasmine. Anyway, Jasmine had arrived and brought one big bag of potato chips which she began to consume all by herself.

Emma had turned the sound down, and switched the channel to escape the visage of Reagan. "How's it going, Slut?"

"You know, not so good today. Can't stand it when it's like hot in my apartment it's really nasty. I got a new mouse down there."

Get out of the basement, I suggest.

"Can't afford anything else," she whined, between crunches of potato chips. You had to see that basement of a Soho warehouse, walls and floors painted black, doors and windowframes painted blood red, photos of war criminals, engravings of medieval tortures, a library full of torture books, Kraft-Ebing, de Sade, Genet, Burroughs—I only went down there once. Which was enough. I remember our conversation was a variation upon this dialogue:

Jasmine: Want to hear some from my book of Nazi atrocities?

Gil: No Jasmine, not in the least.

Jasmine: Okay, maybe some other time . . .

Her tables were crates and boards balanced on crates. She had this sofa she'd found thrown out in the street. She'd restuffed it with newspapers. "It's still a bit wet, you know? I had to drag it home in the rain." Being with Jasmine always put this question in my mind: How could Emma have ever lived with Lisa and me (happy, fun, positive people generally) and been so miserable, and then lived with Jasmine for a year and been so happy?

"Every day is like scraping bottom," Jasmine was saying. "The record hasn't made any money at all. Scrapings, it's always scrapings."

Your next one will do better, I bet.

"Dregs," she said, putting a chip in her mouth, "I'm so tired of dregs, you know?"

Want something to drink, Jaz?

"You gotta start calling me Slut, Gil."

Okay: Slut.

"I mean, I gotta get used to it, you know? Ever think about changing your name as an actor?" She didn't wait for an answer. "You know it's like I walk down the street? Someone yells, hey Slut, you know and I think, fuck off buddy, but he's like one of my fans."

You'll get used to it.

The phone rang and Janet answered it. Kevin in pantomime and whispers hissed "I'm *not* here, I'm not here . . ."

Janet cleared her throat. "No, he's not here . . . No, I don't even know a Kevin. Thank you, bye." She hung up. "Kevin, why did you give out the number if you didn't want people to call you here?"

"I wanted to be called, I just didn't want to talk to him. I wanted to see if he'd call me. That was Nicholas . . ." Apparently tonight was another ongoing fight between Nicholas and Kevin. "Now I'm going to go home and ask if he called me and if he says no, trying to act like he doesn't care what I'm up to, I'm going to confront him. I am."

Jasmine—Slut, I mean—was halfway through her bag putting handful after handful of potato chips in her mouth robotlike. "Gil, how much did you get for the commercial?"

Three hundred and fifty dollars. For a day's work.

Emma ran to the TV. "Look, the show's over . . ." She turned up the volume again. First up was a carpet outlet ad: . . . *thousands of carpets, thousands and thousands of carpets!*

Kevin: "Geez that guy is *such* a moron—where'd they find those cheap suits he wears? And he also does those TV-appliance store ads."

Janet flopped down in the beanbag chair. "That's where Gil's gonna end up, sugar. He'll can the theater and do TV ads."

I'll have you know that guy makes $1000 a shot, I said. Pay me a thousand bucks an ad and I'll sell carpets too, thousands and thousands of carpets—

Emma: "Quiet! The next ad's up . . ."

It was mine. It starts with Dad walking out his door into his front yard—we hear lawnmowers, birds, children playing. It's America, all right. *You know, it took me fifteen years to purchase my family's home . . .*

Kevin: "He's cute, Gil. That's your daddy? How about Sugar Daddy?"

Everyone ssssshed.

. . . I think insurance is the wise decision, not just for me and my money . . .

"No black person," said Janet, "has *ever* stepped foot in that neighborhood."

"The garbagemen?" suggested Emma. A pillow was launched by Janet in Emma's direction. Jasmine shovelled potato chips into her mouth, staring intently at the screen.

I'm with Garden State Assurance Trust for her sake. His "wife" walks out the door, wiping her hands with an oven cloth and her apron on: *Come to dinner darling!* she sings.

"Don't do it," said Kevin, "she's no good for you!"

"Where are you, Gil?" asked Janet.

And I do it for my little girl . . . Here comes the Little Girl, about nine years old, a real pro, her fifteenth commercial, according to her stage mother who was with her on the set. Little Girl rushes in: *Daaaaddy!*

I'm about to come on, I warn.

And I do it for my boy . . . (This is me. In a football jersey, ambling up the front walk. I pitch that football to Dads, a nice spiral: *Catch, Dad!*)

Everyone is in hysterics watching this. Emma is doubled over and Janet is shrieking with laughter. It gets better, I yell.

. . . and one day it'll help my son go to college. Father is mussing up my hair, heh heh heh, father and son, football. It's time for my next great line: *Don't worry Dad, I'm going on a football scholarship!* Mom, Dad, and the Little Sister all laugh: *hah hah hah hah hah . . .* And now the announcer breaks in: *Garden State Assurance Trust . . . For the whole family.*

End of ad. Scorekeepers at home will realize this is football role number three.

Applause all around the room.

Emma laughs, "Brilliant! A masterpiece! We've got to get it on videotape. Ask the station for a copy."

My voice was so high, I said. I don't have that high a voice—

Everyone: YES YOU DO!

It was like a Mickey Mouse imitation . . .

Jasmine put down the potato chip bag, shaking her head. "Anyone recognize that family? Is that *your* mom and dad?"

"A little too white for me," sang Janet.

"My father would have hit my mother by now," said Kevin.

We delighted ourselves by recasting the commercial with Emma as the Little Girl: *Daddy daddy, does it cover my psychiatrist's bills?*

Later on:

"Gil," said Emma, pulling me aside from the conversation and into the kitchen. "Can I ask a question? Why didn't you invite Betsy to this? I did ask you to invite her."

She couldn't make it.

"She's in publishing. They lead boring lives there; I'm sure she had nothing better to do than be here."

Okay okay. I didn't ask her, actually. She wouldn't fit in and Kevin is an acquired taste, so is Jasmine, Janet can be sharp sometimes and hard-line dykeish and you are much smarter than Betsy and I had this vision of it being socially awkward and weird, that's all.

"Well okay," said Emma. "I'll meet her one of these days. I'm sure she's a swell person." Emma was making an effort here and so I felt almost guilty for not asking Betsy. Emma had also noticed once before that Betsy didn't get invited to my opening-night parties, when there were opening nights. That's because I always wanted to end up drunk with the cast or go back to the Village with Emma and get blasted and not sit up until three a.m. talking about anorexia, herpes, who did what to her at work, her ex-boyfriends, her salary disputes, the new very boring yuppie outfit she'd bought—god, that woman was NOT my style.

Speaking of my opening nights, there were only three others

that year. After *Bermuda Triangle*, I stayed at the Chelsea for the next show, *Children of Auschwitz* (a real downer based on journals and poems and drawings from young people in concentration camps; I was a reciter). After that I got sent out to a Long Island community theater to do *View From the Bridge*—not a banner career move but my agent was keeping me working. Odessa, my agent. The one Bonnie got me signed on with. I hated that woman with a passion and . . . wait, we can't go into her atrocities here. Let's just say that for the whole of 1980 she would put her arm around me and say, "Gil, HUHNEY, 1981, I *swayre*, is gonna be yoooour yeeeeuh." The last thing I'd done was play F. Scott Fitzgerald in this thing called *Aficionados* (another stab at trying to make Paris in the '20s come alive). It was an odd audition.

"My god, Mr. Freeman," cried the director who was also the writer, "you ARE F. Scott Fitzgerald. The Midwesterm naïve! What an accent."

I really sound that Midwestern?

"You are the incarnation, Mr. Freeman, of an ear of corn! You are Nick Carroway—I see you before the green light, tomorrow we will run faster, waves ceaselessly borne into the . . . dark night of the, whatever."

So I got the role. Which was mostly me fighting with the woman who played his wife, Zelda. The central plot turned around Ernest Hemingway and Gertrude Stein getting drunk and screwing while abusing each other, she rides him around like a horse, he boasts he's the best lover in the world as he passes out—lots of Paris-in-the-'20s squalor. Lots of dialogue like James Joyce walking on and saying: "Gee, Ernest I have this great idea for a modern book!" and Picasso walking on and saying: "Stop! I must paint you all!" Real historical recreation. This gem had closed three weeks before my commercial hit the airwaves.

Anyway, back to my Commercial Debut Party:

"One more thing," said Emma, about to leave the kitchen with me, "do these jeans look all right?" She spun around and took a step back so I could observe her.

They're great.

"My butt is as fat as you've ever seen it in your lifetime, isn't it?"

(You know, dear reader, between you and me, *yes* it was. In the year Emma and I weren't speaking, she'd gained a little weight. Late-twenties female, perfectly acceptable earthy Italian-American weight—not remotely a turnoff, nothing that required the language of elephantiasis and obesity that Emma invoked.)

"I'm a beached whale. I am not just pear-shaped, I'm the whole goddam orchard down there—"

Give it a rest, Em. You look *fine*. Now can I ask you a question?

"What?"

I've been thinking about my commercial—the all-American kid. And *Aficionados* where the guy said I was the Midwest Incarnate. Don't I project anything . . . dangerous? Exciting? Even a little bit exotic?

"No, not at all."

Nothing?

"You are the cream of the Midwest, Gil. The guy you take home to Mother."

But not the guy you take on a dirty weekend to Acapulco.

"Well, yeah, maybe in real life, but onstage you're pretty clean-cut." She smiles here, looking away. "You know, you're a bit of a prude, Gil."

I AM NOT.

"Come on, let's go back to the party dying in the living room without us. First I'm changing jeans, though—I'm throwing these fatass WIDE LOAD jeans away. I'm going to buy a corset . . ." She went to her room to change.

I went into the living room and sat between Kevin and Jasmine. I asked Jasmine if she was free this month to do some work for the theater. We needed a soundtrack to our experimental show and since she was an "audio artist" it would be great if she could do it for us. The money wouldn't be much—

"Gil, what do you think I make? I make no money at all. I'll, like, sweep up your theater if you pay me."

I thought if you made records, you made money.

"Well think again. Dregs, I'm so tired of dregs . . ."

Emma craned her head out of her bedroom: "Gil? Could you come here a minute, please?"

I went into Emma's bedroom and she shut the door. I could tell something was wrong.

"While we were sitting out there . . " She sat on the edge of her bed, shaking her head in disbelief. ". . . I've been *robbed.*"

Robbed? But we were—

"The goddam open window. I opened the gate so the breeze could get in, while I sat there and typed today . . ." Emma's desk with all her writing paraphernalia was by the window, which led out onto the fire escape. There was a folding, padlocked grill that Emma always kept locked. But on this scorcher of a day she had opened it as she sat there and worked on poetry. Then there was the party for my commercial. Maybe two hours had elapsed, but that had been long enough for some crook to crawl down the fire escape, reach in, get her typewriter, her clock radio, her cassette tape player, her Instamatic camera, a cheap wristwatch that was lying on her dresser, and a twenty-dollar bill lying near her bed. The burglar must have ransacked her room while one room away the party carried on loudly.

"Gotta give the guy points for audacity," she said, numb. "My own damn fault. Leaving that gate open. You turn your head for a minute, relax your guard for a moment and POW the City reaches up and . . ." She trailed off.

You're not insured, huh?

"Of course not."

Emma, I'm sorry. I sat beside her on the bed and put my arm around her shoulder.

"I want to blow some street punk away with some big gun, Gil."

I know you do.

"God. Such cheap old crap too. That typewriter is used and dented and the fraction signs don't work and . . ." I know, I know. "And that camera. It's worth nothing—no pawn shop would give you a ten for it. But the film—my god!" Emma realized the film of Janet's and her surprise birthday party for Jasmine was still in the camera. "I'll NEVER get those people together again, behaving themselves . . . Cock and Jasmine didn't even hit each other once."

(I had missed this occasion because of a rehearsal. Jasmine was thirty, so they had thrown her a Happy Twenty-first Birthday party. The band was there, her manager was there, three of Slut's ex-boyfriends were there, including Cock. When Lisa caught up with me to tell me about her and Jim's engagement, she told me that Emma had been living it up with Jasmine in Williamsburgh: 1) Emma had gone to a tattoo parlor for a skull-and-crossbones but chickened out, 2) Emma had shaved the sides of her head and sported a mohawk but was so embarrassed that she didn't go out of the house for a month, 3) Emma had lived with Cock for three weeks when Jasmine went to L.A. for some record-promotion thing, 4) Emma was getting wildly drunk and trying a variety of drugs hanging out with that crowd, and finally, 5) When Jasmine went west, Emma took over some of Jasmine's phone-sex clients. I had assumed that, in that environment, the celibacy was a thing of the past. That guy Cock. Every suitor's nightmare: a six-foot-three skinhead bass player with great biceps, a biker tattoo, biker's boots, looked like the Fascist-dreamboy in leather and an SS cap, a legendary sexual endowment and an IQ off the low end of the scale—a guy if he was any dumber you would have to *water* him. Every woman's dream. I wasn't going to ask about what they were up to because I didn't want to know.)

Emma was steely: "It's back for a while to the phone sex, I see. I need a lot of money quick."

I hate the thought of you having to do that—

"I got no choice. It's quick cash . . . see what I mean? In your heart, you're a prude." Emma vowed to make the money back in a month and this time buy all new things, nice things, decent typewriter. "And while I'm at it, I'll get a .45 Magnum too."

Emma, I said, you don't get robbed everyday. I'll take you out tonight. We'll get drunk. We'll do bad things. We'll have an East Village night out.

"You got it."

8:45 p.m. The St. Mark's Bar and Grill. Kevin went back to Soho, Janet stayed in to work on an article for the *Womynpaper*. Jasmine, Emma and I are having double chilled Stolichnaya vodkas, no mixers.

"Soho," says Jasmine, "if you're not in a big rich decorated loft, is a cesspool. Third-world living conditions. Dregs, I'm so tired of dregs—"

Get outa here. I'm on Avenue A, stepping over junkies, dodging the gangs, avoiding the drug busts, living in a century-old Puerto Rican slum and you're handing me SOHO?

"I have mice."

So? I got rats.

"I got cockroaches. This big."

I got cockroaches THIS big. They fly around my apartment holding lamps and kitchen implements aloft.

(A favorite New York pastime: the Who-Has-It-Worse game.)

9:30 p.m. The Grassroots Bar.

"Any jukebox in town that claims to be good has to have a few things to pass Emma's strict and unforgiving guidelines," Emma began. "The presence of His Holiness, Ray Charles. Obscure Ray Charles—like here in the Grassroots with 'Ruby' scores a full ten bonus points."

There should be a lot of one-hit wonder groups, i.e., The Dixie Cups, Question Mark and The Mysterians, The Box Tops, and . . . who was it that sang "Those Were the Days"?

Everyone could agree on Mary, but not her last name.

"There should be either Nat King Cole singing 'Mona Lisa' or Louis Armstrong doing, for twenty bonus points, 'What a Wonderful World,' lots of Roy Orbison, at least five Elvis—obscure Elvis, again worth many points. There should be two or three country-and-western, i.e., Emmylou Harris, Patsy Cline, Tammy Wynette's 'Stand by Your Man,' Webb Pierce's 'There Stands the Glass.' The last being the song that converted me to loving country music."

Yeah?

Emma considered "There Stands the Glass" pure American poetry. As we sat there with Jasmine buying us double shots of Jim Beam, Emma attempted to sing (always good for a laugh).

" '*Theeeere stands the glass . . . Fill it up to the brim . . . Until my troubles grow dim . . .*' Now here's where you know a man with an understanding of drink wrote the song, the tag line: '*It's my first one todaaayyy . . .*' "

Jasmine, who seemed not to recognize anything we had been talking about, suggested a proper jukebox needed New York Dolls, the Ramones, the Sex Pistols, the Dead Kennedys, X, and one day, with any luck, herself.

10:30 p.m. The Holiday Cocktail Lounge.

"Yeah you call Sheila," Jasmine was telling Emma, "and she'll fix you up again in the phone-sex business. In a month you'll have enough money to pay for the new phone line and replace everything that bastard stole from you."

"How much is a Magnum .45 these days?"

Jasmine thought about it. "I'll call my Uncle Harry. He got me my gun."

You have a gun, Jasmine?

"Yeah, like, it's not a serious gun. It makes me feel better. It helps in the recording studio to get your producer's attention. You know, Gil, Sheila was saying they're starting up a *male* phone-sex line. You could get some extra cash too, talking to housewives, old women."

No thanks.

"Gil's a traditional Midwestern kid," Emma said, enjoying irritating me. "You're going to end up in the suburbs with a fat wife in a station wagon driving your dog to the vet while you fashion little hamburger patties out on the patio for the barbecue you're having to kick off your yard sale—"

Quite finished?

"I'm just telling you there's nothing to the phone-sex business. I have an affection for these guys, actually." Emma and old men, a long-standing connection. "It's sort of sweet in a way."

In what way?

"Don't you see? These guys don't want to cheat on their wives, or go buy a prostitute—they tell me their stories: I love my wife but she doesn't do anything for me, she just lays there, she doesn't talk dirty . . . So they lock the office door, call up Sunshine Entertainments, Inc.—"

Sunshine Entertainments, Inc.?

"We take credit cards, Gil. If the wife pays the bills, she won't think it strange, something called Sunshine Entertainments."

So these guys aren't all losers, huh?

Jasmine explained: "They got American Express gold cards. They're businessmen, they're like salesmen in boring hotel rooms in boring cities. What gets you is, you know, the *averageness* of them—these are people's dads and uncles and church deacons. They just want to be talked to. The whole thing lasts five minutes tops."

At $35 a shot, five to ten minutes a . . . a session, you could have a $350 afternoon. Why did you ever quit doing it, Emma?

"Well, there was this one old guy, Charlie," said Emma. "And he said he fell in love with me, and his fantasies started getting all tied up with me. He was going to leave his wife for me. Please, he'd say, tell me your real name, I love you, I love you—I'll pay anything to meet you. Started creeping me out, he threatened to trace the number. At that point, I said, enough of this."

Jasmine yawned. "Look," she said blandly, "there's Crank."

We looked. A guy with puke-green dyed hair which he had shaped into horns and spikes with superglue. He was trying to light his leather jacket (yes, he was wearing it at the time) with his cigarette lighter. "Burn, you fucker," he kept saying.

"You know him?" asked Emma.

"He comes to my gigs," said Jasmine, numbly sipping her Jack Daniel's. "Does a lot of ludes. He's really into fire and stuff, you know?"

He was standing beside a girl in a checkered, wholesome farmgirl's dress. Her head was shaved to reveal a FUCK YOU scalp tattoo.

Wonder what her mother thinks of that, I wonder.

"You *would*," said Emma. "See what I mean? Traditional values. Playing shuffleboard on your carport with your 2.4 children and their braces and their lead roles in the sunday school Easter pageant—"

You start up again, Emma, and I'll start letting you pay for the drinks.

She smiled. "That really gets to you, doesn't it?"

Crank had meanwhile set himself on fire. The Ukrainian barman then rushed out and picked Crank up by the collar—burning leather is not a pleasant smell—and hurled him through the door (which the bouncer opened) and out into St. Mark's Place: "Don't you know we gotta fire code in the city?" The bald girl with the tattoo sweetly apologized for him and followed soon after.

Like this crowd, do you Emma?

"Sure."

And after Jasmine had gone to the bathroom, Emma added, "I always feel very SANE in this kind of environment."

12:25 a.m. The Gates of Kiev Saloon.

Jasmine has stumbled home to Soho, which no public transportation served from the East Village—a long walk. Me and Emma, together again, booze still flowing. It's confession hour.

"I'm sure Betsy's nice," said Emma. "You shoulda brought her tonight. I'm sure she'd have loved the Holiday."

I'm sure Betsy wouldn't go in these places.

"Does she like diners? Run-down bars? Old jukeboxes?"

Probably not. She's the kind of woman who orders a salad at a trendy uptown café and picks over it and talks about how many calories are in the dressing, she drinks Diet-everything, and I've never seen her drink much of anything alcoholic.

Emma was behaving. "Hmmm. I'm sure though that you have, uh, other things in common. She reads books doesn't she?"

Yes, in publishing, I suppose so.

"No one in America reads books anymore. She gets credit for that."

How about you?

"What about me?"

Jasmine's crowd is pretty liberated sexually, so to speak. Sex, drugs and rock 'n roll. Guys like you-know, what's his name.

"Who?"

That Cock fellow.

Emma smiled again, enjoying teasing me with this topic. "That's not his real name, of course."

I didn't think so.

"His real name is Penis. Cock is a common nickname for—"

Very funny.

"Stupidest human being I think I've ever met."

Yeah. Did you sleep with him?

Emma giggled. "I was gonna . . ."

But?

"Well, he was living with us for a while—"

Lisa said you and he were together for three weeks. Alone. Together. In Williamsburgh. In the same house.

"You were keeping tabs on me while we were feuding, huh?"

Of course. *You* were with *me*, as well.

"Cock came out of the shower one day and I took a look at him and sized up the situation and I said, uh-uh, no way, that ain't going anywhere near me." She assumed the demeanor of the Virgin Mary you see in religious-store statues: "My celibacy is intact, five years and counting."

You don't miss sex at all?

She picked up her glass and clinked mine. "I've never been happier, more in control of my own life."

2:15 a.m. We're hungry. We walk through the West Village, down Christopher Street, looking at all the dangerous S & M gay clubs, the leathermen at the entrance, the pseudo-bikers, the live shows where you can see . . . well, you name it, you think of it, you can see it. Then we wound around up to Chelsea, home of a number of chrome, late-'40s, all-American time-capsule diners, open 24 hours. Down one street we saw three guys approach, walking together, exuding menace.

"Oh great," whispered Emma, "a mugging to cap off the day of my robbery."

We crossed the street to walk by them on the other side. This attracted their attention.

"Hey Mama," yelled the tallest of them, "come here! I wanna show you some'n." We walked quickly on. "Huh? You hear me? Where you walkin' with yo' FAT ASS so fast?"

Emma ignited: "*Fat* ass? I'll show that son of a bitch—"

"Hey you, faggot!" (I think he meant me.) "Where you goin' with that fatass bitch, eh?"

Emma was about to yell back, but I squeezed her arm: NO. Just keep walking. It's obvious they're not going to kill us or beat us up or rob us, they just want to taunt us—so walk on, before anything escalates.

We round the corner. We survived, I said.

"Yeah," she said, unhappy that our evening had included that note. "Starting Monday, I'm going on a diet. That's all I'm going to say about it."

3:30 a.m. The Korner Kafe, a long rectangular chrome box of a diner with a long lunch counter with a row of barstools before it. An overweight, overworked but efficient man, Mediterranean-looking, was presiding over the graveyard shift tonight. At the far end of the diner was a garishly dressed, tall black man (well, he was clearly a pimp) and a streetworn-looking woman who was surely his whore. They were exchanging tense remarks of which only a few became audible ("I got other bitches on the street Chantelle who ain't gonna pull short-ass trap money shit on me . . ."), and it was all unusually civilized considering how violent, abusive and intentionally humiliating most pimp-whore confrontations are. There was an old man in a booth with a *Racing Form* and a coffee. Emma and I sat at the long lunch counter and got breakfast specials, $2 a piece.

"Told you I had a fat ass," Emma began, when the coffee arrived.

Forget what those streetcrud said. Do you defer to them in all aesthetic judgments?

"Yes," she said, suppressing a smile. "It was probably one of their homeboys who took my typewriter. Heard there was some bad poetry being written on the block. Nip it in the bud."

You're looking very pretty tonight. Forget what they said.

"Yessiree," said the old man, out of the booth, preparing to move his paper and his coffee to the stool beside Emma's, "pretty you are, indeed." Then he started singing big-band crooner style to Emma, with a sweeping hand gesture: "I won't sit under the apple tree with anyone else but yoooo / Anyone else but yoooo . . ."

Emma turns to me, arching an eyebrow.

"Ah, my sister Vera—don't ask me about my sister Vera," says the old man, settling in beside Emma. "Her husband—don't ask me about him!"

I would have acceded to that wish, but Emma was game. "What's wrong with Vera?"

"My sister Vera?" he asked, his lined face a caricature of an addled, nattering old man. "Ah, don't ask!"

He told us soon enough:

"Her husband, Frank—a man without a heart. Throw the bum out he said, throw the bum out. But he's my brother, Vera said, and Frank said, throw the bum out. Now I'm gonna ask you a question little girl, and you . . . you think about the answer to this question I'm gonna ask you right now. Is blood thicker than water? Hm? Is blood *thicker* . . ." He paused, having enunciated "thicker." ". . .Thicker than water? Huh?"

"Should be," Emma said, as our breakfast specials were slid in front of us.

"Am I my brother's keeper? You know where that's from? It's from the Bible, little girl. No one reads the Bible anymore. Am I my brother's keeper? That's in, uh, the Gospel according to . . . it's in the Bible. So is 'Is blood thicker than water'? You're gonna need a napkin for that," he added, pointing to the breakfast special.

"I got a napkin, thanks," said Emma.

"Hey Stavros!" cried the man to the short-order cook and waiter. "Get the little girl a napkin. What kinda place is this? Can't even get a napkin . . ."

"She's got a napkin, Arnie," said Stavros.

"I got a napkin," said Emma.

"She can't even get a napkin around here . . ." Arnie went on.

Look, I said, here's a dispenser full of napkins, right beside us.

"Used to always get a napkin when you went in places—but that's yesterday, and as Vera says, yesterday's gone, Arnie, yesterday's gone."

"Vera," Emma mindlessly repeated.

"Don't ask about Vera—don't even ask," Arnie said, waving off any attempt.

In the corner the woman with the pimp stood up. She was in tears. The pimp grabbed her arm and tried to pull her back in the seat, but she struggled. Still their voices were lowered—it was an emotional disagreement as opposed to a business disagreement.

Stavros slammed his hand on the counter: "Hey, hey, hey, hey, HEY! None a that in here—you take thata sheet outside, eh?" The pimp let go, raising his hands in indifferent surrender; the woman rushed through the door. Quiet returned to the diner; the pimp stayed there staring out the window, drinking his coffee, thinking. There was a bell-tinkle as another customer came in, a man about forty dressed like a schoolboy, baseball cap, unwashed sweatshirt (New York Yankees, very faded print), something a little strange about him around the eyes. He sat next to me.

"I wanna chuh-Coke. Chuh-Coke, chuh-Coke, chuh-Coke."

Emma flashed me a look: OH BOY.

"All right Georgie," said Stavros, "you want your chuh-Coke."

It must have been the regular's hour.

Stavros went to the soda fountain and poured some cherry syrup into a big glass, then filled the glass with cola, stirred it up, gave it to Georgie who went on saying chuh-Coke chuh-Coke chuh-Coke. As the drink stood in front of him freshly fizzy, he went *Sssssssss* in imitation of it.

"You're gonna need a napkin for that," said Arnie.

Emma cleared her throat, getting the cook's attention. "Uh, Stavros. Could you give me a napkin?"

He grunted yes, and handed her a napkin from the dispenser six inches away. "And my name's not Stavros," he added.

"*Ssssssss*," said Georgie, still imitating the fizzy drink. "I wanna stroo. Hey hey, I wanna . . . I wanna stroo."

Stavros-or-whoever handed him a straw. Georgie began blowing bubbles in his cherry Coke.

Emma and I began eating our two fried eggs, butter-sodden

toast, greasy bacon and home fries, curiously done up in red peppers and chili to the side.

"Oh my god," said Emma. It became obvious to us at roughly the same time: the home fries were bathed in tabasco. We both dived for our water.

"Waa-waa," said Georgie, giggling.

"God that's hot," Emma said, beseeching Stavros. "That's the hottest home fries I've ever had . . ." She began panting.

Stavros shrugged. "That's how we make 'em at home in my house."

"I didn't think Greek food was hot."

"I'm not Greek, I'm Puerto Rican. An' my name's not Stavros."

Georgie counted out 75¢ meticulously, out loud, nickel and penny and dime at a time. "That's good," said the short-order cook, "that's real good, Georgie. You tell you mama *buenas noches*, eh?" He laughed at his own harmless joke.

"Bye-bye," said Georgie and everyone said bye-bye to him, even the pimp wearily raised a hand bye-bye.

Emma and I were in pain, sweating now. Of course we could have not eaten it, but there's a distinctly un-macho effect to not eating something spicy brought before you in a New York diner. Whatsa mattuh? You can't take it or some'n?

"I'm gonna die," said Emma, pulling out two napkins and mopping her brow.

"I told you," said Arnie, "about the napkins."

"C'mon Arnie," said Stavros, "time to pay up, eh?"

"Ehhh, I just got in here—"

"You been here two hours—so let's settle up."

"Eh, I already paid ya!"

"No you didn't Arnie. We go through this every night. You didn't pay me—"

"I paid you when you brought it out," said Arnie, all indignation, with a tinge of bad lying, a tinge of senescent guilt.

"Now Arnie, I gonna have to ban you from comin' in here—"

"No, no, Stavros, you can't do that, you can't do that—"

"Arnie," said Stavros, firmly but with respect for the man's age, "you gotta pay for what you eat."

And then Arnie made one of those sad down-and-out New York conversions to pathetic old man: "Stavros . . I got nothin' this week, I . . . I pay you tomorrow, or when—here look . . ." Out came the *Racing Form*: "Here, here see? Arnie's Choice in the fifth at Belmont, that's a sure thing, I got connections, I got an ear at the track, I got . . . Look, seven to one, *seven* to one, Stavros—"

Stavros, not impressed: "Yeah, yeah, yeah."

Emma told me later that she'd noticed the old man's *Racing Form* was a month old, all the circlings and markings, winners and losers, just hot tips in the old man's mind.

"Seven to one . . . Look, I ain't got it now." Arnie pulled out his pockets, his lip trembling, his eyes watering, an old routine still keenly felt: "I give you an IOU. You know I'm good—you know me! Seven to one—it can't miss . . ."

Suddenly the pimp was standing beside me, rapping a big gaudy ring on the Formica counter for Stavros's attention. "Hey, Luis," he said, "how much is the old man's?"

"$2.35."

The pimp pulled out a ten and paid for his, his lady's, Arnie's and told Luis to keep the change. "The old guy reminds me of my old man," said the pimp. "My old man got like that toward the end." And he turned and walked out into the night. And I thought:

Emma, you and your poetry, me and my acting—what are we trying to do? We can't top this city. We poor would-be artists can't compete with or improve on the rich density of human experience on any random, average, slow summer night in New York—who are we trying to kid? In the overheard conversation in the elevator, in the five minutes of talk the panhandler gives you before hitting you for the handout, in the brief give-and-take when you are going out and the cleaning lady is coming in—*there* are the real stories, incredible, heart-breaking and ridiculous, there are the command performances, the Great American Novels but forever unwritten, untoppable, and so beautifully unaware.

"You know the problem with that pimp," said Emma as we trekked back across town, skipping rapidly by the maze of dark alleys and dangerous warehouses of lower Manhattan. "He fell in love with her, and I bet she fell in love with him. That messes everything up. You can't use each other properly once you get love in there."

You really think love messes everything up?

"Sure do. That's what's so compelling about it."

Since it's 4:30 a.m. and we're bleary drunk and tired and most anything would be allowed, I slip my arm under hers and pull her closer.

"I never minded love, Gil, you know that."

Just the sex.

"Right. The love business is all right, it's the sex bit that stinks."

Well she didn't have to worry about me (if the sex warning then was for my benefit). With herpes, there was *no way* that Emma would sleep with me now—in fact, herpes sort of settled the whole issue. I didn't ever see any reason for telling Emma I had herpes—what was the point? Emma and I were now friends, just-friends for life. And I was glad to have it all settled—no more secret longings, no more master plans, no more jealousies, no lies, no fuss no muss. God was in his heaven (somewhere on the Upper East Side, in the sixties) and everything was in its place: Gil and Emma, best friends.

5:10 a.m. Good night Emma.

"Yeah, seeya . . . when are you coming by again?"

All the time, whenever I can, of course. Oh yeah, two weeks from now: Lisa's party. Don't forget.

Emma with distaste corrected, "Lisa and *Jim's* party."

We gotta go.

"No we don't."

EMMA. This time we do, and you know it.

"You should talk. You didn't have to go to that funereal wedding reception." I had been in *Bermuda Triangle* back then, so I had had an excuse.

"I guess I'll go if you go."

Put it on your calendar and *don't forget*.

In the intervening days, I asked Jasmine around to the theater to discuss her music for *Chambers* (a production to open in October). The theater, actually, was only a warehouse. What we'd done was build 25 sets connected by doorways; little rooms. We'd painted arrows between all these little rooms so the audience member could find his way through. Now, we gave each audience member a cassette recorder—one of those portable small ones you wear around your neck with earphones—and he got to go alone through all 25 rooms, four minutes a room, about ninety minutes to do the whole thing. On the tape there was a little *beep* to tell you when to move on to the next room—any fool could find his way through this. Each chamber was a complete world. You'd enter a living room and the furniture would be overturned, the lamps broken, etc., and on the tape would be the sound of a family fight. You were free to go and touch things, move things, explore. We wanted Slut Doll to provide music for some of the horror chambers—Jasmine had a tape collection like you wouldn't believe.

She had a collection of cassettes with every imaginable kind of sound on it—executions, murders, massacres, anything you could name that was macabre and unusual. One cassette was marked BLACK BOX. "That's from a plane crash, the pilot's last words and all. That thing out in San Diego where the two planes hit and the pilot knew he was a gonner." Here was a tape marked RAPE. "There was this security service that had videotapes of elevators and hallways in this apartment complex, and this woman got raped while the night-guard was asleep, in the elevator. The tape recorded not only the visuals but the sounds and screams and his cursing, his humiliating her. Maybe for the Pink Room."

The Pink Room is so innocent-seeming, though, I said. We had a room that was dainty and pink and Valentine's-day mushy.

"That's right," she said, brightening. "I was thinking of playing music-box, tinkly childlike music and then fading in the sounds of this woman being raped. I mean the whole defenseless-woman stuff, dress the little girls in pink, ribbons for the hair stuff starts in the crib, and it leads to woman as victim. There's a connection."

Yeah, I guess . . . What was this tape? I gave her one marked J.J. 1978.

"That's a goodie," she said eagerly, slapping it into the cassette player: There was the sound of a man singing, maybe yelling, a high-pitched battle whoop and thousands, it sounded like a stadium full, of people joining him; it echoed and reverberated and rang dreadfully. A man's voice sang forth above the din: *No there was no man be like that man . . . no man at all—we had not seen his like nor again shall we see him. If they come for us . . .* (the crowd noise nearly drowned him out) *. . . better that we die for this man than go out among the world . . .* (enthusiastic applause, the screaming, the held note eerily re-emerges to full strength).

"It's the last recording made of Jim Jones before he and the 900-some of his followers committed the mass suicide down in Guyana. Creepy, huh? But get that noise they made, all of them together, in some kind of trance. I'm going to use that noise, get a tape loop of it over and over, for the Black Room."

How did she get hold of that thing?

"I have a friend who gets this stuff. I used some of that on my last album. I've got all kinds of stuff here . . ." She rummaged through a cassette carrying case. "Manson interviews, Vietnam atrocities, gas chamber noises, South American torture accounts—"

Right. Have you and Nicholas agreed about the Blood Room yet?

"No. He wants me to use like a heartbeat sound. I mean, Gil. It's like boring, a cliché, you know? We oughta use this rhythm instead." She slapped another tape in her tape-player. It went *ka-dump CRACK ka-dump CRACK ka-dump CRACK . . .*"

"It's from a hanging," she said. "Those guys who up in Idaho went around forcing women driving alone in cars off the road, raped them for hours, tortured them—"

Yeah, okay, I remember. Back a while.

"Yeah, well they got the noose and they made a tape of it officially for last words and all. Anyway, the *ka-dump* sound is where they go through the trapdoor, the crack when the rope goes taut. I isolated it and bounced the tape back and forth until

I got about four minutes of it, then spliced it into a permanent tape loop. One of my songs on *Innocent Victims* is set to that rhythm."

Yeah, all right. I'll get Nicholas to put a noose in that room.

Emerging into the light, leaving the Soho Center every afternoon, escaping this temporary world of corpses, executions, death rattles and suffering screams, was strangely therapeutic. I think I see why Emma got along with Jasmine. After a dose of Jasmine each day, life seemed positively JOYOUS, one gave thanks for every moment that didn't include war crimes, torture or psychopathic activity.

Then it was the Saturday afternoon of Lisa's party. I was a good boy, got up on time and everything, and made my way to Emma's. I'll admit this: Lisa wasn't as fun as she used to be and neither of us were crazy about her husband Jim who was the kind of advertising guy people who have no sense of humor find funny. But I still liked Lisa. Emma was weirder about it—there was a deep resentment of Lisa for something. It was as if she had never forgiven Lisa for growing up and leaving the Apartment of the Gods years ago.

I buzzed for Emma on the street.

"Gil? What are you doing here so early?"

I KNEW IT. You've forgotten Lisa's party. Now get up and get dressed—

"I can't go."

Would you please let me in so we can discuss this? She buzzed me in and soon I was in her apartment with Janet, half-awake, milling about in the kitchen trying to make us coffee.

"I've got to do phone sex this morning. I'm committed," said Emma. "It's a call from Murray. I can't refuse Murray."

Murray the big tipper. Emma, I told her, I'm not going to this thing without you—I need moral support.

"I'll show up later, I'll—"

No you won't. You won't show up at all and I'll have to lie for you. Do your phone sex and let's get out of here.

Janet emerged from the kitchen with a yawn. "I spent five minutes hunting for the coffee. I take that as a sign I oughta go back to bed."

"It's in the broom closet, like always," said Emma, as the phone rang. "You don't think it's Lisa do you?" Emma picked it up. It was Sheila, chief switchboard operator for Sunshine Entertainments, Inc. "Yeah," said Emma, "patch him through but we gotta hurry, Sheila. I got a date I can't miss at noon."

Emma arranged the TV so it faced her. "Jasmine said that Murray called her four separate times during the Democratic Convention."

Murray had this thing for public events. He liked to fantasize he was out there at the conventions, the U.S. Open, the State of the Union Address, the Indianapolis 500. He liked to pretend he was in the stands with a beautiful woman talking dirty to him. Emma's TV set was warmed up. I turned up the sound, and put it on the channel Emma told me. It was Jim and Tammy Bakker on the PTL Club. This morning they were talking to a group of severely retarded people.

Tammy: *You know, Jim, I just can't tell you how strongly I think that these are very special special people . . .*

Jim: *That's right, Tammy Faye. Come on over here and join us as the graduating class of the Mecklenburg Center for Special Education sings us a song . . .* (the young adults wave her on over, poor things, spastic and palsied)

Tammy: *You know, Jim, I don't think of these poor people as retarded at all—it's WE'RE who're retarded, you know?* (tepid applause) *I think of these young people as Angels Unaware.*

Jim: *Angels Unaware, yes, yes . . .* (more applause) *Now come over here and join us, Tammy.*

Boy with thick glasses, slobbering: *God doesn't make mistakes.*

Jim: *Glory Hallelujah! Did you hear that Tammy?*

Tammy: *I couldn't understand him, Jim, what—*

Jim: *God doesn't make mistakes! No he doesn't! God doesn't make mistakes!* (enthusiastic applause)

"That woman is made up," said Emma, shaking her head in disbelief, "like the Whore of Babylon."

Surely, I said, your caller doesn't want to use this segment.

"Oh god, they're singing now; please turn that down."

I did. Silence.

"I hope Lisa isn't going to be too upset. There's no way we can make this little affair by twelve. Oh look, the song is over."

The phone rang.

Emma picked up the phone. "Hellllooooo," she breathed. "Why hello, Murray. You remember me, don't you? Where are we today? Oh yes, how exciting . . ." She gave me the cue, I turned up the volume for her:

Tammy: (near tears) *And you know, Jim, I prayed, I* PRAYED *to God to save Choo-Choo, I said, Lord, Lord, don't let Choo-Choo die, he's been a good little puppy for . . . for . . .*

Jim: *Now Tammy, this subject always upsets you and–*

Tammy: *LET ME FINISH, Jim, I was getting to the point where I realized that everything has its purpose in the world. And maybe, yes* (sniveling) *yes, maybe Choo-Choo did scratch the furniture and spray the curtains—you remember, Jim, the time when—*

Jim: *Yes honey, but now let's go on—*

Tammy: *I'M STILL GOIN', Jim, and I realized that maybe it was Choo-Choo's time . . .*

Emma suppressed a smirk. "Yes Murray, it's true, we're sitting just two rows from the front. Isn't it exciting? What if they come over to do an audience participation segment . . . maybe we'll get lucky. I see you have a raincoat in your lap . . . I know what you're up to, and Murray we're going to get caught . . . All right, all right, just so you won't yell out, I'll do what you say, I'll slip my hand under the raincoat and . . . oh Murray, you're so incredible! This mammoth pulsing strapping . . ."

Tammy: (going out into the audience) *Hello hello, do you like this dress? Yes it is nice isn't it? I wish I could get my hair to do what yours does—where ya from? Ada, Oklahoma? A lonnnng way from home!* (mild applause) *What brings you to Heritage Village? Hm? Isn't that sweet, Jim! They get one week of vacation and they decided to come here to see us! Of course, many people don't know about our extensive amusement and Christian-oriented theme park here at Heritage Village . . . you're camping? Yes, by the Sea of Galilee—isn't it lovely there?*

"You're unzipping your fly, I just know you are, you bad bad boy!" Emma went on, with an eye to her stopwatch. "And what if Jim and Tammy see what you're doing? What Murray? Oh you are so bad! I have no choice but to get this over with as fast as possible . . . OH MURRAY, I scarce had imagined . . ."

Tammy: *How old are you? Nine?*

Pale, freckled dumb-looking white boy: *Yeah.*

Tammy: *Have you been going to our classes for young folks?*

Boy: *Yeah.*

Tammy: *This week is Crucifixion Week at Heritage Village and in the classes and presentations we've been concentrating on the crucifixion. Do you know who was crucified for you?*

Boy: *No.*

Tammy: *Jesus Christ, that's who! Do you know what crucifixion is?* (silence) *Well, I'll just sit right down here on the steps and tell you, how's about that?* (silence, distracted looks) *Give me your hand . . . yes, that one is fine. Now have you ever played in your daddy's basement with hammers and nails? You know how sharp nails are, don't you? Here, hold out your hand, honey—now can you imagine having a nail put right through your hand, just hammered into you till it came out the other side? No, I see you can't . . .*

"Oh Murray, you're so bad!" Emma continued, looking up at the set. "Oh I know she's coming over here, Murray. My god, the ruin, the disgrace, they'll say you're a pervert, a sick degenerate, worthless slime, Murray . . ." Emma winked at me, as if to say that this was doing the trick. "Ah, here she comes, my god, she's in our aisle, she's going to talk to you, she's coming, she's coming, she's here . . . ah, but lookee here, Murray—what a mess you've made!" Emma gave me the thumbs-up sign.

Tammy: . . . *and it's important that you keep those contributions coming in or we won't be able to serve you as we have, and we just love doing the Lord's work, serving our television audience, and our audience is rising Jim, rising and reaching new people each and every broadcast . . .*

"Bye Murray," cooed Emma. "You're so bad but you know I love to meet with you, and you know I'll be there for you next time. The Carter-Reagan debates, right, right . . . *Au revoir* . . ."

She gently set the phone down, then turned to me: "Let's haul ass, we'll never make it by noon."

We ran three blocks north and slammed our money down for the L train, which on weekends is slightly more nonexistent than on weekdays. Silence, wait, anxiety, smells, time ticking away. "I hate this train, I spend half my time waiting for it—half my life," said Emma. Finally we saw a light in the tube. It came as close as one station away and parked there for ten minutes. Emma was tense because she was in a hurry, but also because of the event—I was uneasy about what lay ahead too. It seemed surreal. Eventually the train creaked into the station taking us two more stops to the transfer to the 1-2-3 lines for the West Side. The two platforms were connected by one of New York's longest tunnels, over a block in length—Emma called it the "Rapeway," and nothing could induce man or woman to make this deadly connection at night. The usual Saturday morning wino dregs, addicts, bums with nowhere to sleep, were there—dodge the urine here, skip lightly by the impossibly colored pool of vomit there . . . then finally, we stood waiting for the 1 train. And waiting. And waiting.

"It's 12:20 already. I'm calling to say we'll be late," Emma offered.

Nah, Lisa knows us, don't be nervous. But we were nervous, and we couldn't stop ourselves.

We went past the doorman, into the elevator (which took forever), down the hall ("This hallway smells nice," Emma said. "Hallways aren't supposed to smell nice") and rang the doorbell. We could hear some vague partying noises inside, like bird-chirping sounds.

"Get ready for the performance of your career," Emma said out of the side of her mouth.

The door opened and it was Lisa, thinner, paler, older than we had ever seen her, but beaming and happy: "Oh you're late, you're late, you're late!" A kiss on my cheek, then one on Emma's. "Emma you look so good, so so good."

Emma shrugged: "I look like shit."

Jim approaching from the right: "It's the Emma! And it's the Gil! Stars in our midst, stars in our midst."

How you doin', Jim?

"Great, great. You know me. But now the pièce de résistance . . . what we've been waiting for . . ."

Lisa lightly slapped our arms. "We told Phoenicia to wait to bring him out—we were waiting on you!"

To the oohs and the aahs of all the assembled guests, out came Phoenicia, this big kindly black woman, with Jim and Lisa's one-month-old daughter. "Heeeeere's BAY-BEEEEEE . . . woah woah woah," Lisa looked like a grouper swimming through the crowd to intercept Baby: ". . . woah woah woah, here's Mah-mah, you know your mah-mah don't we, huh, don't we?" Lisa took Baby's hand and waved it hello to the guests who were still cooing over the pièce de résistance.

"There's Dah-dah," said Lisa, aiming Baby at Jim. "Recognize your dah-dah? Hmmm? Woah woah woah . . ."

Jim poked a wiggling finger into Baby's stomach: "Hatcha hatcha hatcha . . . whoa-ho-ho, Baby says don't do that! Baby says hey man, what are you doin' to me, huh old man? Ha ha ha, Baby says who are these people?"

"You know Mah-mah don'tya honey, my little honey honey honey?"

I look at Emma. Emma looks at me. Other guests before us slip in to see the baby. I look at Emma, and Emma looks at me, again. "I want to end my life," she said distinctly.

"Heeeeeere comes Bay-bee-Bay-bee-Bay-bee . . ." said Lisa, lifting the baby over the heads of the throng, flying it towards us. I felt myself back away. Like, what if I dropped it? Be a different kind of party then, wouldn't it? Oh that Gil, he's such a downer at parties, like that time he dropped Lisa and Jim's baby . . .

Jim: "Baby comin' in for a landing, *rrrrrrrrmmmmm* . . ."

"Oh I don't know," said Emma, shying away from the incoming baby. "Oh Jim, I don't, I'm not good with, I . . ."

Emma held Baby. Emma had this sick look on her face. She drifted to me—no you don't Emma, no Baby Hot Potato here;

YOU hold it. "It's alive," said Emma to me quietly, "it's a living thing."

"Baby says who's this? Baby says who's this cray-zee girl? Baby says where's Mah-mah? Huh where's Mah-mah?"

"Mah-mah's here, woah woah woah woah . . ."

"Hatcha hatcha hatcha—Baby says, cut it out, cut it out!"

Then Phoenicia, who was making me feel guilty with all her deference to these white people, took Baby in her arms and laid her to rest in her crib ("Time for Baby to lie down, yeahhh . . ."). Emma stood there with her arms cradled a moment longer as if Baby were still there, overcompensating for our drop-the-baby fears.

"Quiche and cocktails by the pantry," said Jim, tapping us, all smiles, the proud father; and then he and Lisa meandered to the crib with their fellow employees.

Refreshments, I said.

This was a catered affair. There was a nice, clean gay boy behind the table: "Some quiche?"

Two Bloody Marys with quadruple shots, lots of tabasco, three slices of quiche, those little things in the bowl—

"That's Russian yogurt," he said helpfully.

—a spoonful of peanuts there, those things on the crackers, those meatballs, tons of them.

"Want it all on one plate, do you?"

Emma smiled. "We can expand."

We took our bounty to a corner, away from the throng. "The temptation to drop this pile of meatballs on the shag carpet . . ." she sighed.

Now Emma . . .

"Have you see *Andy Warhol's BAD*, where the woman throws her baby out of the skyscraper and it goes splat?"

Emma, really.

"Just thinking aloud, thinking aloud . . ."

We got drunk, very drunk. So did the other advertising people and marketing people and research people and corporate people and Lisa's old friends. No. Wait. We were the only old friends. Everyone else was Jim's old friends, or business contacts.

Lisa came over to our corner to tell us about Towelies. "Remember my work for Wipe-Away? Well, they were impressed and I'm getting to manage Towelies now—hey, I'll send you a case. It's a real challenge making paper towels interesting."

"Well," said Emma, taking another cocktail off a tray, "there are people like me, of course, who read everything they can get their hands on concerning paper towels, who find the topic naturally stimulating."

Lisa laughed a bit unsurely. "Oh Emma, here, here"—she dragged Emma toward a round woman with a nasal voice—"this is Marge—Marge, Emma, Emma, Marge. Marge keeps me sane at work." Emma watched Lisa walk away and was stuck with Marge, who talked to us about Bathroom Blues, a thing you hang on the side of your toilet bowl which turns the water blue.

"What do you do?" Marge asked at last. "Could I have met you before, Emma?"

Emma brightened. "Was it the Celibacy Support Group?"

"What? Ahahahaha . . ." She had an even more irritating laugh.

"What do I do?" Emma continued, tottering with her sixth Bloody Mary. "I'm in telecommunications. Phone service. Phone sales."

"Oh really? That's going places they say."

"Up, up, up—getting bigger every minute."

"Like whadya do exactly?"

"I work in Onanistics."

"Oh. Yeah I've heard of that. Exciting work."

"It's a coming industry."

Emma darling, time to go home.

We went to the door, or stumbled toward it. Suddenly, Lisa had us blocked. "Oh you're not going are you? You know Emma, there's a guy at Simon & Schuster coming later to watch the baseball game on Jim's big-screen . . . I mean, you ought to stay, you'd get along so well and you never know how it might turn out."

"What do I care about a baseball game?"

Lisa laughed. It was a new laugh, a New Lisa laugh—she

hadn't laughed this way a year or two ago. "Oh silly you! No, a publishing job. Don't you want to get out of the East Village and all that? Honey, you could edit. And make contacts, contacts for publishing a book of poems or a novel . . ."

"Contacts," Emma repeatedly flavorlessly.

"And I thought," added Lisa charmingly, "that we could, you know, talk over old times. I wanted to talk old times."

Old, old times. Just having "old times" implies a larger looming sadness somewhere. I told Lisa we had to run.

"Yeah," said Emma, "gotta go. I do my phone sales all afternoon on Saturday while people are home, you know."

Yeah gotta go, another time, blah blah blah.

Jim joined Lisa at the door. "Come back and see the two of us—"

Lisa squealed: "I caught you, Jim! The THREE of us!"

Jim slapped his forehead like on a commercial. "Can you believe it! Did you just hear me? Don't tell Baby!"

Bye-bye.

Emma didn't say anything until we got to the elevator, and then she said we oughta keep drinking, drink all afternoon long, call Janet and tell her to warm up the blender. Which is what we did. Going home the long way by the liquor store (put it on Emma's credit card), the junkfood store on 14th Street, getting some of that pretentious foreign ice cream that was big then, some homemade cookies, Pretzel Stix.

"Now you see," said Emma, scooping the goodies into her arms, "that's what Jim and Lisa have given their lives over to. Deciding to spell words like S-T-I-X. Stix, Pretzel Stix. God, I hate CRAP."

She put the Pretzel Stix back on the shelf, having said that.

On that principle, I pointed out, we had to put the Cheez Crunchies back too, but Emma conceded that we had to bring home *something* to junk-out on.

"Well that was an exercise in bullshit, huh?" Emma said, mouth full of cookies, as we walked back to her place. "Ugh, have some cookies—I'm getting nauzed already."

Cookiezha. Thanks. I don't want children, by the way.

"Holding the kid wasn't as bad as I thought it was going to

be," Emma said, tossing two remaining cookies in the pack in the gutter.

Hey, you just littered.

"Jesus, Gil, New York is the one place you can litter in the world and not feel guilty." She reached into the shopping bag, fished out the Cheez Crunchies, opened them, began eating. "Janet's seriously making the moves on me these days."

Really?

"Yeah, she's determined there's a lesbian in me somewhere."

I shrug. What's it to me? Why not give it a try, I tell her.

"You're supposed to be jealous and say you'll slap me around if I do that."

No, I got it: I take pictures of Janet slapping *you* around—we can make a film. It's a short step from phone sex, porn films, you know.

Emma and I arrived at her place, and she cursed everything and everybody as she tried to locate her keys in one of four pockets, juggling the shopping bag all the while. "Anyway, Janet's acting weird lately. Hurt that I don't sleep with her, except she's not hurt she's just bored and between girlfriends. So can you stay over tonight? Hang out a while?"

Can't, I said. I was going to see Betsy.

"I'm tired of behaving about her," Emma groaned. "Betsy is a blah."

Well, soon enough Emma got to check out Betsy in person. I invited Betsy to the opening of the Soho Center's *Chambers* production. As no one understood a damn thing about this show, it was a critical success—Slut Doll's sound effects were praised everywhere, and we even got a few punkers curious enough to attend and pay admission in the show's four-week run. Monica from the Venice showed up to the opening-night festivities too. There they were: THREE women in my life in one room. No catfights though. Just once, *once* I'd like to see two women go to it roller-derby-like, tearing out each other's hair, bashing each other with chairs, overturn the punch table —*Gil's mine, all mine!*

"You could do better," said Emma, after talking to Betsy at the refreshment table, "but you could do worse."

(I sort of missed Emma savaging my love interests.)

"However," Emma went on, "if she gets in my way, I'll mount an offensive. At the moment she seems too insignificant to exercise my venom upon."

The first Emma versus Betsy incident followed the very next week. If you didn't know any better, you'd hear this story and think I was still in love with Emma.

"Let's go up on the roof," she said. "Now look, you don't have a rehearsal tonight, so look what I've done . . ." She ran into the kitchen and came back with a tray. What was on the tray was covered by a pile of paper towels (Towelies, courtesy of Lisa). "*Ta-da!*" she said, unveiling two bottles of the world's cheapest beer. "No, don't thank me, its was expensive, yes, but Gil . . . for you, *anything*."

Uh, I said I was going to see Betsy tonight.

"POOH on that girl. You don't love her. You want to stay here with me; you want to go up on the roof and look down at St. Mark's and urinate on passersby and . . ." She trailed off glumly, because I looked resolved to go.

She's making dinner and I haven't seen her this month except once, because of the play and all.

Emma looked genuinely disappointed, instead of her usual affronted. "Oh yuck. I was in the mood to tie one on with you."

The thing about people who rarely demonstrate any direct affection for you, is when they do get around to making a heartfelt request for your company . . . well, it's rather touching and you can't refuse them. And I never could refuse Emma much anyway.

I compromised. I called Betsy and said something came up at the theater and I'd be late.

Up the stairs we went to the sixth landing, then up another small flight to the rooftop door. Emma singing ahead of me: "*When this ol' world starts a-gettin' you down / and . . . blah-blah blah-blah blah, up on the roof*. Why hasn't Motown signed me yet?"

Absolutely no singing talent? Could that be it?

I loved that roof, though you couldn't see a thing (except in the neighboring windows, which could get good) other than the street below when you looked over, taller uglier buildings to our sides, an ever-so-small bit of the Twin Towers sticking up above the building across the street.

"They have to keep the lights on all night, because it's too expensive to turn the buildings off and then on again," said Emma.

I know. You told me but I can't remember when.

"Sorry. I'll get some new Emma-Facts." She took a swig of beer and it was musictime again: "*Way on up at the top of the world*—no, *stairs / I got no problems there / Up on the rooooof* . . . No that's not right either."

Way on up on the . . . The thing about Emma and lyrics is that she massacred them in such a way never to get the real ones back into your head.

"I shoulda been a Platter. Or was that the Drifters?"

Just bring the beer over here, huh?

Emma was hyper tonight; she ran over to a slanted part of the roof, a skylight once perhaps, now tarpapered over. "Hey get this!" She leaped about. "*I want to leeve in America / Everything's free in America . . . La la la la in America*—"

You don't know that one either.

"That was a great movie, *West Side Story, Romeo and Juliet* urbanized. Hard to think it was ever slummy on the West Side. Hey, maybe we could do a musical version of *Titus Andronicus*. And we can set it in the East Village."

Never read *Titus Andronicus*.

"Everyone gets cut up and it's very bloody, just like an average night on Avenue A." Emma sat beside me and we each took a swig of the cheap beer. "I've never read it either," she added, after a moment.

We sat there and Emma sat unusually close to me and we stared across the street at people about to go to bed or get dressed to go out or about to make out with/make love to their dates—

"My god, we are going to see something," said Emma, pinching me, whispering (as if they could have heard us). "Three floors down, the orange shade. She is nude."

She is not nude. She's wearing a flesh-colored sweater.

"Those are breasts, I tell you."

She's watering her plants and those are not breasts. Where are your contacts?

"And here comes the guy . . . he's going to kiss her and fondle those breasts. And I bet *he's* naked from the waist down."

It's a sweater, I'm telling you.

"Maybe she has very fuzzy breasts."

It was time to go to Betsy's.

"Another half hour won't hurt. Oh come on. They're going to be copulating in the window ANY minute, I promise."

No, Emma—

"What if I call them up and ask them to?"

I gotta go.

Emma laughing. "Wait, wait—let's, uh, talk about this . . . Can we negotiate? What'll it take for you to call her and say you can't make it?"

And so we bargained for a while, but only for another half hour. Fifteen minutes later we agreed on the half hour.

"Starting from right now."

No, *including* the fifteen minutes' bargaining time.

We started bargaining again. Emma said she'd make sandwiches. She would even make a peanut butter and mayonnaise sandwich, which repelled, nauseated, violated, reviled and disgusted her, but for me she'd do it. "Better'n what you'd get at Betsy's, I bet," she said.

Oh poor Betsy. Here we go, readers, Entry 5689 in Gil's Hall of Shame:

Betsy on the phone: "Gil, where *are* you?"

. . . uh, still at the theater. Everything's taking longer than it's supposed to.

"I thought you had a night off tonight at the theater."

Well yeah, it was a late night off, I should have been free but we've got to repair some of these sets that are falling apart.

Pause. "Ha, you'll never guess what I bought today, dear."

What?

"A Slut Doll album," she said, with a small laugh.

You can record it on the back side of your Barry Manilow and Carole King tape, I said.

"How do people listen to this stuff?"

Some people like it.

"I thought, since I met her at that play and all, I'd go check it out." She sighed. "And so I got it. I thought you could explain the lyrics to me, since I'm not up on all these trendy things like you."

Yeah, I'll do that, Betz.

"How 'bout later tonight? When you get off? I mean, you know me, nothing to do. I mean, I'll be up."

Yeah sure. But if it's too late I may be tired and I may go on home, and we can do it tomorrow.

Pause. "Yeah, I guess. I got some food for you . . ."

Oh shit Betsy, you didn't go to any trouble did you darling?

Pause. "No. I just . . . I just ordered out some Chinese stuff. Sit here and pig out myself, I guess. No, it was nothing special, don't worry."

Yeah well, sorry.

A big sigh, then she brightly says, "Love you."

Emma is standing at the fridge looking at me complacently. And I say, yeah Betsy, same for me too.

I know: I'm a bastard.

It's easy to do that kind of thing with someone you're having sex with and don't love. Oh, and hell, I could fill *a book* with things she did nasty to me, though. She'd read one-thousandth as much as Emma and was determined to make me feel stupid. She always kept toying with the theory I was gay because "most actors are" and I hung around with Kevin at the theater. And she kept needling me "Why don't you tell Emma, if you two are so close, about your herpes?" And I dressed like shit, too. Didn't do anything with my hair—I'd get more parts if I just shaped up, she'd say, Miss Expert all of a sudden. And as for sex—

"Something the matter, Gil?" Emma asked, shoving a peanut butter and mayonnaise sandwich in my hand. "Look, was this some big date you had going, or just some average get-together thing? I didn't mean to mess up anything. Well I did, but not anything important, I mean."

Back to the roof.

"Guess what I brought . . ." Emma nudged me with an elbow.
What?
She considered not telling me, but then did: "A new poem."
THAT'S GREAT, Emma, you're writing again!
"Oh I'm always writing, but not always writing well. I think it's all right, for a change." She uncrumpled a piece of paper from her jean jacket.

NOW THAT WE HAVE LOVED

Now that we have loved,
what do you bet death must be a sure thing.
We will destroy ourselves (you, me and Mankind),
and earth will become as barren as the moon
and the sun shall lose its hard-earned colors
and again be that cold unfortunate star
left to argue against the darkness
in this corner of the void.
With smoldering earth as barren as the moon,
the moon forgets her envy and consents to dance,
quarter moon and quarter earth,
lunar white and jagged,
circle each other in an eternal minuet
of ceaseless symphonic silence.

On the other hand,
maybe not.
There may be other nights with you beside me,
and me and the night thinking of endings,
endings grand and final, worlds in flame,
even the judgment of God cut short by a louder bang,
the so many deaths to be had . . .
But we have loved,
and so I guess I'm going to have to be a big girl
about death etc. and say
it's now all right. Forever.

It's a love poem, I said slowly.
"Yeah."

It's interesting, I said (and she gave me a copy of it, and that's why I still have it). Is it about anyone?

She laughs to herself, shakes her head, looks at the roof a moment. This would have been a nice time to say my name, Emma.

"No one," she says. "No, someone, just no one . . . no one I've met yet. A future love, I think."

Yeah, I thought, and maybe because I'd been such a jerk to Betsy the moment before I was capable of being better than my usual rotten selfish self, and I thought: Yeah, Emma, I hope one day you do find your future love and I hope it lasts and I hope I like him and I hope it's been worth the wait and, mostly, I hope you're happy.

"I think you're still hung up on Emma," said Kevin, giving an unsolicited opinion, over at my place on Avenue A for the third time this week. "But I sort of liked Betsy too . . ."

You go out with her then.

"Too many women, Gil. Too much Drama in your life."

If I missed Drama, all I had to do was follow the Kevin and Nicholas and Soho Center saga. Kevin told me the whole story. Nicholas had this wife (now ex-wife) and they married when Nicholas was in law school and they were twenty-five or so. Nicholas dropped out and opened up the theater with this gay fellow named Michael. Nicholas fell in love with Michael, divorced wife. Wife sued for half the profits of the theater, half Nicholas's income and many other spiteful things, her spite perhaps justified. Michael's ex-boyfriend Randall kept pursuing Nicholas behind Michael's back . . . This paragraph could finish out the book—hundreds of twists and turns. What it amounted to was Nicholas, this slightly exhausted, suffering presence in his mid-thirties, with a beard and beret, was now living with Kevin, this perpetual teenager who seemed to precipitate a weekly fight. By mid-September it was, according to Kevin, a daily fight. As he began to drift away from Nicholas, he started coming to see me. He was terribly camp and I used to cringe walking down Avenue A with him as he flamed out like a Texas oilfire, being as outrageous as he possibly could. Mostly, he was harmless.

"Gil honey look what I found," he said, traipsing into my

room one time, having worked his way through Ruiz's store. He had picked up a Spanish teenybopper magazine that Manuela must have left lying around.

You are going to give that back, aren't you?

"Nonsense, finders keepers." He flopped down on my bed. "I love these Puerto Rican boys . . . look at these Menudo kids."

They're like thirteen and fourteen, Kevin.

He arched an eyebrow, peering over the magazine: "Well, you gotta break 'em in young these days. Gil, listen, listen—this one is for me . . ." He read from the magazine: " 'Pablo is fifteen. His favorite color is purple.' Gil, *my* favorite color is purple. We're meant for each other."

Would you put that down?

"Purple huh? See, he must be a budding little faggot already—purple, for christ's sakes." Kevin read on: " 'Pablo loves to play futbol.' Probably loves it when all the other hot little Puerto Rican boys pile up on him in a tackle."

You're thinking American football, that's soccer, I reminded.

Kevin, still reading: " 'Pablo likes cars. Pablo's favorite group is the Beatles. His favorite food is chicken.' I can DO chicken, Gil—I can give the Colonel a run for his money."

Finger-lickin' good?

"You are so bitchy, Gil—you'd make such a good faggot, you know. I'm making you my project. And there's absolutely nothing—NOTHING, do you hear me?—between me and Colonel Sanders at this time. Don't know how these rumors get started. Of course, if the old boy dropped enough money in my direction . . ."

Give me a break.

"Hmmm," Kevin grimaced as he read on, putting down the issue of *MenudoMania*. "Problems in paradise. It asks Pablo who his best friend is and Pablo says: 'Jesus Christ.' This one is going to take some doing. A LOT of ground work. God knows, though, I have the time."

Is it really that bad with Nicholas?

"We still do a lot of things together. Like fight, say awful things about each other, complain, bitch, run out of money. Between his ex-wife and Michael poor Nickie isn't the least bit fun anymore. I'm going to become celibate like Emma, that friend of yours."

Yeah? Well I'm not supposed to be going around telling everyone about her celibacy, so be subtle if you see her.

"I do want to talk to her about it. I think it's the only way I can keep sane. I don't want any more involvements in my life, unless it's with Pablo. I have *always* loved Pablo and you know that's true—I've been saying it for years."

Since he was nine, right?

"You know . . . oh I am *not* going to tell you this."

Lemme guess: that tired old story where you lost your virginity on the bus with some nineteen-year-old serviceman in South Carolina when you were thirteen. You have told that story at parties, Kevin—at family gatherings, to your mother, at the White House, they show reruns on TV of you telling that story . . .

"Enough with the jokes, already. I only told Kathy at the theater and see where it gets me. It's a good story and if I'd had a head on my shoulders I woulda taken the soldier's name, because when he gets out of the army—"

Dishonorable discharge?

"Would you cut it out? I'm supposed to be the bitch here, not you. Anyway, a man in uniform—darling, like Dietrich in *Morocco*, I'd follow my soldier across the dunes, French Foreign Legion-like. Orlando can't leave the Navy alone, by the way."

I gave Kevin a beer. Once in every visit we talked about his friend Orlando. Orlando was this SCREAMING black faggot trying to make it in the drag queen circuit (saving his money for Paris, etc.) and most of Kevin's stories about Orlando were PURE fiction, I'm sure. Kevin kept telling me he was going to bring Orlando by, or we would have to visit him at the sex shop where Orlando worked days, but it never happened, enforcing my suspicion Orlando was a fake front for Kevin's stories. Orlando, I always said, wasn't his real name—

"It is *too*."

No one is named that.

"Oh you should hear him on this subject. *Orlando* is a book by D. H. Lawrence or somebody where the character Orlando changes sexes. He says his mother named him after that. I said, bitch, she did not, she named you after Disney World. Oh it gets him so mad!"

And what's Orlando up to this week?

"Well they've got new things in on 42nd Street. We really should go down and see them. They have these new motorized vaginas. I mean, straight people are beyond me anyway, but good god, who would want to sit there and put themselves in a plastic slit that makes a noise like a blender, you know? They say *we're* perverse, ha! They've got new dolls now, ones you don't have to blow up with air. Skin approximation is getting better too, Orlando says—it's not so plasticky anymore. And the new dolls—get this—come with REAL pubic hair—"

Get outa here.

"NO, it's *true*, Orlando swears. There's a company in Ohio that puts them out with real pubic hair. I mean these girls grow it, shave it off, hand it in and then they attach it. And they've gotten vaginal scent now. I mean, honey. I mean, that was the good thing about the doll in the first place, right? You didn't have to mess with vaginal scent—that was the PLUS, right? How you can go *down there*, Gil, is beyond *me*."

Well I'm not going down there very often these days. Why is it, Kevin, that when you visit the level of the conversation doesn't even make it UP to the gutter?

"I'm only this bad around *you*. And guess what Orlando says they have in now."

Okay tell me.

"Rejecta. She's the new doll, Gil. She comes with a tape cassette with several ten-minute routines. She rejects the man who's pumping away on top of her. She has this bitchy voice: 'What? You call that a penis? It's so small.' And 'You're so disgusting, I bet you can't get it up . . . you'll never come . . . you miserable worm, why don't you get off me, you fat piece of shit?' "

I don't believe that for *one* second.

"Honey, it's down there. You never believe me—this stuff exists on 42nd Street. Rejecta. I'm buying her for your birthday, Gilbert, so you won't be alone. I worry about you."

Thanks a lot.

"Rejecta, she exists, I swear. What you straight people *won't* do to get off, I mean it. Anyway, Orlando says hi."

I almost let Kevin have his way with me one night.

Yeah, it's true. We went and had two pitchers of beer and he got me camping and being bitchy just like him, and said, Hey, let's make passersby think we're lovers and so we walked arm in arm around Sheridan Square and got stares and winks and offers and reactions of all kinds. I was just waiting for Aunt Sarah to round the corner on her Garden Club Convention, up for the weekend. Or Betsy. Though that would serve her right.

"I *bet* money you've done it," said Kevin, after we left the liquor store, picking up some gin. He could only drink gin and tonic.

Done what?

"Slept with a guy," he said, taking my arm again. "C'mon, tell Uncle Kevin. Church camp, Scouts maybe? Freshman year. You HAD to in Scouts, that's all anyone does on those camping trips is learn how to masturbate."

Afraid not. Although . . .

"C'MON, Gil, *tell* me. I know you're essentially straight (not that I couldn't ruin you, ruin you in *five* minutes for other women). Tell Kevin *all*."

I was eleven, Sammy Henderson was twelve, we were tentmates in the Platypus Patrol. Sammy had torn out this picture of a woman on her knees, showing us her ample buttocks, from one of his father's porn magazines. He started doing something and I asked what he was doing in his sleeping bag and he said, boy Freeman you don't know anything, I'm doing what you do with a girl except with no girl. You know what you do with a girl like this? I was too intimidated to answer. You dummy Freeman, you get hard and . . .

"What? Stop laughing, tell me!"

. . . you get hard, Freeman, and you stick it up her BUTT.

We both, drunkenly, got into hysterics over this.

"Well Sammy had the right idea," said Kevin, doubled over trying to breathe.

Sammy Henderson, I went on, was also the guy who had a

birthday party for his thirteenth birthday and we stayed up late after Mr. and Mrs. Henderson had gone to bed, and there was this late sleazy '60s movie with Dean Martin or someone, and Connie Stevens, and Sammy thought Connie Stevens was the hottest woman in the world and had written Connie Stevens letters, and he pulled out his prick and ran up to the set with all of us watching saying: I'm gonna fuck Connie Stevens on the TV . . .

More hysterics, drunken rolling about.

"I gotta meet this Sammy Henderson. Where is he now, Gil?"

Married, has a kid, works for the Army recruiting office or something.

Kevin and I laughed all the way home. He told me stories that were alternately heartbreaking and uproarious about trying to get straight boys at Christian Church Camp to sleep with him, finally ending up with the born-again counselor.

Kevin asked if he could stay over, as it was raining, and I said yes. And he asked if he could sleep beside me on the one and only mattress and I said yes.

"Just like a slumber party, huh?" he said after being quiet for a while.

Yep, no Connie Stevens movie though.

"Can't have everything." Kevin put his hand on my shoulder and I didn't pull away. He began: "Now you see how harmless it is to be in bed with me. This is as far as I'll go. I will not go any farther unless you tell me to. I want to point out to you how very little technical difference there is between my hand on your shoulder and, say, my hand on your arm. You would concede this, wouldn't you?"

Yes Kevin.

Kevin put his hand on my arm. "Now I'm going to sort of . . . here, slip in right here, beside you, close like this. Now *no one* would say this is queer. This is not technically anything like homosexuality. I am a homosexual and I know homosexuality when I see it and this is not it. This is friendly affection."

I was laughing. Right, Kevin.

"Now if you're wondering about the difference between say this and, say, real homosexuality . . ."

I think I know the difference Kevin. Let's go to sleep.

"Gilbert you are a drag. Let's just conduct a little experiment here. This is in the interest of science, darling—I want to know what a straight boy thinks of as *too far*. I will behave as I'm inclined to behave and you tell me when I have crossed the point at which you are not inclined I should go further." He put his arm under me and hugged me.

Okay . . . that's, that's all right.

"Right," he said. Then he stroked my hair.

Dubious.

He put his arm across my chest and nuzzled closer.

Borderline.

He slipped a hand down to my inner thigh.

WHOA THERE.

"Afraid you were going to say that," he sighed. "Oh well. You give it some thought, Gilbert Freeman." And then he kissed me good night and we drunkenly drifted off to sleep.

I miss Kevin. He, like so many gay men, moved west to do some modeling or TV work or see a lover or all of the above —he just knew he had to get west. Hope he's all right, what with AIDS and all that.

Of course, why move west when you can have the rootin' tootin' Wild Frontier right in your very own neighborhood. I refer to when Ruiz's store was robbed at gunpoint. I'm in my room and I hear *KRRTAO KRRTAO!* which sounded like gunshots on TV except realer . . . Then yelling and screaming outside ensues, commotion upstairs as Señora Ruiz must have heard them too. Should I go out? What if the robbers are still there? I'm not armed . . . yes, go out and see if he needs help—WAIT, of course, calm down and call the police. Señora Ruiz couldn't communicate. I called 911, fingers trembling, voice shaky, throat dry, my hands emptied of blood, cold as ice . . . yeah, Avenue A, Ruiz's Caribbean Foodstore, hurry, I said. There was someone running toward the house, bounding up the steps of the family house. A criminal? No it was Rickie, and he and Señora Ruiz were screaming, crying, barreling back down the next second. I had to go out too.

The aisles of food and cans and boxes had been overturned,

everything knocked to the floor. Señor Ruiz was standing there—thank god, thank god, I thought, he isn't lying on the floor in a pool of blood. He saw us, sort of registered our presence, cursed, shook his fists, bellowed, "The stoopid kids —they were kids, they were stoopid kids, I see them every day—*you*!" He seized Rickie by the collar: "I see YOU hangin' out wid thees kids all the time, my own SON." He threw poor Rickie forward into the pile of boxes in the aisle—Rickie tried a faint protest. "If I ever see you with those riffraff again," Señor Ruiz threatened in a muddle of Spanish and English, "I keel you my own SON. You go to the police, you tell 'em everytheeng you know about those boys—my own son!"

"Papa," Rickie managed, "I don't know 'em—"

"So help me I gonna . . ."

Señora Ruiz screamed, tears flowed, she cupped Señor Ruiz's face in her hands, she implored the Virgin, she shook her head in disbelief, she was in a despair I had never seen a human being display . . . and then *I* saw: as Señor Ruiz was ranting and waving his hands above his head, his jacket revealed a patch of red on his shirt. It was growing. He had been shot.

Police sirens. The police came in—

Radio for an ambulance, I said.

"*No ambulancia* . . ." muttered Señor Ruiz, not quite registering what had happened to him. "No, I no shot, no ees no necessary . . ."

The policeman took Señor Ruiz's arm and led him outside, all the while Señor Ruiz mildly protesting going anywhere, he had to clean up the store, look at the mess, look what they did—ah, he had to pick it all up, no time for police reports, for the ambulance. Manuela had run home bawling as the news spread through the neighborhood; Johnnie was out somewhere. Manuela and her mother fell upon each other, crying, screaming, denouncing the world in Spanish.

The ambulance arrived.

"Tell the Señora that he is all right, he is just hit in the shoulder, he is all right," said the policeman, raising his voice to add, "Señora, he is bueno, muy bueno . . ."

Señora Ruiz yelled something frantically about going with

him; they forbade it. A taxi had been called and she and the family were to follow. No, no, no, she protested, she had to be with her husband—it was insane! In Puerto Rico they would not have rules like this!

"Thees is a terrible country," she told me, her tear-filled eyes cutting deep into me; she clutched my arm, hurting me: "Thees a terrible place, America. *Qué horrible, qué terrible* . . ." And she released me, almost in shock—her children and the officer helping her into a cab . . .

Between questions and locking doors and writing a note for Johnnie and talking to two policemen, I numbly made my way through the crowd, the spectators, the gawkers, went out into the city in the direction of Emma's—not home, not back to my flat, I could not go there, my heart was beating too fast to lie down. I had to walk, walk briskly, stopping for nothing, not for stoplights—I almost got myself run over, I heard a car horn, a curse—stopping for nothing. My walk became a run. This is panic, isn't it? This is weird—a minute ago in the presence of gunfire and emergency I was calm and efficient and now I'm falling apart. I should stop and calm down. But I can't stop.

"Hey man, what'sa mattuh, brothuh?" said one member of a gang of youths I walked into. I'm hyperventilating. I'll kill them if they touch me—

"You on some kinda trip, my man?"

"Those pockets look full to me, T. G.—"

"He's freakin' out, man—"

I don't know what I yelled at them, but it scared them enough to back off and I am running again, hurtling past strangers, pushing people, damn them, out of my way. Where am I running to? I have nowhere to run. I belong to no one. My mommy and daddy live one thousand miles away and my older brother is in Des Moines and my theater friends aren't really my friends, and I'm panicking not only because there are gunshots and gangs and danger and death in this city, but I'm just so goddam tiny and floating free unattached to anything and I have no one no one no one . . . except Emma.

"Gil, what's wrong? You're white as a sheet!" Emma said, bringing me inside, taking my arm, leading me to a chair.

I stammered out that Ruiz's store had been robbed at gunpoint, shots were fired. Señor Ruiz . . .

"My god," she said kneeling beside the chair to face me. "No one was . . . poor Señor Ruiz, he wasn't shot or anything, was he?"

He's on his way to the hospital, I said.

"Oh good god, Gil . . ." Emma had no more to say than I did. "Where? Like City Hospital? Those quacks and butchers?"

I guess. I had given Señora Ruiz a ten-dollar bill to take her and her kids to the hospital. That awful city hospital. You heard stories about the free clinics and city aid emergency rooms . . . people dying from knife wounds waiting for attention, old immigrants dying there not able to make themselves understood, being treated for a life-or-death illness by second-rate medical-school students. Perhaps I should have gone with them. Emma, I said, I should have gone with them—Señora Ruiz's English is so bad—

"Gil, Gil, calm down, it's a ghetto hospital. They speak Spanish there, they'll be fine." She patted my arm. And I started breathing slower; my mind wasn't calming down but maybe my body was.

"There are some whiskey dregs, if you want some."

I nodded numbly. She got up to get the whiskey but I wouldn't let go of her arm. She looked up at me with concern, and sat back down on the arm of my chair. "All right, honey, we'll get the whiskey in a minute." I started breathing normally so I let her arm go and she got two glasses and we split the whiskey. I drank it in a shot. She came back from the bathroom with two pills.

"Valium. From my weekly prescription. This is five milligrams which is small potatoes. Here."

Thanks. Didn't know she had a Valium prescription.

"Well, you remember that analyst and the masturbation therapy and all that silliness? Finally he gave up on me and gave me a Valium prescription. Last resort. I'm so happy with those little pills. Valium was made for me—I'm whom they manufacture those pills for, Gil." She held my hand. "You're doing better now, I can tell."

It's amazing what hand-holding will do for you. It's gotten a lot of bad press, I said.

"Yeah and it ain't bad, is it?"

Emma, I said, you're the only person in this city who'd notice if I disappeared, who knows or cares if I'm dead or alive.

"Oh Gil, there's lots of people—"

No, I mean it. You saved my life—if I hadn't had you to run to, what would I have done?

"You'da done something," she said, tightening her hand in mine.

No really—I'm repeating myself—you saved my life.

"Well," she said, half-smiling, "that'll be $1.50 then."

Emma went to get me some cocoa. It was 85 degrees but there I was sitting drinking cocoa, which Emma's mother gave her after nightmares. My hands were still shaking around the mug.

"I'll turn on the TV and find something escapist," she said, doing so.

I asked to stay at Emma's place that night and she said yes. I wanted some more whiskey but that would have meant going out on the street and I wasn't ready for that just now. It was very clear in my mind; I could close my eyes and see that red stain when Señor Ruiz opened his coat, as he saw himself for the first time what had happened . . . that look in his eyes of dissociation, of somehow not admitting the reality of what had happened to his own body . . .

"Gil, stop dwelling on it. You can stay here tonight, if you like. Janet's at her wimmin's music festival in Michigan."

The phone rang.

"My god, I forgot . . . it's a phone-sex night," said Emma. "The debates."

Debates?

Emma answered the phone. It was Sheila, and Murray's call was coming through when the Carter-Reagan debates began in five minutes.

"I'd put it off, Gil, but I need the money—"

Please, be my guest.

"Murray never takes very long anyway. Better get it on the right channel."

Carter: . . . *and this administration has improved life in the United States, the future is as good as it's ever looked; this administration has created more jobs, more employment opportunities than any administration in American history* . . .

Emma and I exchanged looks and small laughs—oh I was feeling better already.

. . . *and people are happy and secure in this great land—*

Moderator: *Time, Mr. President. Governor Reagan, your rebuttal.*

Reagan: *Well . . . all I can say is . . . there he goes again!* (much laughter, appreciative applause) *Mr. Carter has only to read the newspaper, to ask the average man in this country to find out what the mood of the country is under his administration* . . .

Emma sat looking at the set, shaking her head. "Scary thing," she said, "watching the man who destroyed the country debate a man who if he gets elected will probably destroy the world."

The phone rang.

"Showtime," said Emma. She picked up the phone.

Pause. In the interim while he talked, Emma lit up a cigarette.

"Yeah, I've got it on now, Murray . . ."

Reagan: *I foresee an America that harkens back and remembers its past, hard work, honesty, dignity* . . .

"We're sitting five rows back from the stage and Governor Reagan is talking . . . yes, he does go on, doesn't he? I can tell you're a reporter for the *Washington Post*, you've got your pad and pen and . . . yes, what an exciting life you must lead. I too am a journalist. I've seen you in the press pool many times but I didn't dare say anything, but I guess it's pretty obvious that I'm attracted to you. Am I mistaken or are you aroused sitting beside me listening to this? What? Yes, yes, I see I'm right. Yeah, that's right, why don't you move your raincoat up to your lap . . . no, it's cold in here and nobody would think it strange. I hear you taking down your zipper . . . are you going to show me something? Oh I never suspected, what a beautiful, mammoth, rock-hard instrument you've got there."

Reagan: . . . *the natural goodness, decency of the American people. I think the leader of the country ought to feel and know that decency, be in touch with that spirit* . . .

"Oh baby," Emma continued, taking a quick drag of the cigarette, looking at the stopwatch. "Oh god, I just want to pull off that raincoat and do it right . . . but, but people would see, the whole auditorium, the whole nation . . . but I want you so bad . . ."

Reagan: . . . *and I think one such necessity is a president who will see that prayer is put back in the schools. When I was a boy in Dixon, Illinois, in a classroom right before the Pledge of Allegiance we had a short nondenominational prayer, and, well, I don't think it did me or the thousands of Americans who knew this too, any harm at all* . . .

"Ooh, yes, yes, slip your hand under my skirt I don't care who sees yes that's it oh how do you know what to do? You too? Yes I can tell . . . here it comes, here it comes . . ." Emma gave me a wink and the thumbs-up sign.

Reagan: . . . *and well, I just think that America needs leadership, someone who can help the American people rise to that decency and pride and strength for which they're known. And, well, if I may add—*

Moderator: *Time, Governor.*

Emma was finishing up her business. "Yes, we'll meet at next week's debate too, Mur, you bet. I'm so hot just thinking about it. I'll see you then, Murray. I'll be so hot for it . . ." She set the phone receiver down quietly, and turned to me:

"Forty bucks."

1981

THINGS had been going so well for so long, that when Señor Ruiz sold the store and house to move to Jersey (the speculators had offered him the moon) AND when I was cast in the worst production of my life (*Rigatonio*, details forthcoming), I had mistakenly assumed that the bad stretch of a week ago, ending April 25, 1981, would go in the books as the Official Low Point in My New York Years. I felt so dismayed that I was dying to see Betsy—I hadn't seen her in over a month. We met at 11 p.m., Jackson's Diner in the theater district, on 54th Street.

"Eat in this place all the time, do you?" said Betsy with a sigh as she slipped into the booth across from me.

Great breakfast special here. Can I get you one?

"I think not," she said, trying to smile, "I don't want to die of food poisoning. We have something to talk about, Gil."

Don't we always, Betsy?

"We can't see each other anymore." She looked resolute. I wasn't going to argue because I figured one of these days this scene would be played out. But why when I was one step away from clinical depression?

"This can't be a big surprise, Gil," she went on, looking down at the place setting. "You haven't seen me in over a month. You don't call me at all—"

But last week I called from the theater—

"For five minutes and it was two weeks ago and you asked me to check the TV listings to see what time a movie was on so you could catch the late show when you got home."

True, all true. I would now be quiet and sit there and take what was coming to me.

"I know you don't love me. I can't say I love you either. But we like each other—at least I think you like me. And even as just friends we should . . . you should have done better by me, treated me with a little respect."

(I had suspicions suddenly that Betsy wouldn't be playing out this kind of irrevocable grand scene unless she had another guy to run to.) There's someone else, isn't there? I asked.

She was enjoying this, that feminine love of romance-novel drama. "Yes," she breathed, looking away.

(Good riddance, I'm thinking.)

". . . Yes, it's true. Roger is back in my life."

(The clown who gave her herpes! Back again! The key here, I think, was I treated her indifferently but I didn't treat her brutally. If I had treated her like Roger, been a real Grade A bastard, she'd have been eating out of my hand. And so, no doubt, Roger had sent her down here to break it off with me. Fine. In my heart, some time ago I had already dumped her. Well, she had never been in my heart, really.)

"I know this is going to be rough on you . . ." she went on. This part of the bad-TV-movie scene was all right. What was less all right was that desire of ex-lovers to give you those special words of advice upon leaving.

"You know Gil," she said, "you'd be a lot happier if you took more control of your life. Sometimes I wonder if you know who you are."

(Darling, I know who I am. I am the guy who is still here. Everyone I began this New York odyssey with has packed their bags—Tim, Crandell, Monica, even half the staff at the Venice Theater, Mandy is in a women's commune thing in Oregon, Janet is now moving to be with some girlfriend in Hoboken, Jasmine is living in L.A. now being the toast of the punk scene, Lisa is supermarried being a super career woman and a supermom (and that is just as good as moving considering how far she is from the artist she wanted to be) and Matthew, my best former pal at the agency—they are all gone now. I've come to that stage every New Yorker fears: I'm the only one left, the last holdout. Except for Emma.)

". . . and I think you ought to be more . . . more self-actualizing, Gil. You go where you're pushed a little too much. You're miserable in this play because you couldn't say no to Odessa. Stand up to her, change agents, *do* something. And you were talking about moving back in with that Emma woman . . ."

I swore I'd never do it, but I had nowhere to move, and Emma—with Janet leaving on short notice—was equally strapped. I smile, sitting there not listening to Betsy in the booth. There was a time when my life would have been fulfilled by the idea of Emma and myself, one apartment, living together, couple-like. "You gotta watch what you live for in New York," Joyce Jennings back at the Venice always said, "because you gotta live *with* it."

". . . and of course, I can't pretend not to mind your moving in with *her*. She obviously means fifty times more to you than I ever will. I can't still see you while you're living with her."

Fair enough. And accurately assessed. It's pitiful really—even in her drop-dead goodbye-forever speech, Betsy's self-doubts and insecurities surface.

"I know I was never as smart or funny or whatever it was that you liked so in Emma. I wasn't as pretty, I . . ." Then she remembered I was the one who was supposed to be made to feel bad. "Anyway," she says, picking up her purse and standing, "good luck, I really mean it. Hope you see your name up in lights." A chaste cheek-kiss and then she was through the door.

And I didn't mind watching her go, I didn't mind never seeing her again . . . until she was five minutes out the door. And I felt

(1) all alone again, single for life, we're back to square one in the sex department, (2) sad for the opportunities I didn't create for the both of us—why didn't we take a weekend trip somewhere? why didn't we have activities other than sitting around her apartment eating take-out Chinese?—and (3) because all the Gil-was-a-bastard memories floated to the surface, I wasn't so much guilty as I was sad that I wasn't as nice and good as I always thought I was.

Okay, we'll update that. *Tonight*, May 2, 1981, is my new nadir. I got nowhere to live, except with Emma—and I have deeeeeep misgivings about that prospect. My career is yet again in a holding pattern, a classier, more visible one than the holding pattern I was stalled in at the Venice Theater, true enough, but career stagnation has set in yet again. I'm twenty-seven. I am doomed to play young men's roles, teenagers, streetkids, rebellious sons. I am on the verge of aging out of the *only* way I will *ever* make a living. The hairline is receding. I'm flabbier than I used to be (not that anyone can tell when I'm dressed). I don't have the theatrical teenage bounce and energy needed to convince an audience I'm nineteen and when I try to stoke it up, it's forced. I once dreamed of movies and TV but that's looking less and less likely—theater's my ticket and I'm stuck doing summerstock, walk-ons, desk clerks, townspeople, First Stranger, Policeman 2, Young Man 3—these are the roles I have to wrench into respectability on my résumé. But *Rigatonio* was the worst.

"S'more coffee, babe?" said Valene, the waitress at Jackson's Diner. She was a sharp-looking sixteen, a black girl wise beyond her years with reserves of open-eyed innocence, the daughter of the husband-wife team who ran the night shift. Only so much could be wrong with New York as long as Valenes could be produced on Manhattan Island.

"Starin' out into space a lot there, Gilbert. You got no cream. I'll getcha some cream." Valene made off with the empty cream tin.

It was Saturday night. I had thought Betsy and I would be going home together, back to her place. I had used some of my after-shave, wore my clean shirt. Not the evening I had thought I was going to have.

"Here's some of our special cream, Gil. I got the special stuff just for you."

Milk the cow yourself, Valene?

And then she explodes in this high-pitched unrestrained laugh. It didn't take much to make her laugh—that good heart of hers, I think, was a little closer to the surface than in most ordinary people. I wonder how many waitresses or bank tellers or coffee-wagon ladies know that they are sometimes the only connection to humanity for some depressed people in New York—everything goes wrong and there's the coffee-wagon lady, the sweet girl at the cash window, the Valene who gets you a nice full cream tin: All right, I guess I'll live another day after all.

"Cheer up, honey. Don't like to see you looking so down. You in any plays this week?"

I'm in a real stinker, Valene. Everyone's gonna laugh at me.

"Is it a comedy?"

Supposed to be.

"Well there you are. They's supposed to be laughing."

If they put you in it, it'd be a hit.

"I'm gonna be a star one of these days, Gilbert. You remember I said it."

I don't doubt that, Valene.

"This turkey you in is gonna be over soon, right? You got some'n else lined up?"

Nothing at all.

"'Well they's saying it's a bad year for Broadway," and then she laughs her high-pitched laugh, and walks away. Valene: it's pronounced *Vay*-lean. It sounds like some kind of petroleum product; put some Valene in your tank. A customer put a quarter in the jukebox and suddenly it's an old Marvin Gaye song and Valene is dancing, up the aisles with the coffee, dancing in place at the table, moving this way and that way, sometimes she'd get into a groove so good she'd just have to stop and dance it out. "Coffee at number twelve, Valene," her mother would yell from the register. "I can't Mama, I'm workin' out." "I'll work you out girl if you don't get the coffee to number twelve," said Mrs. Jackson. Valene also sang. She had all the vocal moves down pat, all the Aretha-notes, but it just wasn't . . . wasn't *quite* on pitch somehow. She sang in her church choir, she had a solo now and then—Mrs. Jackson, though I never heard her, was supposed to be dynamite with a gospel number. Mrs. Jackson invited me to church up in Harlem one time and I don't know why I didn't go . . . well actually, I do. I didn't go because I'm a white Midwestern wimp who didn't want to be the only whiteboy for miles, so I missed out and I'm the schmuck. But I'm getting ahead of myself telling about the Jacksons. I'd like to tell about the Jacksons because I loved that crazy family and that crazy diner, and the rest of my life was pretty grim by comparison.

Like my agent (ex-agent now, of course) Odessa Benbow.

Foul old ugly Napoleonic five-foot mutant woman, gray dirty moplike wig balanced sloppily on her round head, a face that looked like a cross between Queen Victoria in later years and a purebred boxer, lipstick that would always turn clotted and brown and a cigarette always one-inch long, always dangling from those greasy brown lipstick-lips, all wrinkled and anus-like from years of smoking. I danced with her one time at some social function and she grabbed me in her pudgy tiny sweaty hands and I thought of England and put my arms around her and it was like hugging a lawn-sized garbage bag full of water, and she talked up at me nonstop, swaying drunkenly, blasting me with martini breath and hors d'oeuvre breath (she drank constantly, her breath was always some amalgam of booze and the last thing she'd eaten). She had no sex or social life, so her clients—controlling them, invading their privacy for professional reasons (ha ha)—became her life, her obsession.

Each visit to Odessa meant being pressed into Odessa, subsumed, envaginated by Odessa: "Give your Odessa a huhhhhg, there . . ."

Conversely, there were days she could not bring herself to move from behind her desk and that chair piled with pillows that stank of her. Odessa immobile: "Huhney, on that thayre table, could you git poor Odessa her pahncil, ovuh thayre, THAYRE on the table—no, to the right . . . yezz, that's it, huhney . . ."

Odessa's one joke, delivered in her thickest most put-on

cheesy Texas drawl: "Yes, my name's Odessa. Guess where I was born. Hm?"

Odessa, Texas?

Amid shrieks of hyena-laughter: "Hyoooston, darlin'. But you can't name a girl *Houston*, now can you? A-ha-ha-ha . . ."

Most Southerners you meet in New York are a blast. But she must have been Confederate Revenge, hatched in the last days of Sherman's March, 1865. (Or . . . maybe she wasn't even Texan. She was such a thorough old phoney, she might have been putting that ridiculous accent on for the last twenty years.)

Bonnie McHenry, my actress-friend from *Bermuda Triangle*, had recommended me to Odessa as Odessa was her agent too. This was her big favor to me. "Odessa's a bit much, Gil, but she gets the job done," said Bonnie.

"Gilbut, huhney, 1982 is gonna be *yawr* yeeuh—huhney, it is, I *swayre*. Listen to your good buddy Odessa!"

She also *managed* some of her clients. Her spiel:

"Now, I can be your agent, huhney, but you can also have me as your manager. I can manage you, darlin', the way you need to be managed—the press, the right people on your arm. A great careeuh is a finely managed thing . . ."

Yeah, and a manager-agent gets 20% as opposed to the 10% an agent gets. But, you know, it wasn't greed that motivated this push to be my manager (she brought it up every time I saw her). She mostly wanted to manage my life, my personal life, gossip columns, affairs, sex, she was a voyeur, she wanted to live a life through her clients, she wanted to own them. What made her worse was all the frustration she felt in never knowing anything about our personal lives, because we never told her *anything*.

The phone would ring, Odessa's pudgy hand would grapple with the phone, prop it under her jowls and chins, and listen, sucking intently on the cigarette. "Uh-uh . . . ugggh . . . yeah . . . mmmmmm . . ." All varieties of grunts and nasty guttural noises. "Yeah, I know, I know, baby, I know about him. He *is* a rough director—he's a complete bastud, you're right . . ." She'd roll her eyes. "Nancy huhney, darlin', you *cayn't* walk out now, it's gotta go and it's too good for yawr careeuh . . . Just put up with him, darlin'. You're a professional." At this, she nearly left the chair registering the opposite. "That's right. You get famous in this and you can traysh the man in the *Times* when they interview you. You know I'm with you, darlin', alllll the way—Odessa loves you, yes she does! Yes, bye-bye, baby," and then she'd set the phone down: "Neurotic bitch, worryin' my pretty little ass to death over her booolshit."

Odessa thought backstabbing her clients would endear her to the ones in the room, but we all figured we'd be the "neurotic bitch" or "stupid queen" or "dumb-ass boy" when she hung up the phone on us as well. And the merest hint that we were dissatisfied with her agenting, that we wanted more pay or better roles, would be met with high indignation, beating of breasts, the stricken gestures of Greek tragedy.

"My doctor says Odessa it's gonna keel you dead working your heart out for those *ungrateful* people. I cayn't believe Nancy said that about me—we'll just see if she gets invited to Odessa's Famous Texas Barbecue this year, won't we?"

Oh yeah, the Barbecue. This annual trial took place in the late summer. Odessa would set a date and cancel, set a date and cancel—apparently we were supposed to hold open whole months to accommodate this affair. ("Of course, Gil, people would give their eye-teeth to come to Odessa's Famous Texas Barbecue—the whole theater *wuhhrld* is gonna be there. It's a *thang*—an event!")

No one came for pleasure, actually. It was just another of Odessa's loyalty tests.

"Gil, now you ARE gonna be there, right huhney? Hm?"

And we heard her talk of nothing else for weeks before:

"It's difficult trying to do a full day's work and plan for this extravaganza—it's about to keel me. I wonder sometimes why I do it, but we who have a natural gift for entertainin' are *obliged* in New York to persevere. My doctor says Odessa don't do it, don't work your fingers to the goddam bone for these people, but what would a year be without Odessa's Famous Texas Barbecue, hm? Besides, you, my clients, are my *family* . . ."

As far as I could see, all she ever did was melt down a block of Velveeta cheese and plop down the pan next to a bag of Doritos. Sometimes the Barbecue would not even include barbecue, but something much cheaper like tacos, which you made yourself from her bowls of dog-food orange-greasy meat, brown withering lettuce, pink tough tomato cubes, and the ubiquitous grated Velveeta. Odessa would be running about in a Stetson hat and, help me Lord, *cowboy boots*, being the most ridiculous person in New York, drunk out of her mind by mid-afternoon (terrified that no more people were going to show up), vindictive and petty by late afternoon ("This is the *second* Famous Texas Barbecue Henry has missed—I'll fix that no-talent . . ."), and ready to pass out by five. Her passing out was preceded by her being deposited on the sofa for a half-hour of chain-smoking, barking out orders ("Don't put so much ice in my goddam margarita this time," adding as an afterthought, "Huhney"), squawking and laughing maniacally after her own repeated jokes, and sometimes a morose period where all her bitterness and muttering scorn was given vent before she fell asleep.

My friend Matthew, a fellow-actor and Odessa-client, would turn to me and say, "Well the old girl went all out this year. She dropped *at least* twenty bucks."

Matthew ran seriously afoul of Odessa and was kicked off her client list—in fact, he's been in a movie since, so the best thing he ever did was to depart the Odessa Benbow Agency. Matthew always seemed to be leaving Odessa's office when I was coming in, and often we'd stop and compare our going-nowhere-fast careers. We'd meet for drinks some afternoons and we'd leave notes for each other on the agency bulletin board, scribbled quickly and stapled shut. We agreed one drunken night that Odessa really did have anus-lips, and it was impossible to watch her suck with her wrinkled lips on a cigarette, and even worse to watch her put on lipstick, that slimestick applied to those puckered, wizened lips, then the play of her mouth as she patted her lipstick and smeared it all evenly . . . ullch, I'm getting sick just thinking about it. ANYWAY, Matt would leave me notes like:

> Anus-lips was in good form today. Shoulda heard her sucking up to Neuro Nancy today on the phone. Drinks tonite? 8 at McKinley's?
>
> —MATT

> Anus-lips is on a diet now! If you come at lunch hour you can see her eat this cottage cheese shit with raw vegs. Imagine Anus-lips chewing cottage cheese, talking with her mouth open, her big fat face. I need a drink—8 at McK's?
>
> —MATT

Well Odessa got curious and opened one of these messages one time and freaked out—"Aynus-lips! Aynus-lips! How cuuuuld he SAY such a thing about me, Gloria, Gloria . . ." And Gloria the secretary, fighting off laughter (I suspect), said it was some kind of joke. I got called in and asked about this and I said that I didn't EVER know Matthew to call her names and that the note must not refer to her—

"I know it's about me, Gil. I sat right there and offered that boy cottage cheese and raw veggies from my own little contaynuh! I'm so huht, I'm so huht I cayn't sleep. You don't feel that way about me, do you Gil? Hm baby? You think I should be called AYNUS-lips by the people I love and work my finguhs to the bone for?"

ALL I could do not to laugh, so help me god . . .

"Tell me, Gil, tell me you dawn't feel that way about your old friend Odessa, hm? You'd never call me AYNUS-lips, wouldya?"

I knew it was going to cost me.

It was going to mean the dreaded bear hug, or worse . . . kissing the . . . NO! NOT THAT! Anything but that! I decided I better cut this short before a real demonstration of fealty was called for. So I ran to Odessa, tried to embrace her, got it over with, assuring her that neither Matt nor I had ever slandered her—I tried, Matt, I promise I tried to get you out of it too. Alas, Matt later denied nothing and stormed out, ending their affiliation. Odessa—we both realized—made this big show of being the sensitive best friend, your surrogate mother ("Huhney,

I'm an artist too in my own way—you are my work, you are my devotion . . .") but in reality all the hurt-Odessa, wounded-Odessa stuff was crap: she was a MEAN old bitch who was plotting her revenge, she would get you back. I heard her afterward, after Matt got signed for this movie, say, "He'll be sawwry he ever crossed my path—just wait till I get ahold of the Page Three at the *Post*—I'll call Tommy at the *Post*, I will, and tell him about Matt's *boyfriend*. That'll make intristin' reading, won't it?" Then an evil cackle. I made a mental note: Leave on good terms.

I would always depart Odessa's office on 42nd Street and feel worthless, prostituted, for having hugged Odessa, and I repeatedly fought the feeling: *It's starting again*, it's turning bad—every three years or so you hit the slump and this is it.

"But Gil, huhney, if this show goes to Broadway—"

Odessa, NO WAY. *Rigatonio* is two hours of actors degrading themselves, the jokes aren't funny, it's an insult to Italian-Americans everywhere, the music is thin, the book is nonexistent, the producer is an idiot—

"Gil darlin', this is not your first time out, huhney. A little professionalism, hm? Would you rather *not* have a paycheck?"

Yes, here, Betsy, was where I should have spoken up and told Odessa *yes*, I'd rather starve than sink in a project that was willfully, inevitably doomed. But was I bringing in the big bucks for Odessa? Was I some kind of big-name star that could afford not to take a job? No, I wasn't. Odessa might well have been relieved to get rid of me, one less unemployable actor on her books. So I was a trouper about it.

As Betsy reported, I intended to move into a place with Emma within the next month. Emma's lease was running out, mine was running out at the Ruizes'. It was a simple matter: we had to go out and find a cheap place we both liked in a fascinating neighborhood near a subway stop. With twenty days to go before moving day, I don't think either of us had as much as opened the Real Estate page in the paper.

After rehearsal, I would trudge to Emma's (formerly Emma's and Janet's) place and drink all her booze.

"Another fun afternoon in Queens?" she'd ask, proffering a

bourbon and soda in the act of opening the apartment door to let me in.

(On top of everything else, this bomb was opening in *Queens*, at the Jackson Heights Playhouse. It couldn't even crawl respectably to Boston or New Haven or Philly or downtown at a small experimental theater. Queens. As close to the heart of the New York Theater World as Saskatchewan.)

"See how packed up I am?" Emma asked, with outspread arms.

I can't say it looks like you've done a thing.

"That's because I *haven't* done a thing. After enduring work it's impossible to come home and do more work."

Emma had this full-time job now. She had made more money, actually, doing temp work. She had landed this primo set-up where she typed in law case books on a computer for law firms through the night—$14 an hour, $20 an hour on weekends. But she claimed that wasn't enough money for her.

"I gotta get a permanent job with major medical benefits," she kept saying. "These psychiatrists and pharmacists are eating me alive." You could not go to see them, I suggest, not take so much medicine, I add. "My life is completely *together* these days, Gil. Why stop doing what's brought me back to mental health?" And so she stopped temping and took a job at Hutchinson & Parks, a public-relations firm. She wrote hype for various products.

Emma flopped down on the sofa. "Today was a red-letter day in my writing life," she said.

Yeah?

"Wanna see what I produced, what I wrote, what my mind and talents and *craft* engendered?" She craned for her purse which hung on the back of a nearby chair. She fished out of it a folded Xerox of a letter. "Enjoy," she said, handing it to me.

> Dear Client,
>
> Congratulations! Our man in the field told us your Pansy-Fresh Room Deodorant display rack and poster was *front and center* in your place of business . . . and WE appreciate that. We really do. Accept the pocket calculator as our way of

saying thanks for your support on the 1981 Pansy-Fresh "Always Fresh" campaign.

As you know the Pansy-Fresh giveaway is underway—some lucky customer from the New York area is going to an island paradise of their choice (in connection with the ad: "A tropical paradise in your living room"). But read the fine print! One of our lucky distributors is going to be Tahiti-bound as well! Could it be you? Please don't miss the opportunity of filling in your entry blanks. Only three weeks left to enter! Figure it on your new calculator!

Once again, thank you for your support. By providing a consistent outlet for the Pansy-Fresh Room Deodorant giveaway and by selling our scent-sational product, you are a valued member of our Pansy-Fresh team. Keep up the GOOD WORK!

Sincerely,

Kay-Anne Madden
Vice President,
Pansy-Fresh Marketing

This woman is a vice president, huh?

"Oh she never sees it. We have one of those automatic signature machines that signs hundreds of these letters. It's all a sham to make the distributor feel involved, and not just a tool, a cog, a stooge."

Well, I say, smiling. It's money.

Pause. I was waiting for it: "I'm a complete whore, Gil. What if future literary historians discover I had anything to do with shit like this? 'Scent-sational,' Gil. Did you catch that?"

Yeah I caught that.

" 'Scent-sational.' *Utter whoredom*. God, I felt better about the phone sex." Sadly, the phone sex had ended as before, with some middle-aged creep trying to trace Emma's number, calling her up, saying he knew who she was, that he was going to get her and consummate his love for her. She called the police, she got new locks for the door, she got paranoid, and now, just as well, she was moving.

"So no, to finish my thought," she went on, "I haven't packed. And when Janet left for Jersey, she left me all this crap of hers, every feminist gazette and newspaper for the last twenty years. I'm supposed to haul this library around with me, I take it."

Let's have another bourbon. I poured them.

"Any luck on a new apartment?" she said, after a sip.

None whatsoever.

"Well hell it's getting desperate. Let's go to a realtor and pay a fee. We're both working."

I'm not working, I'm digging my own grave out there in Queens. We got our co-stars signed today. Florence Crayfield is the actress—

"That old bag still alive?"

Yep. And the daughter is going to be someone named Charity Glenn.

Emma stirred. "I've heard of her."

I couldn't tell you from where. She's done a lot of TV work I think, playing teenagers, child prostitutes, young girls raped in prison, usual family TV fare.

"I know that name from somewhere else . . ." Emma mused. "Well, they're not exactly big names are they?"

No, they pitched the thing to everyone respectable. Florence Crayfield does local game shows, opens shopping centers, turns out for the celebrity car wash. No one really "working" would touch this thing: a fledgling, sure-to-close musical in Queens.

"Gil, you've been in worse things," Emma offered.

Yeah, at twenty-three, at twenty-five. It's getting old. I'd rather do waiter work than this.

Rigatonio, music and lyrics by Gale and Audrey Cooper, responsible for *Beaver!*, a musical romp based on *Leave It to Beaver*, very camp, very bad, closed in three days, and for *What's Your Sign?*, a revue based on the signs of the Zodiac, everyone in stupid costumes (imagine Pisces, imagine Cancer) singing songs and telling jokes about their respective characteristics . . . Their last two projects hadn't gotten *this* far. The book was by Dik Kline (yeah, he spelled his name D-I-K) who had never written anything produced before. Do you think he had some connection to Garth W. Kline, our producer? Garth W. Kline introduced himself the first night:

"Hello, cast, crew, staff, my name is Garth W. Kline, from Garth W. Kline Enterprises, and this is part of a new, a brand-new division of Garth W. Kline Enterprises, Garth W. Kline Productions, and you'll be seeing that name on your paychecks, heh heh . . ." That was a joke. "I want you to know that we're family, that I'm open to you and your ideas and together we'll take Garth W. Kline Productions to the same success we have had with Garth W. Kline Enterprises . . ."

Lord, if you could grant us lowly thespians one wish: Save us from *businessmen*, show us Thy mercy.

We had a director, Silas . . . Damn, I can't remember his name, but then he had no personality, no purpose except to sit beside Garth W. Kline and agree with everything Garth W. Kline said. If Silas dared to direct an action, block a scene—"A little to the right, Gil"— Garth W. Kline would be up, saying, "I think left, actually," and Silas would go yessir yessir. Garth W. Kline, founder of Garth W. Kline Aluminum Siding, Garth W. Kline Plastics, and Garth W. Kline Refrigeration Units, all subsidiaries of Garth W. Kline Enterprises.

The plot? It was sort of a free-form rhapsody on the subject of Italianness—on the stereotype, rather. We're all running around in Renaissance costumes, as if it's Verona in the 1500s. Mrs. Lotsamoola is Florence Crayfield (drunk before lunch each day) and she has a lovely daughter, Charity Glenn (an insufferable BRAT who seems five but was actually a little older than me, who was making $20,000 up front to my $275 a week before taxes). Meanwhile, there's a lowly pasta-maker in town (modern dress, chef's hat, not-so-comic anachronisms) and he has a son, Rigatoni Fozzuli. Papa Fozzuli has two great numbers in the first act; "Meatballs"—

There's a speecy spicy speecy spicy meatbaaaawwwlll,
On top of a pretty pile a spaghetti for yoooóou
A speecy spicy speecy spicy meatbaaaawwwlll,
Plate a pasta for your luncha

It don't costa very mucha
But you musta not say BASTA/to my pasta
fazoooo!

You don't have to know the music to that one to get the idea. The second showstopper was "Rigatoni," the title number. Papa Fozzuli comes out on stage cradling the baby Rigatoni and is trying to think of a name for him . . .

A name upon ya/like lasagne
Ah, that ain't right for yooooo . . .
Call a fella/tagliatelle
What's a papa to do?

Papa Fozzuli goes through every pasta name in the book until he decides to name his kid Macaroni Pepperoni Rigatoni Fozzuli—his mama calls him Rigatoni for short. This number includes a pizza tossing sequence where instead of a dough pie, Papa tosses the dollbaby up and down like a pizza. Inevitably, the man playing Papa (usually in the bar with Florence Crayfield, also drunk by noon) would drop the baby in rehearsals.

I played Antonio, the greedy suitor for Charity Glenn's (Elisabetta's) hand. Of course, I'm going to lose out and Rigatoni, poor boy from the streets, wins her favor. By the end of the play we get (1) a peasant grape-stomping scene, (2) a lot of godfather-Mafia jokes as Rigatoni is pursued by Verona's sixteenth-century equivalent of the Mob (in '30s gangsters' suits, of course), (3) a subplot of drunken friars and nuns, (4) a Mussolini take-off, and (5) an Italian film director who wants to put Elisabetta in the Commedia dell'Arte. A jumble of stereotype, a rich interwoven tapestry of insulting kitsch.

"*Rigatonio*, huh?" said Emma, giggling over the script. "I feel it is my duty to point out that *rigettare* is the verb 'to vomit.' " Otherwise Emma loved it. "It's brilliant, Gil—makes me proud to be a quarter Italian-American. Why are you complaining? If you *tried* to write something this bad, you couldn't do it . . . It's a masterpiece!"

And as rehearsals went on, it became obvious to me that I was going to have to throttle Charity Glenn.

"Mr. Kline," she'd nag, in mid-scene, 10:50 at night, everyone tired and cranky. "I think this needs another verse. Why would she wander out on this balcony waiting for love and just sing one verse?"

Garth W. Kline explained that the songwriter only wrote one verse of her first-act song. It would be reprised in full at the end.

"It's not worth my while singing just one verse. I want another verse—look, people are here to see this Elisabetta fall in love —I mean I need a bigger scene."

And what a stage hog she was. Lingering at doorways, holding notes forever, always a piece of business to distract from other people's scenes. And the worst thing for me was I HAD NO ALLY, I had no Bonnie McHenry, I *alone*, apparently, seemed to think this was trash.

Neither Emma nor I could deal with apartment hunting so we gave in and called a realtor. In a week we found one acceptable place, Seventh Avenue and 26th, a big ten-story building full of old people hanging on to their leases and their beautiful, spacious, last-century apartments.

It was up-and-coming, promised our agent.

"What's the name of this up-and-coming neighborhood?" Emma asked.

"It's so up-and-coming," said the agent, "it doesn't even have a name yet."

Five hundred a month, $250 apiece. Lots of space. Elevator smelled like a urinal though, no doorman, halls were long and ill-lit and suggested rape and mugging and untold dangers. On the other hand, lots of buses, a nearby subway stop. The neighborhood was dull. Deserted by fashion people, button-sewers, alteration tailors, cloth-cutters by night, it was desolate by eight p.m. No nearby bars, no movie theaters, no street action—what a comedown from the East Village. I remember moving in, Emma being all aflutter having packed up at the last moment.

"God, I'm falling apart—I've forgotten everything! I've thrown out all the things I wanted and packed all the shit I'd just as soon lose—"

Emma, we'll sort everything out later. We got a cab waiting downstairs full of boxes, come on—

"Be with you in a second, Gil," she said, rushing to the bathroom. Then I heard the jingle of a pill bottle. She's taking a tranquilizer. Moving is stressful, why not? I'll tell you why not, Emma, because you're taking them at the drop of a hat. But this was not a time for a confrontation.

We weren't very happy, either of us.

Emma comes home from work:

"Today at work, I typed this bitch's letter to Bow-Wow Doggie Biscuits—the woman probably keeps a supply of Bow-Wow in her desk drawer to nibble on. Anyway, I was writing this letter and she types fifteen rough drafts before she gets this crappy letter just smarmy enough to send. And I'm typing it up and I come to the salutation. It says 'Anyhoo, Anyway,' then 'Carol Freeney.' What was this? I ask her what all that is and she says 'Oh that's just a thing I do, it's just how I end my letters.' So I suppress the vomiting urge and go back and type 'Anyhow, Anyway' at the end of this letter, as I thought she had misspelled *anyhow*. So I take it in to her and she goes no no no, it's 'Any*hoo*,' and I ask 'Anyhoo?' and she says 'Yes, that's just a little thing I do, you know at the end of letters, something distinctive so the client feels something personal is going on here, he can get a sense of my personality.' " Then Emma sighed, smiled a placid, untroubled smile at me. "I just thought I'd make it perfectly clear why I'm going to kill myself. I can't take it, Gil. I'm quitting."

You cannot quit. I am going to quit *Rigatonio*. We both can't quit; someone's gotta pay our rent.

Emma nodded grimly. "I'm not quitting, I'm just talking. I've been there four months. If I can make it to the sixth, I get major medical and they can pick up my analyst and prescribed medicine."

Emma, a personal question but please answer it: how much is this Valium prescription costing you?

"Oh it's all on the big bill from the clinic since they have a pharmacy up there and it's all jumbled into the total charge and I ought to work it out sometime, really . . ."

Go get a bill, let's work it out right now.

"Why do you care so much?" Emma picked up the purse she'd just put down.

Going somewhere?

"I don't want to be late for the group therapy session—it's Tuesdays now, remember?"

I knew she took pills. She'd been doing that for nearly three years, on prescription, all legitimate, and maybe she was the one person who tranquilizers were designed for. She was, after all, more stable than a a few years back; she *had* calmed down. But it made me nervous. Each morning as she was getting up I heard her reach in the medicine cabinet for the pills. When she got home, the same thing (at her lunch break too?), and I even heard the medicine-cabinet door squeak when she was going out with her friends Dina and Joanna, two complete bores who thought everything Emma did was a laugh riot, crazy Emma, kooky Emma, isn't she wild? Isn't she the fast lane with her pills and her wicked mouth and her boozing it up? Emma was slumming with them. She wasn't after friends with those two, she was after an audience. It was from people like me she got lip. Such as: Emma, think how much money you'd have left over if you dropped all the medical nonsense.

"Gil, if you don't pay a lot," she explained one time, "it's not official therapy. I've been to the free clinics and you don't get taken seriously. I have more respect for someone who takes $100 off me a week, you know?"

Think of the movies, think of the theater, think of the booze, think of the occasional travel we could have with that money—

"There is no discussion here," she'd say, adamantly. "I need to drop that kind of money so it will hurt me, punish me for being neurotic. Do you see what I mean?"

Not really, then or now.

"Besides, I have to get on my health plan because of my father. I've been on the family policy since I was in college, and now my dad is going in for some kind of tests and my mother wants me off the plan. So I gotta get off."

All right, all right—do what you want with your life, have your major medical, drop tons of money on doctors and pills.

As for me, I'm on the way up. I've passed my Low Point in my New York Years. True, I don't have a girlfriend, no career prospects, I'm in an apartment I don't much like with a friend who needs a drug rehab program, but it's turning the corner, getting better each and every passing day, yessir! In fact, 1982 is gonna be mah yeeeuh . . .

Then Gil had a bad day at work:

"Mr. Kline," whined Charity for the hundredth time.

I was in the middle of my scene, of course. Antonio, played by Gilbert Freeman (in the same bar as Florence, Papa and most of the techies, drunk by noon).

"I have to say," said Charity, "as a professional, I don't much like the pace or blocking of this scene . . ."

It was my scene she referred to. I am front, center stage. I have a monologue. It follows a courtship sequence with Elisabetta. We sang a song at each other in which the gimmick was that every word ends in an extra *o*, like:

ELISABETTA: My Antonio-io/I think you should go-io
Lest my mother and my father find us here . . .
ANTONIO: Oh my caramissima/how about a kees-ima
To my earnest wooings lend an ear . . .

Naturally, Charity didn't want to get off the stage.

"I think," she said, pacing, a look of concentration on her face, "it would be better if, while Antonio is talking about me in his monologue, I could come out on the balcony to hear him, you know? And while he's talking about me, I hear what he says?"

Uh, I think it's a bad idea, I say. He mentions all her money and her fortune, right? Now if she hears that she can't possibly be torn between him and Rigatoni which is necessary—

"I think Elisabetta's a more complicated character than that. She might know he's after her money, but not mind—"

Charity, that's just *unbelievably* stupid.

"Excuse me, I've been in the business for a lot longer than you, and I think I know a little bit more about theatercraft than you, Mr. Freeman—"

All you know how to do is hog the stage, baby—

"All right, all right," said Silas, standing in the front row of the theater. "I think—"

Garth W. Kline (of Garth W. Kline Enterprises): "I think the girl's got a point, Si. They're here to see Florence Crayfield and they're here to see Charity Glenn—"

EXCUSE ME MR. GARTH W.—which stands for WHO-THE-FUCK-ARE-YOU—Kline, *no one* on the Planet Earth or the surrounding galaxies would show up, would shell out money, would expend any energy for the likes of CHARITY WHO-THE-FUCK-DOES-SHE-THINK-SHE-IS GLENN! Why don't you turn over the whole goddam play to her—make it a one-woman show! Inasmuch as this collection of WASTE PRODUCT is a show. And what you know about theater can easily be put in the driest, emptiest SMALLEST, TIGHTEST place imaginable which conveniently for you happens to be Charity Glenn's—

(It gets a little obscene here.) Let's just say I was home early that day. Emma found me when she came in the door from work.

"The fact that you are halfway through that bottle of bourbon suggests a hard day at work," she observed.

A *last* day at work.

"Uh-oh."

I couldn't take it another day, Emma.

"Pour me one, too. And tell me about it."

I'm at a crisis point, Emma. My career as an actor is over. I no longer have the will to do shitwork. I will starve in obscurity for worthwhile projects, I will rake in money for trash, but I will not starve for trash. Goddam Charity Glenn. She was running the place, her and that old asshole, Garth W. Kline . . .

"Of Garth W. Kline Enterprises," Emma repeated deadpan.

I smiled. Pour me another.

"We're going to celebrate your walking off the set," she said after I filled in the whole story. "Like me and the robbery last year, I'll take you out for an East Village crawl. Let me get out of my yuppie costume . . ." Emma went to the bathroom, ran some water, locked the door. I was waiting for it. I walked over to the door so I could be sure: the pill bottle jingled. Oh well. Emma's a blast on those pills, relaxed, confident, together. She can probably kick the habit when she wants; Emma has a way of picking things up and dropping them, like her punk phase—

Aaaaiiiiii!

Emma! What is it? What's wrong?

The bathroom door opened, Emma was wide-eyed. "Charity Glenn! Lollipop!"

Huh?

"She was Lollipop! I knew I'd heard the name!"

Uh, Lollipop—

"Lollipop, lollipop, la la la lollipop / Lollipop—"

The worst TV show in history! The child star! The one you've always wanted to murder!

And we started laughing. One's career destroyed by Lollipop! Imagine, nearly twenty years of being a horrible spoiled child-star theater brat—we couldn't breathe! Lollipop! The phone rang.

Breathless, I answer . . .

"Gil, this is Odessa," I heard. Her most joyless, serious no-nonsense tone; the Texas drawl nonexistent (proves my theory . . .)

"I heard about your little stunt today. Do you want to explain yourself?"

You're my agent. You're supposed to get me work that will build a career, not end one. That was amateur local two-bit doomed-to-fail one-week-close theater. You gotta do better by me or I'll go elsewhere. Get my career out of the goddam basement.

"I think that's enough. You go back and you apologize to Charity Glenn and the director and Garth W.—"

NEVER.

A pause. "Our professional relationship is terminated. Bye-bye." Click. Emma is looking on, biting her fingernails. I ask her what the date is.

"Thirtieth of May, Gil."

New update. Gil's Low Point of his New York Years: May 30, 1981.

Time goes on here. I don't have it in me to go audition anywhere. I sit around the apartment all day and watch the morning movie, the afternoon movie, take the bus to the Village and watch a movie there, come back in time for the evening movie—

"Gil, get a job," said Emma.

I got enough money for this month's rent, don't worry.

"I mean, so you'll be occupied. You got to pull yourself back from the abyss." She looked at me seriously. "You want a Valium?"

Yes I did want one. But I wasn't going to take one.

I wandered the theater district instead. The only drug I could use that day was Jackson's Diner coffee.

"You out of that play you hated, sugah?" asked Valene, refilling my cup.

Sure am.

"So why you so sad?"

Everything's going wrong, Valene. I'm twenty-seven. I'm supposed to be famous by now.

"Look Gil, I'm sixteen and I ain't famous. It takes time. I'm prepared to wait till seventeen . . ." And she was off to take another order. I watched her wait on tables, followed her as she passed the jukebox, followed her as she passed the window with the HELP WANTED sign in it. Wait.

"Gilbert," said Mrs. Jackson behind the cash register, "it doesn't pay what you're used to, I'm sure. Two dollars an hour, plus tips—you keep your tips—11 p.m. 'til 6:30 most mornings. It ain't easy work now."

I'll take it, Mrs. J.

"You shittin' me?" said Valene, absolutely amazed I was going to work nights with her. "You? You sure? You shittin' me?"

"Better watch that mouth," said Mrs. Jackson behind the cash register.

"We gonna have a good time, don't you worry," said Valene giving me a wink.

Jackson's Diner was owned by Grant Jackson, and it was his brother Tom who was the Mr. Jackson I knew, who as Grant's little brother got to run the night shift. Tom never got to see his wife Evelyn so he brought her in to work behind the cash register. Moses the dishwasher and part-time cook (we called him "Moze") was an old crony of Tom's father, about in his late sixties. Valene had just dropped out of school last year and the family wanted to keep an eye on her, I suspect, so she was a waitress. She was a great New York waitress—a natural talent: the care and attention to the water glass, the coffee cup, her omniscience, as she refilled cups and glasses without bothering the customers. She knew when you wanted some more to eat:

"Better get to that cherry pie, Smitty. It's gonna get all dried out and nasty. You wanna piece of that right now, hm?"

And she knew when you didn't want to eat:

"You don't want that chili. Daddy's just opening a can back there—it's old storebought stuff. I'd go for the beef stew 'cause I had some of that myself. 'Bout the same price."

There were cabbies and ticket-box workers and janitors and policemen who would take their breaks or get off work at certain times through the night and Valene had a little pad behind the cash register that listed the exact ETA—John the barman at 2:30, coffee light; Ed the cab driver at 3:15 on the dot, black coffee, two cups, etc.

Moze the dishwasher was an old bachelor man and his glory days had ended sometime in the '50s I gathered. But he had the raciest, lewdest old jokes—jokes so rife, so low and dirty that . . . well, you know, now that I think of it, they weren't that dirty, *he* was that dirty. He had this greasy laugh, this wheeze, and this low whisper and a way of licking his lips and looking about him to make sure no women heard what he had to say. That was a definite peril, actually. Mrs. Jackson hated smut and wouldn't stand for Moze and Mr. Jackson to be cutting up back in the kitchen. Moze drank a little now and then ("About one time a month," Valene told me, "Uncle Moze goes on a bender and has himself a time") and once, but only once, I recall Moze and Mr. Jackson coming in at 10:30 a little drunk—it was someone's birthday.

Mrs. Jackson had come down on the bus with them and had a look of stern disapproval: "You two have got the devil in you tonight. Now you both get some coffee in you, and stop talkin' this trash."

The more Mrs. Jackson got after them, the more they kept telling these foul old stories. "So she tells me," said Moze, through laughter, imitating a girl's voice, " 'Moses, you sonuvabitch, that's the LAST time yo' hands are touchin' my booty!' "

Mr. Jackson and Moze were in hysterics, and Valene laughed along.

"I think we've had enough of your foul mouth tonight, Moses," said Mrs. Jackson, hands on hips. "Buncha twelve-year-olds, you are, sniggerin' over *booty*."

Moze: "You had to see this woman's booty, Evelyn—"

"Tom Jackson," his wife began, "now you straighten up. You got fifty orders there, now get to it 'fore people up and walk outa here."

At five-minute intervals this incredible burst of high-pitched hysterical laughter would explode in the kitchen, way up high where only drunk men who've been laughing all night or little girls can laugh. Valene couldn't stop laughing either. "They's talkin' 'bout Booty Patootie, this stripper Moze used to go with," Valene whispered. "He always talks about Booty Patootie when he gets drunk. I don't think she ever was, myself—I think he made her up."

I got tickled too. Everytime I went to pick up my orders both men were back there trying to keep a sober face, but we'd all make eye contact and we'd all start giggling again.

"I swear it's been an *hour*, Tom Jackson," said Mrs. Jackson. "We're slower 'n a stopped drain tonight, 'cause y'all can't straighten out. Now you got Gil goin' too with your wickedness."

As the night went on and things slowed down, Moze pulled me aside and showed me a flask. I swigged and Moze patted me on the back.

"I saw that," said Valene coming in for an order.

"You tell your mother and it'll be the last thing you tell her," said her father.

"I won't tell if you let me have some. What is it?"

"Get outa here, young lady."

"C'mon, tell me, what is it?"

Her father ushered her out. And Moze told about Booty Patootie, the best-ever stripper to work above 125th. Booty could do the usual things, like straddle the corner of a table where someone would leave a dollar bill, and then—no hands and with great vaginal control—back away in possession of the bill. "There was nothing she couldn't get in there," said Moze. "You put a pencil in there and she'd write you a letter." Booty worked this runway. The men would hold out dollar bills for the first act rolled up lengthwise and Booty would sidle up to them and work herself down to it and—gee, there aren't verbs for this, you had to hear Moze tell it—clamp down on the bills. For the second act, the guys who had a little much to drink would roll the dollar bills *width*wise and hold them in their mouths while Booty closed in and took the money."But that was nothin' compared to the grand finale," said Moze. In the grand finale Booty Patootie would come out and all the men would be sitting there with their long-necked bottles of beer. She would squat —and it took her a good long time to work herself down in increments of elevation—and pick up the long-necked beer bottle, with the beer inside. Now a first-timer at the club, some poor boy, sixteen or seventeen, who wandered in trying to be adult, got put at the Seat of Honor. If you sat there, Booty picked up your beer bottle, then shook it up and let it foam all up inside her and then fall back into the bottle; then as the other men in this gentleman's club clapped in rhythm, the poor kid had to turn the bottle up and drink it in one take.

"Whatcha all doin'?" said Valene.

"Young lady I told you to look after your business," said Mr. Jackson, laughing and hiding the flask behind his back.

"Never you mind," said Moze.

Valene put the new orders down on the big metal cooking table and stormed off. "I just wanted a little sip, that's all," she muttered.

Moze started talking about poontang, and Mr. Jackson said he hadn't heard anyone call it "poontang" since he was in the army. "You know HOW it got to be called 'poontang,' don't you?" said Moze. But I didn't get to hear the end of this story as I went out with some orders, as Valene came in.

"What's that I smell, Gilbert?" asked Mrs. Jackson as I breezed past the cash register, laughing, with gin on my breath.

Uh, wouldya believe the Nightowl Special, Mrs. J.?

Valene brought me a cup of coffee and whispered to me, in conspiratorial tones: "I know what y'all are drinkin' back there."

Really? What, Valene?

"Poontang."

A plate broke and there was more laughter and Mrs. Jackson had had quite enough. She grabbed Valene's arm and took her into the kitchen. "Now you tell me young lady what your father and this no-account man are up to!" Valene looked at her father who knew the gig was up, so he pulled the flask out of his back pocket.

"And what's in there, Tom Jackson?"

And when Valene told everyone she heard them say it was poontang *even* Mrs. Jackson cracked a smile as Mr. Jackson and Moze rolled on the floor in near-death hysterics. "What?" said Valene. "What's so funny? What'd I say?" Now that Mrs. Jackson turned away to smile and shake her head, her authority was GONE. The whole night was a bit of a Lost Night for Jackson's Diner. Everyone was on their best behavior for about another week.

"How'm I supposed to know what they called it a hundred years ago," said Valene, concerning the poontang incident. "I ain't gonna be here this Friday, Gilbert, I'm givin' you warning. I got a date. This is THE date and I need to get myself lookin' good. You never seen me when I'm lookin' good, Gil, but when I'm lookin' good I am really lookin' good. You never seen me lookin' good."

You look just fine in your waitress uniform, Valene.

"Well thank you, but I'm not talkin' 'bout lookin' all right, I am talkin' 'bout lookin' good, Gil. And you never seen me when I was lookin' good."

Unfortunately, Inez, the earlier waitress, wrenched her ankle and Valene had to work a part of the evening shift. I told her that I could work the whole place and cover for her, though Mr. Jackson didn't approve. "Take your date another time, girl," he said. But he finally relented, after Valene put the daddy's-little-girl moves on him.

"Shit Gil," she said looking at the clock, having half an hour to get ready for the Big Date, "I'm gonna lock myself in the john and use the sink for one of my PTP baths."

PTP baths?

"Yeah," she said giggling: "Pits, Tits and Pussy."

She ran to the sink before Mrs. Jackson caught up with her, not quite sure she had heard her daughter say what she thought she'd heard her say.

"You're crazy," Emma reminded me. "You're getting $100 a week at this joint—that's nothing compared to working at some classy restaurant down in Soho."

Emma, darling, it was worth $100 a week to hear about the PTP bath.

Summer wore on and soon it was hot and miserable again and as a break from Life before The Fan we decided upon another Subway Adventure. We'd never done the Number 6 out to Pelham Bay. There's a little-known place called City Island, an unbelievably unaltered little fishing village surrounded by the metropolis. You could mistake it for a small Connecticut seaport; the Long Island Bay was at the end of the main road (after a connecting bus ride) and there were hundreds of sails and little boats and, most superb of all, a breeze.

"I want clams," said Emma. "Let's eat 50,000 clams."

We sat at this outside picnic table while some greasy teenage boy fried up a batch of equally greasy clams. We got beer. We sat and stared out at the sky and ocean; two sailboats sailed toward each other and seemed to be on a collision course on the horizon but for a moment they were one white sail and then two again, having passed through each other.

"This can't be New York City," said Emma.

No it can't but it is, I said.

"Yeah," said Emma.

We sat there some more and stared at things, then our clams were ready and we ate them and they were greasy and good and there was sun and breeze and more beer, and a rare sense of calm.

"I want a child, Gil. I want to have a kid who'll be mine and love me and give me something to devote myself to. I know you laugh, but I'd be a good mother."

She had said this before; I always pointed out that . . . well, you can guess, the thousands of reasons a single mother would have a problem in New York.

"I haven't been sleeping lately at all," she said later. "I wake up violently in the middle of the night and can't get back to sleep. I've been having all these rape nightmares. I can't even go out anymore; I keep thinking everyone is a rapist, that that jerk from phone sex is out there stalking me."

Well it could happen, but you've been careful and lucky for almost eight years. It's not something to dwell on, Emma.

"I know, I know."

How about some more food, beer?

"Yeah maybe later. I feel like my celibacy is my strength—I know that sounds like bad wimmin's poetry, but I think that way. A rapist could just destroy all that—it would shatter me . . ."

Emma, please, what's the use in dwelling on it?

"My poetry really sucks lately," she said, as a way of changing the subject. We then talked about all the new social diseases and how at least Emma wasn't going to get gonorrhea or herpes or syph or VD (no, I'd not told her about my problem yet—WHY BOTHER, huh?). And we talked about all the looneys on the street.

"I was reading where Hinckley was going to be released one day, after shooting the president," said Emma. "He'll probably end up selling the TV rights, writing a best-seller like the Watergate criminals—it's all pretty disgusting. I used to find this kind of American-circus thing funny."

Yeah, me too.

"Reagan is an actor. He was shot by a creep with TV crime-show fantasies who wanted to shoot the president to impress a pretty actress—and the whole thing is played out on TV, the shooting, the hospital heroics . . . I love TV but this is ridiculous.

You know, I could understand some Nicaraguan rebel or some Arab terrorist knocking Reagan off, some Berkeley protestor who had a heartfelt belief that Reagan was evil—I could have lived with someone like that shooting him. But I can't accept the mediocre American kook with the mediocre motives, who doesn't go to jail even, who is negotiating publishing packages when I can't get ten years of serious poetry published—no, no, Gil, *this will not do*."

I know.

"And this last, this last six years or so . . . what kind of garbage era has this been? Ford, Carter and Reagan. It was folkies then it was disco then it was country and western and urban cowboys and then it was '50s revivals and then it was punk and new-wave and '60s revivals, and I'll tell you one thing they won't revive: ANYTHING from the late '70s and early '80s. What a goddam washout."

Well there's been no war, no major civil strife, no riots—

"No nothing; there's not been anything. I'm sorry, Gil, I wish I didn't feel like I was living in lousy times but that's the truth."

Yeah, but the '20s had gangland violence and Prohibition and virtual fascism and head-busting; the '30s had the Depression; the '40s had the war; the '50s were as backward as a decade could be; the '60s had Vietnam and riots and assassinations . . . when would you have preferred to live, Emma?

"Oh right now. But those decades, Gil," she said, raising her finger, "had *style*. I miss style. It redeems so much."

Ah c'mon Emma, this is the Golden Age of Cynicism—things are just bad enough to set up your jokes. You can't make one-liners off Auschwitz or Hiroshima. When else would you have been happy to live? Make peace with the late twentieth century.

Emma smiled again. "I'll make peace with some beer. Your turn to buy."

On our long, hot walk back to the bus stop, Emma stopped at a public restroom and had me go in to make sure no rapist was lingering inside. After inspection she went in and I heard the jingle of the pill bottle. I tried to convince myself I did not hear it but I heard it.

"We've really settled down, huh?" Emma said in the subway train on the ride back.

Whadya mean?

"We're a regular married couple. We oughta get married for the tax break."

What about sex, children, all that?

Emma smiled, she was flippant: "Take a mistress, then."

It was pretty companionable, so comfortable, day-in day-out routines, watching the TV together, our spare time spent with each other. No doubt at all we cared in our own exasperated way for each other. But something was missing—no, not just the sex, not just the physical thing. Something I couldn't put my finger on.

"Just stop nagging me about the pills, bozo," she added, nudging me.

I would hear the pill bottle jingle each morning when I got home from the diner, and she was about to leave for work. Why would anyone need a tranquilizer to get up in the morning—you need other drugs then, caffeine-like, upper-like. Wait. Maybe she *is* doing other drugs . . . I knew someone like that at the Venice Theater, uppers in the morning and downers in the afternoon and up and down it went, every day, for years. I'm lying there in bed thinking: Ah, maybe there's no harm in this. No, maybe there's lots of harm in this. I should have it out with Emma, I'd tell myself. It would do no good, I'd also tell myself.

So I did what any friend would do. I discussed this issue behind her back with another close friend. I went to see Janet in Hoboken.

Should I be worried about her?

Janet shrugged, and ran the spoon around her coffee cup again. "Lots of people pop pills all their life, all the time. What's a pill or two in this city?" But she looked as unconvinced as I did—we weren't talking about most people, we were talking about Emma. So I ran the issue by a disinterested third party . . .

"Gil, darlin', lovechild," began Valene, "are we talkin' 'bout your woman here? Is this your woman?"

No, Valene, she isn't my woman.

"If she IS your woman, you tell her to get her shit straightened out or you're gonna move in with Valene—you tell her that."

She's not my woman, Valene.

"You were talkin' 'bout her last week too. And you're livin' with her, right?" Her gaze was inscrutable.

Yes, but we're only good friends.

"Uhhh-hmmmm," she said unpersuaded. "Look, it's just a few pills and the doctor tole her she could take 'em." Valene dragged the table-wiping cloth over the table, a wide arc to catch the ketchup stains and water circles.

I said I was still worried about my friend.

Valene wiped at a cigarette burn on the Formica top as if she could wipe it away. "Well Gilberto, she's got herself a problem and you've got yourself a problem, and your problem's *her*."

Tell me something I don't know, Valene.

Two dramatic scenes come to mind . . . (it was about the only theater I was involved in that summer, come to think of it).

Dramatic Episode Number One:

Gilbert (to be played by an immensely handsome late-twenties leading-man type) standing with a bottle of barbiturates in the bathroom; Emma (to be played by a tired-looking, peevish late-twenties . . . uh, who am I kidding? She never looked better than when she was mad, all that Italian-American passion) standing in the doorway to the bathroom.

"Gilbert Freeman," says Emma, "I warn you—as god is my witness you are a DEAD MAN if you put those pills in the toilet. I expected better than TV-movie drama from you."

What clichéd TV drama did she mean—my dumping pills in the john or her becoming bright-girl-turned-addict?

"Now you will do just as I say," she said taking a slow step toward me, like a policeman dealing with a gunman, ". . . you will give me that bottle and we will cease fighting and I'll go make Chinese tea and we'll calmly discuss this and stop calling each other names. Let's not do anything I'm going to regret . . ."

I give the bottle a shake to show I mean business—a pill falls into the water.

"You owe me five dollars, bastard—"

Wanna go for fifty?

"I didn't mean to call you bastard, I'm sorry," she said, taking another step—a desperate woman: "What are your terms?"

One, tell your doctor of your dependence, that is if he isn't the unfeeling quack who gets these things for you; two, go to the barbiturate rehabilitation workshop Janet told you to go to; three, make a promise—even a feeble one—to cut this shit out, as barbiturate addiction is rougher to shake than heroin and I cut out the article that gave me that information, which you crumpled up and hurled into the trashcan—you will fish it out and smooth it down and read every word of it.

"That's it? No perverse sexual acts?"

Four: Well now that you mention it, maybe you would be less tense if you stopped pursuing celibacy at all costs, go get a boyfriend, have some sex, exchange some affection—

"Gee, it was sounding all right up to that point."

Which brings us to the point behind all this, which is that I care about you, Emma, and you know I'm not being an asshole or a prude—you are hurting yourself.

"My life is my business, Gil. Look, let's make that pot of tea and talk about this calmly, lucidly . . . give me the bottle."

And I gave her the bottle back because I knew if I dumped them in the john and flushed them she would hit me or slap me and I really HATE being slapped. And it wouldn't change anything anyway, so I gave in and gave her back the bottle and we had tea, and she made many promises.

Dramatic Episode Number Two:

Gilbert (see if we can get that same incredibly handsome young man we got for the last Dramatic Episode), his bags are packed, a check is written out for the next month's rent which he puts into the hand of Emma (etc.) who doesn't understand.

"You can't move out, Gil. You've just been here three months. You know you can't find a place in the fall . . . it's, uh, impossible. You're crazy . . . now just sit down and I'll make some tea—"

NO GODDAM TEA. My terms or I'm leaving leaving leaving.

"I've already told my doctor," she said weakly.

He's the scuzbag who got you in this mess, so to hell with

him. Stop going to him. He's getting some kind of kickback from Downers Inc. or whoever makes that shit. His East Side office is a front for society-women Barbie dolls.

"I'm not going to beg you to stay."

(Now that was a bad time to call my bluff. A simple: 'Gil, don't leave me like this' would have sufficed and melted me and kept me by her side, changed everything, maybe even the Course Of History.) So I leave. I'll come back for my other things, I say, when Emma is at work. So she lets me go.

I drag my bag to the PATH station and go to Jersey. Janet asks how it went, and I say here I am at your house so how do you think it went? Then we worried that Emma might do something rash.

"Call her, Gil," said Janet, "give her another chance."

No, it wouldn't do any good—wait, YOU call her.

So Janet calls Emma: "Em, hey, it's Janet . . ." Janet flashes a so-far-so-good look to me. "Sound sorta down. Hm? Oh really? What'd y'all fight about?" Pause. "Well you know how I feel about that too. He's probably got a point, kid. No he's not here. Emma, I promise you"—Janet crosses her fingers, wincing—"he's not here. Yeah, I'll take a message." Janet looks at me as Emma gives her a message.

She told me to drop dead?

"No," Janet said after putting down the receiver. "She said for you to move back. She gives in."

And so I go back with my suitcase onto the subway and three stops later I'm back home. Why did I have to pack the world's heaviest suitcase for dramatic-exit purposes? I get there and Emma's left me a note on the table: *Sorry. We'll talk tomorrow. Love, Emma.* And I call for her but there's no sound. I check her room and she's in there asleep, out cold—a momentary panic, did she . . . no, it's all right, she stirs and rolls over, smiling at me. I ask if she's all right and she nods.

"Yuh, I'b tok wib du tomorrow . . ." She's doped up and can't speak without slurring.

I close the door and turn off her desk light and then go over to the bed and lift her off her blanket and put her blanket on top of her and tuck her in and then I go to the door but turn back to her bedside, kneel down, look at Emma at her most defenseless, and as she can do little about it, I kiss her on the forehead.

Good night, Emma.

Things looked up from there. Briefly.

Janet made her go to this clinic for a consultation. She dropped the quack doctor-dispenser. She kept up the group therapy and joined an A.A.-style discussion group.

"I sort out my sex life on Tuesdays with the group, and then I sort out my drug life on Fridays with this other group. How long," she'd joke, "until I get a problem for each day of the week? *Ha ha ha*, just kidding—these are the jokes, folks. C'mon lighten up. Get that look off your face. Gil, my man, you should see some of the people at this clinic for the downer addicts." Emma came in and sat on my bed to give me her nightly progress report. "They vary all the participants. Each group gets a few low-level users who caught their habit in time"—Emma waves her hand to signify herself—"and there are some speed freaks who got hooked on downers trying to come down from going up so high, and we've got some East Side middle-aged executives' wives types. Some can't think or move right, some talk like there's mush in their mouth, one woman has a paralyzed arm—yuccch. Lot of shitty lives out there, Gil."

Yeah well be glad you've kept the shit at a minimum.

"My new goal in life," she said.

And she patted my leg, got up, went to bed, the New Emma, and I sat there, feeling, of all things, a little sad . . . no, I REALLY can't confess this. Well, all right: I think I didn't mind it so terribly much as I might have that Emma was in trouble. Now that is just *terrible*, I know, but I thought I might be needed, I thought I might be called upon to help in some way. Yes, it's crummy even once in a while to think something like that about a friend, but it's also crummy never to feel necessary to someone, just along for the laughs, a place filler.

So there was plenty to think about that summer and lots of time to think, as it turned out. I liked night shift for that purpose. When you work night shift you can at any time fall dead asleep—the body has decades of training in sleeping at night and suddenly you reverse all that, but the body remembers, and even with eight hours of good sleep during the day, if you put your head down, shut your eyes for even a minute, you're GONE. The only recourse is coffee and lots of it. Around 2:30 a.m. it thinned out in midtown Manhattan and Valene and I would get to rest, get to sit down and rub our feet for a while. We would pray to the Restaurant God not to send us any more customers—after you sit down for twenty minutes or so you're *shot* waiting tables, you might as well go home and go to bed, further movement is out of the question. Valene and I would look antagonistically at each other as a customer would come in:

"He's yours babe. He's got your name all over him."

No Valene, he's yours. Wait. If he sits at a table with a ketchup bottle, he's yours.

"It's a deal . . ." Valene started smiling as he headed toward a ketchupless table, and he almost sat down, but no . . . "Hell, don't go there, old man, no—don't do it . . . oh, *damn* you, damn you . . ." Valene groaningly, with superhuman effort, got to her feet to take the order.

And I could get back to my new hobby, staring out into the night, that vague reflection of myself in the window; out there was the New York Night, inside I was warm in the fluorescent-white glow and touch of red from the neon MEALS TO GO • 24 HOURS sign. If I had a quarter I'd put a song on the jukebox, sometimes just to get Valene dancing, sometimes just to make her mad ("Don't put on that new-wavey-punk shit thing," Valene warned). Outside the traffic would whiz by, or in a nicer memory, it was raining outside and you'd hear the slish of cabs and passing cars, young people outside running about, snatches of conversation, a predictable burst of noise as the last movies would let out, the midnight strip shows, the bars closing. Some drunks and some bums came in, some streetpeople, and Mr. Jackson would show them to the door or give them a cup of coffee if they were a nice bum, it all depended.

Around 4 a.m. Phelia came in, an older black woman—she had this wild pair of cat-eye glasses—a friend of Mrs. Jackson's, a neighbor up in Harlem. Phelia cleaned floors in Rockefeller Center and this was her "lunch hour," and she'd always decline everything on the menu, everything on special for just a little toast and coffee. Mrs. Jackson and Moze, who took his break now while Mr. Jackson loaded the dishwasher, sat and gossiped with her every night over coffee, not at a New York pace, but a slow middle-of-the-night, hard-day-at-work pace. Lots of pauses between the comments, everything good repeated and repeated, mused over, nodded to, considered.

"A man," said Mrs. Jackson, winding up, "a man will go elsewhere in his marriage." Pause. "He will go elsewhere, and I know what I'm talking about, he will go elsewhere," she takes a breath and raises a knowing eyebrow, "for a little *sweetness*."

"Yez, he will," says Moze, nodding.

"That's right," said Phelia.

"If he ain't getting the proper sweetness at home," Mrs. Jackson went on, "he's gonna get it elsewhere. He will go elsewhere for a little sweetness."

"Yes he will," said Phelia, setting down her coffee cup.

No one says much and more cabs and cars pass by rattling the windows, an occasional honk.

"I'm not talkin' 'bout loving," said Mrs. Jackson.

"I know you're not," said Phelia, pursing her lips. "You're talkin' 'bout sweetness."

"I'm talkin' 'bout sweetness," said Mrs. Jackson.

"Like with Mavis and her man," said Phelia.

"That's *'zactly* what I'm talkin' 'bout. Mavis and her man. That's what I'm talkin' 'bout right there. Now she come to me all teary-eyed, all messed up and cryin', she come in here at three in the mornin', sat in that booth right there—oooh Evelyn, oooh Evelyn, woe is me she says, he's goin' back to her again, I jus' know it. Evelyn, she tells me, I gave him my best lovin'. That man want for *nothin'*. She's tellin' me all this. Now Mavis could give Bernard the lovin'."

"But she couldn't give him the sweetness," said Phelia, shaking her head.

"A man will go elsewhere for a little sweetness."

"Yeah," said Moze.

"He will," Mrs. Jackson continued. "Now you know, I see a lot in here—"

Phelia: "Yes you surely do."

"—and I seen some things. And I know who Bernard was with, 'cause I saw 'em both in here. Right in that booth."

Phelia shook her head. "*No*? Bernard brought that girl right in here, in front of you?"

"Uh-huh. And you know why? 'Cause I don't think nothin' was goin' on. They weren't doin' stuff. No ma'am. I was watchin' 'em—there was no hand-holdin' or touchin' or nothin'; they's just talkin'. Just talkin'."

"Talkin'," repeated Phelia, after a sip of coffee.

"He weren't steppin' out on Mavis for the lovin'. I'm sure of that. He wanted someone to listen to him. You know Mavis. You can't tell her nothin' and she gets all this nonsense goin', never lets poor Bernard be."

Moze nodded: "Man ain't after booty night 'n day. He wants some unnerstandin'."

"Mavis thought," said Mrs. Jackson, crossing her arms, "that he was goin' out on her for a little piece of leg, but she didn't get it right."

"Gotta have unnerstandin'," said Moze.

"It had nothin', nothin' to do with sex," said Mrs. Jackson, raising that eyebrow again. "It was sweetness. He wanted to get him some sweetness."

"I wouldn'ta let Bernard get out my front door, ehhmm ehhmm," said Phelia, with a slight cackle.

"A man will go elsewhere for a little sweetness," said Mrs. Jackson, pouring some more coffee all around.

And on and on the story would go repeating itself, with new touches here and there, Mavis who couldn't keep her man. And I'd listen to this advice from people who had seen a lot of life uptown. And of course, I think Mrs. Jackson put her finger on something: a man will do a lot for a little sweetness. I never thought of myself as "a man" you could generalize about with all the other men when people talk about "men this" and "men that," but I wouldn't have minded a little sweetness a little more often in my life.

Mr. Jackson would come out of the kitchen after loading the washer and listen to his wife go on about "sweetness," and then he'd sneak up behind her and hug her and get her laughing, asking for a little sugar, or he was going to have to go elsewhere for his sweetness, and Phelia would laugh, and then he'd come after her (she was about sixty, churchgoing, unmarried all her life) and he made her blush looking for a little sweetness, while she waved him off, "Now you go on—I swear Tom Jackson, Lord help you," etc.

And so it went, the talk and the coffee and the handful of customers until the dawn. It was 6 a.m. and soon the New Yorkers who hadn't been awake all night, up for less than a half hour, stumbled in, untalkative and curt and dreading work, and we'd give them their coffee and keep ourselves going until the morning crew came in to relieve us. And soon I was saying goodbye and dragging home in needlessly bright sunlight, noticing the relatively fresh air of Manhattan before the cars invaded, and I took the empty subway home—yes, that part was nice, everyone was coming in to work and you were going home with maybe a few other night-shifters for company, you could recognize each other.

And Emma would be up and jittery ("I can't sleep worth dog-do these days," she'd snap) or she'd be impossible to rouse, and I'd have to shake her awake, point out to her her alarm had been sounding for half an hour already. Everything depended on whether she'd been able to resist taking pills or not. She *was* trying to quit, so I wasn't harsh . . . but in the morning light, sitting at our dinner table, listening to the city rouse and begin to vibrate, I often felt myself not caring about anything except the sleep I had been fighting off all night long (perversely, you never wanted to sleep when you *did* get home). I don't know if it was the mind-wearying job or the way I truly felt but I could have let it ALL go, let all the important things fall away; pure indifference. My world had become very small—the newspaper crossword, counting the loose change of the day's tips.

The Theater seemed wonderfully far away, and it could stay there for all I cared. There was a small longing for something better, something passionate and soul-baring, but this was longing for the moon, and like my other dreams it fell quietly to rest, abandoned with my other cares as I would finally give way to sleep at 8:30 a.m.

Emma was on the phone one night and she needed to find an address in her address book which was in her desk and she asked if I could get it for her. So I ran to her room, tried all the drawers (one was locked, which I thought was odd), got her address book and started wondering about the locked drawer. Pills, I thought. That's where she hides the pills. Very calmly, after she got off the phone, I told her I knew she was sneaking pills—any fool could tell—and I figured they were in that locked drawer.

"They are not. You don't trust me at all, I see."

All right—open the drawer and I'll be proven wrong and I'll apologize and I'll buy a whole pizza.

"I don't have to open that drawer. I'm not on trial."

Of course, you have your right to privacy and I'm out of line, and I'll not mention it again, I'm sorry. But if those are pills, I added, then you'll be in for it and I'm moving out.

"They're not pills, Gil, I promise." She looked sincere. "There is something you probably wouldn't like in the drawer, but they're not barbiturates. Really."

Silence for the next ten minutes. Am I going to ask her what's in the drawer? Nah, I know this girl: She'll tell me if I don't show any interest.

"I know what you're doing," she said from the kitchen. "You think if you show no interest I'll tell you what's in that drawer. I *would* tell you but it's something you're going to disapprove of. So I'm not going to tell you."

Pills, I said. I bet it's a mountain of pills.

"Let's not talk about it."

What on earth would *I* disapprove of, *I* who encouraged her to go solo in the phone-sex business? Ah, it's probably something ridiculous, I said, so let's forget it—

"It's not nothing. You'd hate it. We'd have a fight."

All right, c'mon, tell me. Tell me right now.

"No."

If I promise not to disapprove?

"You'll disapprove anyway."

She seemed sincere about not wanting to show me . . . and yet she *sort of* wanted to show me, I could tell.

"All right, I'll show you so you'll shut up about me taking drugs. It's not narcotics, I swear—narcotics of any kind."

So we went into her room and she got out her key and undid the drawer and then stood back for me to open it up. At this point I figured it wasn't barbiturates and I was going to have to buy her a pizza. Maybe . . . my goodness, birth-control pills, maybe? She was sexually active again? My heart froze! Why didn't she tell me if she was— god—SEEING someone, someone male, someone who wasn't me. Oh the day had come, hadn't it? All right, be a MAN, Gil, open the drawer . . . which I did. Inside it was a gun.

"It's a gun," she said.

I know it's a gun. You're right: I disapprove—but I'm being calm about it, okay? Why do you have a gun? How did you get a gun? Good Lord, Uncle Harry. I thought you were joking about Jasmine's Uncle Harry, NRA member, gun-nut Veteran's Association conservative red-blooded American to the right of Hitler. Emma NO, please no. Did you know it's a felony for a private citizen to own a gun in New York City? Did you know that could kill someone?

"Gil," she said, doing a Ronald Reagan impression, "I think we both know that, well, guns don't kill people . . . people kill people."

You think this is funny, Emma. You bought this for amusement, to camp around with. Is it loaded?

"Ammo's in the box there. Hey! Wanna load it up, pick off people from the window? Clean the streets? Dirty Emma?"

I slammed the desk drawer shut: no.

"After Lennon got shot, I got to thinking: My life is in daily danger in this city. Then my stuff got ripped off while we were having a party a room away. It's a jungle. And every looney out there wants to rape me, beat me, steal my few precious things, and I want a gun. What's so controversial? Lots of single women in this city have guns for their protection. Do you blame them?"

Not really, but why do you think you ought to have one?

"Because I want one. It's a symbol. I feel better knowing I can blow my potential rapist away, that I can clean the streets. I'm not gonna clean the streets, Gil, get that worried look off your face."

Wouldn't a can of mace be better?

"It's a statement I'm making, Gil. I don't want to burn a rapist's eyes and run away, leaving him to go free. I want to kill him. Blow him away. Obliterate him. Waste him."

Would you stop talking about blowing people away? You'll probably blow me away one night when I come back late.

"I've had this for some time and haven't blown you away yet."

And Emma, it's a *tremendous* gun—it looks like it could go off by itself.

"I wanted a phallic gun, okay? A penis."

Since when do *you* want a penis?

"Don't make fun of the gunlady, Gil. I'm armed now, so watch it." She pulled open the drawer and took out the gun, stroking it lovingly, smiling, enjoying the outrage.

What kind is it?

"It's a 9-millimeter—Uncle Harry means business. That's where Hinckley fouled up. He shot Reagan with a .22 caliber, which wouldn't kill your grandmother—a pea-shooter. If you're going to kill a president you're gonna need a man-sized caliber—if Hinckley had been packing, say, a snub-nosed .38, with hollow-point 'cop-killer' bullets, we'd be calling George Bush Mr. President today, Nancy Reagan would be working *Hollywood Squares*. You know, the hollow-point bullet saved the .38-caliber from extinction—the .33's only partially effective, and of course the .45s tear your arm off on the recoil—"

What is this? EMMA THE GUN-NUT?

"It's important to know your firearms, Gil—this is America. Did you know that I could have bought an Uzi 9-millimeter submachine gun, fully automatic, and that's *not* illegal yet in

New York because no one has made a law against it. Two thugs in Brooklyn knocked over this bank with Uzis and they couldn't charge them for weapons possession—they didn't have a chance getting it out of grand jury. I was thinking of going for the heavy metal, Gil, the Uzi submachine gun—you know, for a joke—but if I concealed it, that would be an offense. So you'd have to walk around with it on your belt or in your hand, out in the open, so you wouldn't be breaking the law." She smiled nicely.

You're a real comedian tonight, Em.

"Just talking legal practicalities. In this city if someone came in here and murdered you, tortured you to death, and then came in to get me, and I shot him, the Manhattan DA would probably charge *me* for firearms possession. Now how about that pizza? My usual: pineapple and anchovies." (She only got pineapple and anchovy pizzas so she wouldn't have to share it as no one else would touch it.)

I demanded: Put that thing away before you kill someone with it. This isn't frontier America.

"Oh isn't it?"

Now how are you going to feel when you kill some fifteen-year-old creep, from the slums, who harasses you in the street?

"If he tries to rape me, I think it'll be upsetting for a week or so, but being raped will be upsetting for a little longer, maybe my whole life—"

Stop waving that thing around.

"You are really cramping my style these days, Freeman. If I can't have my Valium, then I get to have my gun. I have to maintain a secure environment somehow. Why are you always undermining me?"

Well in point of fact Emma, you *are* having it both ways, since you are *definitely* still popping pills—

"Go and look in the medicine cabinet yourself—there's not a thing to pop in there—"

Your pills, Emma, are in your purse.

"You LOOKED in my purse?"

You always take your purse in the bathroom, which tipped me off; I did not look in your purse.

"I am cutting back, and furthermore, I have a legitimate prescription."

You are becoming a drug addict and you can be a drug addict on doctor's orders, Emma—that's the preferred way these days. It's gonna end up like Elvis Presley.

"Oh *that* little tactic is below the belt," she said, pointing the gun at me as she might point a finger.

WOULD YOU PUT THAT GUN AWAY?

We hadn't seen the last of the gun, I promise you. A drunk in the hallway one night fiddled with our door and Emma slipped in her ammo cartridge and aimed it at the door while I tried to disarm her. As I did I noticed she was having trouble keeping her eyes open. That tore it.

We fought weekly until I said in so many words:

All right. I'm throwing in the towel. I'm walking away. That's it, I've had it. Really, no kidding—I know, I know, you've heard me say this kind of thing before, but now we're talking gunplay, neuroses on top of psychoses, self-destruction—

"You're pissed off at your own life," Emma yelled during Our Final Fight (which came in September, when I moved out). "You're frustrated with your career, with your life—and you're getting mad at me. I'm the same old Emma I've always been—you're the one who's changing!"

That was one of the printable things she said. I packed a lighter bag this time and realized, as I stormed out, it was midnight and Janet was away. I showed up on Lisa and Jim's doorstep.

"Hey Gil, it's a bit late, I—"

Lisa, just for one night, the sofa. It's an emergency. I synopsized the Emma pills story.

"Right sure . . ." Jim came out and was strained but cordial. I got shown the sofa. Lights got turned off, doors closed, their West Side apartment was quiet except for the air-conditioner hum. Great, I'm saying to myself, not able to sleep. Here you are imposing on Lisa and you haven't seen her in six months—it's not as if she's your close friend anymore. Why should the Gil and Emma show break in on Jim and Lisa's quiet evening? Then I hear them discussing something rather loudly from the bedroom. Arguing over me, I guess. No. Something more substantial. I put my head under the oblong sofa pillow. I can still hear them. I see why they were so strained; they'd been having a fight. Ooops. There goes the baby, bawling away. Great. I try to figure out the date.

Final Report, September 3, 1981: Gil's Official Low Point in his New York Years. Lisa would ask me to stay that week until I found another place and in that time Jim and she would have three major fights. Where was it that people loved each other and it worked out right and everyone was happy? What had happened to all our good times?

I knew one thing for sure. That was it for Emma. My life had had enough of that woman. Yes it had had its moments, it had been fun—for maybe four out of nearly eight years—but I'm going to start looking for a higher percentage. And a new career and a new agent. And a new apartment, and maybe a new girlfriend. So there it was, decided for eternity on the sofa in Jim and Lisa's West Side apartment: no more Emma, the conclusion of the friendship. I felt better already for the decision. And I meant it too. Emma, you're never going to see me again.

1982

"IT'S right in the brown satchel there, under this bed," Emma said, giving directions. I fetched it for her and she rummaged through it: "I should show you this poem first . . . no, wait, maybe not . . ."

When does this poetry book of yours come out?

"It'll take about six weeks to get it printed up, the woman said. I want the Women's Consortium Press to print a second edition so *everyone* I know has to buy fifty copies, I'll reimburse you for your raid on the bookshops." Emma found a tattered envelope and passed it over for my inspection. "That's my letter of acceptance. The editor is a friend of Janet's."

Small world.

"Not that that had *anything* to do with anything," she winked.

One good thing about your being here, I said (trying to be Mr. Cheery), is that you have plenty of time to write.

Emma was electric, as enthusiastic as I'd seen her in years, excited about all her literary projects—at last a book of poems was to be published. She held forth, as in days of old, about writing, about how little the later twentieth-century American had to say, how she wished she were from the third world, how she was limited by being terminally bourgeois:

"I'm handicapped, let's face it—I'm a martyr to the American middle class," Emma said, falling back convinced into her pillow. "Proust had Paris to contrast with the provincial life—think of Dickens's London or James's international salon set or Mark Twain or Fitzgerald—I mean, they had backdrops, they had lives and times to write about. Now how can I touch that?"

Well, you can write about anything if you write about it well enough (. . . I said, sounding like someone's mother).

"Indianapolis? Brownies in second grade? Cruising the Food Fair with Gilda Hoad hoping to see fourteen-year-old Tracy Stanbrook who worked as a checkout bagboy on Tuesdays and Thursdays? My Monkees lunchbox? This is my life, my memoirs, middle-class Indiana. It's hopeless, Gil."

Well, write about it and make everybody laugh.

Emma nodded blankly. "You're missing my point. There's no beauty, there's nothing of lasting interest in my childhood or . . . the rest of my crappy life. I'm thinking of papier-mâché palm trees at the prom—the theme was South Pacific Night: Some Enchanted Evening. I'm thinking dance classes at Mrs. DeVon's School of Ballroom Dancing and her annual recital where I was a Dancing Daisy. I'm talking about the sheer mediocrity of my life. If I were black I'd have something to write about. I don't have anything to write about."

We're not living in uninteresting times, I said.

Emma considered this, falling quiet for the first time since my visit began. Then, as if to fill the silence, she laughed. "Do you remember our toys? Our wonderful '60s toys we grew up with?"

The Golden Age of Toys was the '60s.

"Did you know I had a Little Miss Kitchen EZ-Bake Oven?"

God, Nancy Brooks next door had one of those. You could make cakes the size of a chocolate chip cookie.

"They tasted like dirt. They were shit I think. I mean, really, they put excrement in those little cake packages, I'm sure of it.

It wasn't a real oven—I guess they were worried little girls would burn down the house or something. It was this quick drying excrement you poured in the cake tin and then you put it inside this ovenlike chamber . . . oh god, my set came with a little apron, a little frilly apron. Get those girls in the kitchen early, mothers!"

I had an Etch-a-Sketch. And I had at some point a Close-and-Play record player. It's amazing any record survived the plastic technology. Remember gyroscopes, all those pseudospace-age toys.

"Barbies. I had lesbian relations with Barbie—I loved Barbie. When my breasts came in looking like normal breasts and not Barbie's breasts I was convinced I was a freak. Mind you, Barbie peaked after I outgrew her, when I was in high school. My little sister got Skipper and Francie and there was a black doll . . . Darn, who was that? Oh and *Ken*, the Ken doll without the penis. My little sister had the . . ." Emma broke off giggling. "Oh god, the Barbie VAN. The hippie van, Gil. The LUV VAN with decals of flowers you could peel and stick on. MOD Barbie with the miniskirts and go-go boots!"

Confess, confess—did Emma have a pair of white go-go boots?

After initial denials, a guilty nod. "Yes. Yes, when I was twelve. I would dance in my room with Gilda Hoad next door and we both pretended we were Diana Ross and we'd fight over who got to be the Supremes—doing STOP in the name of love with the gestures. We had white go-go boots. Oh god, do you remember *American Bandstand? Hullabaloo? Shindig!* I never missed those shows. I'd close the den door and dance dance dance—the Swim, the Frug, the Monkey, they had a new dance each week. And once I had a slumber party and there was a *Bandstand* with Herman's Hermits, Peter Noone with all those teeth . . . 'Missuz Brown you've goht uh lufflay daught'uh . . .' "

Great Cockney, Emma.

"I can do the 'Enery the Eighth' song too—or was that Paul Revere and the Raiders? Anyway, my slumber party got to screaming and yelling like girls did for the Beatles, carrying on so that my father marched in and told us the party was over, young lady, if we couldn't behave ourselves—I was SO embarrassed, thought I would *die*."

Remember the Pony?

"Honey, I do a MEAN Pony to this day. Oh wow. Well okay that part of growing up was good—but that's nostalgia, not the makings of great art. What did boys get?" Emma straightened herself in the bed, eyeing the clock, waiting for the nurse.

Chemistry sets, I said. I discovered one hundred ways to mix things together to produce a smell indistinguishable from a fart. And of course GI Joes. The great Korea-through-Vietnam-era toy.

"Dolls for boys, in a way," Emma said.

Very macho dolls. GI Joe came with machine guns, tanks, jeeps, a variety of outfits, the real-live-working-plastic bazooka. Tommy Meepers next door to me in Oak Park had a GI Joe too and our GI Joes often went on group tactical military missions—

"How did GI Joes talk to each other, as they were all named Joe?"

How did Barbies?

"Hadn't thought of that. Kids can get around anything, huh?"

Tommy Meepers and I loved to climb trees and we climbed up the tree in the Meeperses' front yard and made parachutes out of a handkerchief and string and we'd throw our GI Joes out of the tree and watch them float to the ground, except they never floated to the ground, they just broke and got their chutes tangled up in the lower branches, hanging there for days.

"Just like Vietnam—realistic games are good for kids."

My younger brother, I said, chewed on my GI Joe and I eventually stopped playing with it. GI Joe also terrorized neighborhood Barbies.

"My sister had better toys than I did, and I secretly, even in high school, wanted to play with them. Remember Creepy Crawlers?"

I remembered Creepy Crawlers—boy did I ever. You weren't a child unless you once threw up from overeating those Creepy Crawlers. There were the kind that were plastic, but there were also the edible ones. You poured goo into a mold—a spider, a snake, a scorpion, whatever—then you put the mold in this press and created your own Creepy Crawler which you could put on the squealing girl's desk at school or down her dress or in her face or somewhere like that.

"Oh god, *games.* Do you remember how many games there were? Did you ever play Twister in high school? That was right up there with spin-the-bottle for social bravery." Twister was where you spun a spinner-thing and a colored dot came up and you had to put your hand or foot there on this big dotted sheet that took up the whole room, and you invariably ended up in some impossible position with your face in some girl's breasts or some guy's crotch as you tried to touch all the assigned spots you had to touch.

It was the Golden Age of Saturday Cartoons too.

"Yeah that's the damn truth. I watched cartoons last Saturday as I was so bored here in the hospital—pathetic. All this Scooby-Doo shit, all this young kids solving mysteries and finding ghosts or going to outer space. Trash, cheaply made too. What happened to Tom and Jerry, the Road Runner, Bugs Bunny, Heckle and Jeckle, all the violent cartoons where animals got accordioned and MASHED into pancakes and boulders fell on them and there were trapdoors and live wires and DEATH around every corner. God, that stuff prepared me for real life. That wasn't entertainment, that was a complex moral philosophy: You want to eat the tweety-bird, then you have to get steam-rollered for it, go over cliffs. It was better to make friends."

It was the Golden Age of situation TV comedies.

"Oh ain't that the truth. Andy Griffith, Dick van Dyke, *Leave It to Beaver*—pure fantasy America. The whole country modeled their families on this junk—twin single beds in our parents' bedrooms! Mother always in an apron. I love those reruns. *What* do people see in TV nowadays? There's not a decent thing on now. Gross kids and gross families and sappy moral lessons and *applause* at everything, these live studio audiences killed quality TV. Geez, what I wouldn't give for the days of canned audiences who were given appropriate responses. Life should have a laugh track, too."

There was a stirring outside in the hall, the nurse's voice.

"Oh god, here she comes, Nurse Ratchett in *One Flew Over the Cuckoo's Nest*. I'm waiting for Simon Wiesenthal to catch up to her . . ."

The nurse was complaining about something loudly in the hall, to an underling perhaps.

"I wonder how many she's killed. Like those nurse-murderers in Ohio that were knocking off patients for fun. In another century she'd have been burned as a witch. I need drugs to look at her she's so ugly. These state hospitals skim the bottom of the barrel for staff, that's for sure—"

Quiet Emma, really. Here she comes.

"Visiting hours are over at three young man," the nurse snarled.

Yes ma'am. (Whoa, she *was* hideous.)

"Here's your pill," said the nurse, taking Emma's wrist in her beefy, truck-driver's hand. "You're fine, just fine," she said, not taking a full measure. "I'm going to watch you take your pill now."

Emma reached uneasily for her water glass and took her pill, trying not to seem nervous or anxious. But she had been fidgeting for this particular pill ever since I'd arrived. She took it and sank back into the pillow, closing her eyes.

The nurse left, grumbling a reminder about three o'clock, she would be back with another pill, she didn't want to still find me here, people think they can just break the rules and they can't, three o'clock is it, and then it's time to go, rules are rules . . .

"The woman should be a guard in a women's correctional institution," said Emma, breathing deeply. "They've really got me going now. I can't tell if this is a placebo or a real downer. The body relaxes in any event. There'll come a time when, I hope, I'll be taking all placebos—the worst of it, last week, I mean, is over. It won't get that bad again. I think."

I had nothing to say for a moment. Eventually, I said, I hope you'll tell me how you ended up in Bellevue in the first place. Why not stay in a regular hospital—

"Aw c'mon, let's not . . . let's not go into that now. I'll tell you . . . in a minute, I guess. Like my Christmas lights?"

Janet had brought in and strung up this cheap $2 pack of colored lights around the window, the unopenable window with a metal beam through it, since there were suicides on this ward. Emma pointed out two get-well cards, one from Mandy one from someone at work; the flowers were from Dina. After I'd left, Dina moved in. Dina was a nagging whimpering secretary at Emma's PR firm—part of this double act, I mentioned earlier, with this woman named Joanna who came over to the house and listened to Emma's ramblings, cosseting her every neurosis. They were Crisis Junkies. Their own lives were dull so they enjoyed watching Emma's lurch up and down—I always suspected they waited for disasters like this to strike, hoping for them at some level. I imagine Dina on the phone: "Yes, it *was* good I was there . . . yes, I did save the day. No don't call me a hero, I have a duty to Emma . . ." If I'm caustic about these women, perhaps it is because at one time I could have been accused of the same thing: nobly cleaning up after Emma's messes and not giving her the kick in the behind she needed. Well, it hardly mattered now. We were out of each other's lives. She could have her Dinas and Joannas.

"When it's late and I can't sleep and I'm wired, waiting for another pill and the TV's shit, I just curl up and look at the Christmas lights blink on and off and think of Christmas and . . . I don't know, who can get neurotic in the presence of Christmas lights?"

They must think you're crazy here, since it's July.

"Are you kidding? This is Bellevue. I'm so sane compared to some of the girls in the solarium. Jeeeeeezus." She did some quick imitations: "Hi I'm Jenny. I'm dead now . . . Hello, I'm Helen and I can't breathe for the guilt, the guilt of killing my children, which I didn't really do but tell everybody . . . Hello, I'm Christina, and I have these attacks of acute nymphomania and self-disgust when I take a knife and fork and try to cut off the offending parts . . ."

I winced. Bellevue Hospital is a nasty place and I wished Emma were not there. She deserved to be here and it would do her some good, I supposed, but still, this is a last stop on the line for people—Emma had cracked it before turning thirty, and that takes dedication, you gotta give credit where it's due. Dina, relishing her role as bad-news bringer, manager of the crisis, had deliciously told me the news over the phone, something like . . . Emma had trashed the city hospital on the Lower East Side, had to be sent to Bellevue—something along these lines. Okay, I broke down and decided to come see her for the first time in nine months.

"Sorry about the clitorectomy story, that's depressing," Emma said, straightening herself up in bed. "We were having such a fun visit. What are you thinking about?"

Wishing you weren't here.

"Yeah, I thought that at first, but this is going to do wonders for my literary standing if I ever get big. Some of America's best and brightest have entered these portals. I mean, drugs are my excuse. It looked like I was doing myself in Sylvia Plath-like, but no, it was an accident. The way I fear death? ME, a suicide? You didn't think I actually . . ."

No, I heard all sorts of things but I knew you didn't try to kill yourself. But maybe Emma should now tell me how all this—

"No, no, no, not yet," she said, waving a hand to delay me. "I want you to see how positive I am. I am so positive lately. I am never going to be depressed again. You smile but it's true."

I wasn't smiling.

"No, you're afraid to smile, afraid I'm really crazy and belong in Bellevue and you're treating me carefully. People have been treating me carefully for some time now. Like when Lisa came."

How is Lisa these days? I ask (changing the subject).

"Oh. Not so good. She came and talked about her problems with Jim nonstop. They're going to separate for a while, she with the kid. She kept going on about not wanting to be a single mother, how hard it was to be a single mother. I said reconcile with Jim, she said no way, not for a while. I told her, Hey if you don't want to be a single mother, let me adopt your daughter—*I'll* be a single mother. I'm gonna kidnap that little girl. But I'm sounding crazy again, huh?"

That's not good news about Lisa.

"She treated me like I was going to cry or break or something weird. Only the kid was great. She crawled in bed with me and we played with the bed-control and went up and down and up and down . . . She is so goddam cute now."

Yes, last time I saw her, she was cute. As kids go.

"Yeah, I looked at Lisa and Child, the complete love and dependence and unconditional caring and all. The kid just needs and loves the mother so thoroughly—I mean, I was taken aback. I thought to myself: I'm gonna get one of those. Just me and it, though. No husband, no marital duties, no sex. I bet they won't let me adopt, though."

A kid.

"Yeah a kid. It would stabilize me, give me someone to matter to, someone to behave for. When my life drifted out of control I could say, Hey Emma, bimbo, get it back on track, your little girl is in need of a sane mother, you're all she has in the world, so get right with god, fly straight."

It seemed an odd idea for having a kid. No weirder, I guess, than any other one, though. I hated kid-and-marriage talk so I started poking through Emma's writing satchel and she didn't seem to mind.

"That, what you're holding," she said, pointing to a stack of notebook-paper leaves attached by a big paper clip, "is my new, my first, my debut book of poems."

I'm very proud of you, Emma. Congrats.

"Hey, I told you: the new positive Emma. You know how Janet always said the Women's Consortium Press could publish a volume of poetry if I'd go through the motions of calling this woman Naomi who knew Adrienne Rich and went to parties with Denise Levertov? Well, I called her from the pay phone at Bellevue—I mean, that clinched it. I must be a first-rate womanpoet. Crazy with the stress of living in the phallogocentric world."

Phall . . . phallogocentric?

"Like that one? Phallus, *logos*, centric—male-dominated words and language that hinder us, constrict us, persecute us women poets."

Hmmmm.

Emma laughed. "Don't worry, they have some nonlooney stuff

they do and if you publish with them all these other women go out and buy the shit and you get reviewed in the women's press and Janet said she'd freelance the review and PRAISE me to the hilt. Ah, the corrupt literary world. *Village Voice* will review me, I hope. I can then take my new book and maybe get a real contract with Grove or Faber or someone, work my way up."

I hope so.

"Looks like we're both in the old papers, huh? I'll get reviewed just like you."

Saw my notices, did you?

"Lisa brought me the clip—what was it? 'Up-and-coming star, Gilbert Freeman.' I mean you're BIG-TIME now—the *Daily News* doesn't go on like that about everyone."

Wellll . . .

"Weren't you gonna tell me?"

(More modesty:) Wellllll . . .

"You were gonna sit there and not tell your old buddy Emma about your new success—your monstrous, GIANT Broadway success?"

No, actually, I'd brought the same clip and I pulled it out and gave her an extra. (Two people panned me so, really, No Big Deal.)

"Must be a great feeling to be up on the Big Stage with the stars now, huh?"

I could not tell Emma the whole of my dissatisfaction with this production, this great production of my dreams, My Big Break. I had spent, I think, eight years waiting for someone to look across at me and say gee it must be nice to be up onstage with the stars and get your name in the *Times/News/Post* magazines and be working in the Theater. And as a younger man (even as late as last year, I think) I had rehearsed answers in my sleep, practiced them before mirrors, but now shrugging and acting nonchalant or any kind of phoneyness put me in the same league as Rosemary Campbell and I had this *dread* of doing anything that got close to that. I wanted to say: Emma, in all honesty I liked doing two-bit avant-garde theater where five people came better than this. This is the desk job of acting. I'm not fulfilled, I'm disillusioned and what did it was *Mother's Day* starring Rosemary Campbell, legend, Rosemary Campbell, the peak of the business.

Mother's Day by Cecil Praed. I play one of the four children. I get $650 a week, by god. And this will run for AT LEAST six months, as long as the old girl wants to do it. Summer season just began and no New Yorkers were coming to theater anymore, it was all Ma and Pa from Nebraska, into the city on their two-week vacations or package tours of family outings or conventions, and they all want to see someone famous like Rosemary Campbell in her vehicle and Katharine Hepburn down the street in her vehicle and Lauren Bacall across the way in her vehicle. Serious vehicular congestion on Broadway this summer. *Mother's Day* was pap, completely predictable, just an obstacle course: Rosemary laughs, Rosemary shows that ageless grace and brittleness still apparent through the years (and makeup), Rosemary lets her lip tremble, Rosemary wrenches her soul, Rosemary Rosemary Rosemary.

The last act is a throwaway for me and Martin who play her two sons. We sit offstage and listen to Rosemary out there having it out with her thankless daughters—yelling, screaming, emoting. Martin is almost as cynical as I am about this production.

"Listen, here it is, listen for the catch in her voice," says Martin, craning forward.

Rosemary out onstage: "Grow up, for god's sake. You can't be a child forever—when are you going to stand on your own feet . . ."

"Get ready for it," Martin would say, "here it is—"

Rosemary out onstage: "Oooooh Stephanie dahrling dahrling girl . . ."

Martin would make wretching motions, contortions. "Every night the same friggin' way. 'Ooooooooooh Steffahnay dahhhhrling . . .' Pickled and cured in her own juices, this one."

Our stage manager, standing to the side, allows a dry smile as he exhales, "Surely you can't be talking about the First Lady of the American Theater, Queen of the Footlights . . . THESPIA herself."

Rosemary, it was beginning to occur to me, was a creation

of a lifetime in Show Biz. She did the worst thing you could do in the entertainment world: She bought her own act. It wasn't just being a prima donna or full of herself or egotistical because she deserved to be all those things, one expected that; it was that she didn't have anything behind the persona, she was a shell, wasn't all there. She didn't know our real names and called us by our character names. She told us the same glorious memoir stories repeatedly, within twenty-four hours of the last time she'd told them—every word the same, every smile, nuance, arch of an eyebrow identical. She worked off a script she didn't know was a script.

"What would happen if a bomb went off in the audience?" Martin asked. "Or if we gave her a line like 'Mother, you old bag, you look one hundred years old.' I wonder if she can ad-lib. She's on automatic pilot."

Like some kind of Oriental princess who never was allowed to touch the ground with her own foot, Rosemary lived in a sheltered world. Her agent and manager/husband, a rich banker, delivered her by limo to the theater at the right time, her makeup boy, her costume advisor, her hairdresser and press person (three solicitous faggots—"Rosie, you're DIVINE, you hear me? You're AGELESS, do you hear me?"—and one icy WASP bitch respectively) all in tow. They told her all she had to know of the world, all that should concern her. If there was a good clipping or mention of her in the paper (the world loved her, this twice Oscar-winning Hollywood Great now treading the boards), the boys took turns reading it to her while she considered it: "Ah yes, we will write him a thank-you letter and I shall sign it. The difference between stars now and stars of my day—"

"This is still your day, Rosie, and don't you think otherwise," says Hairdresser.

"—is that stars of my day cared so about their fans. Harry Cohn once told me . . ." The hand delicately rises to rest lightly on the lower neck, her smile, her legendary smile warmly begins to glow, the eyes widen as Memoir 6783 comes to the surface: " . . . Harry Cohn said Rosemary, darling, for every letter you write that's a hundred more people who will stay loyal to you forever. Write a letter to a fan in a small town and America will love you forever . . ."

"And they *have* loved you forever," says Makeup Boy. "From all over the country they've come to see you, Miz Campbell. They remember you, they love you . . ."

Rosemary exuded a state of grace, you saw the scene in *Life Turns Round* (1943): "I have been so favored in this life . . . I have been, you know, my friends, so very very lucky . . ."

"You've deserved every minute of it, Miz Campbell."

And now the modesty à la her Oscar acceptance speech: "Do you . . . do you really think that, dear? Are you not just telling an old woman" —the voice softens, the eyes have that distant noble look—"an old woman what she would so like to hear?"

I always wondered if Rosemary knew who the president was, or what year it was, or if World War II was over. Her world had no connection to fact or modern life or normalness or strife and conflict of any kind. One could fantasize about her limo getting hijacked to the South Bronx and her getting turned out somewhere along Southern Boulevard to walk back to the East Side (although with her charmed life she might well have walked back without incident). Scary thing, this kind of insularity that happens with American presidents so they don't even know what's happening and what everyone is thinking, and American pop stars in their own little fantasy worlds—god, the cossetings, the emoluments, the unsparing and unceasing effort not to contradict the SUCCESS, these crazy Howard Hughes worlds of yes men and twenty personal bodyguard-staffpeople scurrying about to make sure you never have to soil your hand with opening a door or taking a cap off a pen. I guess you live in that nonsense long enough and you too can be Rosemary Campbell with all the dimension and scope of a touched-up airbrush '30s movie still.

Mayor Koch declared June 10 Rosemary Campbell Day, as it marked her fortieth anniversary in Show Business. When just nineteen (yeah right—this old girl was in her late sixties if she was a day) she starred in *Glory of the Dawn* (1942) released on June 10. (The mayor's office must have slaved overtime to unearth that little fact—any excuse for a photo opportunity and to promote another Broadway vehicle that brought in the tourist trade.) So there was to be a special performance, black tie, limos for miles outside the theater, a theater party of champagne and caviar and inedible pretentious pâtés on cardboard grain-meal crackers like the kind you feed the giraffes at the Bronx Zoo.

The Construction Crew (as we called the Hairdresser, Makeup Boy, Press Lady and Costumer) were there working for all they were worth to restore the sheen and polish on Rosemary. She talked glibly and confidently about her second Oscar and the press and when you get up in front of millions of people there was no reason to be nervous about an affair like this, no reason at all, laughter, light girlish laughter, ah how she'd seen so much in these forty years, had she ever mentioned the time Cary Grant and Fredric March took her dancing at the Savoy, the moon above them and the stars and BLAH BLAH BLAH.

"You realize," said Martin, "that she's going to be even worse than ever tonight. Not a piece of scenery left unchewed. She'll be all over our lines, playing with the props." Right you were, Martin.

Mother's Day was written by Cecil Praed, who had conjured up Rosemary's last two vehicles (*A Dream of Cambridge*, about a *Corn is Green*-like schoolteacher coaching her poor student into Harvard against ignorant parents, etc.; and *So Many Pretty Flowers*, about an invalid wife fighting for her man against his philandering), and Cecil knew that you had to send the others of the cast out there and warm up the audience with lines like "You know Mother," and "Mother is crazy, but we love her," and "There's no stopping Mother when she gets something in her head" so the audience was well ready to see this LEGEND come out and whirl about the stage. And so it went, Martin and myself and Gertrude (Daughter No. 1) as we worked the crowd up for the Great Entrance. Finally, the cue —Martin: "Quiet, let's not let her know we know. I hear her in the drive . . ."

The door opened and in came Rosemary in an ensemble devised just for this evening, this zillion-dollar society-woman ballgown (a little much for the role, but if you started picking at details on this play there'd be nothing left), and the place exploded into a prolonged ovation for Rosemary who made a slight eye-acknowledgment of the applause . . . no, no, she seemed to say, don't prolong this, don't make me break character, don't stand, oh you mustn't, but now that you are all right I will step out of character and yes absolve you with a recognition of your worship (yes, her face COULD say all that). So soon she is bowing a grand opera bow as the audience, tuxedo- and evening-gown-clad, is standing and cheering and honoring and adoring.

Every act started with this nonsense and then GOOD GOD the orgy of endless encore and curtain call at the end of the play, the once-glamorous face registering: Oh me? Again? No you are too kind . . . And of course a speech was demanded as she stood there, fourth curtain call, holding a bouquet of roses, the stage strewn with flowers and petals.

"Thank you ever so much," said her voice, trembling slightly in imitation of some long-lost, remembered genuine emotion. "I have always felt the Theater to be my first home—"

Martin to me backstage: "Ha, her first play here was 1978."

"—and New York is and has always been where my heart belongs. It is my home now and always. And the Theater is where I meet with YOU my friends . . ." The hands extended to include everyone. "I feel such LOVE here, LOVE flowing out, LOVE flowing in, from the stage to you, from the audience to the stage, we are together in a LOVE of the MAGIC . . ." (A slight pause as if the word *magic* just occurred to her.) " . . . the MAGIC that is the Theater. Without LOVE there can be no MAGIC . . ."

This went on.

And then there was the party.

And during the party I watched Rosemary accept more kudos and scrapings-and-bowings and people were saying things to her like "Oh Miss Campbell, my husband's and my favorite film was *Monday's Child* and we've seen it fifty times and even saw it on our honeymoon," and "Oh Miss Campbell you're my all-time favorite actress, could you please sign this," and then the person held out one of those $75 glossy books of movie stills devoted to Rosemary Campbell, and "Oh Ms. Campbell I get tears in my eyes every time I see *Let Me Live Another Day* and your words at the end, when you say goodbye to your daughter, well when my own daughter this spring passed away I took her hand and I said the exact same things and—"

HOLD IT. I should go up and go: Oh Ms. Campbell, you old overrated bag, explain to me how these fellow human beings are debasing themselves before you like some goddess when 50,000 amateur-housewife-actresses in local little theater productions around the country have more sincerity, more talent at this point than you. What sociological phenomenon do you represent?

And this is THE TOP, this is success, this is ALL THE WAY HOME, this is presumably the fame and fortune I had always dreamed of. Now tell me, I wanted to demand of the entire party, *why* is this repelling me? Why is this whole sham of the theater seeming more like a medicine-show faith-healing act than anything else? All right, I tell myself, having another champagne, it's obvious you are having a Crisis of Confidence right here and it's best to keep it to yourself, Gil. In fact, only one person ever appreciated this kind of crisis or at least made you laugh about it and that was Emma.

And (back to Bellevue) when she asked me, "Must be a great feeling to be up on the Big Stage with the stars now, huh?" I should have attempted to go into some of that.

But I said: Yeah, what a relief. Sure is great, and about time too.

"Get me the old battle-axe's autograph, okay? Although she didn't deserve an Oscar for *Pillar of Fire*—shoulda gone to Bette Davis that year. Don't tell her I said that. Just get the autograph. Now tell me about Sophie."

Sophie? Who told you—

"Never you mind my sources."

Oh yes of course: Janet ran into us at Rodrigo's—

"You little *yuppie* you, Rodrigo's. Workin' the West Side now, huh? Coming up in the world. They must be paying you better."

Yep Emma, they *were* paying me better.

My new apartment was in a fine old brownstone on 96th Street in a not-quite-yet-regentrified old neighborhood; the occasional drug deal, wino asleep on the stoop, mugging here and break-in there, marred what was clearly destined for Yuppie Renewal. How gauche of lower Harlem not to take the hint and leave . . . For a long time it was less my apartment than Allyn Farrington's *ex*-apartment. He had picked the gray tasteful carpet to go with the light blue pastel wall paint, the faint pink foyer, the mauve bedroom, all with matching curtains, shades, which complemented the sofa. As it was a furnished apartment, he had to leave all his decorations behind.

"And I'm leaving you that plant," he lamented. "You are good with plants, aren't you?"

Great, I lied. (I could make the Congo wither and die . . .)

"Oooohhh," he minced, "it's one of my favorites too."

Why don't you take it?

"Oh I just can't . . ."

Allyn (yes, he spelled it that way) was another actor in the stables at Gardiner & Gardiner, my new agents (two sisters, known in the business as Jerry and Janie). Kind, decent, caring people, a real concern for their clients—I had been meeting the wrong people, that was for sure. I should have come to these two my first week in New York. Matthew (the guy who was thrown out of Odessa's before me, during the Anus-lips Scandals) had gone over to Gardiner & Gardiner. I called him up, begged him for an entrée, Jerry took a liking to me. Here I am a working actor on Broadway. I had to say it out loud to myself half a dozen times each night before I'd believe it: ON BROADWAY. Gil is on Broadway. You know Gil Freeman, back in high school? Did you hear he was in some Broadway play this month? Excuse me cab driver, could you take me to the Summerscale Theater on Broadway, my makeup call is 7:30 . . . Every other sentence out of my mouth contained the word Broadway—I was bragging, yes, but also I had to keep saying it in order to believe it. If I kept saying it often enough I might even convince myself how happy it's made me. Richer, more famous, nice apartment, less happy. Figure that one out.

Oh yeah, back to the apartment. It was Allyn's: thirty-three years old, thinning hair, dressed like an eternal frat boy, had the uniform gay mustache. I had always dismissed him as a pretentious, irritating, prissy homosexual. "Can you belieeeeeeve," he said, when Jerry and Janie took their younger actors out on a business lunch, "that they would put *this* tablecloth with *these* napkins? Pleeeease." But I had misjudged him. He was in reality a pretentious, irritating, prissy homosexual with a soon-to-be-free West Side rent-controlled apartment. Actually, having stared at those mauve walls for two years, I have decided his taste wasn't that great—he just had opinions.

"I can't belieeeeeeve I'm moving," Allyn exhaled as he took down a framed sketch of a near-naked dancer, silver, thin frame, navy blue backing to match the light blue walls. "I said I'd never move in with anyone again and here I am doing it. Looks like I'll be decorating all over again, as well—Jason's place is . . ." He couldn't find the correct word of revulsion to finish.

Anyway, that was my apartment. I put up show posters (ones I was in), I put up my prints I'd bought from the Metropolitan, my poster of Brando as Stanley Kowalski next to my poster of Gielgud as Hamlet—all my artifacts and souvenirs. Never felt like my home, though. I should have repainted it or ripped up the carpet or trashed it somehow to make it more like what I was used to. Emma had never seen the place.

There wasn't a New Gil, but there was a New Gil Lifestyle:

I hear Emma's in Bellevue. I call a cab. I don't have to take the subway everywhere anymore. I step outside into the front hall. I see my *New York Times*, my *New Yorker*, lots of junk mail. The junk mail is a result of the magazine subscriptions, which are a result of having a bit more money. I get into the cab. I tell him to take me to Bellevue but by way of Broadway Florists at 79th Street. I go in and point to the standard $25 bouquet. Will that be cash? No, I will use my credit card, which I now have. The card I used to take Sophie to Rodrigo's for a $120 splurge. At which time I wore my new suit, managed the time by looking at my new watch. I know MBAs were starting out in the city with first salaries of $40,000 and my new pocket money was small change, but everything's proportional remember. For the first time I had to let the government take my taxes out of my paycheck—in fact, like a lot of actors, I was thinking of going to a tax lawyer who knew all the loopholes about self-employment expense write-offs.

"So Sophie, huh? Not another Betsy, I hope,"

Sophie, I said, is a very—

"Sweet girl? Good lay?"

—sophisticated and intelligent woman who was valedictorian in my high-school class—

"Tits? Big tits there? Bazongas? Honeydew melons? You can tell me. Never known a Sophie with pert breasts."

She stayed in Chicago and went to the university there and got a bachelor's in sociology—

"A bullshit major."

—and stayed for a master's, and now she works at Northwestern conducting social research—

"Bourgeois paper-pushing bureaucratic academic ivory-tower worthless work, it sounds like. Probably puts out for the professors . . ."

—social research about social norms in the ghettos in the South Side of Chicago; she thinks ghetto culture, though horrible, is in some ways more valid than suburban white culture—

"Oooh yuck, a liberal do-gooder, self-righteous, I bet. I hate people devoting their lives to Good Works—she probably works with handicapped children on weekends, works charity telethons, vegetarian, right? Into animal rights."

Are you quite done? It's nice to see you back in form, Emma. Savaging my love interests.

"The Girl Next Door, after all these years. The Girl Back Home. So, when you moving back? You can live in Oak Park, maybe get your parents to rent your old bedroom to you. It'll be as if you never left the Great Midwest."

It's not a full-fledged affair yet, so save your ammunition. She ran into my mother in a supermarket and they talked and Sophie then asked about me because she had a conference in New York and she wanted to look me up—

"My blood chills at the prospect of the woman you love going to . . . ugh, *conferences*. How is she in bed—that's the important thing."

Emma, you never change. And whether that's the good or bad thing about you, I'll probably never be sure.

And there was a pause and we had come close to an odd and hard-to-deal-with subject: our relationship. I could walk out of there and not see her anymore. I could start back up again and be a loyal friend, be supportive and do my Dina imitation and get used as before. I could do what I want—hey Betsy, hear that? If you didn't know any better, you'd think I was becoming more SELF-ACTUAL.

"What's going on in the outside world? Have I missed anything? Nuclear war?"

Reagan's working on it. We're in El Salvador and Nicaragua pretty heavy. Recently the administration, in cutting back money for school lunches, declared they still met health guidelines because ketchup could be counted as a vegetable.

Emma laughed. "Oh I hate being in here when I hear stuff like that. America never lets me down in that regard."

It's three; I'm going to have to go soon . . .

"You're fine until Lucrezia Borgia comes back, so settle down, kick your shoes off."

Why don't you tell me the story now? How you got in here in the first place.

Emma sighed, looked to the Christmas lights serenely. Maybe she had rehearsed this, maybe not. "It's sort of funny in retrospect. If it weren't my life, I'd laugh about it. In fact, it *is* my life and the other day I *did* laugh about it."

(I wasn't going to say anything for a while.)

"Anyway," she sighed, "you know how depressed I was last year before you moved out in a huff—"

You can't blame me, I began—

"No, no, of course not, not that I wanted you to go, or thought you should go . . ."

I am quiet again.

"Anyway, there's my dad with lung cancer from smoking all his life and I'm sorry he's dying but I still don't want to go back and play sappy TV-movie reconciliation, you know? I guess it's expected of me, to go back and pretend we never hated everything about each other and spent our lives criticizing each other—I'm supposed to fall down and say how much I really have always loved him and that I'll always be Daddy's little girl and *yuck*, none of that's true."

How's he doing, by the way?

"Same. Still sick. Chemotherapy is hell and he still sneaks a cigarette now and then—THAT much I like about him. You and I, Gil, weren't talking in November," she clears her throat, "so you managed to miss the great drama of my going home for his fifty-sixth birthday. It might be his last, so we all came home—even my brother Vinnie who hates Dad more than I do—and we sang happy birthday and I wanted to shoot myself for the emptiness of it all, the sham. God. Where's my piece by the way?"

Piece?

"My piece, my cannon. My ROD."

Dina and I took your gun to a pawn shop and she'll write you a check; we flushed all extant pills in your apartment down the toilet. Your place is habitable again.

"Sure know how to take advantage of a girl when she's down and out," said Emma, not too upset however. "Well, anyway, it's my mom and dad's thirtieth wedding anniversay next month, another Last Chance occasion, right? And I tell Mom that I'm not taking time off from work to come out for another dog-and-pony show, and we fight and scream and say things. She was just here, this week."

Your mother?

"Yeah, and she wants to take me back home to Indiana for a while, and I said yes, so maybe we'll be back in the rolling Great Plains together, we can visit, me with my kidnapped child, you with your big-titted sociologist vegetarian friend—"

How long will you be gone?

"Indianapolis? Are you kidding? I'll be on the first bus back as soon as I . . . what do you call it? Dry out? Clean myself out? Whatever. And I think I can do that pretty easily in Indiana as I was a scared Catholic schoolgirl there, never took a drink, never did anything bad, never smoked a cig, no sex."

Just like now.

"Yeah just like now."

Pause. Still waiting for the Big Story.

"So no one's around, right? Janet's in California doing something on university discrimination, Dina's up in Connecticut at her mother's, I can't find Joanna; Lisa—I'm so desperate I even call Mrs. Yuppie herself . . . she's not available, she's doing something with the kid, she and Jim are having problems, etcetera etcetera. I even call the girls from work and that's no good. I've seen all the movies ever made by this point. YOU, of course, aren't speaking to me."

Go on.

"And I'm really vulnerable, so I'm taking a few more pills than I should have taken and I go to my analyst and he trashes me out, calls me self-indulgent, calls me self-involved, selfish—"

I thought you had this guy trained to lick your boots.

"Well I thought so, but he took this day of all days to use the 'kick in the pants' strategy and I left feeling shittier than ever."

And that's when you went home and took too many pills?

"Gil, I've told you, this wasn't a suicide, this was an accident."

Keep talking.

"So I sneak another pill on the way to the group-therapy session, and I remember shit, it's my day to talk and have my guts spilled and have everyone give their sanctimonious advice about my life and what's wrong with it . . . so, for good measure, I take another pill."

Oh Emma.

"Anyway, I go on motormouth-mode, I tell these people everything. You should see them trying to make sense out of my life—which, as we both know, is impossible. We talk about my dying father, we talk about my failed friendships, we talk about pills, we talk my celibacy. Lot of theories on that one: Was I secretly date-raped once? Was I abused as a child? Was I actually still a virgin? A lesbian maybe? I heard it all."

Anything sound good?

Emma laughed mildly. "You know, Gil, apparently I will suffer all my life because I don't want to have some guy's urogenital organs within my body. I must be the freak of the world. I find the male sexual apparatus vulgar—it's like a . . . a popgun going off. Am I certifiable because I don't think it's a good time having this thing go off inside me once a night? I got a lot of problems, okay, but I have NEVER felt my choice to be celibate was one of them." She was done with her speech. "I think it's one of my few triumphs over the human-animal state."

And you told the group this?

She laughed more fully. "Oh no, I really let them have a good session—I cried, I confessed, I was vulnerable, I broke down, I put on a good show. I'm *never* going back there. I told them . . ."

What? Emma was getting the giggles again.

"I mean, what *didn't* I tell them? I told them things I never told anyone before. About getting rid of my own virginity, for instance."

My eyes must have widened.

"Oh come on, I'm sure I told you that one. No?" Emma seemed rather proud of this. "Paul, my first boyfriend always said he didn't want no Catholic schoolgirl virgin so I went home and thought about it and went, hey why not, let's get this over with, so I broke my own hymen so I could be a woman of the world at sixteen. In retrospect, I'm glad I lost my virginity to myself. I wouldn't want it any other way," she added laughing. "*Well*, you should have seen the vultures, the amateur psychiatrists fall all over themselves to analyze this. This was the cause of my celibacy, this was the cause of everything ever bad in my life, etcetera."

Maybe it does have something to do with it.

"*No* it doesn't. Anyway, the Bitch Cheryl asks what therapies I've been taking and I tell all about the masturbation therapy and how it seems to be working and loosening me up and making me . . ." She buries her head in her hands. "I mean, *how degrading*, to sit there and talk about your masturbation therapy—I mean, I'm at an all-time low. I tell them that just this week—hot off the press, folks—I became comfortable enough with myself to engage in penetration. And I started tearing up, tears of joy, because I had reached this landmark." Emma picked up the pillow underneath her and buried her face in it: "Just let me DIE, put me to sleep, put me down . . ."

I stifle any laughter and say *everyone* tells things at those groups, no big deal.

"Oh but there I was having this drug-induced crying jag with these creeps and the Bitch Cheryl comes and hugs me and there is *applause* and support and nurturing and group positiveness and everyone pats me on the back and hugs me and GOD, I saw myself. I said to myself: Emma, you're at rock bottom. You've officially just become someone that you'd make horrendous fun of."

Don't be too hard on yourself.

"And so I run to the bathroom and get some tissues to stop being emotional and stop crying and I feel like such an idiot for doing that psychoanalytical striptease out there so I take another pill."

Sounds like a mistake.

"Right. So I'm walking back home just to be moving and not sitting around feeling bad and who should I run into but Joanna."

Joanna, whoopdiedoo.

"From the temp agency, remember? I know you hate her and think she's a bore, and she is, but she cares about my problems. Anyway I'm desperate enough to go out with Joanna and we go to a bar. I tell her I'm depressed and I make up something just to justify my being so down—I tell her you and I broke off our engagement and we're not speaking."

Me and you?

"Yeah well I needed some sympathy and that's what I said. And we weren't speaking, that much was true. So Joanna is a pal. I have one tiny vodka and orange juice and then, since she's buying drinks (so desperate for company she'll foot the bill, I figured) I keep telling her just an orange juice please, just an orange juice. Well she thinks I mean the same drink over and over again and to be a pal she has the bartender put double and triple shots in there and I can't tell because I could be drinking shoe polish at this point, I was so out of it, my tongue wasn't working—"

So you got drunk and had too many pills in you?

"Well I had this fifty-milligram bottle, right? And I had this illegal other bottle I'd gotten hold of and I thought the latter was the former so I thought I had three medium pills in me and I really had much too much. Well anyway this wave of nausea hits me, the abyss is opening before me, I sense all that stands between me and the void is my ability to keep myself awake. I tell Joanna to get me to a hospital except it comes out like Joooo uhnnnna, gib me to duh hahhhhhspill . . . It's like I have cotton in my mouth. NEXT thing I know I'm in the bathroom and someone is splashing cold water on me, then someone's trying to get me to throw up but even my gag reflex is asleep here, and then I'm being led to an ambulance."

But how did you end up in Bellevue?

"I'm getting there, hold your horses. I'm in the ambulance, right? I'm stabbing myself with my fingernails to keep myself awake. The attendant pokes me and slaps me so I won't pass out. I mean, this is it, Gil, *me and death*, the Distinguished Thing, hourglass and scythe. You know what's odd? There's a very reasonable part of me that's still thinking quite clearly and that reasonable part is sort of laughing. Like when the guy slaps me, it's thinking: Hey buddy, watch those hands, you enjoying this? And when Joanna threw water on me in the bathroom at the bar, it's thinking: You're really messing up my blouse here, Jo. You know, Joanna, if you did something different with your hair you might just get a date or two. I mean, this still small voice is cracking jokes."

You were delirious maybe.

"No," she said excitedly, "it was impeccable. It told me in my own voice—I mean, it was MY voice—that I had to stay awake or fall off into a possible coma. So I sat there and fought to keep awake. Out I'd go for a second and then I'd shake myself awake, digging my nails into my arm—see?" She raised her right arm and showed her scars.

Oh my.

"So I get to City Hospital downtown and the still small voice is going 'Oh boy Emma, you're in for it now. Hack city. Amputate first and ask questions later.' There's a gunshot wound over here, a knifing there, a rape a mugging an assault—your basic weekday night. I'm on this table and then next thing I know here comes Doctor Kildare—no, handsomer, this is a *General Hospital* dream, this is the doctor little girls dream of playing doctor with. And the still small voice goes, 'Great, Mr. Hot comes along and you're too zoned out to end your celibacy here and now.' He sticks a tube down me and I'm all for that —I'm easy at this point, motorcycle gangs, Shriner conventions, just pile 'em on boys, I'm in great spirits here."

What was this tube?

"Stomach pump. They pour this vat of water into the tube and I have this sense of it going into me and then they lower the end of the pipe and siphon everything out of me—oh, the humiliation. Dr. Kildare, forgive me, what a bad first impression. And then something odd happens. That last little spurt of energy and consciousness was like some kind of last reviving before *death*, and I start losing it, going black and the doctor is looking worried and looks at his nurse and then I'm out. It's because I'm breathing so shallowly I just about shut down right there."

Let me guess. Here's where you died.

"Ha ha. So next thing I know I wake up and I'm looking at the ceiling and my heart is racing. And that voice is back, funnier than ever, going, 'Well, maybe you've been reincarnated and you're back.' And then I touch my chest as my heart is beating so hard. Nope, I have breasts—not that these are breasts—so I'm not a child again. My heart starts really racking around in my chest and NO ONE is around me. I've been rolled over to some hallway and I guess some other emergency came in and I got parked and I'm having a heart attack. I'm sure of it—it must have been two hundred beats a minute and I think, shit, it's gonna burst or jump out of my body or tear itself apart. So I rear up to get off the table, but my *head* is still full of drugs and I fall back."

What was all this?

"They gave me a shot of adrenaline fearing I was fading out. But this shoots straight to my heart and something's gone wrong and I'm having a heart attack. So I steady myself and get up—where is Dr. Kildare? The downers and the uppers are fighting it out in me and I start panicking in a big way—I freak out as I've never freaked out . . . I'm absolutely sure I'm dying, my heart is pounding and that's all I can hear and I'm running about trying to get help, running into walls, into all kinds of emergency-room junk. And I come face to face with the big attraction, this guy who'd been cut up in about fifty ways and they're all attending to him and I can't get their attention. So I start trashing the hospital."

You *what*?

"I started pulling over IV racks and turning over tables and hitting the walls and going seriously crazy—all these free-clinic type doctors staring at me, restrain her, tackle her, someone says—"

But weren't you telling them you were having a heart attack?

"You know, that's the interesting thing, Gil. I don't think I was. I was yelling it in my head but maybe not to them. Anyway, here comes some Goon Number Two with a syringe and someone near me says 'angel dust,' as if I'm freaking out on angel dust, and I see the syringe and enough of my brain is working enough to know that they're bringing out a sedative. No, NOT a sedative, I'm yelling to myself—and I fight them, hit the doctor, make a run for it, all the time this crushing pain—it's like someone is standing and jumping up and down on my heart. Someone tackles me, someone holds me, but I kick and bite and I get away, turning over big metal trashcans in my wake."

But they got you, huh?

"Yes, so they got me. I had two rounds of sedatives and one of uppers in me and with that I checked out. I gave up: I said to myself as it got black, all right, stupid girl, this is it, look at those fluorescent lights getting dimmer, there's the last thing you'll ever see, that crappy cork-paneled ceiling and that light and I guess I'm not the first to die seeing that as a last sight, all the middle-aged businessmen being wheeled in here a minute too late to save them, they see the cork-paneled ceiling too and the fluorescent lights . . ." And here Emma sighed.

Why didn't you die?

"They figured it all out, that I was the barbiturate and booze case left unattended in the hallway and that they had given me a sedative on top of it, and there's nothing as efficient as a hospital in the face of a major malpractice suit. I got hooked up—I mean I was out for two days, I don't remember this—I got hooked up to a life-support system. I mean, compared to major Marilyn Monroe booze and pills-takers, I was small change. What? Five or six shots of vodka, a few hundred milligrams—that's not good but it's not heavy-duty death."

And then to the addicts' program at Bellevue.

"Well, I was a dangerous patient—after my little rampage—prone to violence, a risk to society. They sent me here to help their case if I filed for malpractice. It had to look like my own grandmother would have given me that sedative, that it was a well-intentioned accident. And it was, I guess. They didn't mean to nearly kill me. And I like being in Bellevue—I mean, Delmore Schwartz was here, this place has *major* street cred, you know?"

I smiled.

"It does, it does. Everyone good came here. My hospital stay is going to be on all my press releases, but no Anne Sexton screwed-up mess routine as that's been done and done. I want to be the Jerry Lee Lewis of women poets—I'm looking for Kerouac here, Dylan Thomas, living on the edge, living too wildly, a doomed self-destructive figure. If I check out I want to go out like Janis Joplin and not Alice James, if you see what I mean."

Whatever you say Emma. But you are going to have to quit the pills now, right?

Emma looked to the Christmas lights in the window. "Did you know getting off barbiturates is harder than kicking heroin?"

Yes, *I* told you that.

"This is going to take a while."

And suddenly as she looked away to the window I was glad,

glad and relieved that it wouldn't be me that stood to her side, helped her along. A purely selfish moment I had there: Thank God, you got away free and clear, away from these meteoric rises and descents. And then I looked at Emma. Life was always going to be like this for her. And yet, it also came to me, she would always survive herself, somehow. Despite the follies there was something strong in Emma, a will to selfishness, an indomitable ego—I'm not sure what—but it would keep her alive and complaining and stirring up the dust all her days. Admit it, Gil, there was something attractive in this woman, something fierce and opinionated and gifted, whatever the calamities. But also realize, Gil, that she will never need you or anybody, she is self-sufficient, she may be impervious even to those who love her.

"I want to be Whittier, I've decided," said Emma.

Gee Emma, I think you're witty enough for—

"No. John Greenleaf Whittier, minor poet."

I thought you wanted to be a major poet.

"No, I want to be a minor poet. It's better being a minor poet, I've decided."

Hmmm.

"No, now think about it. You say Auden or Eliot or Tennyson or anybody major and you get an argument—Auden's trash, no Eliot wasn't any good at all, Tennyson's a hack. Yeats was good at the end—no, you're crazy it's only at the beginning he's any good, before he fell in with Pound, that crackpot. Crackpot? He's a genius! See, you can't get any agreement on the really great ones. But you stop anybody on the street and go, quick, who was Cullen Bryant, who was Longfellow . . . and they'll say, those guys were poets. No argument. I don't want there to be any argument."

Yeah but Whittier's a trivia question. Have *you* read him, Emma?

"Of course not. Minor poets aren't read—that makes them minor poets. I don't care, after I'm dead, if they read me or not, I just want to be thought of as a poet, no questions asked." Her face brightened: "I want to be Stephen Spender. *No one* says he isn't a poet, no one argues he's anything but a good minor poet. That's bliss. They'll be debating Berryman and Stevens until the cows come home, but they won't be debating James Russell Lowell and Stephen Spender."

Well I wouldn't know, I said.

"I got a positive attitude now, Gil baby. I'm Miss Positive now. A year ago if I couldn't be the female John Keats I was going to kill myself, now I want to be Whittier. I think that's healthy."

Whittier.

"Yeah, Whittier. I want schoolchildren in future generations to have to write papers on me, memorize my name. I want high schools named after me—aah aah aah . . . almost slipped back into delusions of grandeur there. I've still got to watch myself. I want . . . I want shopping malls named after me. I'm setting my sights a little lower now."

Yeah, I sighed, I used to think if I hadn't won the Tony by thirty that I couldn't live with myself.

"Well you got some time left still."

We both broke into an imitation of Odessa simultaneously: "Gil, huhney, 1983 is gonna be YAWR YEEUH . . ." And Emma added, "You know, Gil, it just might be your year. This thing you're in now is famous; it's been written up everywhere."

Well not for me, for the star, Rosemary Campbell—it's her vehicle.

"It's not as if you're a spear carrier, c'mon."

No I'm very happy about it, I said. But I wasn't happy about it. Why couldn't I tell Emma—the only person I knew who wouldn't criticize me for not being grateful for how far I've come, etc.? Because she was not part of my life anymore, that's why. If she couldn't need me I wasn't going to need her. I'd been absent from her life and vice versa nine months—that was a good start. She has her habit to kick, I have my habit to kick.

"God I wish I had a job where I got to have a room full of people clap at me and cheer me every night. How could you miss, doing that for a living?"

Oh Emma, if you knew how much I wanted them to get their clapping over with so I could go home and get on with my life. I'll act for the two hours they paid for but do I have to give rhapsodies about how wonderful the applause is when it's just a bunch of people scrambling for car keys thinking about the crowds and the quickest way out of the city or hailing a taxi, and me up there thinking about getting home in time for the late movie? I really wanted to let her know that I didn't love the theater like I used to, that I'd changed somehow—perhaps she could put it into words for me, help me. NO. Resist temptation, boy. You've done your duty call here; say a polite goodbye and leave.

"Has anyone asked for your autograph yet?"

I stood up and walked to the window with the Christmas lights and looked at them blink on and off and make red-orange and blue-green forms and lines and shadows. No, I told Emma, not yet.

"One of these days. We'll be sitting at a café on the West Side and fans will hound us and the papers will take paparazzi shots of famous poet, famous actor, out getting drunk together—that'll be something, won't it?"

Yeah. And I look out the window, beyond the lights, looking out beyond the security fence and the dreary-looking park below, and there's a piece of the Queensborough Bridge and some part of Queens, and the East River before me, a dirty barge floating with the tide.

"It's time to go isn't it?" Emma said with a sad voice.

Oh my, someone had to say the words and she said them: It was time to go, time to pack our bags and leave and try somewhere else. No, I often told myself, *don't* leave New York yet, not so soon, not so soon after you had some measure of success. The city holds plenty for you still; don't overreact. Didn't I still love it? Yeah, the idea of it, but the living-day-to-day of it not as much. You're in a slump, Gil, I told myself. Another voice said: No you're not, dummy, you're riding high. This is as good as it's gotten. Why aren't you happy then? Well I was for a week, I think—the week after I got cast. And the day I met Rosemary Campbell was exciting. There have been moments—but not as good as you thought the moments would be, huh? Oh Emma, if only you hadn't pulled the thread: that it was time to go. I was being silent so I said: Yeah, I guess within the year or so I'll be moving out of old New York. I've been thinking that way lately.

But Emma stirred herself up in bed. "*Are you crazy?* Leave New York?"

I thought you said—

"Time to leave Bellevue, yes, but not New York! Gil *life* is New York, when one tires of New York, to paraphrase Samuel Johnson, one tires of life! What are you going to do? Go live in a cave in Illinois? Remember the Village People Principle . . ."

(Only Emma could hit Samuel Johnson and the Village People in a single stroke of rhetoric.) The Village People Principle is simply that New York functions at one level of sophistication, the country at another. Remember the Village People? This disco pop band of the late '70s. They dressed up in all the gay-stereotype uniforms (the leatherman, the hardhat) played in gay clubs, sang about San Francisco (the big gay city), sang about the YMCA (the big gay pickup place in smalltown America, and New York as well), and sang about being "In the Navy" (the gay magnet of the services). And the Navy and the YMCA were so delighted with the publicity they were thinking of using the hits (and they were big Top Ten hits, too) for commercials, and then . . . then slowly it dawned (after about three years) that this concerned . . . no, *homosexuals!* Now if you lived in New York, you spotted this from the first single. You see the rest of America, God's Country, being so dense and naïve (and then watch them fulminate and bluster when they catch on) and after a while you start thinking that the whole country is a backwater and you better never leave New York.

"I don't want to hear anti–New York talk from you ever again, young man!" Emma said, fully exercised now. The nurse came in a second later to run me out. "I *am* New York! Don't you forget that, buster!"

Did you know there was a subway—or rather, a mass transit train line—in Staten Island? You can't claim to have ridden them all if you haven't gone over and done that. Emma and I did, the weekend she got out of Bellevue before she went back to Indiana. Indiana lasted four weeks and then she was back in the city, coming up to my 96th Street apartment, and things rocked along. No, I didn't banish her from the door, no big scenes, no goodbye forever. I got out of my mood—it was a phase. Emma was my friend and New York was my city and the Theater was my livelihood—you forgive them their faults. There was one failing in myself, however, that was getting a little harder to overlook, and it took a production the next summer to convince me of it: I wasn't really all that talented.

1983

THE finest actress I met in New York was a co-star of mine, Reisa Goldbaum. Attractive (but not drop-dead beautiful) Jewish woman, early thirties, short thick body, blondish hair. I learned more about acting from her in two weeks than from anyone else ever. I even learned I wasn't cut out to be an actor.

"Gil," said Reisa, answering the door in her bathrobe. "I didn't expect to see you here tonight."

Her apartment was a fifth-story walk-up on First Avenue in the sixties. A box of a place, smartly decorated. I was imposing, it was 10:30 on a Monday night, but I had to talk to her.

"You want some coffee?"

She invited me in and I sat down on her sofa. Beside it on the coffeetable was the script for *Her Gentlest Touch*. She had surely memorized the thing by now, I thought, picking it up, thumbing through it while Reisa made coffee in the kitchen.

"Instant's all right, isn't it?"

Of course. Inside the script she had marked stresses, expressions, pauses, gestures. She was a real technician. Taking home her script each night and perfecting it, given the day's rehearsals. No director could improve on her self-discipline.

She started unsurely. "So, Greg tells me you're not in the show anymore, that you resigned."

True. I'm sorry, it's very unprofessional. But they're calling the actor they almost cast and they think he'll do it.

"They said . . ." She cleared her throat, setting down the coffee. "They said at rehearsal today that you thought you weren't good enough for the part and that I had something to do with your going away—"

That's why I had to come over and explain. I didn't want you to think it was because I couldn't work with you. It's simpler than that—you're too good for me, I can't match you up on that stage.

She laughed. "Pooh! Gil, you were excellent—just fine. You didn't have to go. Greg the director's in shock."

I was adequate. No more.

"*I'm* just adequate, after all," she said sitting down.

No Reisa. You are superb. (She tsk-tsked and waved this aside.) No, really. The fact you don't know it makes it all the more remarkable.

"I think you should reconsider, Gil," she said after a sip. "It's a thankless role, I know. I get to emote and carry on and have mad scenes and you're the patient husband—it's not much of a role, you just react to my acting. Thankless, really. If you're discouraged about it, it's mostly the script's fault."

Her Gentlest Touch was by Morton Handley. It was based on the story of Lydia Proctor, the New England minor poet, very Virginia Woolf-like, intense, neurotic, complicated, suicidal, and I played her young husband Philip who had to cope with her spells of madness and her misbehavior. Proctor's verse was intermingled with the playwright's re-creation—a very classy, erudite production that about a hundred people would appreciate and half of that would actually attend. The director told me: "Gil, I want to see his pain, his regrets at marrying her, his anguish in that he still loves her—dig waaaayyy down deep for this one," he went on. He spouted a lot of decades-old method acting stuff. "Think of a woman in your own life that was impossible, that was difficult and complicated and whom you loved, and maybe she loved you, but you would never *have* her completely! There'd always be a distance you'd never bridge!"

Well that was easy enough.

Philip Proctor had been a small businessman and he had failed in his own pursuits when his wife was getting published becoming mildly acclaimed in hers. So there was the added layer of self-doubt, of unsure talent to make Philip interesting. Sort of like me and acting. Philip, the sympathetic loser. Lydia, the brilliant exasperating neurotic, and, in the end, when she kills herself, a loser too. This wasn't exactly a cheery play.

I don't know, I said to Reisa, if you can understand. But all my life I've gotten by, I feel like a faker—

"Don't we all," she said, smiling, shrugging.

But this play is good and you make it great. I can't match you. I'm not in your league.

She didn't want to hear this. "Gil, I'm dime-a-dozen. I agree you may very well need a break, take some time off, but it's hardly a matter of me being better than you—"

I was laughing: But Reisa you're fantastic, you are!

She looked down in her cup. "Your résumé is ten times better than mine, you've been on Broadway—"

All of that is NOTHING. I can't turn in that kind of hard performance you're doing.

She shook her head. "You're making me blush."

I'll tell you why you're good. You know the scene where you find out your son is dead in the Korean War? And you make a decision to finish the letter you've begun to him, even though it's for nothing? And as you write the letter a poem evolves and you fight with it, wrestle with it, cursing fate, cursing God, and at the end when you arrive at the last line, you smile, smile deliriously. Your heart is breaking, your son is dead but you have wrested some solace, some ethereal arrangement of words from it—you're *great* there. That smile!

Reisa set her glass down and leaned forward. "Yes, I keep waiting for Greg to stop me, but that seemed right, that smile—"

Because it's not expected and it's a smile of triumph, but also of sadness and you communicate that, we're in your mind, we know it's not a happy or selfish smile.

"I worked at that scene," she said softly, almost afraid to give herself her own due. "It took forever to make myself happy with it—"

Reisa, don't you realize that I've never done anything like that in my life! I put on costumes! I fake accents, I imitate, I'm putzing around up there. But you *create*, you bring to life.

She was silent for a moment, then looked up calmly—no one had told her this before (stupid philistines!) and she was allowing herself to be unashamedly satisfied with her work.

It's not just being up there with you, Reisa. It's a lot of things—I'm losing my momentum for the theater. The joy's gone out of it for me—

"Gil it becomes a job after a while, all things do. So many days I don't want to come in, I want to call in sick—there are days I hate the theater."

But your gift will keep calling you back, will keep providing rewards I'll never know.

She touched my face, reaching across. "You go take your break, Gil Freeman. And you come back to New York and you get back on the stage and you knock us dead. There's more in you than you realize."

I just wanted to say thank you, I said, rising, making for the door. There've been nights I've found nothing good to say about the theater. A collection of human misfits and phoneys—

"I know, I've given this speech too."

—has-beens, washups, deluded nobodies . . . and then you see it done right, like when I watch you perform. And the theater is the greatest magic act in the world.

My agent Jerry was a sweetheart about my getting out of the play: "Gil, take it from me," said Jerry, putting down her file folder. "You need a break. You need a rest. You need out of New York. I've seen this and heard this before."

I'm sure I'll be fine, Jare. This talk has helped a lot.

Jerry studied me, not liking what she saw. "Let's get a hotdog, huh?" We left her office, away from the secretary, away from her sister, down to the bustle and noise of 48th Street, half a block from Times Square. We walked toward the commotion, in search of a hotdog vendor.

"How long you been doing this?"

Almost ten years, Jerry.

"And how long have you been away, like back to your hometown?"

A few weeks here and there, Christmas, Thanksgiving sometimes, an occasional pop home in the spring. I'm not big on Oak Park, Jerry—my parents weren't encouraging about my being an actor and now that I'm working . . . (It seemed vain to talk at the moment of my working, as I was trying to get out of a part in a play and causing my agent loads of grief) . . . now that I'm getting my name in the papers, I hate the idea of going home and pretending nothing has happened, as if I don't resent them for not supporting me—

"Your parents are normal human beings, Gil. Forgive them for that. They're probably dying to make it up with you. *Dying* being the operative word—parents die, you know. Get the shit worked out so there'll be no regrets. Trust me on that."

(Jerry and her sister Janie lived together, ran their agency, talked daily to Mother on the phone—a real close family that didn't seem able to admit any new members. Family was one of Jerry's big things.)

"What if I got you in a tour? There are five or six musicals with light singing roles making the rounds this summer. *Grease*, there's a *Hello Dolly!* touring with Donna Lundsford, *'59 Mustang*, *Fiddler on the Roof* is getting trotted out again—"

You mean go on the road? Me?

"You know, as a break. No starring role—chorus stuff, easy stuff. Big casts, lots of drinking, lots of screwing around, put in your three hours each night, see the country."

I'll think about it. Sounds good. We had walked into Times Square, the one place in New York that's never dull, never still, never closed. When you imagine Broadway, you imagine this spot, the blinking lights, the sleaze and sex shows next to family soda fountains and souvenir stores (PUT YOUR NAME IN HEADLINES!!), tattoo parlors, take-out sushi, Thai boxing taught here . . . a New York in miniature. Jerry stopped before a vendor and ordered two hotdogs.

"I don't know what went wrong with *Her Gentlest Touch*, Gil. I thought that part was made for you. It's not as if you've had tons of leading roles, either."

It was perfect for me. As perfect a role as I ever had.

"Can I ask you a question—a personal question?"

Sure. Mustard on mine, please.

"Thanks," Jerry said, handing the vendor the money, leading us away toward the traffic island in the center of the square. "Are you unhappy because you're not on Broadway anymore? I know *Mother's Day* was big-time and this off-Broadway deal may seem small-time to you—"

No, that's not it, Jerry.

"It's hard to come down off the mountain, but it's not always Broadway in this business, you know? I gotta little girl who did the youngest daughter in *Family, Family*, got on the cast album and everything—she's in Staten Island doing the umpteenth local *Sound of Music*, 'doe a deer, a female deer'—that old shtick. Staten Island. You don't get to Broadway every year."

I know that.

"If you love the theater and it's in your blood, it doesn't matter if it's Peoria. Can you play Peoria, Gil?"

(Jerry, that's nice talk, that's real pretty talk. But neither I, nor most of my fellow actors, wants Peoria, wants Staten Island, wants Queens. I guess I *was* spoiled, by the salary, by the perks. When Rosemary was in her last week, we had limos pick us up to take us to the theater, a gesture from the producer. And now I was back in Chelsea, small struggling theater, good cast, good play, working at a five-week run, a smattering of an audience, with—if we're lucky—a few mentions in the press, a spare paragraph or two. Some part of me didn't want to be back there. But, as Jerry explained, it was a step up, to a leading role.) I don't know, I said to Jerry, doing her the justice of not pretending to be better than I was. I need some time to sort out this theatrical career of mine. I need to come to grips with Peoria.

In the meantime I told Jerry to put me down for the road show auditions, male stuff.

I think half of moving out of New York is running around telling people you're leaving, getting used to the idea yourself. I decided to start with Janet. I got on the PATH train to Jersey, and as I walked up the street where she lived I thought to myself: What does Janet care you're going? You and Janet have never been close. To her, you've always been Emma's friend. You never got past the surface with her, this black lesbian separatist with a chip on her shoulder a lot of the time. She's now living with this redheaded sportswriter. Another white girl. Wonder why it is all of Janet's girlfriends have been white, most of her friends are white? You could never ask something like that. All you've got in common is Emma, and ten years of New York, being aware of each other on the sidelines.

"You better come back," said Janet, after coffee, seeing me to the door. "There are not many of us originals left. Come back and help us keep the East Village and Hoboken the proletariat slum we've come to know and love." Good old Janet. That woman could wrench the political sentiment out of day-to-day life like no one else.

I'll be back, I said. I'm just leaving for a short break.

Janet squinted at me. "You sure you'll be back? A lot of people say they'll be back and they don't get back."

SURE. I'll be back in New York before you know it. I just have to see home for a little while, catch up with some people, I have a friend Sophie out there in Evanston, I'll see Mom and Dad. Very few people in New York have moms and dads of course, and I watched Janet's eyes glaze over as I mentioned them. We transplanted New Yorkers all were hatched somewhere near Central Park.

"Great dyke scene north of town in Chicago, I hear," said Janet. And there was a goodbye pause. A last burst of nostalgia ensued:

Remember that snapshot I took of Janet, Gay Rights Day parade (which they tried to drag me to and I received abuse for not going), Janet's big Angela Davis afro, medallions, black power badges, lesbian protest T-shirts? Remember Susan's party for the resignation of Nixon? Remember that trip out to the Hamptons with Janet's girlfriend, that rich heiress Jewish American Princess who ended up fighting with Janet about whether she flirted with the woman at the gas station? Do you remember the dinner Emma and everyone made where Lisa forgot to put whatever it was in the pumpkin pie and it turned out liquid?

"Honey that was *nothing*: Do you remember how the turkey had been in the oven all day and Emma was so busy running us out of the kitchen and being Miss Head Bitch that she forgot to turn the oven on! The *last* Thanksgiving dinner with Emma—or so I swore at the time."

Oh god, next Thanksgiving we ought to have a reunion of that comedy show.

"You're right, we really should," she said laughing, remembering no doubt Emma being useless in the kitchen, getting drunk, wearing this dumb homemade black construction-paper Pilgrim's hat. "Oh god that was funny—yes, yes, we'll have that reunion. I'll get on it right away."

It never happened—those things never do happen—but we ended laughing, Janet and I, and I felt warm walking down the stairs on my way home, warm and a little sad.

Peoria wasn't all that was wrong. The last few years I felt as if I had been given a vision of how I didn't want to end up:

Rosemary Campbell, success. Success at the cost of her humanity. Tucker Broome, washup. A life alone in the theater, the bottle for your friend. Charity Glenn, fame addict. She was someone once and now she can't live without it again, she'll give her life to win that moment of glory back, in cheap TV, in second-rate projects, she just can't let go, just can't walk away. There were the heroes too, weren't there? Bonnie McHenry and Joyce Jennings? Neither were married, both went home alone, a little drink before bed maybe, a little late-night TV. No, true, they're not unhappy housewives in the suburbs but can you be so sure they're not making the best of a lot they found themselves stuck with? Where do you end up, Gil? Bit parts until you're sixty-five? Retire to one of those old showmen's homes, old actors, sit with the music-hall leftovers reminiscing about the good times before visitor's hour in the solarium? And who's going to come visit you? I made a mistake somewhere, didn't I? Emma's got me spooked. If you have a long-term relationship with a good considerate woman, maybe even marry her, have kids—that's Suburban Death, it's average and normal (Emma's worst condemnations). It doesn't have to be. Ninety-nine % of humanity has thought love and constancy and children were a pretty good idea, why did I listen so much to Emma Gennaro who was competing for flakiness with the late '70s?

On the other hand, I know exactly why I listened to her. I had been in love with her.

"So you're going to go on a road-show tour, huh?" said Emma. "I bet, knowing showpeople, that'll be one long orgy."

I hope so.

"What is this city going to do without us? Can it survive without one of us here?"

That's another thing. Emma, Miss I'll Never Leave New York herself, was leaving New York. She had applied to Stanford's program for creative writing, sent in her book, they had given her some money, and she was going to do it, Emma in the Golden Land.

"Stanford's got this grad accommodation *mobile home park*, Gil," she said gleefully, looking over her forms and folders and questionnaires they sent. "I see volleyball parties with Emma at the net. I see surfing, I see becoming a hippie. I see barbecues every night, I see eighteen-year-old California beach bunnies pouring out their hearts to Mother Emma, 'Todd doesn't love me anymore . . .' "

I thought you hated barbecues. The suburban connection.

"Well, we might as well both be suburban since you're going back to sink into the abyss with that Sophie woman."

And that was one more thing. If I took a break in the Midwest, I at least had a place to stay. Sophie had been to New York twice since I saw Emma at Bellevue, she had even bought a book of Emma's poems. "One complicated young lady," said Sophie, smiling, putting down the book when she'd finished. The book purchase had softened Emma's smear campaign for a few months but she was back in force again.

"Don't marry that girl, Gil. It'll be Jim and Lisa all over again. Marriage leads to misery!"

Speaking of Lisa, I got another party invitation.

"Me too. Another advertising party, ooooooh boy."

We oughta go, you know. Tell Lisa we're leaving. Emma had seen lots less of Lisa than I had, so she was squirming uncomfortably. C'mon Emma, you can play with Lisa's little girl.

"All those advertising yucks—I can't take it. And we shouldn't tell Lisa we're leaving town at a party. I guess we'd better invite her out."

Which we did. Down to the Village to the Café Prato near Carmine Street. Emma and I staked out a booth inside, ordered cappuccinos, Emma insisting on a plate of fries.

"I can't believe I'm almost thirty, Gil."

Gonna tell me your birthday at long last?

"Nope," she said munching fries. "But I'll be in California for it. Hurling myself off the cliffs of Big Sur." She laughed. "I really don't care about turning thirty. I feel my twenties were a write-off, but I'm going to get my thirties correct."

You met ME in your twenties.

"Oops sorry. You know what I mean. Have a fry."

Why don't you offer them before you goop them all up in steak sauce?

"Because you'd eat them all—ah, I see Lisa and progeny . . ."

In came Lisa, slipping in the booth across from Emma and me.

"God this has been forever!" she said, setting her daughter down to her side on the booth. "It's been years since I've been here. You remember Gil, your first day in town?"

It has crossed my mind.

"I associate this place with fierce nicotine fits—remember?" Lisa looked as good as we'd seen her in years, freer, more relaxed. "I thought I'd *never* quit smoking, particularly living with Emma the smokestack—we'd get each other chain-smoking pack after pack down here, remember?"

Yeah, we said, hoping to keep nostalgia at a minimum.

"But I did quit," Lisa added, ruffling her little girl's white-blond hair. "I quit when I got pregnant, for *you*, didn't I honey?"

We have some news, I began.

"Just a minute . . ." Lisa's daughter had squirmed under the table and was now in the aisle, threatening to topple a waitress. "Honey, you get in here, you . . ." Daughter, giggling, ran down the aisle. "I said come here. Come here. Look young lady . . ." She used her last-straw voice: "NOW." Daughter came running, Lisa scooped her up and set her firmly beside her. "Just sit right here and don't get into that . . ." Lisa moved the steak sauce out of reach.

"Yeah we had to come here one more time," Emma said, hoping to open up the discussion of our departures.

But Lisa had plenty to talk about. Jim, mostly. She spoke in a serious adult tone so as not to interest her three-year-old.

"So I was right, there was someone else," said Lisa. "Some copywriter at J. Walter Thompson. I mean, not that I blame him in a way, I've been a holy bitch to live with. But still. Anyway Jim and I talked it over and we don't want to get a divorce, at least not right away. So we're going to separate and see how that works for a while—I said PUT THAT DOWN, now . . . oh honey, look what you've done . . ." Lisa quickly whisked a few napkins from the dispenser and dipped it in her ice water and dabbed her daughter's dress now streaked with mustard. "I swear, would you . . . oh, honey, please just sit there, can you do that for Mommy?" Then back to us, continuing about her marriage's failure in an even and almost businesslike tone: "So anyway, I'm going to leave McKendrick Advertising, and go elsewhere. I've started sending out résumés. It would be too weird to be there at work with him every day—that may have been the problem anyway, seeing too much of each other."

Why doesn't he quit *his* job at McKendrick, I asked.

"He was there first. I've been there five years, he's been there seven, his salary is higher, he has a future there, and I don't think I do. I mean, it's reasonable, very reasonable that I should leave—we're in agreement on that. And I want a change anyway. But we're not telling people that we're splitting up, as that might reflect on Jim or me and gossip in the advert biz is so bad, and we just want to be above that, you know?"

Yeah sure, I said. Emma was untypically saying nothing.

"So we're having this party. This party for all the people and I'll announce that I'm leaving to stay home with my kid or something, and people won't think we're splitting up. It's important that people aren't running around talking about your private life. So we're giving this party. *Please*, I want you both to come. It would mean a lot to me."

Uh Lisa, she's in the salt now—

"Oh damn it . . . young lady I swear I . . . Would you look at what you have done?" Lisa gathered the pile of salt from the unscrewed saltshaker and swept it with a napkin into the ashtray. Lisa gave a light pop to her daughter's hand as she reached for something else and before she began to bawl, Lisa snatched her up and said, "NO, not a word out of you, we're going to pick out an Italian pastry now, all right? You want one, don't you? Here we go . . " She picked up her daughter and went up to the lunch counter, out of earshot.

Emma turned to me. "I don't know this woman, do I? Do you know her? I don't know her."

Now Emma. She's got it rough and she's happy to be with us.

"Yeah, talk good ol' Gil and Emma's ears off when things go bad. I don't want to hear about her rotten husband when she doesn't call us but . . . what? Four times last year?"

She's a working mother and she came to see you in the hospital, and she invites us to parties and things—

"Those godawful advertising parties, no thanks, no thanks—"

Sssssh, she's coming back.

"So, anyway," said Lisa sliding into the booth, her daughter still in the aisle, "that's that. We may reconcile, but you know . . . this is terrible, but I *want* to be single again. Not to date or anything, I mean, I've had enough of that. I mean to be by myself. I'm looking forward to getting out from under things. I want to start up my painting again. Remember? I was going to be an artist. Now I have lots more connections at galleries than I did. I mean, I didn't know anything the first time around—it was real amateur hour, you know? Here," she said patting her daughter, "go sit with Aunt Emma." Emma loved to hold the kid and bounced her on her lap, amusing her.

Painting, I said to say something, sounds good.

"So how are you two for roommates? Temporary, perhaps? Hmm? Anyone want a tenant?" Lisa laughed, grinning.

"Uh, gee," began Emma.

There's something we gotta tell you, Lisa.

"Yeah," said Emma, as it was her news: "I'm leaving New York, it seems. For my mental health." As Lisa was looking stunned, Emma went on, stroking Lisa's daughter's white-blond hair gently. "I think I've had enough. It's time to go. I've gotten my book of poems published with the Women's Consortium Press and I can publish there again if I want. And so I applied to the Stanford Program for Creative Writing and they accepted me, because of my book of poems. And it will mean—I don't know—lots of opportunities and things, connections—"

Lisa looked shell-shocked, but said, "Yeah, that's just so great, Emma, that really is nice."

"And so I'm California-bound, this Tuesday. Term starts next week and I'm pretty moved out and packed and—"

"California," Lisa said numbly.

Everyone's clearing out, I said absently.

"Oh my," Lisa sighed. And then it looked like she was going . . . going to cry, for pete's sake. She shielded her eyes and her voice got thick as she said, "Well doesn't that beat all?"

Emma and I exchanged glances and Emma immediately scooped up Lisa's little girl and announced that they were going across the street for candy, and as Emma left she gave me a nervous look. In a moment it was just myself and Lisa, who began to cry, noiselessly, tears trickling down her face. Lisa, I asked helplessly, what is it?

"Oh nothing, I'm so sorry, this is stupid—"

You're under a lot of pressure, a new job hunt and Jim and—

"No it has nothing to do with Jim . . . Jim the asshole," she added, making herself laugh through her tears. She got a bunch of napkins and blew her nose, wiped her face. "I'm sorry, I really am—this is not what I wanted to do . . ."

Lisa, what is it? Something I can do?

She looked up at last, red-eyed. "You know, I had counted on something I shouldn't have counted on, I guess. I thought we could all . . . oh god, how stupid, I'm sorry—"

What is it?

"I thought we, like, could all get a house again. I'm richer now. We could go back to the Village where we started, get a decent loft. The three of us. I've been thinking lately how that was when I was happy. When it was just us three. Now we had a good time didn't we?"

Some great times there, yes—

"So you see, I thought, thank god, there's Emma and Gil and we can get back to what we used to be—plus one, of course, my daughter. I thought that would be so good . . ." And she teared up again, shaking her head, apologizing.

I decided to finish out our bad news by telling Lisa about my four-month tour with *'59 Mustang*. I went on about it a bit, good career move, I'll get some time off, etc.

"Congratulations," she sniffed, smiling. "That won so many awards."

Yeah the touring company ought to do real well. Pay is good. I even get to go back to my hometown, well, Chicago I mean. My agent sent a picture of me to the *Sun Times* and some lady is going to do an interview with me, local boy made good, all that.

"Yeah you've made it, you've really made it."

Oh Lisa, I wanted to say, a chorus-guy with a few lines in a touring company, a four-month hell of bad motels and hick-town dates, no, no that was not making it.

"Well you'll write, won't you? *We'll* write."

Yeah, yeah sure. Letters from the road—that'll be fun. And you have to keep New York alive and well for me, save my place . . .

"Of course," she laughed, and we laughed and laughed some more and the tears seemed behind her, and for that matter, so did our good times and our youthful past, because there we were talking about writing letters, for christ's sake, which I've never been worth a damn at. Oh we're not going to write letters—who are we kidding? Chapters in life end and when they end they feel like this.

"Now when you get back to town," said Lisa, after blowing her nose again, "you look me up. Maybe we can get Emma to come back to visit and then seduce her into staying."

You know how hard Emma is to seduce, I said. And we laughed at the joke, Emma and her celibacy, still going strong.

She smiled and said something so unexpected from a beaming

face: "I am so sad. I really counted on us doing it all again, things being like they were. That would have made me so happy." Then she gripped my arm, telling me something that seemed to fight its way to the surface to be communicated: "I was as happy as I ever was with you and Emma. Sometimes I think back and go, girl, that was the good stuff, that was your wild time."

Well, I said, maybe taking a wrong tack, we think that *now*. At the time I remember us being miserable and complaining and—

"No, I'm sure about this one. That was the best it ever was. That was the real good time."

And if you can believe this, we actually went to this party of hers and Jim's. We were curt with Jim. We schmoozed halfheartedly among the advertising elite. There was the little announcement that Lisa was leaving McKendrick to stay home and watch over her little girl and everyone awwwwwwed, genuinely insincere about seeing her go, everyone wished her luck, piled on encouragement, love and hugs and kisses. (You never saw so much phoneyness in your life.)

"They're happy to see someone more talented than they are leaving the firm," Emma said, beside me on the sofa, our party-watching post. "I'll give Jim this. The man has a nice apartment. Stocked bar, a VCR. Forget Lisa, *I'll* reconcile with the jerk."

You're going to have to say a proper farewell to Lisa, I reminded Emma.

"Oh yeah? I'll sneak out. It's just better to finish it off, cut it short, turn and run."

Yeah but . . .

"But what? I know what you're going to say, that it's unlikely I'll see her again for a long while, but that's all the more reason not to carry on and get dramatic. I don't *do* goodbyes. I don't."

What about when it comes time to say goodbye to me?

Emma looked at me and we made one of those terrifying eye contacts that chilled us, melted us. "Well now, let's not think about that one," and then Emma got up in search of more refreshments, and I watched her. It sounds like I still love her to say this, but there was never anyone who took up space quite like she did. She moved so gawkily, so awkwardly, almost stumbling toward the refreshment table, all elbows and wild gestures . . . and yet it was all perfect, completely consistent. And her voice, lilting and unendingly cynical, all sentences musically soaring to great heights always to end up with a big punchline delivered in a cynical alto. She was nasal and could whine and sing her complaints and—how do I explain this?—if anyone else carped and carried on like she did without that face, that tone of voice, those gestures, well it wouldn't work, it would be intolerable. On occasions like this I had to remind myself just how much I was not in love with her. But indeed I wasn't.

"Well, I don't understand why everyone's so down on nuclear war," I heard her say, standing in a foursome of ad people. "I mean, god, the whole business in Beirut—let's put Lebanon out of the world's misery, there'll be no more massacred peacekeeping forces, no more hostages. Drop the bombs. You Reagan fans promised me this man was gonna drop bombs, and I wanna see some fireworks."

Her foursome was amused, everyone laughed, suggesting a few other places nuclear bombs ought to be dropped: Iran, Cuba, Libya, New Jersey.

"I've said it for years," Emma went on, "there's a chic to post-apocalypse; it's not gonna be so bad after it all blows over—"

"If you survive," said one woman.

"Oh it's gonna take much more'n that to get rid of Emma, I tell you," said Emma. "Reagan's a complete disappointment to me. You know I vote for entertainment value and frankly I'm surprised to find the man becoming a cult hero, popular. I thought he would be impeached by now. The damn country's picking up it seems. You just wait, though. When it starts falling apart it's gonna make great viewing."

One woman said through a whiny laugh, "You really vote for entertainment value?"

"Absolutely. So does America, only it doesn't realize it yet."

Emma and her new admirers even got onto John Kennedy and I thought, oh boy, here we go again, it's all over now, but she had 'em in the aisles, she was a hit—trashing Kennedy, sticking up for Nixon, her Antichrist theory of Ronald Reagan, advocacy of nuclear war, her radical reforms of New York City government, why half of what's in the Museum of Modern Art should be burned, a defense of the worst TV shows in the world . . . She was a Constant—this occurred to me as I think it never had. An unbending Force in the Cosmos. After Emma I've limited my crushes and romances to human beings, and it's behind me, my days of falling in love with Forces in the Cosmos. But you can't blame a guy for trying.

Emma did cut out early on Lisa's party, shirking goodbye duties. That should have tipped me off that she might do the same with me, and I shouldn't have been too surprised, on the Saturday before Emma left New York, to hear this from her on my answering machine:

BEEP! *Well Gil, this is goodbye. I can't see you. What am I going to say after nearly a decade, huh? 'Well, it's been fun!' I mean, c'mon, let's not do corny maudlin things we'll both one day regret . . .*

By god, Gennaro, I'm having my soppy goodbye and no one is going to take it away from me!

So anyway, so long Gilbert. It's been fun. Ha ha ha. I'll write of course and we'll visit and it will be as if I never left, right? Hey, there's long distance, you know me and long-distance bills—I think nothing of racking up the big numbers. Then, a pause. Well come on, come on, say you love me Emma. *Bye-bye kid.* CLICK.

No, Emma, no.

I got my coat and went over to 10th Street and pushed her buzzer. I pushed it again. Nothing. I waited until someone in the building came in and let me through the door and I went up to her apartment, where I heard shuffling from within. I tried the door and it was open. If she heard my voice in the stairwell thanking the person for letting me in, she hadn't made it to lock the door in time. I walked inside and all was bare, in packing boxes, in big yard-size trash bags. Oh what emptiness, the abandoned apartment of a friend, those second homes. She was gone. I went into the kitchen, and then to the bathroom . . . WAIT. Her toothbrush and stuff were still there . . . then I heard a tinkling in the closet of coathangers jingling against each other. I went to the door of the closet and tore it open in a sudden gesture.

"Fucking coathangers," said Emma, crouched down in the closet.

WHAT IS YOUR PROBLEM NOW EMMA GENNARO?

"It's for your own good I left you that message. You weren't supposed to come over here. You were supposed to curse my name and forget me."

Would you please give it a break? We have, I informed her, a good 48 hours until you leave for California. We are going to spend it together.

Emma pouted, now standing in the closet. "Go away from me, young boy. I'm no good for you. Your life is elsewhere . . ."

Would you cut this out?

She stepped out of the closet. "I can't deal with goodbyes. And lately . . . oh Gil, I have this plan that came into my head and it's REALLY BAD, I mean EXTRA even-crazy-for-me BAD . . ."

What is it?

"I gotta leave town before I talk myself into going through with my new project."

At that point I could have been persuaded to come back to New York, so I said I hoped she did stay; I'd help her do whatever she wanted short of robbing a bank. She smiled briefly, ironically, and said I'd be sorry I volunteered. We're not gonna kidnap Lisa's daughter are we?

Emma was quiet a moment. "I don't want to commit myself or rule out any options."

I insisted on our final goodbye and Emma conceded to spending Sunday afternoon with me. And Monday, your last night?

"No, I got something I have to do," she said.

I made her swear endless allegiance, no tricks, cross her heart and hope to die. And so I puttered around Manhattan, tried to interest myself in shops and records and a copy of *Backstage.* I sat having coffee in McDonald's looking through Backstage. MY MY, how that little rag still gets to me—it is a listing of cruelty, a roster of hopes one in a thousand can expect to make real. Maybe ten good parts a month pop up in that newspaper and there are probably 50,000 actors who get the gleam in their eye and have their hearts beat faster and suddenly see it all work out, every dream, every ambition. I sat there and read the openings and I shook my head—I hope not to look at you for a good six months, *Backstage.* And I thought to myself once again, maybe this business is for the Reisa Goldbaums, the real talents.

I started enjoying my swan song. I went to the East Village to look up old monuments. The Ruizes' Caribbean Foodstore was gone, the whole block had gone to developers. It would be another few years before they could drive everyone out. Even the East Village—who would have thought it? Eight hundred dollars a month on Avenue D! Impossible. And now there's a chain jeans store near St. Mark's, the streetcrowd is increasingly white yuppie, striped shirts with beige shorts, very frat boy . . . There goes the neighborhood. They won't be happy, Mayor Koch, the Reaganites, half a dozen landlords I could name, they won't be happy until every bohemian, every *real person*, is off the island, will they? Maybe one day Manhattan can be the tasteless condominiumized suburbs people used to flee to. Ah, I'm out of town—it's not my fight anymore.

Slut Doll is gone, no use looking up Betsy, Nicholas at the Soho was his usual bland self, Joyce Jennings welcomed me with open arms at the Venice ("Of course you'll be back!") and here's old you'll-never-make-it-in-this-town himself, Dewey Dennis:

"Well, saw you in the big show last year, my boy—always knew it! Always knew you'd pull it out. Aren't you glad I chucked you out the door so you could go on to fame and fortune, ahahahaha! You were always good, Gil. Damn good. Come and audition for us next fall, I think there's something for you here . . ."

All is fair in the theater world: I shook his hand and wished him well and meant it (the schmuck . . .).

And Bonnie McHenry fit me in for drinks one afternoon at the St. Regis, which was kind. Oh she'd remember me, sorry it didn't swork out with Odessa, wasn't that a time we had in *Bermuda Triangle*, she'd never forget me, John. I didn't even want to trouble that grand beautiful perfected stage smile of hers by telling her it was Gil, not John. And so the summer ended and it became cooler and approached October, and I went by a few old landmarks and let the fall breeze blow through me; I would stand on the Staten Island ferry, looking out at the harbor, and feel the finality of a number of things. It was time to go.

Let's not pretend I'm superhuman. On-again off-again work is very wearing, very insecure-making. I've proven I'm not a wimp, I've proven I can take it—I've survived most everything. But I wouldn't mind putting my feet up for a while, and giving my endurance-survival faculties a break. I don't want to be begging Jerry and Janie for work in barn-dinner-theater Rodgers and Hammerstein revivals through my thirties. At twenty-three that's adventure, at twenty-seven that's a richly lived life, at thirty that's suicide-inducing.

But, I'm telling you, it's truly difficult to leave the stage. For so long people ask, friends call up: What are you up to? And you tell them I'm mad this week because I'm Hamlet, or I'm drunk and homosexual this week because I'm Brick in *Cat on a Hot Tin Roof*, and next month I'll be nobody at all in an evening of Beckett pieces. Then one day you put all those people away, all the masks, all the gestures and reserves of carefully processed emotion, and people ask you what role are you working on this month . . . and for once it's your own life, the hardest role of the bunch. You gotta say the lines with a straight face. I was not a great actor. For me acting was pretending I was someone; learn the accent, develop a little shtick, put on the makeup, use every trick I knew and half the time you'd believe I was who I said I was. But you look at a Reisa Goldbaum, someone with a natural gift, and you see that she can reach down into a deep and rich humanity and draw up a true-to-life Williams heroine, a Greek tragic figure, an Ophelia, a Neil Simon one-liner queen. I put on the trappings, she had it in her heart. There was only one role in my heart, only one in my repertoire that could draw upon everything I had, only one I could pull off, in New York or goddam Peoria: myself. I think it was time I dusted off Gilbert Anthony Freeman, gave him a limited run. Let's see if the show can last.

But first, a few Saturday night goodbye calls:

"Oh my god, it's Gil, it's Gilbert Freeman!" screamed Valene in a little girl voice, like a teenybopper. "Can we have your autograph? Oh pleeeease," and then she fell into giggling.

"Come here," said Mrs. Jackson, preparing to give me a hug. "Now look here on my cash register. You know how I hate junk on my cash register so I wouldn't put this here if I didn't want it here, 'cause you know how I hate junk on my cash register . . ." Mrs. Jackson had cut out the *Daily News* review and taped it to her cash register; my name was underlined. "Good to see ya, darlin'. You come back to talk to all the little people—"

No, no, you're the Big People, I promise.

"You want your breakfast special with the runny eggs?" said Mrs. Jackson. "On the house, on the house, sit down there . . . Valene get that pot for me, it's gonna burn the coffee."

Mr. Jackson dashed from the kitchen, patting me on the shoulder as he passed, "Well well Mr. Broadway star, come back to see us later on tonight, huh?"

Yes I—

"Sorry, gotta go, son. Gotta run get some butter."

Mrs. Jackson explained as he ran out the door that the refrigerator was working about half the time and no one could get a repairman. She dealt with a small line of customers.

"Here's your breakfast. I 'spect my usual 200% tip now, remember." Valene set the plate down and was about to fly off to another order.

I'm leaving town for a while Valene. I'm sort of saying goodbye.

"Goin' to Hollywood?"

No, just on tour with a play—

"Sorry honey, gotta get this order . . ." And she was off to do her job. It was a busy night. It came to me: New York will go on without me. It will not stop. It will continue to pulse and struggle and live and breathe through the nights, like Jackson's, open 24 hours a day, a world of noise and new faces and new characters and new things to talk about and not a helluva lot of time for nostalgia and maybe no time at all for people who thought they ought to move elsewhere.

"Here's some more coffee, Gil," said Valene, swishing by. "I see you're thinking and staring out into space again. You must be thinkin' 'bout my BIG TIP." And then she ran to the call of another customer.

Valene's benediction: "You gonna miss this breakfast special, Gilbert. I know they can't do that right in Chicago."

Valene, wherever you are, when people ask me what I miss most about New York, I always say: Jackson's Diner, 54th Street, the $1.99 breakfast special. And that is no joke.

Then it was Sunday, the official goodbye-to-Emma day. I decided I would take a morning walk on what looked to be an Indian summer morning, a final stroll around the Brooklyn of our lost journals and memories.

I started at the Heights, the tree-lined streets and rich people sleeping in late, and then after a lengthy sit on the Promenade to look at Lower Manhattan, the hundreds of skyscrapers, the nameless buildings for the nameless jobs, those still-miraculous bridges spanning the East River, I moved on to our old stomping grounds, South Brooklyn. Someone was in our old apartment. There was an out-of-season snowflake taped to the window, a family with a child was there now. I had heard somewhere that Sal's had changed hands so I didn't go in search of it for fear of seeing it yuppified into a Parisian café or worse, torn down —no, it will remain in memory forever serving up the Earlybird Special, an infinity of 4 a.m.'s strung together by late-night chatter, waitress laughter, the aroma and sounds of the sizzling grill, frozen in that blue fluorescent glow. I walk along to the Flatbush Avenue Extension and the city within the city is awakening—there's a man by the pay phones talking loudly, attracting attention: "You put down my name . . . you put it on the books right now, yessir . . ." He clutched a beer can in a sodden brown paper bag. He was fortyish, in a T-shirt, Cuban, I think. "Lester T. Maron, M-A-R-O-N—you put it down because I'm going to kill the son of a bitch. I'm an honest man,

I'm telling you . . ." Then a police car pulled up; the crowd, me included, stepped back. "Now Lester," began the officer, getting out of the patrol car. "You know you're not going to kill him, we been through this before . . ." Lester struck a noble pose: "Lester T. Maron, M-A-R-O-N, and I'm just telling you before I do it . . ." Harmless, after all. I walk on to the Donut House (one of a million on Flatbush, the doughnut capital of America, I bet). I order a coffee regular—the nectar of the gods! dispensing that sweet, taut fix on the morning—and a crumbly cake doughnut and the Haitian proprietor brings it to me: "Halloo my friend," followed by this unreally white smile. His relatives are already spreading blankets on the sidewalk out front, an array of homemade trinkets, jewelry, Caribbean wood statues, incense, a few Christian relics, a little voodoo. Two young boys, ebony black, all arms and legs, crouch in the morning sun as the noise of the street gains strength, a loud radio plays to their side, an island beat—zouk music, there's an LP for sale on the blanket. "Skashah the beegest theeng in Haiti meester," said one boy, all smiles, all hope for a purchase. "Used record cheap for you." Five bucks. Okay, sure. Now I'm walking down Flatbush with a Haitian record under my arm, past the Chinese laundry, past the Greek coffee shop next to the Korean fruit stand—three hours in Brooklyn and you touch the world!—and I stop in Franco's Pizza for a cold drink—it's 110 degrees in there, the ovens are going. "They say it's getting hotter every year," said the old man in the tomato-smudged white pizza-man suit behind the counter. He brings my Coke in a big Pepsi cup. "Them damn spray cans, those antiperspirants, that's what's doing it," added the man. "Hey Willie," he went on, talking to the man in the postman's uniform, dumping salt on a slice of pizza. "Watch it with that salt, it'll raise your blood pressure." Willie chuckled: "If I thought it'd raise something else, I'd put it on that too!" The old men laugh. Ah Brooklyn, you eat, you drink, you sweat, you wither poor fragile, neurotic Manhattan across the river. And now I'm rounding back to the subway, back to my Upper West Side tastefully decorated apartment with the gray carpet that matches the walls, my mauve bedroom. Church is out in Park Slope. I see a black woman walking with her tiny six-year-old son in his robin's-egg blue three-piece suit. Mother is tremendous, rocking back and forth as they walk home from the service, a great maternal hulking form that has no doubt been racked by all the injustice and loneliness the American city can provide, but look at that walk, look at the head unbowed—does she know a white-boy transient from the Midwest considers her the bedrock of this nation? She walks on holding that little boy's hand in her orange-pink Sunday dress with yellow lacy trim and a big white spring-garden hat with plastic marigolds affixed. You better leave your Fifth Avenue sense of fashion and sophisticated eye back in Manhattan where it belongs, because in Brooklyn my friend, it will prevent you from seeing the human heart.

Bye-bye, Brooklyn.

"Is booze gonna make this worse or better?" said Emma, after I arrived at her empty apartment on Sunday afternoon.

Worse, I said, if we get drunk. But one drink would be good.

"I have the dregs of five bottles to finish up, that's why I ask," she said, going over to a packing box on top of which five bottles stood. "How about a Kahlúa and Curaçao, hm?"

I think we can do without vomiting on our last day together.

"Could be symbolic," she sang.

We drank a mixture of peppermint schnapps and Kahlúa and a touch of Grand Marnier . . . in Emma's leftover skim milk. It took you ten years, I said to her, but it seems you finally mixed a halfway good-tasting drink.

"It's not bad at all," she said between sips.

Do you remember that Bicentennial beach trip and all the—

"Aaiii!" she screamed, plugging her ears. "We agreed. No nostalgia, no looking back. Just the future, just progress and new directions. Today we're going to keep the level of conversation to Soviet work slogans, okay?"

Okay.

"I should tell you what I almost was going to do."

This is your stay-in-New-York plan?

"Well part of it. I should tell you . . . no, let's save it, save it for wherever we're going." She looked to the window and outside it was gray and overcast but not rainy. "What happened to the sun? It was nice earlier."

City Island again, I suggested.

"Been there. We've never gone . . . shit, where's the subway map?" She got up to poke through a box full of odds and ends. "There's two subway lines we didn't do. The A line all the way out to Rockaway Park and that C extension thing."

I liked the C. We'd never ridden on the C.

"They're both out on the same line really, out to Far Rockaway."

Nope, never did go there, I said.

"Let's do that. That'll take the day. And I want to see the Atlantic. Later next week I'll see the Pacific and that will seem very strange."

Maybe there's a poem in there somewhere.

"Yes," said Emma facetiously, "to be included in my next collection, Emma's Ocean Poems. *Behold the sea / It is so green . . .*"

Sorry I said anything.

And out the door we went, Emma composing doggerel sea poems:

"*Let us go down to the sea in subways*—yes, we see here Gennaro reflecting modern technology in the form of the epic —*Let us go down on ships in the sea* . . . no, *Let us go down on men in ships . . .*"

Where does that come from, I asked. What you're making fun of?

"No one has ever known. An obscure psalm by Carl Sandburg."

I should end this here and say we never got to Far Rockaway. I should be clever and literary and say the line was shut down and we had ridden all the trains in the New York City subway system but the C, and hence we never never got to Far Rockaway, and (swelling strings:) life was like that too, was it not? So often in this world you don't get to that place that sounds so beautiful, seems as if it would be paradise, solve all your problems . . . Emma and I never loved one another, she never (well so far) got to be a major poet, I never got to be a famous actor really, we never really got to Far Rockaway. Unfortunately, this is my life and we DID get to Far Rockaway. There's a lot to be said for never getting to Far Rockaway, I am here to tell you.

"Where the hell are we? This is taking forever."

There are only local trains on Sunday, Em.

"It's been an hour and we're at Euclid Avenue. Where is it on the map?"

We found it. Two-thirds there.

"Now that is a name to conjure with."

What?

"Far Rockaway. It took some poetic sensibility to decide to name the area known as Rockaway that was farthest out Far Rockaway. They usually do East Rockaway, or something boring like that."

Yeah.

One A train went to somewhere called Lefferts Boulevard and the other A train went to Broad Channel where we would transfer to the elusive C. After Kennedy Airport and the stop for Aqueduct Racetrack the train (not under the ground now) goes up on stilts and crosses Jamaica Bay. Now this is a real Unvisited Attraction of New York—this rattling, wobbling, self-disintegrating train teetering on this rickety bridge for a mile over the expanse of Jamaica Bay. I've never seen an equal thrill on mass transportation (save for the railingless Williamsburgh Bridge crossing, but that's death-defying mass transit and this was sightseeing).

"We're all gonna die," said Emma. "I'm surprised they haven't used this Jamaica Bay business in a disaster movie yet."

There were sailboats out on this still, overcast day, drizzle now coming down. Everywhere was marshland and there were long-legged birds in clumps of grass, storks or something (I don't know birds), and the clattering train scattered a flock of ducks and they took off over the glassy bay, just for a few yards, and settled down again, causing ripples to spread out over the calm surface.

"The day is like wide water, without sound," said Emma. "Except for the subway train, I mean."

Something told me that wasn't an original line.

Emma smiled at me. "It is, in point of fact, mine, but it has been traditionally misattributed to Stevens for some time now."

Then the train approached this island causeway and a station out in the middle of nowhere, Broad Channel. The conductor announced through static and mumble that this was the last stop, change here for the A and the C for Far Rockaway. We got out of the train and stood on the platform, looking at whom we had for company.

"Pretty run-down looking lot, huh?" said Emma, a bit chilled, sidling closer. "This *is* still New York, isn't it? This island. Ought to be New Jersey, some old fishing port on the shore that has gone to seed."

There were two teenage boys who looked bored, an old woman who kept going to the edge of the platform to spit, a young fat girl who stared to the vanishing point of the train tracks wanting the next train to arrive before the boys had a chance to remind her she was fat, and old men, those salty beach-type of old men, ex-fishermen maybe, or perhaps tenants of the welfare hotels. There were a lot of faded hotels on these ex-resort beaches that the city used to house homeless and derelict people—it always seemed the old people got sent to the beach hotels. Coney Island was the most striking example. It was possible, I guess, to have spent one's youth living it up when these resorts were thriving, when these fishing villages were prosperous, and then to have been sent back there, old and penniless, to fade away with the landmarks of your era.

"Let's go to Rockaway Park first, and save Far Rockaway for last," said Emma as the C creaked into the station.

These elevated trains out on the sandy banks across Jamaica Bay were really in rotten shape; the mist and the salt rusted everything and the train squealed and made unbearable noises as rust met rust, wheels didn't turn smoothly, and the stations were the least modernized as it was a lost cause to keep them nice. The stations were graffitied halfheartedly, the signs announcing the stops were torn down or so erased in spray paint as not to exist, perhaps a comment from the young people who had to grow up there. The train came to its terminus at Rockaway Park, and we got out to walk to the beach.

"Ah the Atlantic," said Emma, sighing. "The sun sets in the Pacific, you know. Imagine a sunset over something like this every day if I want to see it. Just drive out to the rocky cliffs and sit back and look."

Ha, Palo Alto isn't exactly on the shore.

"Yeah but I could get to the shore in a car faster in California than I can get to the Atlantic by subway here. The mountains too, Gil. Yosemite and redwoods right in my backyard."

Yosemite is in your backyard the way Washington D.C. is in *our* backyard, Emma. California is not the size of Brooklyn.

"I want to drive places. It's un-American to be confined to buses and subways. I want freeways, freeways I can speed on. I want convertibles. New York is the goddam L train, California is wind in my hair, the top down, sunshine. Look at this shit."

I didn't know which shit she referred to, the boarded-up beach shops, the trash-strewn strip of sand, residue of oil spills toward the shoreline, the reeking public toilet under the veranda you viewed the beach from.

"The weather. This drizzle. It doesn't drizzle in Palo Alto."

Oh it does too, come off it.

Emma looked out to the horizon, vague though it was. "No, there's only sunshine in the Golden West, I won't hear otherwise. Let's go inside somewhere."

We got a bagel at this bakery (I had heard the best bagels in New York City—no paltry claim—were in this bakery along the main drag of Rockaway Park and IT IS TRUE), and then we found a diner place and had a wonderful, life-restoring cup of coffee, a big round mug you could warm your hands with. There are no bagels out west, I warned; the Cult of the Diner is East Coast.

"Yeah but the Cult of the Truck Stop, which I like even better, is Western. Would you stop sticking up for this place? I'm trying to leave New York and not be homesick as hell and nostalgic

—and I *love* New York as you well know—and you're not helping me. You should pile on abuse."

I'd stay if you stayed, I said. Maybe not realizing it until I said it myself.

Emma didn't say anything for a moment. Then, "Don't tempt me."

I could be talked back into staying, and I bet you could too. In fact, I bet if—

"NO," she interrupted firmly. "I'm all packed. I'm going to school. True, I'm going to be sitting in some West Coast pretentious poetry seminar with some twenty-one-year-old simp criticizing my poetry, some pretentious professor telling me to restructure every poem I write—"

You hate school, you hated Purdue—

"But I'd love California," she said, looking out the diner window at the drizzle and the gray sky and the evening, which was coming early tonight. "This looks like a gray miserable October day. They don't have October in California, Gil. I wanna go where they don't have October." Then she got up to pay the bill, through with our discussion. And we were off for the final destination, Far Rockaway. Emma forgot her handbag in the booth and I went to run get it—god, what did she have in there, a brick?

"Maybe I do have a brick in there," she said, taking her bag from me. "You're always knocking my hobbies—masonry is a productive hobby for fun and profit, amusing for the whole family."

Back on the rust-train, back to Broad Channel, and then onto *the* most rundown, shoddiest, worst-kept-up subway line in New York City to Far Rockaway. Once again it was all elevated and salt-corroded and the train squealed and whined over the rooftops of this seaside slum.

"Gee," said Emma, peering through the salt-sprayed windows of the train, "I somehow expected a little more out of a place called Far Rockaway."

There was a playground beneath us, muddy and cold-looking, only a few scattered children standing around, as if in gangs.

There was a strip of stores and shopfronts down below a moment later and some of the windows in the top stories were busted out, deserted. All the buildings were Sad America, leftover '50s boom-buildings without grace or style, like old family sedans of the period, ugly now from trying to be too futuristic then—we have rejected their future.

We got off at the final station.

"Well we did it, didn't we?"

What, Emma?

"We rode 'em all. Every subway. I feel a sense of regret of not getting to the 8 line before they shut it down, but we can't help tracks taken out of service."

Yeah, but who are we going to brag about this to? We're the only people who'd care about this.

"Nah," said Emma, "anyone who'd like you or anyone who'd like me would think this was cool."

We walked from the station into what could most qualify as the downtown area. A few stores were open on Sunday, most not; a lonely-looking lunch counter was open and empty, the old waitress sitting in a booth looking at the door. There was something called the Beachcomber Hotel, with a Vacancies sign in the window ("They could probably put the word *vacancy* on the permanent sign," Emma said). Old people were the only people on the street, walking a dog, or each other, at an old-people pace.

Emma and I went to a municipal park, the name of which was on a vandalized sign we couldn't read. We wandered toward it, looking out to the sea, calm, indistinct, churning up a small wave of dirty brown sand every few seconds.

"Gee, a real *garden spot*," said Emma, looking chilly.

Yep.

"Getting cold now. The ocean looks cold, doesn't it?"

Yeah.

And then: That deadly this-is-it pause, pre-goodbye.

"I tell you what," she said quietly. "You just keep looking out at the sea and I'll go and get on the next train back to town. You stay for another twenty minutes and look at the sea and when you turn around I'll be gone. Simple and painless."

Sigh. I suppose that's what we could do.

Already her voice was getting more distant as she took a step or two back from me. "Now we'll see each other soon enough. You can come and sleep under the stars in California anytime. Hell, I'll probably drop out and move in with you in Chicago —oops, I forgot about the Bitch Sophie. You will tell the Bitch Sophie hello for me. Don't take up with that girl, Gil—sight unseen I know she's bad news."

You'd probably like her, Emma, I said. (But you know, that was a lie. I bet they'd hate each other.)

"You're pulling out of the theater and New York and you're going to be insecure back there, no friends, all alone—you're gonna let that woman become too important to you. If she starts talking about marrying you and moving out to the suburbs you call your old friend Emma, y'hear? I'll come to Chicago and straighten her out."

Still I didn't turn around. I said: Emma, you won't like anyone I'd marry or live with. And what does it matter to you?

"Gil, darling, just because *I* won't have you doesn't mean I want you throwing yourself away. I want First Approval Rights."

Whatever you say Emma.

There was silence and I thought I heard the sounds of footsteps. Oh my, there she goes. So I looked out at the sea like she suggested and it was neither calming nor sad making nor inspiring, just gray and there. I called out Emma's name.

No answer.

Well that was that. And when all is said and done, I said to myself, she was the one central person in my youth, she was attached fatally to New York so that one couldn't exist without the other, and as I turned around to walk back to the subway, I . . . I saw her come running back, waving at me.

"Hold it!" she said, running to catch me.

You're not going away?

She caught up to me. "Hi."

You're not gone.

"I know that."

More last words?

"Not exactly. Gil, I think you should make love to me."

Excuse me?

"You heard me. You should sleep with me. Right now."

Let me get this straight—

"At the Beachcomber Hotel. They have a vacancy, what do you bet? We'll pop over there, get a room, and you do whatever it is you men do with your penises."

I was speechless, for once.

"I *wasn't* going to do this, I swear. But once I got the idea in my head, I couldn't talk myself out of it."

I smiled, shrugged a bit. The idea of making love to me?

"Gil, baby, you are so irrelevant to this. It's nothing personal, I promise. You'll serve my purpose—"

Ending your celibacy before you go out to California?

"No dummy, a BABY. I want to have a baby; I want to be a single mother. You see, this is my plan I was going to tell you about. I have to have a kid. Genetically, I can deal with you as a father. I know that sounds a little Nazi-ish but you gotta think about these things, huh?" She took my arm and led me toward the hotel, but I stopped our progress at a bench.

"What's wrong? I thought people who had sex thought it was fun."

I looked back to the sea and was quiet a moment. Well, yes, I'd like to, but . . . Emma, I said, I can't have you produce a child that's half-mine, pretend he or she doesn't exist, a son or daughter—I would want to see it, support it, have it know me.

"Not if you weren't sure it was yours."

Explain.

"I worked this out, Gil. Tomorrow night I'm going out with Morris from work who is a Harvard MBA. A real Jewish intellectual type. After me. The perennial flirting at the water cooler. I'm going to seduce him and that will be Possible Father Number Two. When I get to California, I'm sleeping with the first post-grad student in literature that appeals to me. And as I'm going by way of Indiana to drop some things off at home, I'm going to look up Duane who I went out with in high school. He's probably married but he always had it bad for me. He was number nine academically in our class rank, and that's bright enough. I've got six possible fathers in all."

I see.

"Now one of you is gonna get it right, I figure, and get me pregnant. Yes, you would be a pain in the ass if you thought I was carrying *your* child but I bet you wouldn't be as concerned over a child that only had a one in seven or eight chance of being yours. You'd leave me alone and let me be a single mother. I'm asking this as a favor, Gil."

I looked at her and back at the Atlantic.

"I wasn't going to go through with my plan until I saw the hotel there. And as I walked away a minute ago, I saw it again and thought, shit, Emma Gennaro, here's your chance. It's now or never. You're being very quiet, Gil."

Lot to think about there.

"I mean, it's not as if . . . " But Emma trailed off.

It's not as if what?

She said quietly, coming forward to put a hand on my shoulder, "It's not as if you're in love with me anymore, is it? I mean, you've gotten over that, right? I wouldn't ask if it was going to hurt you, you know that. But now, what's the harm, huh?"

Oh God.

"I mean, you're a normal heterosexual guy, pretty much, right? Just start her up, put it in, let 'er rip, zip up your pants and we'll call it a day. Hey, it's a one-time offer."

Will this be the first time for you in ten years, Emma?

"Aw c'mon, it's not as if I haven't *washed down there* or something for ten years. The parts still work. I think."

I'd feel better about being the second guy, the third guy—

"Hey I could have seen Morris tonight and you tomorrow night. I wanted you to be first. Because you'll be nice about it. You understand me enough not to make this a suicide-inducing experience. I mean, I'm out of practice, I'm not into foreplay here, I'm not gonna be the BEST YOU EVER HAD, etcetera. You'll be my dry run—ha ha, bad choice of words there—for the Real World."

I looked at the Atlantic Ocean which was being singularly unhelpful about telling me what I should do next.

"Don't think about it too much, Gil—let's go."

All the Knowledgeable Voices were going: NO, are you a FOOL? You'll be messed up by this, she'll be messed up by this, your friendship with Emma, your budding romance with Sophie—everything will be messed up by this . . . But TEN YEARS of my past were going in a decidedly high-school-buddy voice: GO FOR IT, Big Boy, *get it in there!* You idiot, you've wanted this for years and now HERE IT IS, so move quickly here, time's a-wastin'. What WAS the hold-up here? Sex, Gil. You know, the thing you like. What's the worst that could happen, I recall saying to myself.

READ ON, for the answer to that one.

"Room three," said the crone behind the hotel desk-counter, who had come out of some dark smoky smelly room with only the TV light flickering inside to answer our bell. She resented us being alive, purchasing a room she would have to clean up, making her get up from the TV news, being young and there for obvious sexual purposes.

"Always wondered how this felt like," Emma said as we went down the hall. "A cheap sleazy degrading encounter in a hotel with a strange man—"

A strange man you've known for ten years.

"All men are strange to me at this point, I promise you," she said, turning the key in the lock. It was a square room decorated circa 1930, faded wallpaper, a yellowish light in a dingy lamp-shade, sticky linoleum, old calendar pictures on the wall.

"This is the end of the world," Emma said blandly. "Give me the beer." (After the $27.50 for the hotel room—I'll spare you Emma's fifty choice comments about paying that much for this dump—we pooled our remaining $1.50, subtracting the subway fare back to the city, and bought some low-grade beer.) "You're not having any of this beer," Emma informed me, sitting on the bed. "Thank god, there's a TV in here."

Gee, thanks a lot.

"Let's make this perfectly clear, Gil: Your genitalia hold *no* attraction whatsoever for me. You are a performing service industry. I would have purchased a whore if I could have as-certained his intelligence. *No* emotion enters into this, okay?"

I didn't know how to commence things. I put my hand on her shoulder, stroking it softly, gently—

"That's really feeble, Gil."

I don't know how to start this thing up.

"We're not doing SHIT until I finish this quart of beer. I needed a fifth of vodka, not this watery stuff." Emma turned on the black-and-white TV.

Not the TV, come on.

"Oh yes the TV," said Emma. "Until I'm a little inebriated."

The set warmed up. It was the network news: *Mrs. Marribelle Higgins will not soon forget the Beirut massacre—her son's last words to her came in this letter. . .* (Mrs. Higgins reading it for the reporter, teary-eyed, trembling lip:) *"You tell Sis hi. And give my love*—a sob here—*to Daddy. . . "*

Gee, I'm sure glad the networks resisted sensationalizing this season's American military tragedy—

"Next channel," said Emma, swigging constantly. "Why don't you go wash up?"

Right, I said, leaving her to a news report from Grenada which Reagan just invaded and allegedly liberated. There were black Grenadans dancing in a line through the street in joy. There were guys making up reggae songs for the reporters, some rhyme about Meestuh Reagan, he our man, Meestuh Reagan understand . . . Emma let out a strange cry.

What is it?

"I just . . . I just wanted you to know that officially I have now seen goddam everything—black third world peoples singing and dancing in a parade to honor Ronald Reagan, their hero."

Emma, more importantly, there is no hot water, no bathtub or shower, just a sink and a toilet and those are brown with rust-stains and—

"Gil, this is an omen of something," she said, fixed to the TV. "Maybe this is telling me not to bring my child into the world, the world which in the last week has adopted surrealism as its guiding philosophy."

I came in from the bathroom and watched the Grenadans dance through the street with posters of Reagan, signs of U.S.

WE LOVE YOU, and then another reggae hymn to an American soldier.

"Good god, it leaves one speechless," said Emma, looking at me seriously. "I think we better call this off. It's socially irresponsible bringing a child into this world." She took a next-to-last swig of the beer.

I think we're committed at this point, Emma.

She finished off the beer, threw the bottle toward the wicker trashbasket, and sighed heavily. "Ten whole years," she murmured.

Yeah. Well, why don't we get undressed?

Emma gave me a scarcely comprehending glance. "Oh no. It's not going to work that way. You're not, for instance, going to see me nude—get that thought out of your head. No one sees The Breasts. The last people to see The Breasts were my ninth-grade gym class in the showers, and they were sufficiently laughed at then for one lifetime. You will never see these Breasts."

You're gonna keep your shirt and sweater on?

"I will concede to taking off the sweater. I will unfasten my pants and pull down my panties as far as the knees but no further. I want the freedom to pull up my pants at any time."

Wait a second. Emma, you *have* to take off your clothes.

"I most certainly do not."

How do you suggest . . . (I clear my throat) . . . I, uh, become sufficiently aroused?

"What do you mean?"

I mean you with your pants down to your knees under the covers in the dark is not going to do it.

"I don't care how you get aroused. Go in the bathroom and do it yourself. I told you this wasn't the deluxe treatment."

Take your clothes off and get under the covers or NO BABY for you. And turn the lousy TV off, willya?

"TV stays on."

Why?

"I need something to distract me from the notion of your . . . you know, doing what you're doing to me." Emma began to wheel the set over to where she could see it easily from the bed; it would be inches from her face.

You are being ridiculous, I said, going into the bathroom. The TV will produce enough light that I will be able to see an approximation of your body parts, maybe a gleaming of The Breasts—

"You have a point there." She turned the TV off. She turned off the lights. "I've got bad news," she said. "It's not dark enough in here."

Maybe we should take these towels and blindfold ourselves, I suggested. Or we could put out our eyes . . .

Emma yanked the blanket off the bed and then stood on a creaking chair and tried to hang it over the already closed curtains. "What are you doing in the bathroom?"

Trying to get some hot water, I said. There was none.

"Make sure it's clean. Put lots of soap on it. I don't want to smell anything sexual."

There was no hot water. I locked the door to the bathroom and then attempted to wash my genitals in the COLD water in the rust-stained sink.

"What are you screaming about now?"

It's fucking cold—this sink is like ice.

Emma got curious. "Does it actually reach to the cold-water tap?"

It won't reach anywhere if this water doesn't warm up.

"You're not going to come out of the bathroom nude or anything, are you?"

Can't say I'm particularly inclined, no.

"I do not want to see your penis, Gil. I'll never be able to look at you again in the same way. I'll look at your face and see your penis. Penises are just ghastly things—I couldn't get it out of my mind if I saw it. It wouldn't be the same between us."

I'm getting a little fed up with all this, Emma. You know, for your information, vaginas aren't anything too appetizing sometimes.

Silence.

I kept on from within the bathroom: What if I went around carping about vaginal odor, huh? Would that make you feel confident? In the mood for love?

More silence.

Me again: I think for the sake of this act we're already committed to, you should get more in the spirit. All right? Emma, are you out there?

"Yes, I'm out here. I don't want to do this anymore. Let's stop this before it's too late."

All clean (and about as capable of sexual excitement as a cold piece of liver), I zip my pants up and come out of the bathroom. Emma is sitting on the bed looking dejected.

"You've broken the mood," she said accusingly. "That crack about vaginal odor."

WHAT IS THIS? You can savage the whole male sex and I say one thing and the whole deal is off?

"That's right. It's *my* sex, *my* baby, *my* hotel room in *my* name. It will be done my way."

We were at an impasse. I looked at her and she looked at the floor, reconsidering.

"Oh turn off the light," she said, slipping under the covers, fully clothed. "Let's get this over with, this horrible thing . . . "

I turned off the light. And stumbled into the TV as I made my way to the bed—I cursed, Emma laughed.

"Watch out for the TV," she said.

Thank you. Is this the bed? I asked, feeling about.

"Watch those hands. You're within striking distance of The Breasts. Everything's off if The Breasts get molested in any way. Keep that in mind."

We both say nothing for a moment.

"I think we should keep a running patter throughout. I don't want this to get too heavy here."

You know I don't think there's a GREAT DANGER of us getting carried away in the throes of passion somehow. But I know we're going nowhere if you keep insulting me and making stupid remarks—

"I'm a little nervous. Can you understand that?"

Yes, all right. Let's get on with it. I think we should start by kissing . . . (I knew as soon as I said that, that that was a NO GO.)

"HA! Freeman, it'd be like doing it with my brother. Now cut the nonsense. Get hard, put it in, come, take it out, and let's get back to Manhattan."

I am not aroused Emma. I need some concessions here.

"No Breasts."

I don't care about The Breasts—FORGET I ever mentioned your goddam Breasts.

"I think we can do without abuse of my Breasts, Freeman. I think we can live without insulting my appendages."

Concession No. 1 is that we touch each other's . . . parts.

"No touching of parts."

EMMA, for Christ's sake. I'll touch you down there and you touch me and—it's obvious, isn't it, we both have to be aroused. Isn't it?

Emma was quiet a minute. "Uh, necessary huh? It's been a while, you know. You can't just DO IT and let me lie here? Please Gil," and she sounded pleading, desperate. "Don't make me *do* anything. I don't care how you . . . just . . . "

Oh good god. All right, all right. But this is like pin-the tail-on-the-donkey. I can't just aim and go in . . . you'll have to help me, directionally, like.

"I should have brought my mittens. I see that now."

That's a minor concession, Emma. When I say I'm ready, I'll roll on top of you sort of, in the right position, I think, and then you close your eyes and think of Brooklyn, reach down there and help me put it in. And another thing: elevate your hips.

"Why?"

It'll help.

"Help what?"

Help things along.

"What things along? Oh. Okay, yeah. Sorry Gil don't get exasperated with me, just a little patience. Patience. What are you doing over there?"

I'm trying to . . . you figure it out.

"Oh. Is it working? What do you guys think of when you try

to get it going there? *Playboy* centerfolds? Naked women? Do you think of the vagina directly or generally, or do you concentrate on what it feels like? What? I'm interested, really. Is it some right-side-of-the-brain longing for the mother's womb or—"

Emma. Darling. Love of my life. Would you not mention my mother when I'm trying to arouse myself?

"Why do I get the sense most guys could have done this already?"

THANKS A LOT, EMMA.

"Okay I'll shut up. I didn't think you had to concentrate that much. I thought you just whipped it out and it hardened right up."

Maybe when you're fourteen.

"Really? It changes? I mean, I know about *old* men not being able to get it up; guys getting impotent and flaccid and LIMP and—"

EMMA, A NEW SUBJECT PLEASE.

Emma tried being silent a moment.

"How's it going?"

Marginal.

"Oh you know," she said laughing, "this is so *stupid*—why didn't I think of this before? I can do a phone-sex routine."

Oh really now—do I look like some middle-aged used-up man of waning virility in need of that kind of trash?

"Yes, at the moment. Here we go . . . " Emma breathed heavily for a few seconds. "Oh Gil, oh my . . . you're gonna do it to me aren't you? You're gonna break me in half with your incredible manhood . . . "

Oh c'mon, Emma.

Emma started making more realistic noises. "Ohhhh yes, I . . . I want you inside me, all the way in big boy . . . "

To my everlasting shame this is working, go on.

". . . Oh baby, you're getting so big and so long, I think it's not going to go in—and I'm so hot for it, I'm just dripping with the thought of it in me . . . Oh yeah . . . "

I think we're getting there. Now Emma, don't be alarmed but

I am going to touch the vicinity of your pudenda, and I think you should be prepared to take my, uh . . . my—

"Your gigantic *manhood*, your mammoth organ into my hands and guide you into my moist valley of desire . . . "

Yeah something like that. You ready?

"Oh yes baby," she said, still in that awful high porn-film actress little-girl voice. "Oh yes, I'm going to take you in my hands and put you in so far . . . " Emma fell silent as she reached out.

Something wrong?

"That is the most disgusting thing in the world."

I think I liked the phone-sex better.

"Oh Gil, you're such a STUD, it's so giant and . . . " She started laughing.

Burning with embarrassment, I ask what is SO funny.

"Nothing, nothing . . . and uh, yeah put that in me, this mammoth . . . " Hysterics from Emma. "*Sorry*, I'm sorry, it's just I expected something a tad bit bigger after all that—"

Emma, I am getting up right now and leaving—

"No, no, no—please, I'm serious now."

So we could be even, I lowered my hand between her thighs. Ha, I said, just as I thought.

"What?"

JUST what I thought, I repeated.

"WHAT?"

You're about as aroused as I am.

"What are you doing now?"

I'm trying to sexually excite you, make you writhe with passion, walk the ceiling, etc.

"Get your hands off of that. I happen to be sensitive there."

I'm not going to be able to slide right into the Sahara Desert, Emma. So get with it.

"SAHARA DESERT?"

A little healthy viscosity would help—

"You know how I feel about viscosities."

SEX IS VISCOSITIES, you idiot—it's a fact of life!

"Bastard, get off me."

Ha, it's all right to run me down and insult everything about me, but I can't say anything about you.

"I told you I'm in charge of this sex. Now you have five minutes to get this over with or we're going home. *The clock is running.*"

Well.

You know, it would be a good time to finish off that list. The kind of women frequented by the Average Middle-Class Heterosexual Male in his late twenties to early thirties:

1. The Good but Uninspiring Woman.

Not too different from the Placemarker of the last list, a woman there until someone better comes along. Except often someone better doesn't come along and there she is, the Old Regular, the old standby. The man who rounds thirty with this woman in his life will probably marry her (but he assures himself he will eventually cheat on her, maybe with the Quality Item), and he'd actually love her more and respect her more if she wasn't so *content* and complacent. He has the gnawing sense that she thinks she's done very well to land him, while he sold himself short by settling down with her. I'd say this describes (now that I'm back in the Midwest, writing this) about 60% of all couples. And most couples are unhappy by this point. Something about the magic 3–0: If you're single you want to be married, fearing a life of loneliness, childlessness, alone at your death-bed; if you're married you fear your youth is slipping away and you yearn to be single again for that last fling. Because somewhere, out there—though vaguer and less likely than ever—is

2. The Quality Item.

The ideal, the ultimate, the one of your dreams. And your dreams have been perfected by this point, taken far from the realm of realistic expectation. How do you kill the desire for that all-encompassing perfect woman who may or may not exist? I'm not the one to ask this question since I don't believe in the Quality Item anymore. The Quality Item, the Woman of Your Dreams, is the last vestige of adolescence and my adolescent notions about most things have been pounded out of me at this point. But it was a handy delusion, wasn't it? It led you further than you might have gone—but then again, you might have broken a few hearts unnecessarily, thrown aside someone perfectly wonderful, holding out for that someone better who never comes along, who never maybe existed.

I never could get through Emma's Victorian tomes on her bookshelves, but I could manage the recent stuff, all those contemporary novels by Roth and Bellow and Mailer and they all have middle-aged men, somewhere between fifty and sixty, throwing it all away—family, money, prestige, self-respect—on some whore, some BIMBO, huffing and puffing away, it was so good, it was so wonderful, she was so right, etc. Good god, I hope by the time I'm that age I'm not like that about sex. What I'll want then, I suspect, is what I pretty much want right now, and that's

3. A Woman with a Little Sweetness.

I'm not talking about subservience or playing housewife or making my meal every night or cleaning up after me—this is not, I believe, an antifeminist concept; it applies to men as well. If I have to explain to you what sweetness is, then maybe you don't know it when you see it. Sophie may not be as point-by-point beautiful as Emma was (frankly, I ceased to regard Emma's looks after 1980), and Emma might be a touch smarter and brighter about things, and certainly life was far more exciting—accidental suicides, new problems each week, hospitals, the unending one-liners and wit . . . but SON, lemme tellya, I would trade ten years of Emma-drama for a solid month of Sophie and a little sweetness. Those unconscious thoughtless considerations, doing on occasion what she hadn't planned on, her being able to dismiss my current problems with understanding and not condescension, her . . . like last night, I'm typing away at this, right? She sits across the room in her flannel nightshirt, pregnant to the max, waiting for me to finish, reading her sociology book, drinking cocoa. I'm gonna be a while, I say. That's all right, she says. I guess she was waiting for me to go to bed at the same time as she does—not for smooching, not to talk, not for anything, I think, but the idea that we ought to get into bed at the same time, and that it should just be that way. There are a lot of examples I could give, but Sophie has told me she had better not figure too largely in this book. So take my word for it. Oh Mrs. Jackson, you are SO right—a man will go elsewhere in his life for a little sweetness.

"All I ask is one fucking favor and you can't even do *that*," Emma reminded me as we stood there at the Broad Channel station, waiting for the A train to take us back into town. "I'm completely humiliated. I am going to put myself in a tub of boiling water when I get home, to rid my body of your . . . ulllch, secretions."

You're an unfeeling bitch, I said (or something like that).

"First, buddy boy, you can't get an erection for half an hour—"

COULD YOU PLEASE not tell the whole subway platform here?

"Then when you finally do have the goods, you don't make it to the target in time."

THAT could have been prevented if you had let me work a little closer to the destination—if I coulda had a little help—

"I TOLD you. The only time you could put it in was when it was time for the damn thing to go off! Just face it, you blew it."

You're making a scene—

"I don't care who knows—*I'll tell the world!*"

You've got that cop on the other platform staring at us now, so cool it.

"Stupid bastard. I bet that cop could do the trick. In five minutes behind the trashcan here."

All right, bitch, why don't you go ask him then?

"How do you think it makes me feel, huh? Slimed all over by your . . . your *parts* without the goods to show for it." Then, abruptly, her voice breaking: "I suppose I'm the ugliest cow in the world."

Emma, you're beautiful to me as always, but don't pretend you were nice to me or did anything to attract me. And you're getting very worryingly hysterical and weird on me—

"I'm having a nervous breakdown if you want to know why. I'm shaking, look at me."

I don't know why or HOW you got so goddam fragile Emma. But I have less sympathy than I might. I see the train. At last.

"So was this just me? Do you have this problem all the time? Did you ever function with the Bitch Sophie?"

Yes, though it's none of your business.

"And that Monica creature. And god, the all-time lowest, Betsy. You got it up for Betsy when you couldn't manage it for me?"

Your rage is taking a very unpleasant and vindictive turn, Emma. (All right, all right, I was less eloquent than that.)

"Betsy looks like she was squeezed out of a tube. Wormlike, clammy. Terminal wimp with no sex appeal. Maybe that's what it takes for you."

I wouldn't have touched Betsy with a *bargepole* if it hadn't been for the herpes. And secondly . . .

OOOOOOH but you can bet I didn't even get to "secondly."

"HERPES?? Why did you fucking sleep with a woman with herpes? Oh GOD, no no no—you bastard! You . . . you criminal—you creep! SLIME MOLD! I'll kill you . . ."

(Oh Emma, I swear, I swear on a stack of Bibles, I'd forgotten ALL about the herpes, I promise, I just got so caught up in the idea of sleeping with you—I wasn't infectious, I promise!)

". . . Piece of human shit!" she went on, as she began to assail me, fists, fingernails, and then she took her ten-ton purse and swung it at me, right into my face, and I went DOWN to the ground, my nose bleeding, and later a black eye (which didn't hurt my playing a hood in *'59 Mustang*, but putting on makeup was hell for the first week).

"Hey what's going on down there?" yelled the policeman on the other platform across the tracks.

Emma swung at me again and this time her purse fell open, spilling out everything, including her brick: a .38 Smith & Wesson.

"My god," yelled someone, "it's a gun!"

The handgun clattered down the platform, coming to a rest near the edge. The policeman on the other platform blew his whistle and ran toward the overpass to get over to us and arrest Emma for possession or me for rape or someone for something—just as the train came in.

I dragged Emma, still hitting me, into the car. OH GOD, please let the train pull out, please . . .

"I'm not leaving my gun," Emma said, attempting to run back and get it.

YOU WANNA GO TO JAIL? I yelled at her. The doors closed, the train pulled out; there was the sound of whistling —the cop blowing this whistle till he was blue in the face. The occupants of the subway car looked up at us, terrified but curious enough to keep staring.

"That's TWO guns you've made me lose, asshole," said Emma, shaking free of my grasp. "You've robbed me of my guns, you've robbed me of a chance for motherhood, and you've given me herpes all in one day. ARE YOU HAPPY?"

Yes, actually. I couldn't stop smiling.

"What on earth are you laughing about?"

I'm not really sure, but I couldn't stop.

"You've fucked up my whole life and this is it . . . I don't ever want to see you again, you jerk. You better not be infectious or I'll kill you with my next gun. WOULD YOU STOP LAUGHING?"

I'm sorry I can't help it.

"I'll never forgive you for fucking me—or rather for fucking me enough to give me herpes but not fucking me enough so I can have a child in California—what are YOU looking at you OLD BAG? This is between this TURD and myself, mind your own business . . . Gil Freeman I'm going to strangle you on the spot if you don't stop laughing—"

Don't you see even the tiniest bit of humor in all this, Emma?

"HELL NO—and you owe me for that gun too, buddyboy, I wanna see a goddam check in the mail." Then she became intensely, furiously quiet: "Would you *please* stop laughing?"

Far Rockaway, I said, catching my breath—what a place!

Emma was distracted, her eyes tearing up, her face red, her lip trembling. She looked out the window, which held our faint reflections; beyond was the distant skyline of the city in the gray drizzly early-autumn evening. "Nice name, Far Rockaway . . . beautiful name. Too bad the place is a dump."

ENDING

AND I guess that's what I wanted the book to say: Lots of things have pretty names, the Theater, New York City, Being a Poet, Being an Actor, Fame and Fortune, Far Rockaway, Emma Gennaro, the Quality Item, pretty ideas with pretty dreams attached to them. Listen to the words: Broadway Star. Isn't that everything you'd ever want to be? But what's in the books, on the billboards, what has the reputation, these things often let you down and—Emma, wherever you are, you'd appreciate this—when you get there, sometimes the place is a dump. Don't get me wrong, there's a lot to be said for the American Dream. But you wake up from dreams.

After the Far Rockaway fiasco, it was very easy to stay with Sophie and that plan of turning around after a rest and coming back got more and more remote. So I didn't go back. I mean, without Emma it wouldn't be the same, would it? And it would take no time at all before I got fed up and irritated by all the hassles of theater life, right? And Lisa writes me every once in a while and tells me how the East Village is more and more white upper-class kids (as we all feared it would get), Manhattan rents are through the roof, $1000-a-month range, all the places I liked to hang out are yuppie-redecorated, and so many places have closed, been torn down, those family-run hash houses, those local Irish bars . . . See? Hundreds of reasons I'd hate it if I went back. In addition to the big reason I won't go back, Sophie, eight months pregnant with the World's Greatest Child, sitting there across the room. No. I can never go back.

You know—and I guess this sounds neurotic—I can't go to the theater anymore these days. If the guy up onstage is too amateur, it's painful because I could get up there and do better. If the guy up onstage is good, if he's stagestruck, if he's got that gleam in his eye and hears in the small-town polite clapping of Evanston the thunderous ovations of New York . . . well, it's just hard to watch, that's all. I've got a job now doing—

Uh, wait. If I tell you what I'm doing for a living now you really *will* yell SELL-OUT! And in a way you'd be right. But hey, I've got a nice little office and a typewriter and a top desk drawer where for several months now in spare moments, during coffee breaks and lunch hours I've been adding to this pile of paper you're reading. And that's been rewarding, looking back over everything before this next chapter of my life starts.

So let's finish up: Emma did not get herpes, hasn't had a child yet, only stayed in California six weeks before returning to New York. The last time we talked was when she snapped "Have a nice life, bozo," and stormed off the subway train at Washington Square. And let's see, that was . . . god, almost five years ago. Sophie says I'm still a bit in love with her. No, Soph, scarred for life is more like it. This book isn't a love letter, it's partly an attempt to try to figure out someone named Emma who saved my life from being unexciting and half-lived a lot of the time: there I'd be, teetering on the brink of normalcy, of averageness . . . of happiness. And Emma you'd pull me back every time.

Sophie says I'm writing this to spite Emma, to succeed in the written word where she didn't. Eh, maybe a bit. Mostly I wanted to tell you about this particular life as it may be the only book this life may have in it, and you get so many success stories these days, so much Yuppie Dream, so much life-at-the-top. There are people out there who don't get to the top, who walk away, who give up, but who also don't mind really, and I thought I'd tell that story.

You know, my last days in New York after Emma left were very quiet and dull and I packed for the last time (God, what a relief not to be hauling myself inhumanly around that city with All My Things). And I decided I needed a New York Moment, a last time of goodbye. And I thought up all kinds of Last Goodbye stuff to do, go up the Empire State Building, go out to the Statue of Liberty, even go back to Far Rockaway. Naturally none of this panned out—I got very busy toward the end with my landlord and my bills and New York Telephone and I kept going out with the cast of *'59 Mustang* and getting to know them and getting drunk and then . . . damn, it was suddenly my last day. I picked up my U-Haul in the Bronx, drove to the West Side, loaded up and prepared to drive to Chicago (later I'd get on a train and come back to join the cast in Boston). So I'm on my way in the Lincoln Tunnel, crawling in a traffic jam about 7:30 p.m., and when you get out of the tunnel there's a spiral highway that winds up to ground level and to your right is one of THE Views of Manhattan—the island is spread out in a panorama of lights and glimmerings, a city shimmering like the hope that it is, a beacon for newer, fresher, younger people, and I looked at it a little distantly and thought: well, that was then and I feel a part of somewhere else already, and then I thought: maybe I didn't get my name in lights, maybe I didn't set the place on fire, maybe all of New York doesn't know my name, but there are scratchings on the wall, New York, little pieces of graffiti in certain off-Broadway theaters, a linoleum floor I put down in Brooklyn, telltale signs that I was there, and maybe one day I'll be removed and assured enough to go back and look for a few of them, point them out to my boy or girl, maybe. Glimmer and shine and pulse over there always, I thought—never let us down in America, always be there for us to expend our youths and dreams and energies and lives upon. It is time to go, New York, and one last thought before I go is—

HONNNNNNK! The car behind me was not appreciating my New York Moment. I wanted to get out of the car and tell him, HEY BUDDY, don't you know this is my swan song? A chapter is ending here? That's how it goes these days, huh? Moving forward at the sounds of horns on highways, at the cue of traffic signals, turnstiles, tollbooths, ushered and rushed to the next stop on the itinerary, and there are days on the commuter train in the winter when it's got dark early and you can't see out because of the reflection and you might put down your paper or put aside your book and really look at yourself, because amid the noise and the smoke and the strangers and what's become of your life: there you are.

So wish us luck on the kid. And I hope you're happy these days. I am.

Which is not to say that there aren't nights when I put on my coat and take a walk here in Evanston and go down to the lakefront near the university and walk along the rocks and get nostalgic and look up at Chicago, all golden and clean, reflecting down the shore to me, and think: that's nice, that's real nice, but I knew a place once where the lights were brighter, and the air was filled with dreams.

TOMA
KETCH